Take So

Take Someone Like Me

Jayne Buxton

W F HOWES LTD

This large print edition published in 2007 by
W F Howes Ltd
Unit 4, Rearsby Business Park, Gaddesby Lane,
Rearsby, Leicester LE7 4YH

1 3 5 7 9 10 8 6 4 2

First published in the United Kingdom in 2007
by Arrow Books

A CIP catalogue record for this book is available
from the British Library

ISBN 978 1 40740 253 6

Typeset by Palimpsest Book Production Limited,
Grangemouth, Stirlingshire
Printed and bound in Great Britain
by Antony Rowe Ltd, Chippenham, Wilts.

For my parents

ACKNOWLEDGEMENTS

They say that second novels are difficult to write, and cause their authors all manner of agony. That I largely escaped such torture must surely be due to the enthusiastic support I received from the lovely people working with me: Euan Thorneycroft, my agent, and everyone at Arrow books – Nikola Scott, Kate Elton, and their wonderful copy editing, design, marketing, sales and publicity teams. I am also immensely grateful to the following people: Rose Blake for her insights about all things teenage; the friends who made up my impromptu market research group; Doctor Gillian Van Hegan and Catherine Evans at Brook Advisory Centres for the information they so graciously provided; Paul Richards for giving me a glimpse into an optician's life; Sarah Bennetts, the original Herself; Lady B, Lynne Mastroianni and Carolyn Holmes for allowing me to pinch their stories; Lauren for her bake-sale tips, and Carrie for the We family; and the lovely Hazel, who sells the prettiest frocks around.

Finally, and as always, thank you to my family, all of whom have been unceasingly encouraging.

LIBBY

It's one of those days when a white mist hovers above the frozen ground long after the sun has risen and the cars have begun roaring along Richmond's streets, trailing their charcoal plumes. A day for huddling. Not a day from which you expect much. Certainly not a day you expect to make any earth-shattering discoveries.

But I make two discoveries before ten o'clock in the morning. The first is that the world is in a truly shocking state. The second is that my fifteen-year-old daughter is almost certainly having sex.

I make the first discovery as I whisk through rooms picking up the debris left by the girls as they scrambled to get out of the house. Of course I've been aware of the upsetting goings-on in the world, but seeing it in black and white gives me quite a jolt. There it is, all laid out before me in a scrapbook with a red cover and dull, mustard-yellow pages. A year's worth of human and planetary drama: a middle-aged banker killed by a bullet delivered on his doorstep; a Scottish family swept over an inadequate sea wall into the North Sea; thousands killed by an earthquake in Turkey;

1

and story after story about damage to the natural world. *A HOTTER WORLD MAY FREEZE BRITAIN; FOUR HUNDRED SPECIES UNDER THREAT; OESTROGEN IN WATER SUPPLY BLAMED FOR FALL IN MALE FERTILITY; LAST DAYS OF THE BLUE TIT.*

I discover the scrapbook when I reach under Ella's bed to retrieve a lone, fluff-covered sock I've spotted after I've swept through the room pulling back curtains and switching off lights and rearranging the duvet. It is obviously something she's been working on for some time and has taken great care over. Each newspaper article is framed in red felt-tip and headed by an abbreviated title of Ella's creation. After I've recovered from the initial onslaught of all the accumulated tragedy, I am torn between pride (that my ten-year-old can assimilate all this information) and grave concern (that my ten-year-old is interested in assimilating all this information). In the end I'm not quite sure how to respond.

I am even less sure of how to respond to the second discovery. I find the birth-control pills in Phoebe's underwear drawer, tucked inside a pristine and obviously unread volume of *Cider with Rosie* I recognise as a gift from the godmother we don't speak to any more. A corner of the shiny pink foil packaging is peeking out from the pages of the closed book and catches my eye, as if winking at me, as I place four pairs of clean knickers in the drawer.

It's pure chance that I am in the drawer in the

first place. I stopped putting Phoebe's clothes away years ago, figuring that she was perfectly old enough to do it herself. But this morning, instead of placing the clean clothes on her bed as usual, I do what I always do for Kate and Ella, which is to put them away in cupboards and drawers. Perhaps I am just on autopilot, having been into Ella's and Kate's rooms first. Perhaps I am distracted by the discovery of Ella's scrapbook. Perhaps I am just meant to find the pills.

I retrieve the knickers from the drawer and place them on Phoebe's bed, then grab on to the bedpost, being vaguely aware of the carpeted floorboards shifting beneath my stockinged feet. There's just no way I can go back to laundry distribution with the same conviction now.

PHOEBE

The funny thing is, I never read *Cider with Rosie* when it was given to me. Now, four or maybe five years later, I find myself reading the odd paragraph, surreptitiously, as if it's the book rather than the pills that I'm trying to hide from Mum. The last time I checked the pills I shoved them back at the start of the chapter called 'Public Death, Private Murder'. It's the kind of chapter that stands as a story all on its own, and you only have to read a few sentences to become engrossed in it. When Mum calls me for breakfast I'm tempted to keep reading about the poor boy who was beaten and left to die in the snow, but I force myself to snap the book shut, with the pills now safely stashed between pages ninety-six and ninety-seven.

I check out my reflection one last time before going down. I have a spot on my right cheek, which is unusual for me. I never get spots. This one makes me feel, I don't know, unprepared to face the world.

Normally I look pretty good. (I know that's a terrible thing to say.) I have a pretty good body, long legs, good skin, Keira Knightley lips. My face is a nice oval shape with a pert nose that my friend Alice says looks like Michelle Pfeiffer's. (Alice says I'm a dead-ringer for a young Michelle Pfeiffer full stop.) And someone once said my eyes were mesmerising, which I liked the idea of. Dad says my hair is like spun gold, long and glossy with just the right amount of wave in it.

Of course I would never say all this to anyone else. I know it's unforgiveably vain to give yourself compliments. But I can't help what I see. There are lots of plain people around, even quite unattractive ones, and I'm nothing like them. People look at me. When I walk into a room I just know that people are straining their necks, trying to get a better look. And when I talk to boys, I can see their eyes getting sort of watery. Like they've lost focus and are in danger of forgetting what they're saying.

People assume that life is easy when you're pretty. But let me tell you, it isn't. Things don't always go my way. And there's so much pretence involved. You have to pretend you don't notice the effect you have on people for a start, or feign insecurity about a flat bottom or short fingers or some other irrelevant little imperfection just to make everyone else feel better.

I've become a master of pretence. Like I said, I never give myself a compliment. And when someone else gives me one, I smile and try to change the subject – maybe telling them I like their sweater or something. I try never to let anyone catch me looking in a mirror and I never, ever brush my hair or put on lipgloss in front of other people. You sometimes see women applying a full face of make-up on the bus, in front of dozens of strangers. I think it's unbelievably tacky, and I would never do it. Besides which, it always strikes me as counter-productive. Make-up is supposed to be about helping ordinary faces masquerade as better-looking ones; what's the point if you're going to blow your own cover and reveal the transformation as it takes place?

The trouble with having to pretend all the time is that it becomes almost like a full-time occupation all on its own. I hate to sound dramatic, but sometimes I feel like being this beautiful has taken over every inch of me and there isn't much room for anything else.

I know that Josh thinks I'm lovely because I always catch him looking at me. Plus, when he first met me he told Max Winters I was the best looking girl he'd ever seen. When I first let him feel me up I thought he was dying. Really, he was practically hyperventilating into my neck. He says it's just not fair to make him wait any longer. That I can't keep getting him all aroused and then leave him there unseen to. But I just don't know. Why is that my responsibility?

LIBBY

The scrapbook explains a lot. Such as why Ella's bedtime routine has become progressively more protracted. For years, said routine consisted of her lying in bed reading until I popped upstairs to kiss her goodnight and turn out the light at the appointed time. I would often be back on the sofa with a glass of wine within minutes. Then one night a few months ago she started insisting that I sat with her for a few minutes before turning out the light. She claimed to have been disturbed by a film she'd seen while at a sleepover – some ghastly horror about the dawn of a modern-day ice age.

'Is that really going to happen to us? Are we really going to wake up one day and find ourselves covered in ice?' she'd asked, eyes wide with alarm, the dishevelled Tommy, a sad-eyed golden bear, pressed against her cheek. *Tommy could do with a wash,* I remember thinking.

'Of course not, that's just a movie. Movies exaggerate everything,' I'd said distractedly, scraping a bit of dried food from Tommy's black button-nose.

'So what will happen, then? What will the ice age be like?'

Knowing little about the first ice age, and absolutely nothing about any impending one, I'd been somewhat at a loss. So I'd opted for the answer I thought a ten-year-old would want to hear.

'Ella, sweetheart, there isn't going to be any ice age. The scriptwriters made it all up,' I'd said, pulling the duvet up to cover her shoulders, nearly smothering Tommy in the process.

'But what about global warming?'

'Well, I guess some scientists think it's a real phenomenon. But if it is, it will all be very gradual. So gradual that we won't even notice it. It's certainly not going to cause any problems in your lifetime. It's nothing for you to worry about.'

That night she'd been quite easily calmed, but it wasn't always the case. The time she brought up the shooting of the Chelsea banker I couldn't seem to find anything reassuring to say. She eventually succumbed to sleep, but I'm sure she remained convinced that a masked intruder was going to break into our own house and shoot Rob at any moment.

Then there were the nights when she just said she felt sad, for no particular reason. It wasn't global warming or rising crime rates in middle-class areas, just a generalised gloom.

Still, I wasn't really all that concerned. I know that children go through phases. When Phoebe was six, she used to go around pressing all the doors tightly shut at every opportunity. Before I was able to figure out whether hers was an obsession with neatness or monsters that threatened to slither through the gaps, the peculiar behaviour stopped. Overnight. I assumed it would be the same with Ella. But the scrapbook is worrying. Maybe my child has developed something of an unhealthy obsession.

'Ella, I found your scrapbook today when I was tidying your room. Do you want to tell me about it?' I say matter-of-factly as I plonk myself firmly down on her bed. You can say these sorts of things to ten-year-olds without undue fear of reprisal. Say them to a teenager and you will be accused of treachery and told to mind your own business before being ordered unceremoniously from the premises.

Ella looks down shyly, then turns her head to face the wall. Her unruly chocolate-brown hair, my hair, is spread out across the white pillowcase like a fan. 'I made it myself. It's not for school or anything.'

'I think it's great, Els. But tell me why you wanted to make it.'

She shrugs under the duvet. 'I don't know really. I think maybe I thought it would make me feel better.'

'Better about what?'

'About everything. All the horrible things in the world.' She turns her head back to face me. Her eyes are wide and apprehensive, her long lashes like exclamation marks. 'It's all so horrible, Mum.

9

There's so much to be frightened of. And at night it always seems so much worse. I can't seem to stop thinking about it then.'

'So you made the scrapbook because you thought it would help. Did it help?'

'A little. But I still think about things.'

'I know you do, angel. It's totally normal to think about things. And it says great things about you that you are so concerned. But I think, instead of cutting out newspaper articles and putting them in your scrapbook, you might be better off talking to me or Daddy about the things that worry you. We'll probably be able to help you. Because things always seem much, much worse when they're in the newspaper. There's so much information missing, and everything is written in such a dramatic way. That's not really how things are.'

I don't even know if this is true. I suspect not. But it feels somehow wrong for a ten-year-old to be exposed to the truth in all its gruesomeness.

'But that is how some things are, isn't it?'

'Like what?'

'Like, global warming is real. And it's true that we are destroying our environment. Why are people so awful? And why aren't we doing anything about it, Mum?'

'Well, because life's complicated, Ella. People are busy earning livings, and going to school, and raising their families. Sometimes they're too busy to think about big things like the environment. It's not that they wouldn't want to help. It's just that they get sort of . . . sidetracked.'

'Well, it scares me that people don't pay more attention. I think they should.' She focuses her brown eyes on me in a way that's almost challenging. 'Don't you think they should?'

There's no escaping the implication, intended or not, that *I* am one of *they*. One of the busy people who are so busy earning livings and raising children that they can't make time to look at the big picture.

I try to think of something I can say that will redeem myself in her eyes, and come up with, 'Tell you what. You promise to talk to me about this whenever you are worried, instead of sitting all alone with your scrapbook full of scary stories, and I'll have a good long think about what we can do to get people to pay a little more attention. Deal?'

'Deal,' she says, yawning and curling herself around Tommy.

When she is asleep I sneak back in and prise Tommy from her arms, planning to have him washed and back in bed without her ever noticing he was gone.

I don't make anything like this kind of progress with Phoebe. In fact, there seems to be no opportunity to talk to her at all. Not the evening of the discovery, which she spends revising for a French test and talking on the phone in her room, emphasis on the latter. Certainly not over the bowls of

Crunchy Nut Cornflakes the next morning, with Rob and the other two as witnesses. When I tell her I think the length of her school skirt is in danger of earning her an order mark, I am scowled at and instructed to get a life. At that point, an inquiry as to the state of her sex life seems unwise.

PHOEBE

I'm not really a morning person. This isn't a crime, just a fact. I don't see why everyone is so intent on my being pleasant before nine o'clock. I just need to be left alone, or at the very least, not actively provoked.

This morning Kate and Ella were sitting at the breakfast bar for ages before I came down, and I ended up with the crumbly remains at the bottom of the Cornflake box. So I made a perfectly reasonable request.

'Kate, do you suppose you could think of others just occasionally, and not hog all the Cornflakes?'

'I didn't hog all the Cornflakes. I had one bowl. It's not my fault you were late coming down.'

'Oh, shut up. At least I take the time to get ready properly in the morning. At least I don't go out looking like a slob.'

'Well, at least I'm not vain. Always looking in the mirror. Wearing a skirt that's halfway up my bum.'

Mum intervened then, hands on hips, a woe-is-me sigh at the ready.

'Girls, do you mind? This is quite foul to listen to at the best of times, but it's particularly unpalatable so early in the morning.'

Then she focused her gaze directly on me. 'While we're on the subject, I do think your skirt might be getting a bit short, Phoebs. Any day now you're going to get an order mark for it. Do you want me to pick up another one for you?'

I considered being nice. Then I decided that she was making it impossible and rolled my eyes instead.

'You *really* need to get a life, Mum.'

What is it about mothers? I wonder. Or maybe it's just my mother. Always hovering, dishing out instructions and reprimands. *Have some breakfast. Your skirt's too short. Your top's too low/too high/too tight. Shouldn't you be in bed? Are you really allowed to wear those hoops to school?*

My mum doesn't understand what it's like to be fifteen. She must have had an idea once, but the past twenty-six years have evidently erased all recollection of it. Whenever she makes an effort to dredge up a relevant memory and tells me a story about When She Was My Age I have the urge to press my hands against my ears. Sometimes I do. When She Was My Age it might have been OK to wear a skirt down to your knees and a big, bulky winter coat like something an old-age pensioner would wear.

Mum's not a shouter. When she disapproves of something she presses her lips together then makes

14

an exaggeratedly casual, throwaway remark you just know has reinforced steel underpinning. God knows what she'd do if she knew I was thinking of sleeping with Josh. Probably faint. Or internally combust.

When I was younger she said I should always talk to her about anything that worried me. She said that the minute I started to think about boys and sex I should talk to her because it was all very confusing and she could help me. *Yeah. Like that's ever going to happen.* I could never tell her about all this. Thank God I don't have to. The nurse at the family planning clinic was just great about the pills. No questions asked. No funny looks. Just a prescription. I know she won't even tell Mum because the little white leaflet she gave me says it's against NHS policy to involve parents once you are sixteen, and I almost am.

So I have the pills but I haven't started taking them yet. I don't know, it's like, once I do that, I'll have to say *yes*. Sometimes I want to, but a lot of the time I don't. Josh is amazing, and everyone loves him. But I can't help feeling there should be something a bit more intense before I give in. I don't know, shouldn't there be sparks or something? Shouldn't I be gagging for it, a bit like he is, when actually I'm quite happy with the way things are?

Laura and Alice say I'm mad not to. Alice says she'd give anything to have someone like Josh as her boyfriend. But then, Alice would do practically anything for a boyfriend full stop.

LIBBY

A week's gone by and I've failed to find the right moment to talk to Phoebe. I did, however, find the time to make seven visits to her knicker drawer. On each visit, I was relieved to find the foil intact.

The day after I found the pills I was struck by a marvellous thought. The pills were unopened, meaning she hadn't started taking them. Meaning, she probably hadn't done the deed. Then came the sobering realisation that the particular packet of pills I'd stumbled upon could be one of several, each one stashed in a different hiding place in her room. I spent a mad half hour one morning rummaging under cushions and beanbags and flipping through books looking for a half-empty pill packet, scouring the carpet for minute pieces of discarded pink tin foil. Nothing.

Pills or no pills, I'm fairly confident that nothing can have happened this week. She's only seen Josh once, when she went to watch him play rugby, so unless she's been sneaking out of her bedroom window during the night, there can't have been any opportunity for a tryst.

'What would you do?' I asked Fran, my very best friend of more than a decade.

'Good question. I just thank Christ I'm not there yet. I honestly don't think Freddie even knows what girls are. But if it were me I think I'd talk to her.'

Fran's kids are younger than mine, and both boys. Freddie is fourteen and Jake is twelve. We met in antenatal class when I was pregnant with Kate and she with Jake. When my waters broke in the middle of a class she volunteered to drive me to the hospital, and somehow managed to squeeze my hands throughout the contractions and shift gears at the same time. The bond between us was assured.

Of course, having a teenage daughter who may or may not be having sex with her teenage boyfriend is child's play compared to the traumas that Fran has endured. Six years ago her eminent surgeon husband Doug left her to set up home with his twenty-nine-year-old anaesthetist, who, to add insult to injury, was tall, blonde and exceedingly perky of both bottom and breast. (I know this because Fran insisted that I accompany her on her one and only attempt to spy on Doug and his new lover. We sat huddled in the dark in my car, and when we saw them emerge hand in hand from the block of flats where they were living, I leaned over Fran and hugged her in an attempt to obscure her view. But it was too late. She'd seen what I'd seen. And it made her believe that Doug had probably never been all that keen on her small, rounded body, or the light brown hair she wore scrunched into a knot at the back of her head. That he'd probably never loved her properly.) When Doug and his perky-bottomed lover had a baby within seven months of his leaving it was all Fran could do to keep herself and the boys from falling to pieces. Freddie, in particular, was inconsolable. Even now he is a solemn, sad-eyed boy, as if he's already seen too much.

After a few years, Fran regained some of her bounce. She took up radiography again, started to go out a bit more. Not on dates with men, but out, nonetheless. At the beginning she didn't have any spare emotional energy to deal with other people's problems. Now she is back to doing what always came naturally to her: helping people to gain perspective and laugh off their more trivial concerns, or digging deep into her emotional stores to support friends whose lives have truly gone off the rails.

'Just be very careful, that's all. Nothing too heavy or you'll push her in the other direction,' was her parting warning to me.

When I told Rob about my discovery he reacted exactly as I thought he would.

'Oh Christ. Here we go.'

'Rob, we knew this was going to happen some time.'

'Yeah, some time. Sometime much later. Not sometime now.'

18

'I know. I didn't even know she and Josh were that serious. And I think fifteen is too young. But maybe we're just being old-fashioned. Do you think?'

'Old-fashioned or not, you'll have to talk to her.'

'And say what exactly?'

'I don't know. That's your territory. But something has to be said.'

So we're in agreement then. Something has to be said. I try out a few somethings, ranging from the liberal to the condemnatory:

Phoebe, darling, I found your pills and I know you're probably sleeping with Josh. If so, that's fine, but there are a few things you maybe need to think about. (Builds bridges by being open and accepting, but risks major breach of trust due to implied snooping in knicker drawer.)

Phoebe, sweetheart. It struck me that you and Josh are seeing a lot of each other and might be getting to the point that you are thinking of sleeping together. Do you think we maybe ought to talk about it? (Wins me kudos as apparently perceptive mother without accompanying breach of trust. But offers little protection against immediate ejection from bedroom.)

Phoebe. I found the pills. What the hell do you think you are doing? (Clearly inappropriate, but tempting, nonetheless.)

Three or four years ago, this kind of dilemma would have been unthinkable. Phoebe and I always had such a good relationship, and I prided myself on being the kind of mother kids could talk to. I was always party to discussions about cruel friends, minor jealousies, horrible teachers, coveted possessions, embarrassing moments. Then after Phoebe turned thirteen, I suddenly realised I was public enemy number one. She started saying things like 'I just can't talk to you,' and 'You're always on my case,' in response to some innocent inquiry or remark I'd made, and I would think, *Who, me?* I couldn't understand how she could interpret my behaviour that way. Often I couldn't even understand what she was saying. She was vaunting disdain in a whole new language, one that took words I thought I knew and dressed them up in an unrecognisable meaning. The first time she said 'Stop screwing at me', I stood there in open-mouthed confusion. 'Excuse me? Stop screwing at you?' I'd said eventually. 'Yes. Screwing. It means haranguing, nagging, shouting at, Mother,' she'd replied. 'And you're always doing it.' (Though I was hurt by the accusation, I have to admit to having been fleetingly impressed by her vocabulary; haranguing isn't a word you hear much these days.)

Before long I realised that it wasn't just a bad day, or a short phase. This was our relationship, and it was no longer a relationship of equals. Somewhere along the line I'd started tiptoeing around her. I began to think of her as someone separate from the daughter I'd once known. Rob and I started referring to her as Herself, though seldom within her earshot. *How is Herself feeling this morning? What does*

Herself have to say about that? Will Herself be joining us? Craving just a little of the physical intimacy I'd shared with her when she was younger, I was reduced to creeping into her room late at night to sit silently stroking her arm or holding her hand while she slept. It was the only time I could be absolutely assured of not being rejected, shouted at, ridiculed. That's not to say she's never affectionate, or that we never share a laugh; just that her tenderness is dished out in tiny, intermittent and unexpected doses.

She's such a beautiful thing you can hardly believe so much ugliness can come out of her. Her good looks seemed to sprout without warning. All of a sudden, the gangliness had become perfect grace, the sporty muscularity was a sensual leanness, and the puppy fat on the cheeks had fallen away to reveal a perfect set of cheekbones. When I'm not furious with her, she takes my breath away. Even crumpled from sleep and with her hair swept up into a messy ponytail, she is mesmerising.

I can't help thinking that all that loveliness must be difficult to cope with, which may explain why I overlook her Nathan Nasty tendencies more often than I should. It pains me to watch her flailing about trying to establish who she is, at times a glossy, care-free thing with the unshakable self-assurance that comes from sensing she's the prettiest girl in the room, and at others, someone small and gauche and uncertain. Then there are the in-between times, when she's just impossibly self-absorbed and unspeakably selfish.

Such a contrast – Phoebe in all her teenage awfulness, seeming to stomp through life without a thought for anyone else, and Ella carrying the weight of the world on her shoulders. Thank goodness for Kate, who defies all the well-established rules about middle children by being good-tempered, easy-going and undemanding, happy so long as she isn't denied her weekly quota of netball, hockey and horses. I never seem to have to worry about her, and she demands nothing of me. I honestly think that if I did nothing other than send her off full of warm porridge each morning she'd be absolutely fine.

PHOEBE

When I get home from school on Tuesday I ask Mum whether she managed to get to Top Shop to pick up the olive green fringed bag I wanted. She says she didn't have time.

'You didn't have time?' I say, incredulous.

'That's right,' she says in an annoyingly matter-of-fact way.

'Oh right. The Waitrose shop take all day did it?' I say, doing what mum would probably call a flounce out of the room.

Didn't have time. Honestly. It's not like she has anything else to do all day, I think, as I throw my school bag onto the bed. I sit slumped on the bed for a few minutes, waiting for my seething frustration to subside. My eyes land on the top drawer of my bureau, the one where the pills are hidden. I decide to check on them one more time.

They're still there, right where I left them. I stare at the package for a few seconds, then I think, maybe this is as good a day as any to start taking them.

I push on one of the little circles of perforated

foil. It pops open, and the pill falls out onto the floor. I scrabble around trying to locate it, then hold it in the palm of my hand for a bit. It's so tiny. So inconsequential. It's hard to believe that it's capable of doing something as monumental as preventing a baby from being conceived.

Right, here goes, I say to myself. Then I place the pill on the tip of my tongue and go over to the mirror to examine it. It looks like an ulcer or something.

For some reason I get stuck in this position, standing in front of my mirror with a pink pill on the end of my outstretched tongue. And the longer I stay there, the more uneasy I feel. Eventually I take the pill off my tongue and force it back into its little pouch, pressing down what's left of the foil on top of it.

Maybe I'll wait a bit longer.

LIBBY

The first real thing Rob ever said to me was that I needed a new pair of glasses. I might have been insulted by his comment but for the charming manner of its delivery, and the cheeky smile which followed it. Anyway, he was right. I'd had the glasses I was wearing since before university. They had a crack all the way along one arm, and were suddenly looking shockingly old-fashioned. But I hadn't seen much point in investing in a new pair when I wore my contacts most of the time.

Rob had a vested interest in persuading me to update my specs in more ways than one. He was doing his pre-reg year at the optometrists next door to the café in Notting Hill where I was working. He later confessed that he was on some sort of commission deal with them, but that wasn't the reason he mentioned my glasses that day as I placed his coffee in front of him and watched it slosh over the edge of the mug and on to the table. He mentioned the glasses because he thought it was a good chat-up line.

As it turned out, he was right. It's unusual to be treated like a real person when you're serving up hot drinks and cinnamon swirls all day. The most I'd usually get would be a smile and a thank you. Certainly no registration of interest. Definitely not any inquiries as to why such an obviously clever and ambitious young woman like myself was wasting her time serving Earl Grey teas and espressos to other people.

So when Rob actually spoke to me, he was in with a chance from the start. In that sense, I suppose almost anything he'd said that wasn't hot beverage-related would have been a good chat-up line. But he followed up the line about my glasses with another one.

'I've seen just the pair for you next door. If you come in after work, maybe I could fit them for you. You know, sort of a fair exchange for the fifty-seven coffees you've served to me so far this year.'

I knew where he worked. I would occasionally see him through the window on my way home, and he came in most days to pick up a coffee and something to eat. Sometimes, like that day, he'd eat in, but most days he'd grab his brown paper bag and rush back next door to his next client. (They were obviously understaffed at David & David Opticians.) I noticed that he had beautiful hands, smooth and long-fingered without being effeminate. And I used to like the way his outstretched legs seemed to take up so much space when he sat at a table, and the way his lean athletic frame seemed so ill at ease in the knee-length white jacket he was forced to wear. There was

26

something ever so slightly Clark Kent about the whole impression.

We spent an hour looking at glasses that evening, and ended up settling on the first pair I'd tried on. They were shaped like a chunky half-moon, with a slim metal frame, and were apparently the epitome of cool. Rob gave me the discount normally reserved for prominent local business owners, and set me up on an instalment plan that I could manage on the pitiful wages I earned at the café. Then he took me across the road to the pub, where we cradled a couple of lagers for almost two hours and I told him how I'd failed to get a job in my chosen field of marine biology and was just filling in time as a waitress until the right opportunity came along.

'I knew you weren't a regular waitress,' he'd said. 'I could tell by your eyes. It's like you're dreaming of something else.'

'Probably why I spill so much coffee,' I'd joked, pleased that he'd taken me for someone with something on my mind. Someone like him.

We went out six times before we slept together. That seventh time I accompanied him to his niece's christening, an event during which we were under so much scrutiny we almost upstaged the baby. Rob's family is a sprawling and unwieldy thing, and all its members seemed to be there that day, beaming quietly at the sight of young love in bloom. I could feel the rising tension in Rob's hands as he held mine all through the service and the popping of the champagne corks afterwards, a kind of urgency that I was feeling too. I knew by then that I loved him, and that, family christening or not, we needed to be together. The idea of having sex for the first time in the cramped bathroom of a house belonging to your boyfriend's brother-in-law's parents, while armies of white-haired relatives sup champagne on the floor below and dozens of small children can be heard roaring around the gardens beneath the window, might not seem particularly romantic. But the way we felt then, a four-poster strewn with rose petals could not have been more idyllic.

God, we were mad for each other then. Insatiable. Almost anywhere would do. And any time. Just after closing time behind the cappuccino machine at the café, or directly beneath the eye chart in examination room two when he was on solo duty on slow afternoons.

Rob was the third person I'd ever slept with. (Is that a lot or a little, or just right? I wonder now. Will Phoebe be expecting to notch up at least a dozen conquests by the time she reaches twenty-three?) The first was Simon, a gentle, sandy-haired boy who worshipped Bob Dylan, when I was eighteen. I'd been seeing him for a year, and it was a nice, safe experience, but nothing to move the earth. After three years with Simon and a year on my own I met Craig, a guy with dark hair and aquiline features who should have come with a warning label. Now, he made the earth move. The trouble was, everything else with him was a moveable feast too. We saw each other on and off for a year or so and I never knew where I stood. It never felt as if he actually saw me, really saw me. Eventually I got tired of feeling invisible. My big regret is that he dropped me before I'd summoned the courage to do it to him. It was a most humiliating scene. When he told me he wouldn't be calling any more (the implication being, of course, that I was not to call him either), I found myself blubbering and clinging to him despite the fact that I'd been plotting how best to bin him that very morning. *These tears aren't for you*, I wanted to say to him. *They are for everything you never were.*

What I wish for Phoebe's first time is something in-between Simon and Craig. At seventeen or eighteen, somewhere in the midst of an established relationship with a boy she'd climb Everest for. If there was a fairy godmother in charge of 'Virginity (loss of)', that's what I'd ask her for.

PHOEBE

You're beautiful, it's true, trills my James Blunt ring tone, and Josh's name pops up in the window. I'm lying on the floor of my room with Alice and Laura flicking through copies of *Now* and *Heat*. Alice keeps tossing her newly hennaed hair around in an affected way I hope she's going to get over soon, and Laura is drooling over a double-page spread of Chad Michael Murray.

I'm not crazy about talking to Josh when they're listening. It makes me feel like we're on show, having to prove we're having *a deep and meaningful relationship*. Inevitably, we end up sounding like the most superficial idiots going. When we're alone it's different. Less like a game, more like an actual *deep and meaningful relationship*.

'Hey, Phoebe, what's up?'

'Oh, hi. Nothing really. Just hanging out with Alice and Laura. What are you up to?' I say, flopping back on to my bed. My head sinks down between my two enormous cushions and for a minute I feel like I can't breathe.

'Just got home from training. Hey, listen, I was thinking. My mum and dad are going out Saturday, so maybe you could come over and watch a movie or something.'

Watching a movie sounds good. It's the *or something* that kind of worries me. 'Hmn, yeah. That would be great,' I say.

'Awesome. Maybe you can get your mum to drop you off, then mine can take you home. It'd be great if you could help me with this English thing I have to do too. It's due Monday and I've left it a bit late. Maybe you can help me cut a few corners.'

'Sure. Listen. I have to go now. Alice and Laura are here. Call me later?'

'No worries. See ya.'

I hang up and try to imagine him lying on his bed thinking about me. I wonder whether he's thinking sweet, gentle thoughts or the more depraved variety.

I contemplate telling Alice and Laura about the conversation I had with Mum last night. I'm wondering if maybe it's just something mothers think they have to do when their daughters reach a certain age. Maybe they're taking a cue from some book they're all reading, or from a guidance note from the Pastoral Care Unit at school.

Alice holds up the copy of *Now* and says, 'God, look at how fat Felicity Wallace looks in this bikini!' Laura says, 'That's nothing. Look at this picture of Pete Ferdinand. He's got man-bosoms!' I decide that now probably isn't the best time to tell them.

She'd come into my room and started speaking

to me in that voice that's full of false lightness. Her parenting-book voice.

'Listen, Phoebe, I've been thinking for some time that we ought to have a talk about something. Can we do that now?' she'd said, as if I really had any choice.

'Sure, but I have to finish my maths, so we can't spend long.' I'd rested my elbows on my crossed knees and looked at her quite openly, as I recall, expecting something along the lines of 'It would be nice if you could help around the house a bit more', or 'We really need to talk about your attitude'.

I was just lining up a range of possible retorts when she said, 'OK. Well, there's no way to say this than to just say it, so I will. I've a feeling you and Josh are getting quite serious. Am I right?'

'It depends what you mean by serious. I am only fifteen, Mum. It's not like I'm getting married or anything.'

'I know that, Phoebs. But you've been seeing each other for a while. So I just thought that probably you were starting to think about, you know, having sex with him.'

I was mortified. More mortified than you can possibly imagine. I wanted to crawl under the bed and zip myself into the body-length duffel bag I keep stashed under there. No one wants to think of their mother thinking of them having sex. It's just so unnatural.

'Mum, I really don't want to talk about this.'

'I know you don't. I don't either. Not particularly. But it's kind of my job to make sure you think about these things before they happen. Has it happened yet, Phoebs?'

'Muumm! No, as a matter of fact!'

'But you are thinking about it?'

I looked down at the maths textbook lying open on my crossed knees. The numbers were swimming around on the page. My face was hot and probably red too, so I didn't dare look up.

'OK , you don't have to tell me. Just bear with me while I say a couple of things, OK? I'm not going to warn you about making sure you're protected because I know you know all that. Though you might not know that you need to take birth control pills for two weeks before they start working, by the way. Anyway, I know you've been told a thousand times about condoms and Aids and sexually transmitted diseases.'

So, what are you going to talk about? she'd left me wondering. *What else is there?*

'What I really want to talk about is how you might feel about it all.'

And then she launched into a long and elaborate story about a guy called Simon and another one called Craig, and how it's never how you think it's going to be the first time so you need to be with someone you really adore who can pick up the pieces, and how it's much better if you wait until you're older because everything makes so much more sense then and there's less chance

33

you'll get hurt and feel badly afterwards. I didn't really look at her the whole time, but I tried to listen, even though the blood pounding inside my ears made that difficult.

When it sounded like she had finished, I just said, 'OK, Mum. I think I get the picture.'

I tried to smile at her then, because she sounded like she was almost as uncomfortable as I was. But the smile signal my brain sent to my lips must have taken a detour somewhere, because the smile came out all wrong. I know it did because her sigh said *I give up*, and she left the room before I even asked her to. (This happens a lot, by the way. The sighing, I mean.)

What I can't figure out is why she picked that moment to talk about all this stuff. *She knew.* How did she know? Perhaps I've been inadvertently giving myself away, wearing an expression all parents have been taught to recognise. Maybe she's overheard me talking to Alice or Laura. Chances are that if she can tell, then Dad probably can as well, and that is just too embarrassing to contemplate. I feel a sudden urge to be ten again, when the worst thing I had to worry about keeping from my parents was the fact that I'd lost my school blazer for the second time.

LIBBY

The conversation with Phoebe wasn't exactly what you would call a success. It wasn't the kind of conversation I'd always envisioned. Somehow I'd always pictured that moment to be full of emotion and meaningful smiles. At the very least I'd anticipated some curiosity on her part, some acknowledgement that I'd been through it once too, and that I might be able to shed some light on the situation.

Then I remembered that I'm a non-person, a person without a past or a future or even a very relevant present. In the immortal words of Herself, '*Yeah right – like that was ever going to happen.*'

I reason that there's a (very, very small) chance she'll reflect on what I've said when she's on her own. Sometimes it works that way. Initially, the response to whatever you've said is violent and outright rejection. Then you discover through some back-door means that they've actually taken on board what you've said. Like the time I overheard Phoebe lecturing Laura about the importance of breakfast, warning her that if she skipped it her body would assume she was starving and begin storing fat mountains.

'How did it go?' Fran asked me.

'Very badly, I think,' I said. 'It didn't seem as if she heard me. And there was a terrible tension between us. You know, it never fails to shock to me that this child who once suckled at my breast and hung on to every word I uttered now finds it so easy to discard me. How can they love you so much when they are little and reject you so readily when they grow up?'

'It's the way of the world, sweetie,' she said with a knowing sigh. 'You aren't the first mother to struggle with teenage rejection. She'll come back in a few years. I know that because it says so on page one hundred and fifty-three of that book you gave me.'

I feel as though I've tried to fulfil my parental duty at least. With Ella, I think I may have done the opposite by trying to expunge her fears through the denial of fact. Today I'm on a mission to make amends by trying to understand the facts a little better. Once I've done that maybe I can do something about some of them; maybe she and I can even do something together. That way she'll feel more like she's in control, less like the poor helpless soul who's fate is to be frozen inside a block of ice.

As I approach the library steps with an armful of books, I spot someone I know I'm supposed to recognise at the top of them. It's the multicoloured silk scarf tucked into the neck of her coat that's most familiar. I slow my pace to give my brain

time to kick into gear. It does so just in
I'm able to greet Claire Thomason as in
waiting to run into her all along.

'Claire. Hello.'

'Oh, hello,' says Claire vaguely, not having
the advantage of my slow approach to the st

'It's Libby Blake, Phoebe's mum.'

'Oh, of course. Libby. So sorry. My mind in
abuzz with so many things I just can't think
straight.' She smiles and rolls her eyes in a way
that manages to be more smug than self-effacing.

'Really, are you very busy?'

'Lord, yes. This time of year is quite frightful,
what with one thing and another. I've no sooner
finished all the paperwork generated by the fund-
raising ball for the Asthma Society than I find
myself knee-deep in the plans for the St Helen's
fund-raiser. It's a red and purple theme this year,
and I can't tell you how challenging that is proving
to be. That's the last time I allow a committee to
dictate the decor!'

'Gosh. Sounds like you have a lot on your plate.'

'Quite. Anyway, I gather Phoebe is coming round
to see us on Saturday. We won't actually be there
for part of the evening, but I'm sure that's fine.
We do so like Phoebe, Mark and I. She's a lovely
girl. And so beautiful!'

'Thank you. We're very fond of Josh, too. I know
Phoebe thinks the world of him.'

'You know, it might be nice for them if we made
a bit of an effort to get to know each other, Libby,

'...here's an opening on the St... ...f you'd be interested. We... ...help.'

'...of you to invite me. I'll... ...a lot on myself.'

'...s face tells me she doesn't... ...of person that would have quite... ...aps it's my unruly hair, which has... ...y started to blow across my face. Perhaps ...e remnants of scrambled egg on the right ...g of my jeans, which I didn't discover until after I'd left the house. Maybe it's the jeans themselves, worn Levis as opposed to fashionable Earls. They certainly don't convey busy and important in the same way as Claire's immaculately tailored cream-coloured coat.

'Well, we'd love to have you if you have time. Anyway, must run now. I've several hundred bolts of purple silk to collect!'

I watch Claire descend the steps and march towards the dark blue Mercedes parked just outside the library gates, noticing with some pleasure that the hem of her coat is hanging down on one side at the back. Not dramatically, but just enough to be noticeable. Forcing thoughts of Claire's committee to the furthest recesses of my mind, I turn and ascend the remaining five steps and push through the swinging wooden doors of the library, which make a satisfying swishing noise as they close behind me.

I love libraries even more than I love bookshops.

The thing libraries have that bookshops don't is a sense of history. Strolling between the racks of dusty books knowing you're in the presence of volumes that have been thumbed through a thousand times, by people who might even now be dead, is strangely comforting. I love it that you might not find the latest Ian McEwan there, but you would always be able to find an obscure edition of John Betjeman's poetry. And that the Jilly Cooper paperbacks and the tomes on ancient Roman armour look almost equally threadbare and well loved.

Phyllis spies me from behind the long desk, and shouts in a whisper as I approach.

'Hello, Libby! Nice to see you.'

'Hi, Phyllis. How are you?' I say, dropping five oversized hardbacks on to the desk in front of her.

'Exceedingly well, thank you, dear. Now tell me, how did Ella get on with these? Were they useful?'

'They were perfect for what she needed. Thank you so much for digging them up,' I say, not missing a beat.

I've prepared myself for Phyllis's question. In fact the books, all variations on the topic of life under the stairs during Victorian times, hadn't even been opened. By the time Phyllis had successfully had them transferred from other libraries, Ella had dug up scraps of information from elsewhere and completed her project on Victorian domestic life. But when Phyllis called I didn't have the heart to tell her all her efforts had been in vain, so I went and picked up the books anyway. They've been sitting untouched on the dining table ever since.

'So what can I help you with today, dear?' Phyllis asks eagerly, pushing her pink-rimmed specs on to the bridge of her nose and tucking her wiry grey bob behind her ears.

'As a matter of fact, I have a little project of my own you can help with,' I say, watching her eyes light up. Phyllis is not just someone who's handy with a date stamp. She's a professional information specialist.

'Go on, dear. I'll see what I can do.'

So I tell Phyllis about my plan, which is to get myself up to speed on the latest findings about the threats to our environment in order to help Ella get to grips with her fears and maybe even help her figure out what she can do about it all. Phyllis listens attentively as I recall the finding of the scrapbook and the nightly agonising about global warming and other demons.

Phyllis says, 'If only other children had parents who were so willing to help them sort out their problems,' then starts tapping madly on her keyboard. 'Tell you what. Why don't you go and have a wander around in racks five and six while I find out what's available from other libraries. I won't be two ticks.'

Most of the stuff on racks five and six is decades out of date, but I do stumble across a compilation of essays on climate change by leading scientists that looks pretty relevant, as well as a book on the basics of the ecosystem that has enormous colour pictures and bold print and looks as if it really belongs in the children's section. I take both of these to the counter, where Phyllis is waiting with a list of other books and reports she's ordered for transfer.

'Marvellous. These look good, don't they? The others should be here in a few days.' Then, with a flourish of her date stamp, she adds, 'You know, if you're really serious about this you should take a look over there on the bulletin board.'

'Really, what's that?' From where I'm standing, the bulletin board looks like a jumbled collage hastily assembled by a few enthusiastic four-year-olds.

'It's a new group that's being set up, organised by that charity Green Link. Are you familiar with them? Anyway, they're organising local environmental action groups, and the first meeting of ours is on the twenty-fourth. I'm going to it, and so is my friend Nancy. She's a health visitor who works a lot around here. Would you be interested?' Phyllis smiles encouragingly at me over the rims of her glasses, and pushes an orange flyer towards me. 'Here are the details just in case.'

'Hmn. I might be,' I say dubiously. I've never been a group action kind of person, and suddenly I have a vision of my private little quest turning into something un-manageable and overwhelming.

'Well, think about it, dear. Bring Ella along if you think it would help.'

I wonder if that's a good idea. I'm pretty sure that Ella will benefit from more information, but doubt she'd profit from sitting in a circle with a bunch of slightly obsessed eccentrics (for this is what they will surely be) raising their fists and suggesting all manner of hair-brained action plans to save the world.

'Oh, I will. Thanks for your help, Phyllis. I really appreciate it.'

As I make my way down the library steps I feel as if my cage has been rattled. Information I can handle, even complex information. I was trained as a scientist, after all, even if it does seem like a lifetime ago. I can even get quite enthusiastic about thinking up some small things that Ella and I can do that will make her feel she's doing something positive. But I'm not sure I'm up to a weekly pow-wow with the local Green contingent. As a rule, I try to avoid sandal wearers and consumers of organic granola. I've got nothing at all against them. They're just not my cup of tea.

PHOEBE

My second attempt at taking a pill isn't much more successful than the first. In fact you'd probably say it was even more pathetic. My hand starts shaking when I try to remove the pill from the pouch where it's nestled, and I put it back without getting it anywhere near my mouth. I think it's Mum's chat that's done it. Somehow, by bringing all that stuff up she's made me feel like my having sex is an even bigger deal than I already thought it was. Also, I have this really weird feeling, as though I'm being watched. I know that's impossible. It's just a feeling. But it still prevents me from putting the pill in my mouth.

The whole thing is vaguely surreal. Here I am agonising over a packet of birth control pills, and not more than fifteen feet away, in another room, my parents are quibbling about mundane things like what's for breakfast. There's a feeling of being here but not really here, which I get quite a lot. No, that's not quite right. It's a feeling of being here, but being a different person to the one that everyone thinks is here.

LIBBY

'Is there any bacon?' Rob shouts out from the bathroom. It's the weekend. Rob likes bacon and eggs on the weekend.

'No.'

'Oh God!'

'Oh God what?'

'Oh God, there isn't any bacon.'

'I did try to get bacon but all they had was Danish smoked and extra thick rind, which you hate. I meant to go somewhere else but I forgot.'

Silence.

'You shouldn't be eating bacon anyway.'

'What?' I can hear the water pounding against the tiles in the shower; Rob's in the habit of turning it on at least half a minute before he plans to get in it. He likes to brush his teeth while the shower warms up, and tends to leave the water running in the sink while he does it, which has always driven me slightly mad. It's not the wasted water that bothers me so much as the din of so much cascading water within the confines of one tiny tiled room.

'I said you shouldn't be eating bacon anyway.'

'What?' he says again, popping his head around the bathroom door.

'Oh, never mind.'

I am the person who's supposed to buy bacon. I'm also the light bulb person, as in the following interchange, which happened last night:

'The light bulb situation on my side of the bed is unsatisfactory,' Rob says, smiling and holding his book right up to his nose for effect.

'Why don't you go and get another bulb.'

'I don't know where we keep them.' He says *we* but his tone says *you*.

'They're in the boot cupboard.'

'The boot cupboard?'

'Yes. You know, the cupboard at the end of the hall where we keep the boots and the coats. And the light bulbs.'

'But you're the light bulb person.' Half joking.

'I'm the light bulb person?' Incredulous and only just joking.

'Come on. You know you are.'

Much of the time I resignedly accept this sort of conversation; I can almost see the humour in it. Rob has a way of saying things that begs indulgence; requests are made politely, if with a certain amount of presumption, and mild condemnations are usually delivered with humour. He's not the least like Andrew, my friend Julia's husband, who barks instructions and delivers decisions on family matters rather in the manner of an esteemed and curmudgeonly judge. And when I moan to Fran she reminds me that being chief peeler of grapes for a loving, faithful husband is far preferable to living with a man who helps with the cooking then buggers off with his perky-bottomed anaesthetist.

On other occasions this sort of exchange will prompt a resentful, bad-tempered retort. I never know which way it's going to go. Only lately it seems to be going more often in the direction of a bad-tempered retort. I am steadily amassing a list of Things That Trigger Bad Reactions. It includes:

- Being called the light bulb person, or the one who empties the dishwasher, or the person responsible for picking up things from Boots.
- When he says he doesn't do salad. Men don't, as a rule. It's far too fiddly, involving the washing and careful chopping of at least five different sorts of vegetable.
- That he doesn't ever put out the rubbish. All men put out the rubbish, don't they? Even utterly useless ones.
- Excessive use of the word *we* in sentences about jobs that need to be done.
- Not making the bed, even when he was the last one to get out of it and you are in as much of a hurry to get out of the house as he is.
- Making the bed badly, so that it actually looks more untidy than before it was made.

Sometimes I can nip a bad-tempered reaction

in the bud by rationalising that this is all part and parcel of the trade-off I made. He bears the burden of breadwinning, which can reasonably be calculated to last thirty-five years with no time off for good behaviour and no chance of early release. In return, I bear the burden of everything else, including being the one who buys bacon, the light bulb person, the dishwasher person, the Boots person, the person who opens and deals with all the post (including bills, letters from the Inland Revenue, and those electoral registration forms they send out every five minutes), the person who assists with homework, the person who uses a screwdriver to fix the loose handle on the fridge door, or, to cut a very long list short, the person in charge of Miscellaneous. Oh, and as part of the deal I agree to relinquish all pretence of an independent life.

Maybe he doesn't think it's a very good trade-off either, but I don't often hear him complain. Except when I forget to get bacon or refuse to get out of bed to get a new light bulb.

PHOEBE

Josh makes a funny groaning noise I haven't heard before. I'm familiar with most of his noises, but this one is new. His hand is fumbling around under my top and my neck is wet where he's been mooching for at least five minutes.

'Oh, Phoebs,' he says, making the strange groaning noise again. It's a little like the sound he made when he got kneed in the groin on the rugby pitch. Or the one he made just before he was sick at Laura's party. Maybe a combination of the two, with an underscore of gentle panting.

'Phoebe, please.'

'Not yet. I can't,' I say. But I don't want to put him off completely, so I gently chew at his lips the way I know he likes and put my hand on the bulge in his jeans. This just seems to irritate him.

'Phoebe, you can't do that! First you say no, then you say yes.'

'I did not say yes! I kissed you.'

'The kiss said yes.'

'That's not my problem,' I say sniffily, adjusting my bra and pulling my shirt down over my jeans.

'What is the problem? I'm so into you Phoebe.

Aren't you into me?'

'Of course I am. It's just that . . .' The sentence trails off while I sit staring at my hands, twisting the turquoise rings on my middle finger.

'It's just that what?'

'I only just started taking the pills. And you have to take them for at least three months before they work properly,' I say triumphantly.

'But I've got condoms,' he suggests playfully, reaching across and twirling a piece of my hair around his fingers.

'Yeah, well, condoms break. Or don't they tell you that at boys' schools?'

He drops his hand and flops back dramatically on the sofa, both arms flayed out across the cushions. He scrunches up his eyes and starts to make mock crying noises.

'You'll just have to wait a bit longer,' I say, moving in to tickle him. 'Tell you what. I promise I'll be ready by the end of May when the three months are up. That's not so long, is it?'

He turns and smiles at me. 'It's fucking for ever!' he says, lunging towards me and squeezing my waist. The tickling leads to wrestling and a full-scale chase around the house and culminates in his lying on top of me on his bed, pinning me down and kissing me. I feel that unmistakeable stiffening against my pelvic bone and I know I have to do something before he has time to think about mounting another campaign. There are lots of options, I know, but at this moment the best one seems to be ice cream.

'I'm starving,' I announce, wriggling out from underneath him and escaping to the door. 'Do you want Chunky Monkey or Chocolate Chip?'

When Mr and Mrs Thomason come home, Josh and I are a picture of propriety. We're sitting at the kitchen table going over Josh's English essay, which was in a pathetic state before I got hold of it.

'Hello, you two. Have a nice time?' coos Mrs Thomason. Mr Thomason nods at us from across the kitchen as he hangs the keys on one of the little hooks above the noticeboard. I notice that the board is incredibly neat and organised, with everything in rows and nothing overlapping, unlike ours which has layers and layers of assorted (and probably long redundant) stuff pinned to it. Old photos, taxi cab numbers, recipes, school timetables from about three years ago.

'Really good, thanks,' I say in my most polite voice. I like Mrs Thomason, but she's a bit scary. You just know she's not the type to put up with anything short of perfect courtesy.

'Phoebe, I forgot to mention earlier, I ran into your mother the other day,' says Mrs Thomason through a sort of stretched smile, smoothing the bow of her silk blouse with an immaculately manicured hand. 'I suggested that she might want to join my committee, the one that's organising the St Helen's ball. Would you be a love and remind her to let me know? It would be such fun to work together and Lord knows we could use the help.'

Although I try very hard, I can't really see my

Mum and Mrs Thomason working together. Mrs Thomason is so frighteningly busy and efficient. She's on the boards of about a hundred charities, and seems to know absolutely everyone. Last month she had dinner with Jude Law and Vanessa Redgrave because she's fund-raising for a theatre they're involved with. I mean, how on earth could Mum compete with that? All she's done for the past fifteen years is look after us.

Then I think, maybe that's the point. Maybe I should encourage Mum to help Mrs Thomason. It would be good for Mum to get out a bit, do something interesting. She might even be able to get herself invited to a few of those dinners with famous people. And besides, Mrs Thomason isn't the kind of person you turn down.

The bottom line is, it just can't be good for a grown woman to spend her whole life thinking about when she last changed the sheets, can it?

LIBBY

I used to go running with Fran until she declared herself more of a Pilates person and gave up the habit. 'I just can't be doing with all that bloody pounding and fresh air,' she proclaimed. 'You'll have to find another running partner.' I mostly run by myself, except every other Friday morning, when four of us go running in the park with a sergeant-major type called Hank. (Before I met him, I didn't think real people were called Hank any more, or ever.) Hank was Gilly's personal trainer until she generously decided to share him with the rest of us every now and then. So Gilly, Karen, Penny and I scurry along behind him, trying to keep up, then endure twenty minutes of sit-ups, press-ups and other similarly undignified exercises in full view of the bleary-eyed commuters driving through Richmond Park.

I know that running destroys the knees and plays havoc with your pelvic floor, but it's the most exhilarating feeling I know. Although I enjoy the sessions with Hank and the girls, my favourite time to run is very early on a winter's morning, when everyone else is still buried under their duvets and struggling to face the day. I love that feeling of getting a head start, so that no matter how else the day shapes up, how much crap it throws at you, you can look back and remember how you felt out there with the cold air on your cheeks. Really alive. And like a whole person, not just the bits of person that everyone else likes to see.

I often wonder what Rob sees. Perhaps a faded version of me, like the wallpaper you take for granted when you've had it on the wall for a while. Then every now and then you find yourself staring at an amazing motif and you remember why you chose it. I've a feeling it's like that with Rob and me. Every once in a while he remembers why he chose me. But there's no disputing the fact that I've slipped into the category of background decor.

I once tried an experiment. I went to Selfridges and bought three unashamedly sexy bra and knicker sets. They were the most gorgeous articles you've ever seen. More lace and silk and cleavage-enhancing construction than Rob had been privy to in years. I wore them in rotation for about two weeks before he noticed. And then all he said as he picked them up from the floor where I'd dropped them and dangled them from his little finger was, 'These new? Not like you, Lib.' And this from the man who'd once been unable to keep his hands off me. I don't think he meant to be so dismissive (I've always known him to be more of a fan of pure white cotton than elaborate lace numbers that try too hard), but I was still bothered by the realisation that he couldn't really imagine me as an Agent Provocateur sort of woman. Ever ready with a sapient alternative point of view, Fran's take on this was that I was *lucky* Rob didn't fully appreciate my expensive lingerie. 'If a man goes gaga for sexy underwear on you, you can just bet he'll be going gaga for it on someone else too,' she said.

Today, I return from my run to find him standing naked in front of an open drawer with his hands on his hips, seething with indignation I can spot even from behind. He still looks strong and lean like the rugby player he once was: muscular legs, firm bottom, sculpted back and shoulders. His only real concession to age is the slight thickening above his hips, the bit I grab hold of whenever we are teasing one another about being at the top of the hill, if not actually over it. Even his hair is youthful, dark blonde and gently curling at the back of his neck. It's only when you look at him face on that you notice the slight ebbing at the forehead, the one or two silver hairs at the temples.

When he hears me come into the room he spins around and heaves an accusatory sigh. 'Lib, there are no boxers in here!'

'Yes there are,' I fire back, not entirely sure it's the truth.

'No there are not. See for yourself.' He steps aside and ceremoniously waves me towards the drawer.

I decide to ignore the melodramatic gesture. 'Well, I must have left them in the laundry room.

I know I washed them. I'll be right back.'

I dash downstairs, noting with mild alarm that there are no signs of life coming from any of the girls' rooms despite the fact that it's gone seven. The boxers are indeed in the utility room, folded neatly and waiting for someone to carry them upstairs, along with half a dozen perfectly ironed T-shirts and several pairs of socks. Of course I'm not stupid enough to suppose that the someone would be anyone but me. Clean laundry could sit down in that room for weeks and they could all have resorted to turning underwear inside out before it would occur to anyone to venture in the vicinity of the washing machine and actually look for an item.

I grab the pile of laundry and head back upstairs. Annoyingly, my foot catches on the heaving stair-basket, sending the damn thing tumbling down the stairs, whereupon it disgorges its contents all over the hall floor. The theory behind stair-baskets is that people pile in a day or two's worth of the clutter that has somehow scattered itself around the place, and then someone takes the basket upstairs and puts all the stuff away. It's another concept that doesn't really work very well, mainly because the someone is always me, and I don't even play by the rules. Judging by the stuff currently spread out over the hall floor – which includes a paperback Rob finished reading before Christmas and a hairclip I remember Ella searching for some-time last month – it's been some time since the wretched basket was put to its proper use.

I quickly stuff the spilled junk back into the basket and place it on the step before running upstairs with my pile of laundry. By this time Ella and Kate appear to be up, but Herself's room is still pitch-black. After throwing a pair of boxers at Rob, who makes an amusing sight sitting on the bed in just a shirt and black socks, I cross the hall to wake her.

The air is heavy with sleep and it's so dark it takes me a second to locate the bed. I stand by the side of her bed and gently touch her shoulder. A more assertive gesture would only invite abuse.

'Phoebe. It's time to get up. You've overslept.'

'Go away. Tired.'

'Phoebs, come on. Wake up.'

Normally it is forbidden to open curtains, but when rousing her promises to be especially difficult I occasionally risk it. Today I go over to the window and draw the curtains aside a couple of inches, just enough to let in a stream of sunlight that casts a yellow stripe all the way across the carpet and up on to the duvet.

Immediately I think, *If only I hadn't done that.* But it's too late. I look down and there it is. A tiny fragment of pink tin foil on the carpet. So close to the baseboard that by this afternoon it might well have worked its way into the gap between carpet and baseboard and never been found.

There was no guarantee she was going to listen to my advice. I know that. But I had rather hoped that I might at least delay things a little. Surely at her age, even a few months can make a difference to the experience. Now I don't know what to do. What does a mother do at a time like this? Acknowledge that something magical and special and potentially life-changing has taken place, or is about to? Tell her I hope Josh was using a condom as well? Or kick the pink foil into the corner and creep out of the room?

I can't have been standing here very long, but it clearly seems like an age to Phoebe. She sits bolt upright and shouts, 'Mum! What are you doing!'

'Just letting some light in, darling,' I say, flicking my heel against the carpet as I leave the room.

'Good run?' says Rob when I walk back into our room. The clean boxers have obviously nipped his bad mood in the bud.

'What? Oh, yeah. Fine.'

'Must have been cold out there this morning.'

When the pause goes unanswered, he says, 'You OK?'

'Fine,' I say. 'Just thinking about what I have to do today.'

'Whatever it is that you have to do, do you think you could squeeze in a trip to the sports shop to get my racket restrung? I just remembered I'm playing Tom on Saturday and the strings are shot to hell.'

Ella appears at the door. 'And while you're out, could you please go to W.H. Smith and get me one of those green folders with 'Glamour' on the front? And it has to be green because Lilly has the pink, so if they don't have it there please try to find it somewhere else.'

Racket restringing? Green 'Glamour' folders? Certainly. And while I'm at it, why don't I pop into the chemist and pick up a year's supply of birth-control pills for my eldest daughter who, by the way, is not very old.

That trick about counting to ten does work, and I use it often. By the time I get to ten I no longer feel unable to restrain myself from shouting, 'What do you think I am? Your fucking servant!' Instead, what comes out is the eminently more reasonable, 'I'll try to fit it in, but I have to go down to see Dad today so it might have to be tomorrow, OK?'

Then I head towards the shower and get in it without waiting to see if it's OK. I turn the shower on full and bend my head forwards in the hope that that the water will massage away the tension in my neck. I wonder when it was that I got so good at burying things. When it was, exactly, that I stopped shouting and resisting and began acquiescing? Did someone tell me at some point that this is what good mothers do? Because if they did, they've a lot to answer for.

Later, I am struck by a memory of Elena Jacob's mother, Betty. I'd been invited to supper and we were all sitting around waiting for it to be served. Mr Jacob was there, and Elena's brother Timothy.

We were expecting Mrs Jacob to come into the dining room carrying a dish of lasagne, but instead she came in carrying her handbag, a mint-green thing with a short, stiff handle and a gold clasp. 'Right,' she'd said. 'I'm going out.'

'Out?' Mr Jacob had said incredulously. 'Out where?'

'Just out. I see no reason why it's any of your business. You go out all the time.' Then she'd turned on her heels and marched towards the front door. A moment later we heard the rubber of her tyres squeal as she sped away in her battered estate car.

Later that month, Mrs Jacob went out unexpectedly again. Only that time she stayed away for almost a year.

When I looked back, I realised that there had been clues, if anyone had wanted to pay attention to them. One time she was sitting smoking at her kitchen table and I walked by on my way to the TV room. She looked so tired and sad that I'd asked her if she was all right and she'd said, 'This family'll bleed me dry if they're not careful.'

Counting to ten isn't always enough on the days when I visit Dad. Sometimes a whole combination of strategies is required, everything from taking deep breaths and smiling inanely to physically removing myself from the room.

As I pull into the drive of his tiny cottage and hear the familiar crunching of the gravel beneath my tyres I can see him through the kitchen window.

He looks up and waves, as he always does, then begins the slow, awkward shuffle towards the front door. I can clamber out of the car a lot faster than he can negotiate the trip from kitchen chair to front hall, so I usually have to stand at the door and wait for a few minutes.

'Hello, my lovely,' he says as the door creaks open.

'Hi, Dad. Are you winning today?' I say, putting my arms around his bony chest and squeezing gently.

'Just about, love. Just about.'

I walk behind him on the painfully slow return to the kitchen, then dash ahead of him to plump up the cushions of his chair before he sits down. I dump the carrier bags full of food on to the kitchen table, where a couple of dirty cereal bowls and a crumb-strewn plate are sitting amongst a few days' worth of old newspapers.

'How's Rob?' he asks as I start putting away the food and moving the dirty dishes to the sink.

'Really well, Dad.'

'And how's that new optician he's just taken on? Working out all right?'

Here we go. Count to ten. Deep breath. Smile.

'I think he's going to work out really well. He's com-petent and reliable, which is about all you can ask for,' I say.

Rob's new partner started working with him almost a year ago, but my father asks about him every week as if he's just turned up for his first

60

day at work. That's the Alzheimer's talking and the reason I take deep breaths for most of the five hours I'm with Dad each week. The other questions I'm prepared for are, in no particular order, and each repeated on average three times per visit: 'So does Phoebe have a boyfriend yet?' 'What do you think of that Tony Blair, then?' and 'When did you last speak to Jaime and Liz?'

Jaime and Liz are my sisters, Liz being the eldest and Jaime the youngest, leaving me in the middle. I think this means I'm supposed to be awkward and rebellious, but it doesn't seem to have worked out that way, on account of the fact that I've been far too busy being a doormat instead.

Jaime, Liz and I had to sit down months ago when Dad's Alzheimer's seemed to worsen dramatically overnight and work out how to make sure he was properly cared for. We devised a sticking-plaster sort of system that has me visiting him every Tuesday and every other Thursday as well, Mrs Tupper the cleaning lady popping in every day for an hour or so, meals on wheels four times a week, and a companion from the local church spending Friday afternoons playing chess with him. (God only knows what that's like for her. I should think those knights and rooks get moved around in an alarmingly disorderly manner.) Jaime has him for lunch every other Sunday if she can manage to prise herself out of her potter's studio for the day, and Liz just does whatever she can, which is to pay for Mrs Tupper and occasionally send other (guilt-drenched) cheques in the post. Liz has such a frenetic lifestyle, what with two young children and a stellar career as a corporate lawyer, that you can't really blame her for being useless when it comes to fulfilling domestic demands emanating from outside the four walls of her Chelsea town house. But that doesn't stop me from doing it. The funny thing is, Dad doesn't seem to notice. He constantly claims to have seen Liz 'just the other day', even when I know she hasn't set foot in the place for weeks.

'Have you eaten this morning, Dad?' I ask, opening the fridge to put away the milk and a block of the extra strong cheddar he likes. The middle shelf is encrusted with hardened egg yolk, obviously the result of an earlier mishap. I make a mental note to scrub it clean once I've sorted through his post and put the washing in.

'I think so, dear.' The strained expression on his face tells me that he's not sure.

'Why don't I just make you a little snack, then? Buttered toast and banana all right?'

'Lovely, dear. How's that young Phoebe, then? Got a boyfriend yet?'

'Bloody hell,' I mutter, resting my head on the steering wheel and pounding it with my fist. Then I look up and smile, remembering that Dad could still be watching me through the window. It wouldn't do to let him realise how thoroughly exhausting and soul-destroying I find these days.

During moments like these I find myself feeling ir-rationally angry with Mum for leaving him to face this awful decline by himself. She was always the fit one, the one with all the energy. Then, like a bolt out of the blue, she has a heart attack and dies. *Women just don't have heart attacks*, I remember thinking at the time. Especially not women like Mum, women who could still march around the block at a clip carrying several string shopping bags laden with apples and onions, women who could still dance the foxtrot given the opportunity.

Mum died three years ago, and already my memories of her are fading slightly. Now, with Dad's mind in such a mess, I can't even rely on him to remind me of how she was. If I ask him how she handled this or that when she was bringing us up, or what she thought about such and such, he gazes wistfully into the middle distance as if he's waiting for some sort of memory prompter to drop down before his eyes. When he does eventually answer me I can never be sure it's an actual story about Mum that he's recounting and not a recollection based on the combined experiences of any number of other women, including his sister Edith and Mrs Harris next door.

I remember once he told me a story so familiar I stopped what I was doing (chopping carrots, I think) and just stared at him open-mouthed. What a coincidence, I'd said, the exact same thing happened to me. Then it dawned on me that of course I was the one it had happened to. I'd told him the story and he was retelling it with my mother in the leading role.

The one thing he will always say with complete conviction is, 'She was a wonderful mother, your mum. Always put you first and never once complained.' I must have heard some variation of that sentence a thousand times. I can even vouch for the truth of it myself. Memories of Mum might be fading, but they're still vibrant enough for me to know that she was always there, unfailingly unselfish, forever giving up her piece of sponge cake so that one of us could have seconds.

One thing she would almost certainly have done, regardless of how drained and run off her feet she felt, would be to stop off on the way home to restring a tennis racket and hunt down a green *Glamour* folder.

With that kind of role model, how could I go wrong?

PHOEBE

When Mum visits Grandpa she always comes home in a crap mood. Crap can range from mildly withdrawn to outright irritable, but it's all crap. Sometimes she'll slope around the kitchen making dinner but not speaking. And when you ask her something she takes for ever to answer, like your question was so complicated she had to work out the answer. Sometimes she doesn't answer at all.

But tonight she's not going to have a choice. I have to decide what I'm going to do for my A levels and I need a parental signature. Dad's got late night at the clinic, so it's down to Mum.

I wait until she's done all the dishes before I spring it on her. When I walk into the sitting room she's stretched out on the red sofa with the newspaper on her lap, but she doesn't look like she's reading it.

'Mum, did you remember tomorrow's the deadline for handing in my A-level form?'

She looks a bit vague for a second, then it's like a light goes on. 'Oh my gosh, yes. I'd completely forgotten.'

'So, can we talk about it now?'

I see her take a deep breath (why *does* she do that so often?) and shut her eyes for a second before she says, 'Sure. Fire away.'

So then there's a conversation that lasts about an hour and is really pretty painful. I want to drop German, she thinks it would be a waste of all the effort I've put in. I want to do drama, which means I have to give up ICT, and wouldn't Dad think that was a missed opportunity? You get the picture.

I want to tell her that she can't really talk about not wasting years of effort. She spent four years getting a degree in marine biology at university and about five minutes working in the field. She sometimes talks about going back to it, but I think *Yeah, right, like that's ever going to happen.* I mean there's not going to be a lot of opportunity to research the habits of starfish and dolphins when you live in London, is there? If she'd trained as a lawyer or an accountant or something it might have been more useful.

I haven't a clue what I want to do with my life. I'm hoping something will hit me. Some passion I can't ignore. As it is I get pretty good marks across the board, even in chemistry, so I can't even eliminate anything on the basis of ineptitude.

One thing I've decided is that I'm not going to waste my brains like Mum did. People are always telling me I should be a model, and sometimes I think I might be, but even if I was, I'd make sure I was an Elle Macpherson kind of model. I'd make sure I got involved in the business side of things. You've just got to stay on the ball.

Which reminds me, just as I get up off the sofa, of Mrs Thomason.

'By the way, Mrs Thomason wanted me to ask you if you'd thought about joining her ball committee.'

'Oh God. Yes, I have. And no, I won't,' Mum says, smacking the newspaper with her fist.

'Muuum! It's a great opportunity. You can't say no.'

'Phoebe. Being on the decoration committee for a charity ball that's going to be attended by a load of self-important ladies-who-lunch who've each invested three thousand pounds in a new ballgown, and the sum total of the proceeds of which will be less than ten per cent of the ticket sales, is not what I would call a great opportunity.'

'But Mrs Thomason has asked you! She knows everyone. So you could get to know everyone too.'

'Phoebe, I'm not interested in knowing everyone. I know enough people.'

'Oh yeah, like who? Penny Bourne? She's a *real* somebody!'

Even I know that's mean. Penny, one of Mum's occasional running buddies, is nice, even if she is sartorially challenged. She wears belts *through* the belt loops of her *high-waisted* jeans, and sweaters with cute *appliqués* on them. Last year she turned up to Christmas drinks in a sweater with a Christmas tree on the front. When she squeezed

67

a button hidden deep in her trouser pocket, the tree lit up and started flashing.

From anyone else my comment might prompt outrage. But Mum just frowns at me and shakes her head.

'Phoebe, I hope you don't mean that. And if you do, I hope you'll quickly come to see how appalling an attitude it is.'

And that's when I say it. The unforgivable. Just to see if she'll forgive it.

'For God's sake, Mum. You don't know anybody important, and you don't do anything important. You're wasting your life. And someone like Mrs Thomason comes along and offers you a chance to get involved and you just pass it up. Well, if you want to be a loser, that's your problem.'

It's my problem too. I know that. Because from the minute the words have escaped my lips I want to take them back. Mum's face goes pale and her eyes fill up. But she still doesn't shout at me. I think she might be in shock. But for the life of me I can't think what to do next.

So I pick up the A-level forms she's signed and walk upstairs to my room. Before I even reach the door I can hear U2s 'Numb' on my radio, which just about sums things up.

LIBBY

There's no mileage in going head-to-head with a fifteen-year-old. Particularly not someone as adept at acerbity as Herself. Even when they've been more insulting and hurtful than you'd dreamed humanly possible. What would be gained? At best a grudging and insincere apology. At worst a sneer and another dose of derision.

Phoebe's outburst hits me just below the shoulder blade, on the left hand side of my chest. A burning sensation spreads out rapidly from its hard, hot core. I always feel pain and disappointment there. Not in the heart, exactly, but near enough.

I don't feel the burning sensation all that often. Ordinary, everyday upsets and defeats might only cause the slightest flutter in my stomach. Some go no further than my head, where they are rationalised away, or buried in the minutiae of daily life. Something has to be extra-ordinarily distressing to reach that spot below my shoulder blade.

When I heard about Mum's death, I felt it then, of course. For days, weeks even. And now every so often, when a thought or picture of her passes through my mind, startling me. Every now and then it's prompted by something between Rob and me. There might have been an argument, the careless exchange of cruel comments scripted for shock value. Then again, it might come out of nowhere, on the back of a period of coolness and ordinariness between us, and brought on by nothing more than a look in his eye, or the absence of a look I wish were there.

It's not just the fact that she sees me this way that hurts. It's the fact that when I close my eyes and look at my life as if from afar, I experience a stab of something that feels like regret, which is even worse than being insulted by my own daughter. I wonder how it's possible to regret a life that includes a good marriage to a loving husband, three wonderful children and a very nice roof over all our heads. But I don't think it's these things I regret. It's the part of me that got lost in their creation.

When Rob and I were first together we talked all the time about taking a year out to go and work abroad. South-east Asia was the destination – a place where I would be able to do groundbreaking research into marine species and he would be able to save the sight of waiflike, sad-eyed children and frail old people living in remote villages. The dream bubbled away for a few years, but with each step on the ladder of respectability and stability it receded. By the time Phoebe was born, it was as dead as a squirrel under the tyre of a ten-ton lorry.

Everybody has dreams, and a great many of

them come to nothing. And who's to say that travelling around Asia studying tropical fish and providing the poor with specs would have been any more fulfilling than loving one another and raising a family? It's not really the loss of the Asia dream that I regret. It's the fact that I didn't get around to replacing it with any other. Rob got his optometrist's practice, purchased from his long-time friend and mentor Patrick Fox when he was just thirty. He's even been able to indulge his love of rugby through the sports-vision side of his business. (His contracts with two of the country's top rugby clubs are a source of great pride for him, and he's spent many an enjoyable day teaching talented players exercises to improve their hand-eye coordination.) He is forever expanding his knowledge, attending lectures and conferences on things like lens technology and corneal injury. Just last month he spent two days in lectures about retinal detachment which he described as 'utterly fascinating'. *And* he has his family. Me? I have a beautifully framed BSc (Hons) in Marine Environmental Science from the Oceanography Centre at Southampton University, and seventeen years' work experience in domestic survival in the heart of suburban Richmond.

Maybe marine sciences wasn't the best choice of degree. Even English graduates were more in demand than marine science grads back then. (The same is probably true today.) And it doesn't exactly lend itself to a flexible life, a life full of starts and stops and moves and compromises. There's one inescapable fact about a career in marine sciences: you have to be near the sea if you want to do more than dabble. And if that's not possible, because the man you love has career opportunities that draw him inexorably to London, your own career is pretty much stuffed.

About seven or eight months after Rob and I met, we did try living separately so that I could take advantage of a six-month research contract back at Southampton. It was a project in 'Sedimentary Dynamics and Diagenetic Processes' – not exactly my desired specialisation. But it was a fully funded position that I'd heard about before anyone else, thanks to an old mentor, Professor Magnus Johnson. So I left the flat Rob and I had been sharing in London and went to live in a ten-foot-square university dorm room for six months.

The research was fascinating, and it was unspeakably thrilling to be looking at the dynamics of anything at all after months doing menial jobs demanding no greater skill than the counting of small change. But being apart from Rob was torture, for both of us. Our relationship was at the stage when separation resulted in real physical discomfort. Weekend visits and nightly phone calls were no cure for the ache I felt not waking up beside him.

When the research project ended I moved straight back to London, and we were married six months later. Soon after the wedding I spent a year as a tutor at the Scarborough Centre for Coastal Studies, which only required me to be away from home two days a week. But after Phoebe was born the mountain that was my chosen career seemed to loom ever more insurmountable. How was I to seek out another of these elusive positions with a baby chewing on my breast twenty hours a day? With what, exactly, was I to pay for childcare when the most I could seem to earn looking at sea creatures was seven pounds an hour?

Besides, when Phoebe came, it all seemed less important somehow. Am I ashamed to say that? I'm not sure. But it was the truth. Even at twenty-seven, when so many of my friends were still galavanting around the world on extended gap years or galloping towards early coronaries in the City, I knew my place was with her, and I quickly came to cherish that place. Ideas of making a name for myself as a marine researcher, or simply losing myself in the search for some comparatively rare species on a seashore, seemed to recede with each stint with the bottle steriliser. I remember once, just after Ella was born, someone asked me what I'd done before the children came along and I was actually stuck for an answer. The girl who had been a marine biologist seemed so far away, so unconnected to me by then, that I must have felt fraudulent in even claiming to know her.

By 1997, when the London Aquarium opened, I might have been ready to relaunch myself back into the adult world. And for a few months my hopes were raised. I scoured their website for details of job openings, and even managed to track down a contact there who'd known Professor Johnson. But it didn't take long for me to realise that what they really wanted at the aquarium were a few bright young things (bright, young, unhindered and willing to work all hours) and a raft of 'information specialists' working on a volunteer basis as guides to the hordes of tourists that soon spilled out in winding queues from the aquarium doors. I didn't fit either category, and I knew I wasn't going to get very far.

I suppose 1997 was the last time I gave my career any serious thought. And with three girls under seven, a husband with a flourishing optometrist's practice and no aptitude whatsoever for juggling (is it a term that even applies to men, I wonder?), it was not a thought that lasted very long. There's been a sort of ill-formed, unspoken sense of unease growing within me since then, but nothing that anyone would notice. Nothing I've allowed myself to pay much attention to.

I probably wouldn't be paying any attention to it now were it not for Phoebe's cruelty. I want to accuse her of a profound lack of gratitude, of not having a clue how difficult it is to subsume oneself entirely to the promotion of four other people's happiness for fifteen years. I'm tempted to stage a sit-in, where we can both test out how she might find life if I weren't someone who'd wasted her own on her three children. But all the while I am muttering these words beneath my breath three others are poised there on my lips. 'You are right.' *You were right*, I might one day say to her.

But I don't say it when she launches her attack, or any time in the days after it. Neither do I relent and decide to become a member of Claire Thomason's Marquee Decoration Committee, or whatever else it is that she has in mind for me. I decide, instead, to *go out*. To the maiden meeting of the Richmond branch of Green Link on Wednesday evening. I'd already been thinking that I owed it to Ella, and it occurs to me that I might also owe it to myself. It must, I think, be better than doing a full-scale Mrs Jacob.

PHOEBE

When she tells me about the meeting she's going to, my first reaction is that she must be quite mad. Then I think, *She's just doing this to annoy me. To prove a point.* Turning down Mrs Thomason is embarrassing enough. But to turn her down in favour of going to a meeting with a bunch of non-entity environmentalists, at the public library? On a Wednesday no less, which is the day she'd promised to take me shopping for new boots, and the day Kate needs collecting from hockey. That's embarrassing and mad combined.

'Jesus,' I moan to Kate. 'Let's get this straight, shall we? Work alongside some of the most influential women around to raise money for charity and maybe get invited to meet Jude Law? No. Hang out with a bunch of vegans in kaftans every Wednesday and moan about climate change? Absolutely. She'll be there. Is it just me or has she lost the plot?'

Kate looks at me and says, 'What's the big deal?' and I realise I've chosen the wrong person to moan to. Kate is so infuriatingly neutral all the time. It's impossible to get her riled up about anything. I sometimes wonder if there's anything going on in her head at all.

'Obviously, you've lost the plot as well,' I tell her.

LIBBY

Rob,
Lasagna warming in oven. Should be ready at 6.30. Serve with green salad (in fridge – dressing in yellow jug). Back at 8.30 or so.
Ella with me. Please make sure Kate puts wet hockey stuff in utility.
Love, Lib.

Kate,
Sorry was not able to collect you from hockey. Just put filthy kit in utility room and I'll wash it for tomorrow.
Love, Mum.

Phoebe,
Kate being dropped off at 6.15. Dad home at 6.30ish. See his note re. supper in case he's late.
Love, Mum.

Fran thinks I make things hard on myself, going to these sorts of lengths. Ever since she went back to work four days a week she's had to demand less of herself, accept the fact that all the surfaces in

78

her house will be permanently adorned with a fine layer of dust or that the boys will occasionally have to eat a Sainsbury's ready-made shepherd's pie. Last year, faced with two bake sales in one week, she purchased three home-made cakes from the first one at Jake's school and took them as her contribution to the second at Freddie's rugby club.

The other day I moaned to her, as I occasionally do, that domestic chores seem to be taking over my life. 'Honestly, by the time I've dreamt up something for dinner, shopped for it, run an incredibly important errand for this person and sewn up the hole in the jumper for that person, then waited around for the bloody washing machine repair man or whoever to show up, the day's gone. And I feel like I have nothing to show for it.' Her response was matter of fact: 'Then just don't do it. Give yourself a break. Domestic chores have a monstrous way of expanding to fill the time available and I think you just have to say *enough!* Leave them to buy their own Pritt stick or fix their own dinner every once in a while. Having tinned soup once a week is not going to kill them.'

Despite Fran's enthusiastic coaching from the sidelines, I haven't quite got the knack of this. I feel much better leaving the house knowing that everything's organised and they know what to do; with detailed instructions, even that lot have to be able to get supper on the table and homework done. (In the wake of Phoebe's accusations it occurs to me that I might also be a little frightened of emptying the day of some of its menial

79

domestic contents for fear of not being able to find anything to replace them with.)

Six p.m. on a Wednesday evening isn't the most convenient time for a meeting. Perhaps the time has been set to accommodate those people who work locally and want to attend a meeting before going home for supper. Or perhaps it's been chosen to lure all those people who could never be tempted to leave the house in the full-on darkness, with dinner still undigested and EastEnders beckoning.

Inconvenient or not, I'm quite glad of it. It makes a change not to be driving around collecting children and standing at the stove dishing out supper at this time of day. I don't even mind the near darkness and the drizzle, which is so light as to be almost refreshing. Ella is in a good mood as well. Every third step is a skip as we walk together up Church Road towards the library. As we near the top of the hill I point at the spire of St Matthias Church, mesmerising against the darkening sky. She nods and smiles up at me, without my having to explain. She must have heard me comment on its beauty a thousand times. I never tire of looking at it. To me it's the most inspiring view in Richmond, rivalled only by the vista of the river and the cows in the meadows from Richmond Hill, which I always think would give a classic Turner a run for its money.

When we reach the library, the yellow light behind its steamed-up windows looks positively cheering. A handwritten sign informs us that the meeting is to be held in the large conference room that runs along one side of the library. It's well-used that room, being home to a Tiny Tots playgroup, a disabled children's art class, a music and movement class for the elderly, and several book clubs. I remember the playgroup from when the girls were young, and I've occasionally witnessed the swaying of octogenarian limbs through the glass panels of the doors.

Phyllis springs from her seat and rushes over to me as soon as we walk through them.

'Libby! How wonderful that you came,' she says, ushering Ella and me towards spare seats amongst the several rows that have been carefully arranged. 'Nancy, Barry, this is Libby. And I'm guessing this is Libby's daughter. Ella, isn't it?'

I remember Nancy as the name of Phyllis's health visitor friend, but Barry is an unknown quantity. He thrusts his long thin hand in my direction, his collarbones straining with enthusiasm, then nods and smiles in Ella's direction.

'Barry Staples. From the Doll's House.'

'Oh, the Doll's House,' I say, with genuine longing. At one time or another, each of my girls has coveted a doll's house from the collection of mini-Victorian buildings sold in the shop that sits at the far end of the parade of shops at the top of Church Road we call the village, between Amandine and Ed's Things.

'I'll bet Ella would love one of those houses, wouldn't you?' says Phyllis, beaming at Ella, who nods eagerly, though I know for a fact she's long since outgrown her desire for the perfect doll's house. Like Barbie, doll's houses seem to be the playthings of ever younger girls. Whereas I remember playing with both when I was eleven, all my girls had acquired other obsessions by the time they were seven or eight.

Phyllis's officiousness is undiminished by the absence of a date stamp. It's difficult to keep up with the pace of her conversation. I mentally prepare myself to be introduced at a clip to everyone in the room, which is humming with quiet conversation.

In fact Phyllis doesn't get the chance to make any more introductions. At the front of the room a tall slender man with a mass of pepper grey hair and a matching beard has suddenly appeared, and is quickly recognised as someone to whom attention must be paid. He smiles broadly before introducing himself. I notice that his jeans have a hole in one knee, but it's the kind of hole that comes from kneeling too much on rough ground as opposed to the kind that comes from taking style tips from David Beckham.

'Hello, everyone. Thank you so much for coming. My name's Derek Foster, and I'm a national team leader with Green Link. Before we start, I'd like to get these chairs into a bit more of a friendly set-up. I've no desire to be standing up here talking to rows and rows of chairs! Can I ask you all to help me move them into a circle?'

People immediately stand up and obey the bearded one, myself included. We're going to have a job getting all these chairs into a circle, I think, but I'm not about to dip my oar in. Let him figure out the geometry.

In actual fact, it's not as difficult as I'd thought. There aren't that many people in the room. Fifteen, twenty maybe. Quite easily accommodated by a large circle if the chair legs are overlapped a little.

'Great. Fantastic,' announces Derek, sitting himself down and leaning forward with his elbows resting on his long, partially outstretched legs. He then leans over and whispers something to the man beside him, a youngish bloke with dark, shoulder-length hair. The dark-haired fellow shuffles some papers around, finds the one he's looking for and hands it to Derek.

In the instant it takes Derek to gather his thoughts I scan the circle at low level. I only spot one pair of sandals worn with socks. The rest are just your average array of scuffed boots and trainers, the exceptions being one pair of pristine burgundy court shoes and a fabulous pair of green suede high-heeled boots. I look up from the sandals with socks combination at Barry's grinning face.

'Right,' pronounces Derek. 'Let's get started! I'd like us all to introduce ourselves, then we'll tell you a little about what we're trying to achieve at Green Link and how you might be able to support us. Let's start with Daniel here, who's what we call a local team leader. Daniel?'

'Hi there,' says Daniel with an easy, almost lazy smile. 'I'm an advisor to Green Link at a national level, environ-mental science being my background, and I'm also a local team leader, which means I'm in charge of setting up and overseeing local action groups. I'm working with three at the moment, one in the Oxford area, one in Nottingham, and this one, which means I'll be spending an awful lot of time on trains. On the plus side it also means I'll be able to share experiences between the three groups. Anyhow, it's great to see you all here. I'm really looking forward to working with you.'

Daniel turns to his right to face a small, elderly woman whose near-translucent hair gives her something of the appearance of an angel.

'Hello, everyone. I'm Daisy Hancock. I live in the flats behind the library,' she says in a voice that's very refined but barely audible.

'And what brings you to the group tonight, Daisy?' prompts Daniel.

'Oh well. I suppose it's something I've thought about doing for some time. And Phyllis over there reminded me that I'm not getting any younger so I'd better hurry up about it. She's right, of course. And with my children so far way and my poor husband dead, I've plenty of time on my hands.'

'Time is what we need here. Thanks, Daisy. And who are you?' Daniel nods towards the woman sitting next to Daisy, whose bright yellow hair is pulled back into a tight bun to reveal a pair of rather dramatic rouged cheekbones.

'My name's Lynnette. I run the beauty salon across the road. I've thought for quite a long time that I ought to do something positive about the environment, especially being in the business I'm in. You know, with all the chemicals I have to use. So when I saw the notice, and with it being so local, I thought you really don't have an excuse any more, girl. So here I am.'

Ella sits quietly beside me as introductions are made, her nervousness apparent in her rigid posture and perfectly still, tightly knotted hands. She leans towards me and whispers, 'Mummy, I'm the only child here.'

'That's OK. They'll be all the more pleased to have you,' I say, squeezing her hand.

After Lynnette, we meet David Peabody, a local vet with a face like a basset hound, and Shelly Davis, who apparently works at the DVLA office in town. She is tiny: five one at the most if you account for the stilettos. She has a small, upturned nose and enormous round eyes. Everything about her says perky. Then comes the owner of the green suede boots, a woman who could be anywhere between forty-five and fifty-five. It's impossible to say. Before she speaks she pushes aside a long strand of ringletted auburn hair that is obscuring her vision, and starts fingering the bright ceramic cross around her neck. Everything about her is earthy and vibrant, right down to the multi-coloured leather bracelet on her wrist.

'Hi, I'm Eloise. I own Lilac Rose, the boutique

just down the street. I also live near here. I'm a bit like Lynnette really. Always meant to do something, never got round to it. When this group turned up on my doorstep I thought it was really time to give it a go.' Eloise's deep Australian drawl impregnates the air with a sensuality that is most out of keeping with Daisy Hancock's floral print dress and Barry's footwear.

Nancy is next. She has a no-nonsense air about her, an impression probably created by her squarish face and extremely sensible haircut. Short, dark, styleless. Sexless. On first meeting, she seems a lot like Phyllis, though perhaps marginally less outspoken. Phyllis follows Nancy, and takes credit for the presence of most of the other individuals in the room. It seems that almost all of us have visited the library in the past couple of weeks and found ourselves clutching an orange leaflet courtesy of Phyllis.

Then it's my turn, and I wonder how it is that everyone else seems to have taken their introductions in their stride, whereas I can feel a tightness at my throat I'm sure will betray me. It's been a long time since I spoke in a group of more than about six people.

'I'm Libby. I live locally, with my husband and three girls. This is my youngest daughter, Ella. She's the reason I'm here, actually; she's been asking me questions I don't really know the answers to. We decided to come here together.' I pause before adding, 'Also, I was trained as a marine biologist about a hundred years ago, and I worked a lot on similar projects at the time. I think I'd really like to get back to some of that.'

'Great. I'm not sure how much marine activity we're going to see, but it's good to have you here,' Daniel enthuses. Then he directs his gaze at Ella, as does everyone else, and there's a brief period of silence during which I wonder whether she'll be brave enough to say something.

'I'm Ella. I've been worried for a long time,' she says finally, in her sunlit voice. 'You hear so many awful things and read terrible stories in the papers. I think there's going to be some sort of huge disaster if we don't start to do something. But it's hard to know what to do. Mum said coming here would help us to figure that out. I'm really, really excited about being here, even though I'm, you know, the youngest one and everything. I probably don't know as much as all of you but I'm really good at helping. Well, except when it comes to keeping my room tidy and stuff like that.'

Ella's giggle is greeted by an outbreak of laughter and a profusion of kindly smiles. Daniel looks directly at her. 'I have absolutely no doubt that you'll be an enormous help to us,' he says. Then he turns to the woman on my right, the proprietor of the burgundy pumps. 'And you are . . .?'

'Julia Harding,' she replies in a voice like the Queen's, only warmer, smoothing the skirt of her burgundy wool suit with delicate, plump hands. 'I'm headmistress at Carlisle Lodge. These two girls with me are Courtney and Michelle, who've volunteered to support me in my effort to get Lodge pupils more involved in local environmental action. We're all very pleased to be here.'

Courtney and Michelle don't look at all pleased to be here. Courtney is slumped disinterestedly in her chair, treating us to the occasional glimpse of her chewing gum as she rolls it around at the front of her tongue and clamps it between her front teeth. Michelle, meanwhile, is sitting upright but with her head tilted to one side, and is twirling the end of her pale straw-coloured ponytail around her fingers.

I experience a twinge of guilt, realising that Courtney and Michelle would probably be Phoebe's classmates if we'd opted to send the girls to Carlisle Lodge rather than cripple ourselves with three sets of exorbitant termly school fees. Julia Harding must be the headmistress I read about, the one who was drafted in to turn the place around a few years ago. Sitting beside her now I feel slightly ashamed of what will surely be interpreted as middle-class snobbery at some point during our mutual association with this group.

Barry goes next, but I have to confess to not listening very carefully during his short monologue, which isn't as short as it ought to be. I drift back into focus just as the woman next to him, Carole Watts, begins to speak. Turns out she and her friend next to her, Marcie Gibbons, live in the council houses close to Carlisle Lodge. They've both been concerned about the lack of respect for the local environment that they witness around them every day, the sprawling graffiti, the cardboard fish and chip trays strewn across the expanses of worn grass, the empty tin cans clattering around in the gutters.

By the time the last two introduce themselves almost half an hour has passed. So you have to forgive Derek when he fails to stifle a yawn just as Peter Ekenberry finishes introducing himself. Peter is 'M&S for Men' personified. Gentle, inoffensive, middle-of-the-road-looking in a burgundy and blue crew-neck sweater and grey trousers. As it transpires, Peter's family live next door to Ron, a fragile bespectacled man who looks to be in his sixties and is the last of the group to speak. Ron has a bird sanctuary in the back of his garden, which explains the extraordinary cacophony that can be heard whenever you pass the end of his street.

Introductions done and dusted, we all turn to Derek for some of the promised enlightenment as to the purpose of Green Link, and of this meeting. I'm still feeling self-conscious, like a bit of an imposter. I've come here as much for Ella as out of a deeply felt concern for the environment, whereas the others seem, I don't know, like the genuine articles. The truth is I can't really see it yet – Libby: wife, mother and . . . environmental activist.

Between them, Daniel and Derek explain the Green Link strategy of setting up hundreds of small local environmental groups to help make the big picture relevant locally. My mind wanders as talk of global warming and the Kyoto treaty washes over me. I force myself to pay attention.

'We thought it might be useful to list out some of the actions that have proven successful in other parts of the country, and to get some of your ideas for things that could work here.' Derek's voice tails off as he becomes distracted by his struggle with an ancient-looking flip-chart stand. One leg appears to be shorter than the other, so the stand ends up leaning precariously to one side and the coloured markers start to slide off the ledge.

Daniel leaps from his chair to help Derek, and manages to catch the markers before they fall to the floor. He goes behind the stand and fumbles about with something, which obviously does the trick, as the short leg suddenly becomes elongated and the whole mechanism is suddenly standing straight and tall.

Daniel then takes one of the markers and writes down the ideas as Derek explains them. With each action idea that's mentioned, I can sense our little group retreating into itself, becoming collectively more and more uncomfortable. Talk of local rubbish collection drives for school children and poster campaigns to remind people to recycle seem palatable enough. But by the time Derek gets to actions like door-to-door visits to encourage each family to make a ten-point energy-saving plan, faces have turned visibly grey. I don't think anyone counted on there being quite so much asked of them. Certainly not so much public action. Perhaps they'd just anticipated being required to stuff a few envelopes, which is what you can sometimes get away with when you sign up to help the local Labour or Conservative Party associations.

Derek and Daniel must be used to this open-mouthed silence, because they don't seem at all fazed by it. When they've reached the end of their list, Derek rubs his hands together and says, 'So there we have it. A host of useful, local initiatives that could really make a difference. What do you think?'

A couple of heads nod weakly, and there are a few audible 'hmmm's, but otherwise the reaction is pretty subdued. I begin to feel sorry for Derek and Daniel.

My thoughts are interrupted by the sound of Ella's voice, its sweet, optimistic note a stark contrast to the gloomy atmosphere.

'I especially like that one about getting people to use their cars less. Sometimes I think we use ours way too much, even when it would be really easy to walk. We have this monster of a car. A great big black Range Rover that costs about sixty pounds every time we fill it up. I don't think we need a car quite that big, do we, Mum?'

There are chuckles all round as the group sense my embarrassment in the face of Ella's revelation. Great. Another grenade lobbed into the great 4x4 onslaught, and by my own daughter, no less.

'It is second-hand, though,' I say defensively, not wishing people to think me profligate as well as environmentally negligent. 'Anyway, the idea of getting people to drive less in the local area *is* a good one. The others are good too. I can see how those actions could begin to get the community involved in this issue and really make a practical difference. It's just a little daunting, that's all.'

I look around the circle to see if I've spoken out of turn. No one else seconds my thoughts, but no one is shooting daggers at me either. After a few seconds someone else does speak up.

'Libby's absolutely right,' says Barry, sitting up straight, radiating earnestness. 'That list is daunting. And it's certainly not what I expected when I came here tonight. But I was wrong to expect anything else! We can't expect to improve the environment by sitting on or hands and listening to nice lectures, can we? We need to put our backs into it.'

I'd never have taken Barry to be a man of passion. But people are visibly moved by his declaration. Faces are just a little less pale and strained, slightly more open.

'Thank you to Libby and Barry for being so open. I hope you all agree with them,' says Derek.

'Hey, listen,' adds Daniel. 'You're not the only ones who find this daunting. When I first saw a list like this it scared the shit out of me.' Everyone laughs in response to this. Even Courtney and Michelle's faces crack.

'And you know,' continues Daniel, 'you're under no obligation to get involved. If you decide this isn't for you, that's cool. All we ask is that if you do decide to help, if you decide to come back here next week, you give us your whole-hearted support. We can do a lot together provided we're really in it together.'

Then he looks around the circle, smiling. The smile says everything. There's forgiveness for those who can't face getting involved, encouragement for those who aren't sure, and comradeship for those who've made up their minds to help.

I glance at Ella, whose ear-to-ear grin immediately tells me which category she and I will fall into. There will be no escaping this now. She is hooked, whereas I feel vaguely nauseous. Maybe it's just nerves, those butterfly-like flutterings you get when you are both excited and anxious. I have to admit there is something a little intoxicating about the thought of being involved in an initiative like this. Something new and fresh that could really change things. At the same time, I have a feeling that getting involved won't be without its complications.

And suddenly I feel unnaturally protective of my Range Rover.

PHOEBE

Caressing the little perforated pouches in the pink tin foil I register that there are twenty-three pills remaining. In each of the other two packs there are twenty-eight. That makes eighty-one days until I sleep with Josh. I lean over to my bedside table and grab the diary, opening it up to the front page that has the whole year at a glance.

I circle May the sixth, which will henceforth be known as The Day I Will Go All the Way. That's when he's expecting us to do it, and there's not the slightest chance he'll forget. No no no. He might not be able to write a decent English essay, but you can bet your life he'll have figured out about May the sixth within seconds of my telling him how many pills I've taken and how many there are in each pack. Without the aid of a calendar.

Looking at the red ring around May the sixth I feel a curious sense of a relief. The whole business of when you're going to have sex and who you're going to have it with is just so wearing. Now the decision's been made I feel as if I might be able to forget about it. I finally managed to start the pills on my third attempt. The first time the pill got stuck in my throat – that tiny little pill! But now, five pills later, I'm a pro.

I remember being shocked when I read in the paper that girls as young as thirteen are boasting about having had three or four partners already. And when I first heard about daisychaining, I thought it was a nerdy nature activity until someone explained that it was a faddish form of teen orgy.

Who are these pre-teens who are going at it like rabbits, I've wanted to know. They certainly don't go to Philmore High. Of the girls I know, only two have lost their virginity: Natalie, because she's been going out with Guy for over a year, and Rebecca, I think. I'm not even sure about Rebecca. She never has proper boyfriends, but occasionally you just hear things. There was a story about her sleeping with some guy from Westbury College she'd only been seeing for two weeks, but that could be just a rumour. I try not to get involved when her name comes up because I'm in a diffi-cult position. I've known Rebecca since we were both about five, ever since her mum Julia met Mum through her friend Fran and we started seeing each other at family lunches and that sort of thing. We're friends, but not really, if you know what I mean. She's not really my sort of person, but I feel a kind of loyalty towards her. And I really like Julia.

Thirteen, even fourteen is definitely too young. The trouble is, you don't want to leave it too late either. If you've not done it by seventeen, well, that could be embarrassing. So if you think about it, you've really only got a window of two years to get it right. And if you don't happen to have a nice boyfriend in that window, you're stuffed.

I remember Mum saying once that she felt sorry for girls today, growing up in such a sexualised environment. She's got a point. Sex *is* everywhere. You can't really open a magazine or look at a billboard or watch *EastEnders* without seeing someone shagging. It's just something you get used to. Truth is I don't even think about it any more except when she mentions it. Then, for maybe a day or two, it's all I see. People shagging. People talking about shagging. People desperate for a shag. Shagging, shagging everywhere.

Fortified by my plan, I pop a pill into my mouth. With uncanny timing, Dad appears at my door. He stands there like he's settling in for a really long chat. He asks me about the deadline for A-level choices and school in general and Josh, and all the while I have this little pill floating around in my mouth. Yesterday I found it so easy to swallow, without water or anything, but this little bugger just won't go down. And I keep thinking *Arseholes. He knows*. I'm sure he knows, because I can't speak properly with this pill stuck to my tongue.

'You OK, Phoebe?' he asks finally.

'Yeah. Just got a bit of a sore throat.'

'Here, let me look at it,' he says, walking towards me. He's forever peering at our tongues looking for the telltale green gunge that signals a throat infection requiring an immediate course of antibi-otics.

'No, no, it's OK,' I squawk, a bit too shrilly, desperately trying to manoeuvre the pill from where it's lodged between my teeth and gum.

'OK, OK,' he says, raising his hands. 'Keep your hair on.'

Then he just laughs and walks out of the room.

Thank Christ for that. Sex might be everywhere, but it's better for everyone if we all just pretend it isn't going on here.

LIBBY

Life is nothing if not full of surprises, thrown out like small reminders whenever you think you're in for a spot of smooth sailing. *Don't take things for granted*, life whispers. *Pay attention.*

Take today, for example. One minute we're all walking along in the spring sunshine swinging our shopping bags, the next minute Phoebe is close to tears.

Right up until the moment of the blow-up I'm marvelling at how pleasant the day has been. The three girls and I out shopping for necessities: jeans for Ella, summer shoes for Phoebe, a swimsuit for Kate. At 1.30, purchases in hand, and hardly a cross word exchanged all morning, we decide to drive to the Organic Burger Bar for lunch. I shove the last of the bags into the boot while the girls clamber into the car. Then, just as I walk round to the driver's side, it happens. There's a loud whistle, and I lift my head to see a swarthy, dark-haired man leaning out of the window of his lorry, banging on the outside of the door with his filthy palm. 'Hey, babe, lookin' good,' he shouts before ducking his head back inside to share a laugh with the two other blokes in the cab of the lorry.

It's innocent enough, and not all that unusual. It's what lorry drivers do, as a rule. I don't think much of it until I glance to my right and see Pheobe's thunderous expression.

'Mum, I can't believe what I just saw!'

'What?'

'Men leering and whistling at my mother!' she says accusingly.

'Phoebe, it's no big deal. Those sorts of blokes do that all the time, to everyone.'

'Yeah, but not my mother. That makes me feel quite sick. Really, you've no idea.' Then she slumps back in her seat, arms folded across her chest in disgust.

'Phoebe, I didn't do anything to encourage those men. It just happens.'

Silence. Silence all round, in fact. I don't think Kate and Ella know what to make of this.

'Phoebe, are you listening to me. It's not my fault, and it's not a big deal.'

She turns to me with a scowl, a thin veil for her bewilderment.

'Whatever. It's just that, I don't know, you don't like to think of your own mother that way. It's just not what you want to think.' She turns away to face the window, arms tightly folded, hostility emanating from every pore.

I don't see much point in continuing the discussion just at this moment, so I turn the ignition and pull away from the curb. Phoebe's frostiness persists all through lunch, despite the light-hearted banter between the rest of us. She's thawed a little by the time we get home, but there's a discernible barrier between us for the rest of Saturday.

Lying in bed that night, I'm left wondering whether I did, after all, do something wrong. Whether I have been doing something wrong all along. The question that plagues me at 1 a.m., while Rob lies beside me breathing the quiet, even breaths of someone in a deep and untroubled sleep, is have I been the right sort of mother?

You could drive yourself crazy thinking about what defines the right sort of mother. I know that. And I know there can't be just one definition of a good mother. But I've always suspected there are some sorts that are better than others.

I remember when Phoebe was little, about six, she became fast friends with Alice, who she's now known for almost nine years. Back then when they met at school, Alice was the eldest of three. She had a sister aged four and a brother aged eighteen months. Her mother Christine was in much the same situation as I was, I suppose, with three children under six. There was something slightly frenetic about all our lives, spent struggling around supermarkets with two or three disgruntled children in the trolley, or dragging tired and bad-tempered toddlers to the school gates to collect an older sibling. But there was always something more frenetic about Christine, and it worried me. She was forever forgetting to turn up to things, failing to return phone calls. She would offer to take another child home from school, then forget and leave them there. Alice was often missing from birthday parties because Christine had either forgotten, or couldn't cope with the logistics of getting her there. If she did turn up, it would be late, and without a present.

Then two things happened that made me decide that Christine really wasn't the best sort of mother. One day she left her middle child, Jemima, outside the chemist while she went inside, and when she came out the pushchair had gone. Someone told me she spent a panicked five minutes searching for Jemima, who was eventually returned to her by the mad old fellow with matted grey beard and wee-stained trousers who was often to be seen hanging around local street corners with his stash of assorted carrier bags and decrepit bicycle. He had taken it upon himself to take Jemima for a walk, and then returned her five minutes later because he couldn't stand her incessant wailing. She was safe and sound after all, and no harm had come to her. But it might have.

A few months later I was driving through Richmond when I spotted a woman with small children crossing the road near the swimming pool. From a distance of about thirty yards, I watched as one of the children ran out into the road and into the back of a passing truck and fall screaming to the ground. And I knew, even before I got to them, that the mother was Christine and the child was James, Alice's baby brother. As I stood beside her handing her tissues to press upon James' forehead to stop the gushing blood, I thought, this woman is not the right sort of mother. She doesn't know that when you are crossing the road with a small child you grip their hands so tightly you can feel the blood pulsing through their palms. She does not know how to keep her children safe.

I liked Christine, but I decided there and then that I would never allow Phoebe to be in her care in anything but the safest, most predictable of situations. Short playdates at their house were OK, but almost anything else was off-limits. No trips to swimming pools or playgrounds unless I could go along, no acceptance of offers to collect her from school. As the girls got older, if there was a sleepover planned, I always managed to engineer things so it was at our house. Alice and Phoebe are still close friends after all these years, and Christine and I are on good terms. I don't think anyone has even noticed all my scheming, or if they have, they've never said anything.

It's only recently, with Phoebe being older and able to look out for herself, that I've lightened up, allowing her to spend more time at Alice's and even spend the night. But I still feel a flicker of trepidation when I agree to let Phoebe go. I still hold my breath until she comes back.

I want to be a mother who knows how to keep her children safe. Beyond that, it seems to me the ground rules are altogether more vague. There are an awful lot of prescriptions, so many you could go half mad trying to keep up with them. For the past fifteen years, I've been carrying around an ever-expanding mental list of things I must watch over to ensure the children are healthy, happy and fulfilling their potential. These days, the list is something of a monster, many-tentacled and out of control. It probably includes, in no particular order:

Vitamins and supplements – C for colds, Omega-3 for brains, calcium for bones. Ahh, but what about cancerous chemicals in fish oils? Find something else containing Omega-3.

Not too much TV. Average child on four hours a day. Really? How do they fit it in? What is acceptable amount? Does news count? (Should they even be watching the news, that nightly parade of violence, sex, death and dishonesty?)

Lots of sleep. Kids today apparently suffering from chronic overtiredness, sleeping two and a half hours less a day than twenty years ago. What to do when young teenager hooked on the OC and One Tree Hill, both of which end at 11 p.m.? What to do when teenager lies in room listening to iPod long after lights out?

Beware violent computer games. Esp. the one that gives prizes for stealing cars and shooting innocent bystanders. What to do when friend's parents have purchased complete box set of 'Night

Killer' games and think parental monitoring is oppressive and unnecessary? What to do if friend's parents have purchased complete box set of 'Night Killer' games because they haven't a clue what's in them?

Exercise: children need at least an hour of the aerobic variety every day. Does dancing in kitchen with headphones on count?

Water! Thought this was just important for adults wishing to preserve skin elasticity, but no. Apparently children need at least half a litre a day for brains to function properly.

The five-a-day rule. Five portions of fruit or veg every day or children will fail at school, fail to grow, get cancer. Chips don't count, even upmarket, chunky ones with lots of potato in them. What about baked beans?

Limit sugar. Leads to energy highs and lows, poor performance at school, and frightfully bad tempers.

Meals in general: make sure you eat together most nights. (Four nights a week a good target?) The family that eats together stays together. Children's table manners will be appalling if they are allowed to eat alone or in front of the TV every night of the week.

Praise. Without it children can lack self-esteem, possibly leading to anorexia and/or drug addiction.

While we're on the subject of self-esteem, your child has a better chance of having some if they have interests and hobbies they feel good about. A child with no interests or accomplishments is a prime candidate for drug-taking rebelliousness in the teen years. Must get Phoebe to focus on something useful.

Sex: you can't afford to be silent on this one. Your children need to be armed with as much information as possible to protect them against at least a dozen STDs, teen pregnancy and Aids, all of which could ruin a life, some of which could end it. But for heaven's sake, don't go encouraging any of that abstinence until marriage nonsense, as it's a proven fact that people who don't have sex until they are married end up running away with someone they hook up with on Friends Reunited in their mid-thirties.

There are so many things on the mothers' mental list, alongside the bog-standard daily fare of making sure every one is fed, bathed, clothed, gets to school on time and does their homework, that it's impossible to remember it all, much less actually do it. I tell myself a good mother must be one who keeps her children safe and can tick off maybe three things from the mothers' 'To do' list every day.

But should a mother be a separate person? That is the question that haunts me as I lie here in the dark. Moreover, should a mother be the type of separate person who attracts the unwanted attention of strange men in passing lorries? Or who fails to purchase critical articles from Top Shop or W.H. Smith on the appointed day? I don't know the answer to these questions. But I think Herself's got her answer all worked out. She's somehow got it into her head that there's only room for one of us to be a person, and it's not supposed to be me.

PHOEBE

For as long as I can remember, Mum has had this thing about us all trying to sit down for a meal together at least four times a week. She's actually said that, like four is a magic number. Whereas, if you ask me, it's better when people do their own thing, eat when they feel like it, in separate rooms if they want. Tonight is obviously one of those evenings. Dinner is just one long argument, every turn in the conversation seeming to lead us back on to the red-hot coals from which we've just leaped, feet in blisters.

It all starts innocently enough, aside from a bit of a scuffle about whose turn it is to set the table. The first sign of trouble is when Ella starts piling the chicken up on the side of her plate.

'Ella, what's wrong with the chicken?' Mum asks, heaving one of her trademark sighs.

'I don't eat chicken,' replies Ella.

'Since when?' says Kate, through a mouthful of chicken and mashed potato that is disgusting to behold. I look away.

'Since I decided to be a real vegetarian.'

'Ella, chicken is the one meat you have always

107

eaten. That's why I chose it tonight. I thought it would be nice if, just for once, we could all eat the same thing and I didn't have to prepare half a dozen different meals. Could you please just eat it.'

'No. You can't force me to eat meat, Mum. That's not fair.'

Mum buries her face in her hands.

'Leave it, Lib. It's not worth it. She can have a sandwich later,' says Dad.

But the chicken turns out to be just the beginning. Next on the agenda is me.

'What did Mr Franklin want to talk to you about today?' asks Kate.

'How did you know Mr Franklin wanted to talk to me?' I say, shooting her a fierce look.

'Amy told me. She was in the office when Mr Franklin stopped you in the hall.'

'What was it all about, Phoebs?' Oh great, I think. Now Dad's in on it there will be no escaping.

'Oh, it was nothing. No big deal.'

'Come on, Phoebe, Mr Franklin doesn't ask to see you if it's no big deal. Tell us,' says Mum, putting her fork down and resting her chin on her hands.

Now eight expectant eyes are locked on to me. Kate and Ella are loving it. They relish any hint of a scandal, so long as it's nothing to do with them.

'Well, if you must know, he wanted to talk to me about my commitment. He says I'm very bright, but I'm letting myself down. Which is ridiculous.'

'What do you think he means?' she says and I think, *There she goes again with that parenting book* crap. *'Ask your child an open, unthreatening question rather than make accusing statements and you're more likely to get an honest response from them'*. A quote from a well-thumbed paperback I found next to Mum's bed about two years ago.

'How the heck do I know what he means? Whatever, it's not true. So I find my subjects boring at the moment, and maybe I don't always spend as much time on stuff as I could. It's not as if it really matters. I'm doing just fine anyway. I still get better marks than half the people in my class.'

Now Dad's leaning on his hands too. I brace myself for a lecture and watch Kate's lips forming into a barely disguised smirk.

'Phoebe, Mr Franklin's right. You are a very bright girl. And if he thinks you're capable of more, if he thinks you should be putting more effort in, then I would take that on board if I were you. It's because you're bright that he expects more from you. He wants you to live up to your potential. So do we all, for that matter. Coasting through life just isn't an option.'

Funny. That's almost exactly what Mr Franklin said. He also said that being pretty and privileged wasn't the passport to a great life that I seemed to think it was, and that I would have to work hard like everyone else if I was to make something of myself. But I'm not going to tell them this bit. They'd only agree with it.

'Well, if he wants me to be more interested in work he ought to get his teachers to make the work a bit more interesting. Anyway, why pick on me? I'm not the one who got forty-five per cent on her spelling test the other day.'

'That's not fair!' shouts Kate. 'I was ill when we got that list of words! I hadn't prepared.'

And so it goes on. By the time everyone has lobbed in a spiteful comment or two we all seem to have forgotten the specific issue that got us started down this track in the first place. I can tell Mum is getting really tired, perhaps regretting the idea of getting us all to sit down together when all we'd really wanted to do was eat on trays in front of *EastEnders*. I see it as poetic justice of sorts when she's next to come in for a bit of a drubbing.

'Anyway, Lib. Next Wednesday,' says Dad, scraping up the last of his mashed potato from the plate, 'Phil Baker from the Optometry Association has invited us to be at his table at the fund-raiser for the Optical Research Foundation. I thought it would be a good thing to do. I'd like to get involved in one of their research projects, and this can't hurt my chances. You up for that?'

Mum looks at Ella, then says, 'I can't. Wednesdays are Green Link nights. Remember?'

'But surely not every Wednesday? It's not like they're paying you. Surely you can miss one meeting?'

'Sure I could, but what's the point in getting involved unless you take it seriously?'

Dad's exasperated now. 'Remind me. Why are you doing this again? Is it really so important?'

'Yeah, I'm not quite sure either,' I chip in. I have

wondered. I saw a programme with Peaches Geldof about some teenagers who spent the whole of their half term picking up rubbish from some woodland in Sussex, and I remember thinking how sad is that? Peaches said she thought teenagers were supposed to be thinking about guys and clothes and having fun, not picking up rubbish, and I was inclined to agree with her. I'm not sure what middle-aged women with three kids and a house to take care of should be thinking about, but I'm sure it isn't litter either.

I look over at Mum. She's making a strange face, looking frantically backwards and forwards between Ella and Dad as if she's trying to make him aware of something but doesn't want Ella to know. Ella catches on before Dad does. Then Mum catches on about Ella catching on and explodes.

'Why am I doing this? Why am I doing this?' she shouts, sitting back in her chair with her arms folded.

'We're doing it together, Dad,' says Ella in that sweet, matter-of-fact way she has, as if it explains everything.

'That's right. I'm doing this because our daughter has some very real concerns about the world she's growing up in, and I thought it would be good, for her and for me, if I could do something constructive about it. And besides,' Mum goes on, quite enraged now in a way you don't normally see, 'since when is it a crime for me to something that I want to do, whether you think it's a good idea or not? Since when is it a crime for me to be *busy*? To be unavailable to do what the rest of you might want me to do for just a few hours in a week?'

'All right. Keep your hair on. Go to your meeting. I'll go to the dinner by myself,' says Dad indignantly, standing up to take his plate to the sink. 'If you'd rather spend an evening navel-gazing with a bunch of Greenpeace types than getting dressed up and going out to a rather glamorous evening with your husband, that's your choice.'

'Yes. It is,' says Mum, staring steely-eyed at the unlit candle in the middle of the table.

So there you have it. A family meal to strengthen those family bonds. Dad storms off to the sitting room to sit fuming behind his newspaper. Kate and Ella slink away from the table muttering something about homework, and I go upstairs to call Alice. That just leaves Mum sitting at the table, her shoulders hunched in anger.

And all those pots and roasting pans still sitting in the sink.

LIBBY

Fran has met someone. After six years swaddled in the bubble wrap of work, domestic responsibility and women-only book clubs, suddenly she meets a man. He seems to have materialised out of nowhere. She met him, not on the Internet, but in an Internet café. She went there when her laptop packed in and she had to send some urgent emails. Seems the two of them were waiting for two termin-als to free up and they started talking. She stretched out the sending of her own emails for as long as she possibly could in an attempt to time her departure from the café with his, then bumped into him accidentally on purpose as they stood waiting to pay. Unbelievably, he asked her if she'd like to go to the adjoining coffee shop for coffee. His name is Paul Carson, and he's a teacher.

'He is also,' she says with a conspirational giggle when she rings me the day after meeting him, 'only thirty-six. I'm seeing him again tonight. The kids aren't too keen on the idea of my going out with a man who isn't their father, even after all these years,' she tells me. 'Well, Freddie isn't anyway. But he'll get used to the idea. I think

113

sometimes you just have to say bollocks to them.'

Bollocks, bollocks, bollocks, I repeat to myself as I drive down to see Dad. I'm going to that meeting whether they want me to or not. The nerve of Rob, assuming that I'll always be available.

I'm driving down to Dad's on Wednesday rather than Tuesday this week. (Tuesday he was invited to a luncheon hosted by the local Brownies.) Aside from the usual domestic mayhem and the hours of torturously circular conversation that I normally face while there, there is an added irritation furnished by my inadvertently locking the car keys in the boot just as I am leaving. I put the keys down in the back of the car while I search my bag to make sure I've got my phone. I turn away from the car for one second, just one, just as a huge gust of wind blows the door shut. I listen in horror as the automatic locking mechanism is activated by the force of the slammed door. When it happens I know immediately that it's something of a disaster, but the AA confirms it to be really quite a big disaster indeed.

'Crikey,' says the AA bloke, whistling down the line. 'The locks on those Range Rovers are about as secure as you can get. And there's no release button, nothing at all, which is a bit of an over-sight if you ask me.'

So I wait three-quarters of an hour for someone called Pete from the AA to arrive and another hour while he struggles to prise open the boot with the help of an assortment of sharp metal objects. Hovering irritatingly close to Pete, Dad asks me at least seven times if I've checked the instruction manual to see if there isn't an easier way. By the time Pete has finished, and I've spent the next hour crawling along a stretch of motorway littered with cones suggesting some alleged road-work activity, I arrive home almost two hours later than usual. So there is no time to write extensive instructions to everyone like last week. I quickly rustle up a chicken casserole which I leave on top of the stove with the briefest of notes stuck to the cling film: '30 minutes, 180 degrees.' Then I swoop up Ella from Lilly's (in the car. I know, it's quite unforgivable) and we drive to the library.

I had wondered whether Ella's enthusiasm might have dwindled, whether she might have already begun to resent the Wednesday evening commitment (which, after all, will almost certainly prevent our return in time to watch *What Not to Wear*, a family favourite), but she's as keen as mustard. I am a little bit nervous and quite a lot curious. I wonder who will be at the meeting this week. There will surely have been a few dropouts, and who would blame them? It's not everybody's bag, all this organising and active canvassing and highly public activity. I'm not entirely sure it's my bag, but I need a bag right now, any bag, and this one will have to do.

I spot Eloise on the steps just as we near the library gates and find myself feeling glad to see her. She seems nice, and interesting. I go over the rest of them in my mind, wondering who I'd rather *not* see again. I know I'm guilty of judging books by covers when Michelle and Courtney come immediately to mind. Then I think about Barry. Verbose, overeager, earnest Barry and his sensible sandals from the Clarks for Men range. Funnily enough, I think he would be very badly missed.

'Hey, Libby, Ella. Great to see we didn't put you off last time!' comes a voice from behind. I turn around to see Daniel leaping up the steps two at a time to catch up. He holds the door open and ushers us inside, smiling warmly and shrugging the strap of his backpack further up on to his shoulder.

'Oh, we're not ones to be put off that easily,' I say, smiling back. I notice a tiny scar on his cheekbone, just under his right eye, and have a bizarre urge to touch it.

'Good, because I'm late, as you can see, and I could use your help with something.'

The something turns out to be the lugging of two enormous boxes full of books from where they are sitting beside the front desk and into the meeting room. When we push through the glass-topped doors with the first box (Daniel at one end, bearing the bulk of the weight, Ella and me at the other), people are already arranging the chairs in a semicircle. It's difficult to tell how many people are here, there's so much commotion. I spot a few familiar faces and try to recall their names with the help of the little memory-jogging adjectives I made up last time. Faithful Phyllis, Lovely Lynnette, Elegant Eloise, Ron the birdmon. I feel bad about Boring Barry, and vow to think up another adjective. The man himself is already seated near the flip-chart next to Daisy Hancock. They appear to be comparing footwear.

The second box of books successfully stashed at the side of the room, Daniel strolls purposefully up to the front, simultaneously shedding his battered brown leather jacket and backpack. He stands next to the flip-chart, hands on hips, and shakes his head.

'Well, I can see you people don't need me to organise you at all. Maybe I should call it a day, let you get on with it.'

'Fast learners,' says Barry, beaming.

'I can see that. Here, let me help you with that,' says Daniel, darting towards Julia Harding, who is struggling to lift a chair from a precariously balanced stack by the wall. The man is a veritable human dynamo, leaping up steps, striding effort-lessly across rooms, springing to the aid of distressed headmistresses threatened by toppling chair towers.

Once we've all settled into the circle it's easier to see who's here. Marcie Gibbons and her friend Carole are, but Shelly from the DVLA isn't. Phyllis's friend Nancy is here (no doubt horsewhipped by Phyllis), as is David Peabody the vet. Lynnette, wearing a tight-fitting white polyester dress with 'Real Beauty' emblazoned in pale green embroidery across one breast, has just sat down on Daniel's left. Just as I'm about to give up on them, Courtney and Michelle slope in, sipping Coke and munching on cheese and onion crisps you can smell from twenty paces.

There was one other person last time. Who was it? Ah yes, Mr M & S himself, who enters the room now with an apologetic nod of his head and attempts to secure himself a chair with a minimum of fuss and noise.

Still, there's one other person missing. Derek, the wise bearded one. As if sensing my mental query as to his whereabouts, Daniel volunteers an explanation.

'Hey, everyone. Great to see you. It's just me here from Green Link tonight. In fact, it'll be just me most of the time from now on. Derek is a national group leader, so he tends to travel a lot.'

So, Daniel is in charge. He can't be more than twenty-seven or -eight, surely. Is he really expected to corral the efforts of a group like this, a mad jumble of local environ-mental enthusiasts ranging from ten to eighty, with all the experience and organisational skills of a first-year nursery school class?

'Aha!' Daniel exclaims, looking over at the two teenaged boys shyly poking their heads around the door. 'Come on in, guys.'

The boys amble over towards Daniel, who puts one arm around each of them. They both smile tentatively at the group.

'This here is Harry,' says Daniel, indicating the shorter, darker, bespectacled one of the two boys, 'and this is Gabriel.' Gabriel gazes at us from underneath a mop of wavy pale blonde hair. His nose is showered with biscuit-coloured freckles.

'I met these two upstanding fellows when I gave a talk at their school last week, and twisted their arms until they agreed to join our group,' continues Daniel. 'They're already working on a whole load of great in-school environ-mental projects, so I know they are going to be a huge asset to us. In fact, they both took part in a half-term litter drive out in Sussex that you might have seen a TV documentary about. Grab yourself a seat, lads. Over there next to Libby looks like a good place.'

I shuffle my chair closer to David Peabody's to make room for the boys. Gabriel pierces my toe with the leg of his chair as he squeezes in next to me, but I stifle the squeal because he already looks self-conscious enough.

Then Daniel is away. He retrieves three books from the boxes we heaved into the meeting room, all of which he holds up for hasty inspection. We are encouraged to buy them at a discount from Green Link. There's a pink one called *Save the Planet*, a lime green one called *An Ethical Life* (that puts me off, for a start) and a third, smaller volume in various shades of green called *The Reluctant Environmentalist*. Apparently, reading these will equip us suitably for the task ahead.

'You know,' says Daniel apologetically, 'I hate to

do this to you, to make you feel like you're back at school. But what would be great is if we could divide into small groups and take an initial look at each of the books. Talk amongst ourselves about some of the ideas in them, then share those with the rest of the group. Then, if you all go away and read the books this week, we'll be in great shape to talk in depth about our own plan next week. Sound good?'

We nod, quietly enthusiastic.

Luckily my group (consisting of Gabriel, David Peabody, Eloise, Michelle, Phyllis, Ella and myself) is handed copies of the *Reluctant Environmentalist*, which looks far easier to digest than either of the other two books. It is full of cartoons and bright, colourful boxes containing wonderfully approachable headings like 'Make your bathroom greener', and 'Watch those disposables!' I'm sure Daniel has planned it this way, to make things easier for Ella. She immediately opens up her book and begins reading, a studious expression on her face.

We agree to give ourselves twenty minutes to skim the book so we've at least some idea of what we're talking about before we start talking about it. As the six of us sit in our small circle perusing the pages, the near silence is punctuated by the occasional gasp (perhaps at the discovery that the toxins within our home are more dangerous than the ones outside it?) and the odd expression of pleasant surprise (possibly it's the revelation that linen sheets are not just the more luxurious option, but the more eco-friendly one as well).

I let out a few gasps of my own, being faintly staggered by the range of things that need to be considered. When I last thought about this stuff for any length of time, more than fifteen years ago, it was enough to be concerned about oil spillages from recalcitrant oil tankers or inadequate recycling rates in rural areas. Now, it seems, these things are mere tips of the iceberg that is environmental responsibility. Now, it seems, I need to worry that I'm drinking the wrong sort of coffee (from beans cultivated in the sun as opposed to under a canopy of trees) and cooking home-made meals in a genuine oven (as opposed to an energy-conserving microwave). *I'm not sure I can do this,* I think.

'I think all this is bloody scary,' Michelle says finally, nodding her head repeatedly in emphasis, a piece of chewing gum fixed firmly between her two front teeth. 'What this seems to be saying is that we're killing the environ-ment with every single thing we do, from the minute we wake up. Where the fuck are we going to start? Sorry, I mean, where are we going to start?'

Ella has been observing and listening, taking in everyone's quiet reactions. Prompted by Michelle's outburst, she decides to put in her own two pennies' worth.

'I knew it was scary all along. Didn't I say that, Mum? I've been collecting newspaper articles about it all. But today, I don't know, I feel a bit less scared. At least this book has some ideas in it.' She holds up her book, opened to a page on green bathrooms. 'It says here that if we just shower instead of taking baths we'll use up to *ten* times less water. That's just so easy. I hate baths anyway.'

Daniel appears behind her as she sinks back into her chair with a triumphant sigh. At this moment, it would only be a slight exaggeration to say that I've never been so grateful for the appearance of anyone in my life. Ella might be feeling bullish, but the rest of us are clearly overwhelmed. Someone has to give us an answer, a strategy, a route through the quagmire.

'I imagine you're all feeling a little overwhelmed at the moment,' he says to the six of us, who at the moment resemble a collection of china dogs with loose, bobbing heads on someone's mantlepiece. 'Don't stress too much about it now. Why don't you guys just try to summarise your impressions of this book and share them with the group in a few minutes. Sound good?'

When the full group recongregates it quickly becomes apparent that we aren't the only ones to feel prematurely beaten by the enormity of the challenge. The *Save The Planet* and *Ethical Life* crowds look equally downhearted. What follows is an hour's rather aimless discussion about the horrors we have suddenly been exposed to. Shelly is particularly fixated on the idea of toxic hot spots in the home, while Daisy can't get over the fact that there is something called a green grave, and her husband isn't buried in one. Lynnette holds up the pages on chemical pollution and wonders if she ought not just close down the beauty salon with immediate effect. By the time the meeting is adjourned my head hurts. Judging by Phyllis's expression, hers does too. The only people to leave the room with apparently buoyed spirits are Ella and Barry, which I suppose I might have predicted. That's it, I think as I watch him go. Buoyant Barry.

While Ella visits the loo I stack my chair on top of some others at the side of the room, then begin fishing my jean jacket out of my bag. As I put it on I'm still in a bit of a daze, so I don't notice Daniel approaching me from the side. I jump when he places his hand on my shoulder.

'So, have we put you off yet?' he asks, smiling in a way that's almost consoling.

'What? Oh. I shouldn't think so. I'm tougher than that,' I say, when what I really want to do is go home to my house full of toxic cleaning fluids, overflowing rubbish bins and the multifarious evidence of rampant consumerism and pretend I've never set eyes on *The Reluctant Environmentalist*.

'Good,' he replies. 'I had you figured for someone who could hack it. Don't let all the fine print discourage you. There's a lot we can do around here with only a small amount of pain and suffering.'

'Oh, I'm sure that's true,' I say, trying to match his affable, optimistic expression and really *be* someone who can hack it.

'Great. I'll see you next week, then,' he says, squeezing my shoulder in a knowing way before swinging his backpack over one shoulder and strolling off towards the double doors. He turns just before he reaches them. 'Hey, thanks for the help with those boxes!' he shouts before disappearing.

'You're welcome,' I say to no one.

I shrug my own bag on to my shoulder and walk towards the doors. I'm conscious of a heat spot in my shoulder, just about where he touched it.

I've always known Ella to be determined, but her resoluteness shows no bounds during the week after our first meeting. By Friday she's read *The Reluctant Environmentalist* cover to cover. When she discovers that I haven't yet made it past the first chapter, she frowns and purses her lips. Then her face lightens and she announces, 'I know, as you're so busy I'll make some notes for you. A sort of summary. Would you like that?'

You can't say no to an offer like that so I say, 'Great. That would be wonderful,' before resuming the chopping of red peppers for a stir-fry. At this encouragement she skips away to the study, and the sound of computer keys being purposefully, if awkwardly, bashed begins to filter through to the kitchen.

By Saturday I've forgotten her promise, but late in the afternoon she seeks me out in the shower, where I am on all fours attempting to dislodge the stainless-steel drain cover in the hope of discovering why the water refuses to drain away on cue after each shower. The stench issuing from the drain is quite revolting, like a blend of rotten eggs and decaying potato peel.

'Mum, here it is!' she proclaims.

'What?' I say, sitting back on my heels and turning to face her.

'The notes I promised to make for you.'

'Oh, great. Why don't you leave them over there on my bed and I'll have a look at them,' I say.

'You really should try to read them tonight,' she says sternly. 'We have another meeting on Wednesday.'

'Well, I may not get to them tonight,' I say with mild irritation, then soften my voice when I detect the imminent onset of a furrowed brow in her narrowing eyes. 'Dad and I are having dinner with Gilly and David tonight, but I'll try to read them tomorrow. OK?'

'OK. It's just that I don't want to be the worst ones in the group. It's pretty important after all.'

'Don't worry, sweetheart. We won't be the worst. Other people are busy too. I very much doubt they'll all have read their books.'

When I finally get around to picking up the notes, I'm amazed by what I find. I thought the scrapbook was pretty impressive, quite remarkable in its comprehensiveness, but it was essentially a compilation of other people's reporting. These notes are more personal, written in Ella's own words, so that her particular anxieties and preoccupations come through even more clearly. She appears to have gone through the book in its entirety, and picked out the most startling points in each chapter. The fourth page contains a conclusion entirely of her own creation.

So, in conclusion, every family needs to do something. And that includes ours!
Here are the ten things we should do!

1. *Recycle more. We could recycle almost everything if we really tried. Can we buy some bins to put in all the rooms?*
2. *Start composting. There's a spot behind the shed that would be a perfect place.*
3. *Turn off the lights. Especially Phoebe and Dad.*
4. *Try to wear sweaters and stuff instead of using the heating all the time. A good plan would be to keep a pile of sweaters in each room. One for each member of the family.*
5. *Take showers, not baths. And showers must only be two minutes long. Especially Phoebe and Dad.*
6. *Stop using the tumble-dryer. (Sorry, Mum, but did you know that tumble-dryers use ginormous amounts of electricity and they ruin your clothes?)*
7. *Change our car. It's terrible. The worst one we could possibly have. A big, black petrol-eating monster.*
8. *Throw away all that cleaning stuff under the kitchen sink and start cleaning with things like water and vinegar and lemons. Lemons are really great for cleaning greasy things.*

9. *Shop at Oxfam. Did you know that you can find some really nice clothes there? Even Phoebe could do this every once in a while instead of getting new stuff from Top Shop all the time. Fashion is the enemy of the environment!*

10. *Buy food that's grown nearby. It's just a sin to buy peas or kiwi fruits that have travelled thousands of miles in a great big dirty polluting jumbo jet when we have perfectly good food in England.*

11. *Go organic. All right, so organic food is way more expensive. But just think about how much better we'll all feel without all those pesticides inside us.*

I think the plan should start on Monday. I could be the manager, sort of like when I was games captain. Please say you agree.
Love, your youngest daughter, Ella.

Oh boy, I think as I'm reading. There really is no turning back now. What have I got us all into?

I sink back into the pillows on my bed and think fond thoughts about my tumble-dryer and my big, black, evil car. Then I picture myself perusing the rails of worn jumpers and badly fitting tweed skirts on offer in Oxfam and feel quite sick.

Damn it, Libby, I think. You're just going to have to be grown-up about this. A good mother supports her child-ren's passions; she doesn't try to squash them the minute they show signs of becoming inconvenient. We'll take it one step at a time, starting with something manageable. Recycling bins. We can manage that. Who knows, I might learn to love all this. It might be good for me.

Fran sends me a text.

Fourth date and I still fancy him! More importantly, he still fancies me! Can this really be happening? xox Fran.

Apparently so. When do I get to meet him? I text back.

Who knows whether Fran's found the real thing or whether it will all end in tears. Will the lovely Paul toy with her for his amusement then cast her aside when he decides he needs to settle down with someone his own age and have children? Or will love conquer all? Whatever the case, there's no stopping Fran now and I wouldn't dream of trying. After six years of nothing, even a passionate affair that turns to dust in her hands has to be something worth hanging on to while it lasts.

PHOEBE

I've been willing to let this go for a little while, seeing as Ella is only ten and she's all excited. But my patience is running out. I'm beginning to get irritated.

It started out innocuously enough. Ella began giving us little lectures, telling us to turn off a running tap or switch off a light. Then suddenly there were these coloured plastic bins in almost every room in the house. Hideous things in red and yellow. Red for rubbish, yellow for re-cycling, apparently. The other day I came home from school to find that the bins in my room had handwritten lists Sellotaped to the front of them. Ella told me later that she'd been checking up on everyone and discovered that I'd put an empty tissue box into the red bin instead of the yellow one. Shock, horror! 'I thought you might need a little help until you get used to it,' she'd said, all sweetness and light. 'Don't go sneaking around in my room when I'm not there,' I warned her, an image of the pink foil pill packet flashing in front of my eyes.

Even Mum seems a bit irritated, but she's going along with it all. I think she may even have been co-opted. I notice that she's doing this weird thing of taking for ever over the smallest things, as if she's dissecting them in her mind. The other day I saw her throw something in the bin. The plastic wrapper off the apples, I think it was. She shut the bin and walked away, then a few minutes later came back and took the bag out. She stood there for what must have been thirty seconds, staring at this piece of plastic in her hands, which was by now covered in yoghurt. I guess she must have decided what to do with it then, because she ran it under the tap and put it into the recycling bin in the utility room.

Then another time I noticed she went to wipe up some apple juice from the counter, but she stopped herself just before the kitchen roll got wet. She actually turned around, stuffed the kitchen roll back into the roll, and wiped up the mess with the J-cloth from the sink.

'What do you think uses more energy, Ella? The manufacture of a piece of kitchen roll, or rinsing a J-cloth out with hot water?'

'Who cares?' I said. But she wasn't listening to me. She was listening to Ella, who said, 'I don't know, but I'll look it up in one of our books.' By 'one of their books' she must mean the pink and green things she's been lugging from room to room all week. Her Green Link books.

Peculiar behaviour must be catching. This afternoon I was at Carlos Coffee in town with Josh, Laura and Dougie, Josh's friend (who Laura fancies in a way that's incredibly obvious and just a little bit embarrassing). Rebecca came in with some girl I've never seen before. She came over to say hello and started to tell us a story about how her class had tormented some poor science teacher by hiding his class notes. She was standing right next to Josh's chair, so I know he heard her, but he just stared straight ahead, almost as if she wasn't there. Then, when everyone else said goodbye to her, he didn't say a word, but I noticed that he and Dougie curled their lips and exchanged a mean-spirited sort of look.

'Why were you being so rude back there? With Rebecca? My mum's really good friends with her mum, you know?' I said to him when we were walking home.

'What do you mean? I wasn't,' he said defensively, dropping his arm from my shoulder.

'You were. What do you have against Rebecca?'

'I just don't like her, that's all. She annoys me.' He put his arm back around me then, but dropped it when a carload of Kings boys sped by and hollered out the window.

'Well, she kind of bugs me too,' I said, 'but she's all right. And I feel sorry for her in a way.'

'Nothing to feel sorry for,' he said. 'She knows exactly what she's doing. Anyway, let's not talk about her. What movie to see this weekend? *Million Dollar Baby*'s still on I think.'

To be honest I wasn't wild about seeing *Million Dollar Baby*, but I told him I'd go on account of his boxing obsession, even though I was feeling a strange sort of detachment from him at that moment. I hadn't liked seeing that side of him. A side that could treat someone like vermin and laugh about it. It had left a nasty taste in my mouth.

Dad pops his head into my room. Coming hot on the heels of the unswallowable pill incident, it strikes me that he's been making an annoying habit of this lately.

'Hey, Phoebs. You OK?' he says.

'Sure. Why wouldn't I be?'

'No reason. Just checking.' Then just as he turns to go, he says, with a barely disguised smirk, 'You surviving the great green assault?'

'God, isn't it awful! When do you think it's going to pass?'

'I fear we could be in for rather a long run of it,' he says. 'You know what Ella's like when she gets her teeth into something. And your mum seems unusually enthusiastic about it all. I go along with it, within reason. We should do our bit for the planet. But I fear those two might be getting carried away.'

'Yeah, well if Ella comes into my room and starts snooping around again, there'll be trouble,' I say, raising my fist and scowling. Then I smile and he smiles back, and we both shake our heads, like the parents of wayward offspring.

LIBBY

I'm sure Rob thinks I've gone mad. When I finally crept into bed last night, trying to avoid accidentally nudging any of his limbs, he rolled over to face me and asked me, with his eyes still squeezed shut, what time it was. When I said two a.m. his face registered a combination of pain (at the thought of my still being awake at this hour?) and disapproval (at the thought of what I'd been doing at this hour?).

'Libby, this is crazy,' he said.

'I know. I just wanted to get through these books before the next meeting, that's all.'

'Why? What's the urgency?' he asked, rolling back over to face the other way. It was clearly a rhetorical question.

Oh, you know, ice cubes where the ice caps used to be, that sort of thing, I felt like saying. If I wasn't aware of the urgency before, I certainly am now. Ella has been dropping these little facts into our conversations out of the blue. No one else seems to hear them. I not only hear them, but seem incapable of shrugging them off.

'Did you know,' she said the other morning just

133

as she was hopping out of the car at the bus stop, 'the ice caps are melting at such a rate that pretty soon they won't exist. Then there will be floods everywhere. We've *got* to do something! Byeee.' Then she scurried off, leaving me stunned in her wake.

That same afternoon, she was setting the table when she suddenly announced, without even lifting her eyes from the knives and forks in her hands, 'Did you know that a quarter of animals and plants will soon be extinct on account of climate change? I read that on the Internet today in ICT class.'

'Gosh, that's awful,' I said. 'What do they say we should do about that?'

'Well, stopping global warming is one thing. But we also have to stop people shooting the animals. Those people who wear fur coats or have, like, elephant tusks on their mantelpiece, they're just evil.'

'Actually, I don't know anyone who wears a fur coat or has elephant tusks on their mantelpiece,' I offered by way of consolation.

Then she stood with one hand on thrust-out hip, the knives and forks protruding from one end like small weapons, and shook her head. 'Just because we don't know them doesn't mean they aren't out there, Mum! You have got to stop being so naïve!'

I've been guilty of lots of things in my life, but I've never thought naivety was one of them. Naïve isn't something I feel proud of being. Besides, these surprise fact attacks from Ella are beginning to take their toll. I needed to create some context for them, to get a little ahead of her, or at least catch up with her. So I started reading.

Now I'm an insomniac as a result of everything I now know about the world.

I hope I get over it, but everywhere I turn there's an environmental dilemma staring me in the face. Can I really pick up those items at Waitrose, where I happen to be, instead of at the local greengrocer's, to which I would have to make a special excursion later, knowing that the supermarkets' super-grip on our groceries is destroying the local economy and contributing to global pollution? Will I use that Cif to scrub the sink, or walk (naturally) to the shop and purchase several dozen lemons for this purpose?

And this new-found knowledge is making me judgemental. I very nearly accosted a woman in the chemist when I saw her buying disposable nappies. I was tempted to seize them and inform her that some eight million are discarded and shoved into landfills every day.

Perhaps Rob is right. Perhaps I am going mad. It turns out that the list of things you need to do to be a good environmentalist is even longer than the one that tells you how to be a good mother. It's impossible not to go just a little bit crazy.

This, too, will pass, I tell myself. Somehow I'll find my way through all this and land upon a sane, practical approach to living green, one that helps Ella without driving the rest of us bonkers.

PHOEBE

'What's with all the lemons?' I ask Mum as I root around for something I can actually eat, like an apple or a pear.

'Oh, that's Ella's doing. She read that lemons are a great substitute for all those cleaning products we use. She made me stop and stock up on the way home from school yesterday. Of course I wasn't allowed to buy the ones from Budgens because they'd travelled all the way from South Africa, so we had to go across the road. The best we were able to do was Spain!'

Mum rolls her eyes, but she's grinning like mad so I can tell she's not really put out.

'Bloody hell, Mum. Do you think maybe you overdid it just a little?' The fruit bowl is overflowing with lemons, and there's a second bowl of them next to the toaster on the other counter.

'Well, maybe a little. But she is right. I was pretty sceptical, but you know, they do work amazingly well. Just this morning I soaked a T-shirt of Dad's in a bowl of water and lemon juice, and it came out bright white.'

'Hmn. That's great,' I say, hardly able to contain my enthusiasm.

'Phoebe, you could try to support your sister a little in this, you know? It's very important to her, and it's not like it's a bad thing all round.'

'Yeah, well, there's only so much one family can do about it. Personally, I think it's all going to work itself out. Car manufacturers are going to invent some battery-powered car any day now and that will solve most of the problem. In the meantime, the fact that you've chucked away the Cif bottle isn't going to make a scrap of difference.'

'Phoebe, don't be such a cynic. You're too young to be a cynic.'

'Cynical, Mother dear, is what I do best,' I say, fluttering my eyelashes. I have to hand it to her. She takes it on the chin. As I scoop up my school books and head towards the door, she doesn't even try to come back at me.

LIBBY

'You know that tree at the end of the garden? The elm that he's always saying blocks out all the light? Well, I told him I'd organise to have it cut down, that it would cost maybe a hundred quid, but he kept refusing.'

I swap the phone into my left hand so that I can stir the spaghetti sauce with my right. During the transfer I drop the spoon into the pot, splattering crimson-red sauce all over the stainless-steel hob, the floor and my favourite white shirt.

'Damn it! Anyway, I turn up on Tuesday and you know what I find? There he is, standing under the tree on that tiny kitchen table, the formica one that should have been chucked out in 1957. He's standing on this thing, with two belts looped together attaching him to the trunk of the tree, and he's sawing off all the upper branches himself. At eighty, for God's sake.'

'My God. He could have killed himself. That table is ancient, and it was never very strong to begin with,' says Jaime.

'And the week before, I phoned and Mrs Tupper answered. So I asked her how Dad was getting on with that new bin. You know how he was always using that plastic bag slung on the door handle, and kept saying there was no room for a bin in his kitchen? Well, I'd taken down this bin and plonked it right there next to the sink. Anyway she said – wait for it – 'Libby, he loves it. In fact, he's kissing it right now.' And she wasn't kidding.'

'Kissing the bin! Christ, he'll be fondling the washing machine next.'

'Pretty soon he won't be able to live on his own any more, Jaime. He'll have to go to one of those homes. Or live with one of us.'

'God. What a thought.'

'I know. I love him to bits, but the idea of going through what I go through on a Tuesday every single day, in my own house, with nowhere to hide, fills me with absolute dread. Then I feel terrible for feeling that way.'

Jaime's potter's wheel whirs into life in the background. I can picture her sitting there, legs astride the wheel, phone wedged between ear and shoulder, hands already coated in a layer of thick wet clay.

'What are we going to do?' she asks. What she really means is, what am I going to do? Jaime and Liz use 'we' in the same way as a lot of men, as in 'Have we sorted out that thing with the bank yet?' or 'We really ought to clear out the shed sometime.'

'I don't know. Maybe we should start looking into what's available. Just so we know what the options are.' Meaning, Maybe *I'll* start looking into what's available.

'That's a good idea. I hate the thought of him in some cold, clinical environment, but maybe it would be for the best. Anyway, I really have to go. This bowl is beginning to look like the leaning tower of Pisa.'

I hang up the phone and turn around to find myself facing a diplomatic delegation. Ella, Kate and Phoebe are standing in a small semicircle behind me, as if waiting to pounce. At least they have waited, rather than waving their arms in front of my face and mouthing their requests through clenched teeth, or shoving hastily scrawled notes under my nose, as is the norm.

They stand there, in order of ascending height and age, looking like an advertisement for L'Oréal Excellence. There's Phoebe with her long golden waves, and Kate with her thick light brown hair, carelessly pushed back from her forehead and with a slightly bedraggled, unbrushed air about it. Then there's Ella, with her shoulder-length dark brown hair spiralling down in soft ringlets. Soft, but still tighter than my own, which have lost some of their staying power over the years.

Are there other families, I wonder, whose children all have such markedly different-coloured hair, such dissimilar appearances all round in fact? I don't think I know one. Their faces don't even resemble one another's. Phoebe's is delicate and perfectly formed, a slight haughtiness built into her very cheekbones. Kate's face is softer, rounder, less defined, less intimidating. Ella is cuteness personified. Her features are compact, elfin-like, fully animated ninety per cent of the time.

It's only in their expressions that you occasionally receive fleeting confirmation of their sibling status. When Kate is worried, her features bunch up in a way that is suggestive of Ella. And when Ella laughs you sometimes see Phoebe. I quite often see Rob in Phoebe, and he claims to see some of me in Kate, but I am incapable of seeing myself in any of them.

All so different, yet united, today, in their aim to solicit something from me. Permission? Money? Sympathy? The resolution of a heated argument perhaps?

'Mum,' says Ella, failing to allow a decent interval between the end of my conversation with Jaime and the announcement of her request. 'Did you see that note from Mrs Howard? The one about the costumes for the school play? Are you going to help, because I was supposed to take the form back today.'

'I'm not sure, Ella. Sewing really isn't my bag, and I don't have a sewing machine. I have helped with lots of other stuff this year, so I think I'll leave the costumes to someone else.'

Ella's face crumples in disappointment. Having a mum who Contributes is some sort of badge of honour for these girls, I've learned. Being part of a costume-sewing circle, doing hair and make-up backstage, miraculously securing an obsolete stage set from a West End show – these are the ways to really make your mark. Something regular and reliable – like Mr Patek's daily fruit stand at break-time – is pretty highly regarded as well.

Your bog-standard running a stall at the Christmas Fair and baking brownies for bake sales doesn't cut the mustard.

Kate lobs in her own request during the few seconds it takes Ella to muster up a suitable retort. 'Mum, you remember that team show-jumping thing? The one at Longridge next month? Can I do it? Elaine sent another email last night.'

'Lilly's mum is helping with the costumes. Why can't you?'

'Well, in principle it would be great for you to compete, but there's the cost of hiring the pony and the horse box . . .'

'I've looked into all that. I can share a pony with Martha, so it won't be so much.'

'And when we did *Midsummer Night's Dream* you were the only one who wasn't at that coffee morning where they made the garlands.'

'Ella, that's just not true. There were lots of mums who weren't there. And I made a couple of togas and sent them in, so I more than did my bit.'

'Please, Mum. It's such a great event, and I've not jumped with a team before.'

'Can you two just wait for a second,' shouts Phoebe, elbowing Kate aside. ' I've got something really quick to ask Mum, and Laura's waiting. Mum, you know there's a party at the rowing club on Saturday and I told Josh I could go? Then I'm going to sleep at Laura's. That OK?'

Hers isn't really a question. More like a carefully worded pronouncement.

'Please.'

'Oh please, Mum.'

'Mum! Laura's waiting.'

My brain finally grinds to a halt and I stand open-mouthed in front of them all. I wonder if Rob's patients badger him like this? I wonder if other mothers are similarly deluged? Maybe the more organised amongst them devise systems to prevent the chaos and the overload. Perhaps a machine that spews out little tickets with numbers on them, like the one at the Waitrose fish counter.

Jolting me out of my stupor, Phoebe holds up her mobile like some sort of self-evident truth and says, 'Mum? Laura, remember? Waiting for an answer!'

I do so hate to keep Laura waiting, I think, but my brain is fried.

'Girls, can we try this one at a time. Youngest first. The other two of you, go away for a second. I'll get to you in a minute.'

And so passes half an hour during which I am subjected to persuasive power equivalent to that of the UN task force on child poverty. When thirty minutes has passed, Herself is going to the party at the boat club (in a new, yet-to-be-purchased skirt from Top Shop no less), Kate is competing in a show-jumping event at Longridge at a cost equating to your average monthly mortgage payment, and I've become an honoured member of the *Guys and Dolls* costume committee.

The truth of the matter is that I feel a bit guilty. The past few weeks seem to have flown by in a flurry of Green Link-related activity, and during that time I managed to misplace a critical school permission slip of Kate's (leading to her being threatened with exclusion from the day-trip to Folkstone) and remain so cheerfully oblivious of Ella's mock SATs that she ambled along without any home preparation until the weekend before they started. For Ella's class bake sale I resorted to Fran's underhand trick and passed off as my own a home-made jam sponge and some chocolate muffins hurriedly purchased at the bun and biscuit sale at the nursery school next to the library. (No one seemed to notice that I wasn't a relation of one of the establishment's pint-sized pupils.)

I've also taken my eye off the pink tin foil situation. It's true, I've been a bit slack of late. So now I must pay the price, which is swallowing my objections and saying yes.

But we've made such progress! After that week when I immersed myself in reading and research and wandered around in a dazed half-sleep, drunk on information and paralysed by an apparently limitless list of essential actions, I managed to calm down. I started to breathe again. And when I did, the fog had lifted, or at least thinned, and I was able to think more constructively.

It was mainly Ella – it's difficult to look at her bright, open face or listen to her cheery proclamations ('Don't worry, Mum, we can do it!') without some of her clarity of purpose and enthusiasm rubbing off. It helped to be able to swap stories with the others, too. Daniel must have seen this scenario acted out dozens of time. The conversion of the clueless.

After that meeting we seemed to surge forward in a great wave of planning, Ella happily thriving in the middle of it all, her anxiety diminished by being channelled into action. (What a relief it is to go upstairs and find her already dozing rather than staring wild-eyed at the ceiling.) Now we have a ten-point community action plan, the last bits of which were finalised yesterday afternoon. Owing to a session of music and movement being held in our usual room, Daniel, Eloise, Barry and I were forced to squeeze ourselves into a tiny room stuffed with books at the far end of the library. Huddling round a table that wobbled every time someone leant on it, we hashed out the last few elements of our plan. Then, at Eloise's suggestion, we took ourselves off to Harry's Wine Bar to celebrate.

My initial instinct was to decline the invitation. It was two in the afternoon, and I had the girls to collect at four. I never drink in the afternoon unless it's a roast Sunday lunch or someone's wedding. But the others were having none of my coy refusals. Barry said he'd got his assistant staying on to look after the shop, so he was darn well going to take advantage of it. Eloise insisted that you have to mark every milestone, however small, to avoid getting discouraged. Daniel said I deserved a drink more than anyone, and he wouldn't take no for an answer.

So we sat in the early spring sunshine sipping white wine as if we were holidaying on the Algarve, not stealing time away from doing the Doll's House accounts, or neglecting half a dozen mundane errands before the school run. And once the first half-glass had gone down, I began to think that I did, after all, deserve a drink. At one point the slow-moving traffic and the busy passers-by and Barry's twittering receded into the background, and the warmth of the sun transported me, just for a moment, to some other place. Daniel smiled and sort of half winked at me over the top of his glass and, to my surprise, I half winked back.

Rob puts his book on the side table and sidles up to me, his arm resting on the covers over my stomach. I've always loved his arms, still muscular, smooth-skinned, the arm of a sportsman. I drop my own book on the duvet and close my eyes, waiting for the familiar feeling to wash over me. It does, eventually, and when his hands have performed their habitual dance across my body and he's moving slowly inside me I feel, as I always do, a mix of warmth, pleasure and gratitude. Not everyone is lucky enough to be sleeping in the same bed as the man they married seventeen years before, I think. Not everyone is lucky enough to still want to.

Then, without warning, a memory of the wine and the sun and the smile surfaces from somewhere and pinches at my heart. I turn my head on the pillow and try to breathe evenly, as if nothing has happened.

PHOEBE

I let myself in and call out to Mum before I realise that Mum has a special Green Link meeting and she won't be here.

I wander into the kitchen and flick on the light and a bright orange Post-it note comes unstuck and floats to the floor. I pick it up and stick it back under the switch. 'SWITCH ME OFF!' it says in Ella's bold handwriting. My irritation is, up until this point, just the usual mix of after-school weariness and pre-homework grumpiness, but the Post-it note takes it up a notch.

I look around, expecting to find the usual array of notes and some sort of casserole on the counter. But tonight there are none of these things. The only thing on the counters is a great big filthy mess. Juice cartons, empty glasses and plates full of crusts from this morning. A bright red British Gas bill lying half submerged in a pool of spilled tea. A school blouse (is it mine?) tossed carelessly next to the phone, a needle and thread sticking out of one of the buttonholes, suspended in mid-stitch.

'Jesus, what happened here,' I mutter rhetorically as I open the fridge door looking for dinner.

But there's no dinner in the fridge. There's not even any food in there, unless you count one egg, a bowl full of grapes going brown at the tips and a half-empty jar of mayonnaise.

'My God, there's nothing to eat!' I shout, just as the doorbell rings. It's Kate being dropped off by Mrs Ireson. I'm about to shut the door behind her when Dad comes strolling up the path.

'Hi, Dad. Glad you're home early. There's nothing to eat!'

'Oh, come on. There must be. Mum always leaves something for us. Let's go inside. It'll be there somewhere.' Then he looks at the two of us. 'Where's Ella?'

'No idea,' I say.

'I'm not sure, but I think I heard Mum saying she was going to Lilly's after netball practice, until someone could collect her.'

'Oh,' says Dad, sighing. 'I guess that's me. Anyone know Lilly's number?'

'Nope.'

'Me neither.'

'Well it must be in the address book. I'll see to that in a minute. Now, let's see,' he says, disappearing behind the fridge door. He emerges a second later, scratching his head.

'You're right. There's no dinner.' Then he catches sight of the mess on the counter. 'Jesus. What happened here?'

'Do you think Mum's been kidnapped?' asks Kate, only half joking.

'Don't be silly. She probably had to rush out. Some sort of emergency, though I can't think what,' he says, shaking his head in puzzlement. 'There must have been a good reason.'

He doesn't sound convinced, but he makes a laudable effort to gloss things over.

'So!' he says, clapping his hands together and marching over to the long cupboard where all the tins are kept. 'Let's see what we can muster up. Looks like there's enough tomato soup for two of us. And there's a tin of those little sausages in baked beans. Who fancies that?'

'I hate tomato soup,' I say. 'Can I have the sausages?'

'I hate tomato soup too,' Kate says matter-of-factly.

'Right, you can share the sausages and have them with bread,' he says, peering into the bread bin. 'Scratch that. You'll have to have them with crackers.'

Then he shakes his head again and heads out to the hall to hang up his coat. I hear him muttering 'Jesus' again when he thinks he's out of earshot.

We find Lilly's number, eventually. It's not under L for Lilly, or S for Sargent, or even E for Ella's friends. It's under W for Williams. As in Nancy Williams, Lilly's mum, who obviously kept her maiden name in case she should ever want to go back and set the world on fire after having her three kids. Dad calls her and gets the address, and Ella gets home safely, but she's not impressed because the beans and sausages have been consumed and she doesn't like tomato soup either. Dad boils up the lone egg, into which she dips the last of the stale crackers.

Mum gets home even later than usual. Kate and Ella are already in bed (probably with tummies grumbling) and I'm in my room trying to create a replica of a Vivienne Westwood gown from papier mâché and scraps of old fabric. When I hear the door slam and Mum's footsteps on the hall tiles, I tiptoe over to my bedroom door and open it just a crack.

'Good meeting?' shouts Dad in an aggressively jovial tone I can pick up even from here.

'Great. Got a huge amount accomplished,' Mum shouts back. She must be in the kitchen because I can hear crockery being clanked together.

'Good. Well at least one of us had a good evening.'

'What's that supposed to mean?' Indignant footsteps across the hall.

'I mean, it wasn't particularly pleasant to arrive home to that mess (he'll be pointing now. He might even have dragged her back into the kitchen to stare at the evidence), to three hungry children and a house completely devoid of anything that might be construed as food.'

No response from Mum.

'Oh, sorry, there were only two starving children here. I had to go out and look for the other one.'

Still no response from Mum. Not that I can hear, anyway.

'Aren't you going to say anything?'

It's not necessary to be poking my nose through the crack any more. I'd be able to hear him even if the door were pressed shut and clad in state-of-the-art soundproofing.

'What would you like me to say, Rob? I'm sorry that I dare to go out? I'm sorry that I have something that distracts me from the ever-escalating demands of this family for just a few hours once a week? Maybe you should be sorry too. Sorry that you can't cope for one night. Sorry that you never learned to cook, or to wipe your own arse, for that matter.'

Now this is getting nasty.

'I'm not going to dignify that comment with a response, Libby. But you and I both know that it isn't just one night. Lately it's a couple of nights, and meetings in the afternoons on top of that, and Christ knows what else. You're hardly here. I mean, you can't be – just look at the place! And even when you're here you're not really here.'

'What's that supposed to mean?'

'You know exactly what it means. You're distracted. Absent. It's like none of this matters to you.'

I shut the door then and go back over to my desk, where my frankly lamentable attempt at Vivienne Westwood is waiting for someone to transform it into the A-grade art project it's meant to be. I don't want to hear any more. I think Dad's right, of course. The house has been kind of a mess lately. And I hate coming home to find out that I've got to organise everything. I wish she would forget about this Green Link rubbish and we could get back to normal. It's definitely making her weird.

But she's got a point. Dad's a pathetic cook. And it wouldn't hurt him to go to the supermarket every now and then.

LIBBY

I'm soaked to the skin and my hair is stuck to my head in sodden clumps. I wish I'd worn a sweatshirt with a hood. I wish you could count on the English sunshine to make more of an effort before giving way to threatening-looking clouds and unexpected torrential downpours.

As I stand in the utility room stripping sodden training pants from my frozen, red legs I can hear the rest of them stirring to life upstairs. I duck into the kitchen in my underwear to peer at the diary. I'm trying to make a point of checking it for essentials every morning, as I seem to have forgotten a few things lately. Forms that must be returned, extra children that need collecting. That sort of thing. The worst was not turning up to the inaugural meeting of the *Guys and Dolls* Costume Committee last Thursday morning. I meant to go. But then we decided to get started on the planning for the litter drive and I completely forgot about the *Guys and Dolls* thing. I got a call from a very concerned Rosie Blackburn asking if I'd come down with something.

I peer into the fridge for inspiration for tonight's

dinner and discover its shelves to be shockingly bare. It seems that no matter how diligent you are about grocery shopping – and by grocery shopping I mean the gargantuan weekly shop involving the pushing of an unwieldy trolley around aisles crammed with fellow shoppers and trays full of unstacked produce, the unloading of approximately one thousand articles on to the check-out desk and the restuffing of same articles into environment-mutilating plastic carrier bags and back into the unwieldy trolley then into the car boot, followed by the unloading of the carrier bags from car boot to kitchen, during which two inevitably split and disgorge their contents along the full length of the front hall, and culminating in the mind-numbingly boring chore of putting the thousand items away, during which process you notice that the fridge shelves are coated with spilled orange juice, decaying cucumber, hardened egg yolk, or possibly all three, and vow to clean it out before the next shop but never quite get round to doing it – within two days it's all gone and someone will open the fridge door and wail, 'There's nothing to eat!' Family food supplies are like every mother's To-Do list: impossible to keep up with.

Food shopping has always been near the top of my list of most hated domestic tasks, but lately the dread I feel at the prospect of a supermarket shop has ballooned out of all proportion. Ever since I cottoned on to the concept of food miles I've found myself in a moral quandary every time

I venture near the fruit and veg section. Should I support the poor Kenyan farmer by buying his green beans, or save the four thousand or so miles' worth of ozone-depleting fuel that's brought them here and buy the sad-looking specimens from Cumbria instead? If I can find them, that is. Quite often it seems easier to go home empty-handed.

'Mum, why are you standing in the kitchen in your underwear?' Ella creeps up on me from behind and I nearly jump out of my clammy, goose-pimpled skin.

'Oh God! You scared me. I had to put my running stuff in the machine because it was filthy and wet. I'm just checking the diary to see what you need today.'

'I found this in my school bag,' she says, brandishing a handful of white paper. She hands it to me and I quickly identify it as a copy of the Green Link draft action plan complete with background notes. The one I thought I'd lost yesterday.

'I was looking for that all yesterday! It must have got mixed up with your homework. Thank you, sweetheart. Remember you're coming this afternoon? We've got that special meeting about our toxic product collection drive. I've not made any plans for you, so I'm going to ask someone, maybe Mrs Foster, to drop you off at the library after school.'

'Cool,' she smiles, kissing me on the cheek before venturing over to the long cupboard where the cereal packets are kept. I close the diary, grab my

Green Link papers and take my shivering, scantily-clad body off towards the shower. I know exactly what's coming next.

'Mum! There's no cereal! What am I going to have for breakfast?' she shouts.

But I'm already halfway up the stairs. No time to hang around. Got work to do.

When Ella walks into the conference room, I'm hunched over a table with Michelle and Gabriel examining their latest poster effort. I'm briefly distracted by one of Fran's increasingly regular text updates: *Paul seen me with bed head and still fancies me. I've seen his v. small, v. untidy flat and still fancy him. Surely this is real thing? xox Fran.*

It turns out that Michelle is a dab hand with illustration, and Gabriel is a whiz with words, so they make a formidable pair. They're determined that ours will be, not just a poster, but a piece of artwork that cannot be ignored; an item of such persuasive power that thousands of local residents will be induced to troop to designated collection points with carrier bags full of toxic cleaning fluids. But I can see a small problem.

'You don't think the bit about foetal death and diarrhoea is a bit over the top?' I ask.

'But it's true, innit,' insists Michelle. 'Too much of them air fresheners can cause foetal death and diarrhoea.'

'I know, but we don't want to seem too alarmist. It'll put people off completely. Make them think

155

we're a bunch of nutters.' I wince guiltily at my choice of words. Looking on from the outside, I would probably have thought the same not too long ago.

It's problematic, this business of deciding just how much to frighten people. And I'm sure some of the ideas we throw around will sound outlandish, or laughable. One thing that's never going to fly is the idea of using washable hankies instead of disposable tissues. Aside from being vaguely repulsive, hankies will never make the leap between the generations. When I asked the girls if they'd ever carry one they all fell down in a fit of simulated vomiting.

'Oh hi, darling.' I say as Ella pokes her head around the door. 'Over here.'

Ella walks over to us and smiles shyly at Gabriel and Michelle.

'All right, Ella?'

'Fine, thank you,' replies Ella in the golden, melodious way that ten-year-olds still have.

'Come over here and I'll show you what we're working on,' I say, leading her over to a table where Eloise is leaning over a map of the local area, sticky-backed red dots at the ready. She looks up and smiles at us both.

'Hi there, hon. Your mum and I are trying to work out where we should have the drop-off points for all these nasty cleaning fluids. We've got to decide and then request permission from the council. Why don't you help us?'

'Sure,' says Ella, dropping her school bag to the

floor with a thud. 'But why don't we just get people to take them to the recycling place?'

'That's a good question. We did think about that. But we decided that we needed to make it real easy for people, so they wouldn't have any excuse not to participate. And we wanted the whole thing to be super-visible, to make a statement, you know? So we're going to spread ourselves out a bit. Man the stations for a whole week. Make a really big deal out of it.'

'Oh,' says Ella, entranced by Eloise. It's hard not to get entranced by Eloise, such is the mixture of earthy friendliness and otherworldly romanticism she exudes.

'We're counting on you to help man the the stations that week,' I say, putting my hand on Ella's shoulder.

Her eyes light up. 'Yeah, that would be cool. Maybe Dad and Phoebe and Kate could help too.'

Pigs and flying come to mind.

'Anyway, sit yourself down and we'll try to work this out. What about one here, Eloise? At Station Road? It's a nice big space, with plenty of parking nearby, and enough room for a couple of skips.'

'Good idea,' says Eloise, carefully placing a red sticker on the corner of Station Road and Mickelson Crescent.

'Skips costs a lot of money, don't they? Who's paying for then all?' asks Ella.

'Er, that would be me,' says Daniel from behind. He's obviously just arrived. 'Well, not me exactly, but the Green Link fund I come with. It's a pretty small fund, though, so we're going to have to do some fund-raising before long.' Then he takes Ella by the shoulders and looks at her with mock solemnity. 'And how are you? To what do we owe the pleasure of your company today, which is, after all, not a Wednesday?'

'Mum had to come and there was no one home, so I came too. I don't mind.'

'Never too young to become an environmental fanaticist,' he says, before ambling off to the coffee pot on the other side of the room. 'Coffee, anyone?'

'No thanks,' Eloise and I say in unison.

I watch him as he lifts the coffee pot up above his head and examines its contents, then pours what little there is in the pot into one of the three chipped mugs sitting on the tray. He ignores the milk and sugar and takes a gulp before turning to lean against the table. Then he surveys the room, and smiles at me before reaching into his backpack for his battered blue notebook, the one he carries everywhere.

I turn my attention back to Ella and Eloise and the red dots. 'Where were we?' I ask brightly.

An hour later Ella is sitting in the corner finishing an essay on tudor life, having assisted Eloise in littering the map with red dots. I don't know how we're going to cover them all. We'll have to eliminate a few, I'm sure. Or recruit another several dozen volunteers, and several thousand more pounds for skips.

Then I have an idea. I wander over to where Daniel is sitting perusing some rather complicated-looking spreadsheets.

'Listen, do you suppose we could persuade a local skip company to support us, maybe supply a few skips for free if we agree to feature their name and logo somewhere?' I suggest.

Daniel stares at my fingers splayed out on the edge of the table, then looks up at me. Suddenly very conscious of my hands, I stand up straight and thrust them into my jeans pockets.

'That's a great idea. You want to draft a letter, make a few calls?'

'Sure, I'll get on to that this evening.'

'She's lovely,' he says, nodding towards Ella.

'Oh, thank you. And thank you for being so kind to her.'

'She's so like you,' he says then, his eyes lingering on my face.

I feel a sharp intake of breath and a swilling sensation in my stomach and I hope he doesn't notice.

'Oh, to be ten again,' I say lightly, turning to move away.

'Well I, for one, am glad you're not,' he says.

I blush, and look down at my feet, searching for an appropriate response. But he doesn't wait for one. Instead he folds his spreadsheets in half and stuffs them between the pages of his blue note-book as he stands up from the table.

'I'll just see how these guys are getting on,' he

says, and walks over to where Michelle and Gabriel are sitting with their feet on the table, laughing and sipping Diet Coke. I guess they must have cracked the wording on the flyer, because they hold it out to Daniel proudly as he approaches. I watch him as he nods his head vigorously and squeezes each of them on the shoulder.

Maybe he does that to everyone, I think.

I need to organise a meeting with the local council. The question is, who at the local council? Daniel can't help. He says that in his experience councils are all organised differently and I will have to do some initial sleuthing.

I try calling the main switchboard. It is automated, of course, and I have to listen to around twenty-one options, none of which sounds like what I want, before I reach the one that will allow me to *speak to an operator*. It must be that everyone chooses the *speak to an operator* option because the line is engaged. It is engaged every time I try for fifteen minutes, so I give up and decide to try sleuthing without the aid of the automated telephone system.

I find a phone book. (Five of them. There are some advantages to being based at the local library.) I peruse the list of departments, and am encouraged when my finger lands upon one called Environmental Service (Inquiries). It too has an automated telephone system, but you only have to go through three options before you reach the one that allows you to speak to a person. Speaking to a person turns out not to be as useful as I hope, though. The person can't help with either my general inquiry (who do I need to speak to about getting approval and support for some community-initiated environmental schemes?) or my more specific one (how do I get a permit to hold a rally in Hill Road Park?) The person has no idea what I'm talking about. Talking to her is like wading through molasses in boots with suction caps on the soles. When we finally get ourselves unstuck she suggests I try the recycling department. 'They understand all about that environment stuff over there,' she says helpfully.

The people in Recycling are very happy to (a) send me another roll of orange recycling bags (b) give me precise collection times for each road or (c) boast to me about a new efficiency improvement drive that will involve all homeowners placing their recycling bags no further than three metres from the road, thereby preventing back injury to and industrial action by the collection men, and maintaining our council taxes at a level to rival the lowest in the country. What they cannot do is tell me who I should talk to about our own programmes, or give me permission for anything, much less the hiring of a local park for a rally – 'A rally? You mean like a car race?' – or the location of skips on street corners to assist in the disposal of household cleaning products.

By the time I've finished talking to Environmental

Services (Inquiries) and Recycling, I've lost the will to live and think I might need to call Respite Homes or Hostels for People with Mental Health Problems instead. It occurs to me that I'm not being creative enough, and that perhaps I need to think more laterally, or backwards. I wonder if I should try the department called Traffic Signals/Bollards, for instance, or perhaps the one mysteriously named Special Services.

I call Daniel to give him a progress report. 'I'm getting nowhere with this,' I say.

'Maybe we should try to find another way in. What about calling one of the councillors themselves. Maybe they'll be able to direct us through the maze.'

When he says this I scan the alphabetical listing of departments and spot one called Councillors – for Information, and feel momentarily hopeful.

'OK. I'll have another go,' I say, as if setting off up the north face of the Eiger with storm clouds looming.

PHOEBE

When I open the fridge I see that it is practically empty except for a carton of blueberries with a Post-it note from Ella stuck to it – 'MUM, THESE BLUEBERRIES ARE ALL THE WAY FROM CHILE!!!' it shouts – and several plastic containers stacked neatly on one shelf.

'What're all these containers? Dinner?' I inquire hopefully as I pull out the milk. There's the tiniest drop in the bottom of the carton. Probably just enough for two cups of tea, but definitely not enough for cereal.

'What? Oh, no, not really. I'm taking that stuff in to the meeting tonight. I've noticed that Courtney and Michelle don't eat properly at all. They subsist on crisps and chocolate and fizzy drinks as far as I can see. So I'm taking them a healthy meal they can have at the meeting.'

'So what are we going to eat?' I ask, not even trying to disguise my exasperation.

'Oh God, Phoebe, I haven't really thought yet. I'll get something today and leave it for you, I promise.'

She looks at me almost apologetically. Or maybe it's not apology I can see in her expression but thinly camouflaged impatience; it's hard to tell.

'Good. Because I don't want another scene like last week,' I say, feeling forty-five all of a sudden.

As I wait for the kettle to boil, it occurs to me how strange it is that Mum should be taking white plastic containers full of food for two girls she barely knows.

'Mum, do you think these girls, Courtney and, what was it? Rochelle? Do you think they're going to want your food? Don't you think they might think you're interfering just a bit? Maybe they *like* eating crisps and chocolate.'

'They do. But that's because they don't know any better. They've not had the benefit of parents who know about nutrition being around to watch what they eat. They're perfectly happy for me to take them dinner. I asked them.'

'You asked them? What did you say?' I ask, incredulous.

'The other night they commented on how they'd never realised how bad their diet was, talking about something from one of our books, but neither of them can cook and their mums are hardly around because they work shifts. So I said I'd take dinner in for them each week, show them some easy foods to make.'

'So you're cooking them dinner every week?' My jaw is slack with disbelief.

'Well, cooking might be stretching it. It's mostly cold food. But I'm making them something, yes. And I thought I'd write out the recipe and stick

164

it to the box so they can make it themselves some-time. What do you think?'

'All I can say is you'd better not let Dad know that's what you're doing. Something tells me he won't appreciate your point of view very much at about six o'clock tonight when he's burning the scrambled eggs,' I say, squeezing past her with my tea.

'He'll live,' she says, glaring at the few drops of tea I spill on my way across the kitchen. I double back and dab them with my socks.

He'll live. *He'll live?* Who is this woman, and what has she done with my mother? Where's the person who used to worry when she hadn't made a pudding for dinner, or that she might have inad-vertently served us mince twice in one week? Come to think of it, where's the woman who used to worry about when she last changed the sheets? It feels as though someone's tipped a bucket of sand over mine.

'By the way, Mum. My sheets really need doing. If you wouldn't mind, that is,' I say with expertly delivered sarcasm. I'm already halfway up the stairs, which is too bad because it means I can't see the expression on her face.

About halfway through the morning I'm desperate for a pee, so even though I know I'm going to be late for maths I sneak away to the loos. When I'm washing my hands I realise there's someone else in there, and she's sobbing. Peering under the doors I can see a pair of regulation black loafers and grey tights with a hole in them. It could be anyone.

I contemplate a hasty escape. After all, it's none of my business, and whoever it is probably doesn't want to be discovered. But the sobbing becomes less contained and more desperate as I'm standing there, so I go over to the cubicle and lean my forehead against the door.

'Hello? Are you all right?'

A stupid question, which is greeted by a derisive silence.

'Can I help you?' I ask, trying again.

'No,' comes back the choked response.

'Please come out and let me help you,' I say, suddenly feeling quite determined.

'You can't help. No one can help,' says the voice.

It's a familiar voice, but I can't immediately place it. Then I do.

'Rebecca? It's Phoebe. Open the door. What's wrong?'

I hear the latch being slid to one side and the door swings open an inch or so. I push it open tentatively, afraid now of what I might find behind it.

Rebecca's cheeks are streaked with wet mascara (I've always thought she wears too much), and her skin is blotchy, but otherwise there are no signs of intense distress. No slashed wrists or needles.

'What? What is it?' I ask, crouching in front of her and looking into her eyes, which are empty, almost dead. Hopeless.

'Rebecca, please tell me what's wrong. I promise

166

I'll try to help you.' Strangely enough, I really mean this. I don't know Rebecca that well, but something about the way she looks now makes me want to reach out to her.

The warmth I feel is not reciprocal. Her eyes become steely and small and mean.

'You can't help me! Do you hear me! You're the last person who can help me! *Just go away and leave me alone!*' This last thing she screeches at me, as if I'm the cause of her distress rather than the innocent bystander who's tried to rescue her.

I stand up and back out of the cubicle, leaving her sobbing into her hands.

'OK. Suit yourself,' I say haughtily, immediately regretting it. This is not a time for cheap shots, I know. It's just that sometimes they come out of their own accord, and they make climbing back extremely difficult. So there's nothing for me to do but leave her here.

By the time I'm out the door I'm already thinking mostly about the detention I'm probably going to get for being so late for maths.

LIBBY

When I push open the doors I see Daniel right away, but he's facing away from me, leaning over one of the tables. The table itself is piled high with stacks of leaflets and cardboard boxes, and a Starbucks Grande cup is perched precariously close to the edge. I can't be sure of what mood he's in, but I've a pretty good idea. Bob Fisher died this morning.

'Who's Bob Fisher?' Kate had asked in response to my sudden gasp at the announcement on the radio.

A couple of months ago, I wouldn't have known anything about Bob Fisher, but now I know him to be one of the greatest environmentalists the world has known. A hero of our time. And a great hero of Daniel's.

Most people have heroes, I guess. Growing up I had a couple of my own. There was Charlotte Rampling, gazing out from the pages of *Paris Match* in her inimitably cool and sexy manner, and to whom I was, unfortunately, never going to bear more than the most remote resemblance. I suppose I should have been admiring the Farrah Fawcetts and Linda Carters and Christy Brinkleys like all

168

my friends, but those glossy, smiling creatures never did anything for me. It was Charlotte I wanted to be, though she must have been forty even then.

Then there was David McAlpine at the National Oceanography Centre at Southampton, who seemed to know everything, not just about his own speciality, but about everyone else's as well. Any question you asked him, any comment you made, he would have something intelligent to say. It could be a question about large marine species (his field) or one about someone's sudden attack of post-viral arthritic reaction, about which he was supposed to know absolutely nothing. But he could always shed light on the situation, could always be counted on to quote a study or two supporting his view. I was twenty when I used to listen to him from the third row of a musty classroom, or sit across from him and a couple of lagers in the student bar, and I thought I would never again meet anyone so worthy of compete adoration.

But I'm not sure any hero of mine ever had the kind of impact on me that Bob Fisher had on Daniel. He can actually recall the moment when he decided to follow in his footsteps. 'He was funny and brave and audacious, and he refused to accept the limits of the practical. He believed in small miracles,' Daniel enthused on the evening two weeks ago when he'd told me how Bob Fisher had first inspired him to get involved in the green movement. Ella and I were sitting with him in the conference room after everyone else had left the regular Wednesday evening meeting. He'd stayed behind to finish stuffing envelopes with notices informing people about our group, and we'd volunteered to help him. As we all folded and stuffed and licked, he talked about how he'd become a full-time Green Link activist after completing his masters in Environmental Science, spurning offers of respectable staff positions at several universities. 'There's plenty of time for me to do that sort of thing,' he'd said. 'Right now I feel like I want to be at the heart of a change effort.'

I said to him then how I loved the way his commitment seemed to come so easily, and to be so devoid of judgement. He attributed that to Bob Fisher too. 'That's the honorary Canadian in me. I owe that to Bob Fisher as well,' he'd said, grinning. 'Canadians are the most consensus-minded people on the planet, you know.'

Today, Daniel turns around when he hears the sound of the door opening. I smile at him. Then my mobile rings and Rob's name pops up in the little screen.

'Hi, what's up?' I say. It feels odd to be speaking to Rob while attempting to throw understanding glances across the room at Daniel. Perhaps it feels odd to Daniel too, as if he's intruding on something, because he turns his back to me again.

'Nothing much. Just wondered whether we'd sorted out that business with next door and the new fence. Only I saw Bill this morning and he gave me a decidedly frosty look. I thought maybe he was getting impatient with us.'

'Oh yes. I forgot. Kind of. I mean, I got the

quotes but then I just sort of let it slip. I'll get on to it,' I say dispiritedly.

'You OK?' he says, suddenly concerned.

'Hmn? Yeah, I'll be all right. Just heading into Green Link.'

Rob makes a non-committal noise on the other end.

'Right,' he says. Then there's a brief pause before he adds, 'Well, anyway, don't forget about the fence. We really need to get moving on that,' he says.

I'm tempted to ask, as my friend Carrie did once when her husband handed her a typewritten list of urgent jobs titled 'Things we need to do this month', Who is this effing WE family and what makes you think they'll be prepared to help us? But he's right. We do need to get moving on the fence, and on the loo that only flushes on the third attempt, and the handle on the loo door that keeps falling off. We need to attend to what appears to be a nascent ant problem, and something that looks alarmingly like rising damp in the front hallway. Then there's the fridge, which is empty again, and the ever-present issue of our young teenaged daughter, who, according to my sporadic investigations, has popped a packet and a half of birth-control pills.

All this has to be attended to. But right now, my biggest concern is the demise of a hero.

'Good morning,' I say as I approach him hesitantly.

He turns around and smiles, but it's a weak, fleeting smile. His eyes are lugubrious.

'Hi there,' he says quietly. 'How are you doing?'

'More to the point, how are *you* doing?' I say. No point in trying to gloss this one over, pretend we're going to get anywhere with a toxic disposal campaign today.

He slumps into a chair and I lean against the table next to him.

'Well, I've had better days. You heard, then?'

'On the radio,' I say, nodding.

Then I'm not really sure what to say, so we sit in silence for a moment, him tapping the side of his coffee cup, me staring at the floor. Then he looks up at me.

'It's weird how these things affect you, isn't it? I mean, I barely knew the man. Had met him three times. No, let's be realistic, I'd seen him three times, met him just the once. But I felt like I knew him. And I knew every inch of his work, of what he thought.'

'I know. You did know him, actually. Part of him, anyway. It's totally natural for you to feel this way. Do you want to give this a miss today, maybe go home?'

He laughs half-heartedly. ' I do want to give this a miss. But I don't want to go home and stare at the four walls. They're a pretty uninspiring set of walls at the best of times.'

'Right then. Let's go out,' I say decisively. 'I'll buy you breakfast, then lunch as well if you want.'

'Now that's an offer,' he says, getting up from the chair. He stands there for a moment, arching his back and raising his face to the ceiling with his eyes scrunched together. Then he looks at me and offers another weak smile.

'Right. Let's go then.'

You can cover a lot of ground during a four-and-a-half-hour meal. We dawdle over two coffees and a couple of pains au chocolat at Amandine for at least an hour and a half, by which time it's almost noon and we've worked up a proper hunger. Not for food, exactly, but sustenance. Wine. More conversation. The kind of conversation you can only have over wine.

There's an awkward moment when we approach the doors of the Italian just along from Amandine. When he holds the door open for me I'm suddenly struck by the thought of how this will look to other people, the many other people who I know in this urban village and who will very likely be strolling about its streets over the next hour or so. With my luck, Gilly – who is always on the lookout for some gentle gossip – will spot me as she goes sprinting by with Hank. 'Maybe we should go somewhere else,' I say, biting my lip. He looks at me quizzically, as if he can't think what could possibly be worrying me about going into this innocuous little establishment, which makes me feel a little foolish. Then he says 'OK, let's walk into town,' and we head away from the village and into the comfortingly anonymous hurly-burly of central Richmond, where we land upon a tiny Greek restaurant in a quiet street well away from the beaten track.

As I watch the waiter twisting the corkscrew and expertly pouring the light gold liquid into my glass, I experience another short-lived feeling of guilt. I shouldn't be doing this, in the middle of the day, with another man, with my husband working no more than a mile away. Then I think, why not? What's there to be ashamed of? I'm with a friend and colleague in need, helping him ride a shock wave. Rob must have had dozens of these kinds of lunches, with receptionists whose boyfriends have upped and left, or male colleagues contemplating divorce. It's what working people do in times of trouble. Bunk off and get drunk.

Small wonder it's what they do; it works. By the time we're halfway through the first bottle, Bob Fisher and Daniel's sadness at his death have been pushed, if not to the farthest recesses of our minds, at least safely away from our frontal lobes. Daniel's eyes have recovered some of their glow, which I attribute as much to the restorative effects of the conversation as to the alcohol.

'So,' he says suddenly, leaning forward on his elbows. 'Tell me how you got to be such an optimist.'

'An optimist? Is that what I am? I hadn't realised,' I say, surprised.

'Yeah. I spotted it from the word go. You're the kind of person who wants things to go well. You want to make things happen. If there are obstacles, you immediately try to think of ways to overcome them.'

'Maybe you're right,' I say, savouring a sip from my wine glass. 'I've never really thought about it.

The thing about giving your life over to raising children is that you kind of lose perspective on what kind of person you are, because you never get any feedback. And you spend so much of your time battling things, small things, that it doesn't feel as if you're winning, let alone being optimistic. Do you know what I mean?'

He'd be forgiven for not knowing. Half a bottle of wine has made me slurry.

'My guess is you're a middle child,' he says confidently, leaning back in his chair with his arms folded across his chest.

'You're right. I am. My sister Liz is a corporate lawyer, very clever and high-powered. Always was that way. And Jaime, my younger sister, is just kind of away with the fairies. She's a potter. Doesn't know what day it is half the time. Doesn't care either. Now that I think about it, I've always sort of been the practical one, the one who sorts things out.'

'There, you see. I think I'll have to call you Mrs Blue Sky.'

'Excuse me?'

'Mrs Blue Sky, as in 'Mr Blue Sky'?'

Nothing. My brain is well and truly pickled. I offer an embarassed giggle by way of apology.

'You know, that song by the Electric Light Orchestra?' he says with mock exasperation, then starts singing.

I recover from my bout of early eighties rock amnesia and join in.

'There. You remembered,' he says, smiling.

'What are you doing quoting ELO lyrics? You can't have been more than about seven when they were at their peak.'

'Ah, but I have an older brother, and he's probably the biggest ELO fan that ever lived. He brainwashed me at a very early age. I never recovered.'

The waiter suddenly appears with another bottle of wine I don't remember having ordered. Daniel nods encouragingly at him, then leans across the table and whispers, 'In memory of Bob.'

'Absolutely. A sign of respect,' I say in a sort of slurred whisper, leaning in from my side of the table. Our faces are so close I can smell the wine on his breath. Another few inches and we'd be rubbing noses. I sit back abruptly and try to regain my composure.

'So, how old is your brother, then? What's he like?'

'He's forty next month. But he won't be worried about that. He's a real dude. Kindest, most balanced bloke you'll ever meet.'

'That's a pretty big age gap.'

'Yeah. I was an accident. But a happy one. After Neil, my mum was told she probably wouldn't get pregnant again, and she struggled with it for years. Then suddenly, long after she and Dad had given up hope, I came along and disrupted their lives all over again.'

'Did you mind? Being like an only child, I mean. Neil must have left home when you were quite young.'

'No, it was great. Sort of like having two fathers, only one of them was a little more in touch with my world, a little better at reading me. A lot cooler. I think I was really lucky, actually.'

'And what does he do? Neil, I mean.'

'He works in sales for a publishing company by day, and he's a musician by night. Plays base for a band called Emerson Jack. And in between times he's dad to two little boys, Cy and Ned. They are just great. You've gotta see them.'

His eyes light up, and he sits shaking his head for a moment, as if picturing some amusing scene featuring Cy and Ned.

'But all kids are great in their own way, aren't they? I'm sure yours are. That Ella is a doll.'

'Yes, but girls can be a handful,' I say, then wish I hadn't. Not a very Mrs Blue Sky kind of comment. A bit of a downer, in fact.

'Ah, but surely a handful is good! A handful means they're thinking, and learning, and challenging. Who wants to raise a bunch of yes-men. Sorry, I mean yes-women.'

'I'm sure you're right,' I say. 'And I'm sure that's what Bob Fisher would say too.'

And I leave it at that, because I don't want to get into a lengthy discussion about child-raising with Daniel. I don't want to tell him about the mind-numbing boredom, the frustration, and the emotional see-sawing that are such a big part of a daily life spent running around after three girls and a husband who operates on a strictly last-name basis with the household appliances. With a bottle of wine inside me, and the knees of this gloriously sanguine person touching mine under the table, I'd rather focus on the joy of it all.

Then, a second later, I realise I want to get off the topic altogether. The juxtaposition of Daniel, here, now, and talk of my family, somewhere else, forgotten for the past four hours, is suddenly uncomfortable. And reality is beginning to rear its ugly head. I am drunk. Very drunk. And in an hour and a half I have to collect the girls from the bus and behave like a person who hasn't wiled away the entire day drinking wine with a very young man who isn't her husband.

What have I been thinking of?

'I need some coffee,' I say with an abruptness that must be comical. 'And then I really have to go.'

Daniel is startled. Wondering, no doubt, what transformed the mellow, indulgent mood that sprouted eighties' song lyrics into the lukewarm demeanour I'm wearing now.

'Oh, sure. I could do with some too,' he says, turning to signal to the waiter.

I keep my eyes down while we sit and wait for our coffee, rummaging in my bag for wallet, keys, chewing gum. Feeling chilled, I pull my jacket around my shoulders.

It's only when I've left the restaurant, when I'm halfway home, that I realise I've forgotten to pick up the library books Kate needed for her geography project. I've also failed to call the fence people and attend to the ants and the rising damp, and the fridge is still empty.

But it's too late now. I'm out of time.

PHOEBE

I don't get a detention after all. Mr Lockhart loves me. Not in the biblical sense, of course. (Bearing in mind that Mr Lockhart is incredibly old, that would be more than a little bit sick.) He just thinks I'm a good girl, and he almost always gives me the benefit of the doubt. I remember once last term there were five of us at the back not paying attention, and he gave everyone an order mark except me. I never question how this has all come about. Maybe his daughter looks like me. Maybe he just has a soft spot for people who manage to stay in the top maths set for two terms in a row.

Whatever. I am relieved, because they've taken to holding detentions on Friday evenings, just out of spite.

In fact, the whole thing has turned out to be such a non-event that I almost forget about Rebecca until she sidles up to me in the lunch room on the last day of school before Easter break.

'Can talk to you for a second?' she says as I'm loading up my potato with cheese and ham.

'Sure. Come join us over there,' I say, indicating

179

the table where Alice, Laura and Tilly are already unloading their trays.

'No, I need to talk to you on your own,' she says, looking slightly panicked. 'Just for a minute. It won't take long.'

So I reluctantly sit down with her at a small table next to the vending machines. I look across at Alice, whose rigid back and hand on hips posture combined with wide-open mouth convey the full extent of her incomprehension.

As soon as we sit down she leans in and starts whispering. This is obviously going to take longer than a minute.

'Listen. I'm really sorry I was so horrible to you the other day. I was just really upset, that's all.'

'That's OK,' I say. Then, trying to purge the coldness from my voice, I add. 'Are you all right now?'

'Well, no. Not exactly,' she says, with attempted non-chalance. Her eyes immediately start to get watery. 'Oh God, oh God. Don't let me cry again,' she says, wiping her eyes ferociously.

I look around me, then quietly place my hand on hers for a second. 'It's OK. Just take a deep breath. Then tell me what's wrong.'

She sits in silence for a few minutes, pushing her ham salad about on her plate. I take a few bites of my potato, the insides of which are yellow and have a sickly-sweet taste on account of the potato having been first overcooked then left to languish on a hot-plate.

'OK. Here's the thing,' she says, finally. 'You have to promise not to tell anyone.' She looks at me for confirmation before proceeding. 'I've made a really big mistake. And I'm in big trouble.'

What can it be, I wonder? Caught cheating on an exam? Shoplifting? I look at her intently, willing her to go on.

'I'm pregnant,' she says, squeezing her eyes shut. Oh my God. 'Oh my God, Rebecca.'

'I know. What the hell am I going to do, Phoebe?'

'How did it happen?'

'I'm not sure,' she says. Then, in response to my confused expression, she says hurriedly, 'What I mean is, there was one time the condom sort of slipped off, and another time we didn't use one, and I'm not exactly sure which time it, you know, happened.'

'Rebecca, how could you *not* use a condom? How could you?'

'Please don't look at me like that,' she says, burying her face in her hands. Then she realises she's attracting attention, so she sits up straight and adopts an inscrutable expression.

'We just got carried away and he promised he would pull out before anything happened. But I don't think he did it properly because stuff was dripping out of me for hours afterwards.'

I screw up my face, recoiling from the image. 'Who's we? Who's he? Have you got a boyfriend I don't know about?'

'No. Not exactly. I can't tell you who it is.'

'But Rebecca, you'll have to tell someone. You'll have to tell him, at least.'

'No, no, I don't!' she exclaims in an urgent whisper. 'No one has to know. I'm going to get rid of it. Can you help me?'

And this was supposed to take a minute? I look over at the others. Laura has gone and Alice and Tilly are talking to Chloe now. They've lost interest in me and Rebecca and why we've cordoned ourselves off over here, but that won't last. At the first opportunity they'll be all over me, begging me to spill the beans.

'Please promise me you won't say anything, Phoebe,' Rebecca says, as if reading my mind. Her eyes are boring holes in me. I think about her mother, Julia, who's always seemed to me to be a really nice, understanding sort of person. Then I think about her father, Andrew, a stern, distant man who Mum once called (and it's quite something for Mum to be *this* rude about someone) 'an opinionated bastard with his head permanently stuck up his own arse'. Apparently he once grounded Rebecca for a month when she came home ten minutes late from a party. Ten minutes!

'I promise,' I say. 'But I don't know how I can really help you, Rebecca. I don't know anything about abortions. Why would you think I would?'

'Who would know?' she asks. She sounds small and helpless, like a four-year-old misplaced by her parents in a theme park.

'I guess I could look into it for you. If you want.'

'Would you?'

'Yes. I'll try.'

She reaches across the table and squeezes my forearm. 'Thank you so much, Pheobe. I really don't have anyone else I could talk to. And you were so nice the other day.'

She's right. She doesn't really have anyone else to talk to. She has friends, but not real friends. She's one of those people who always seem alone, even when they're in the middle of a crowd.

The afternoon period bell rings. Rebecca stands up from the table and gives her eyes a final precautionary wipe. 'I have to go see Mr Wilkes now. I'll talk to you later?'

'OK,' I say numbly, then look down at my potato. Arseholes, I think. Now it's stone cold as well as overcooked.

LIBBY

ouncillors – for Information isn't the lifeline I'd hoped it would be. It turns out to be a number that councillors can call when *they* want information, rather than a number residents can call for information about councillors. Silly me.

But just as I'm about to start tearing my hair out follicle by follicle, Marcie Gibbons drops a solution into my lap. She says she was in touch with a local councillor a year ago when they were having trouble with a neighbour with badly behaved dogs. (Apparently the old man shared his fifth-floor one-bedroom flat with twelve vociferous terriers. When one started, it set them all off and the din of their yapping could be heard even in Marcie's flat down on the second floor.) Not only does Marcie have the councillor's name and office number, but she has his mobile number, and *it still works!*

Clive Prattley is a little like a terrier himself. His ardency is apparent even over the phone, and I get a mental picture of him straining on a lead. He's not the man I need to talk to, of course, nor does he know who is, but he is willing to do some investigating for me. When he says he'll call me back in a day or two with the infor-mation, I actually believe him.

Sure enough, Clive calls back two days later and gives me the names of three individuals, all of whose permission is required for our various events. Park permits are granted by one person, skip distribution permits by a second, and permission for flyer distribution by a third. Clive advises me to telephone them immediately because he's briefed them all and they are expecting to hear from me. 'Seize the momentum!', he exclaims, and I picture him then as a terrier standing at the helm of a warship wearing a captain's hat. I wish he were here in front of me so I could give him a hug.

'I've been thinking we should change our second car. Maybe get rid of it altogether.'

I look over at Rob to gauge his reaction, but his face is shielded by the newspaper.

'Rob? Did you hear what I said?'

He puts the paper down with a sigh. 'Lib, why would we want to do that?'

'Because it does seem excessive, having two cars. And, as Ella keeps reminding me, a Range Rover is absolutely the worst one to have in terms of environmental damage. We could get one of those Prius hybrid things maybe, that run on a combination of petrol and electricity? If it's good enough for Cameron Diaz it should be good enough for us.'

'Lib, those cars max out at about thirty miles an hour, and they probably cost a fortune.'

'But it would do for essential driving. And the rest of the time we would be encouraged to walk or take the train more. It's ridiculous that I drive the girls to the bus stop, for instance. They could easily walk. Twenty years ago kids would have walked twice as far.'

'You know you sound like your father, don't you?' he says, smiling.

'But it's true, isn't it?'

He looks at me sternly for a second, then laughs, as if he can't be bothered to be cross with me after all. I've caught him at a good time. Excessive Green Link activity, inadequate food supplies, rampant ants and failure to call fence people have failed to irk him in quite the same way as usual this week. The drunken lunch went completely unnoticed thanks to his being late home that evening. I don't think the girls even noticed my inebriety. By the time I went to collect them I'd consumed three tall glasses of water and lain on the bed with cucumbers on my eyes until I was sure I'd pass for someone sober.

'Lib, don't you think it's enough that we've got multicoloured recycling bins in every room in the house and you and Ella slapping our wrists every time we even contemplate throwing something in the rubbish? Or that we've got organic bloody everything, every bloody where. I mean, what exactly is that stuff you've got me washing my hair in? Oatmeal? Any more ideas from you and I'm seriously going to have to consider petitioning for divorce.'

I wouldn't blame him for being a little irritated. Ella and I have put them through quite a lot in the past few weeks. There's organic shampoo and soap in all the showers; all chemical cleaning products have been banished, which is mostly fine but isn't proving very effective against the rings around the bottom of the loos; radiators are turned to the off position whenever we're not in a room, which admittedly makes the house feel like a large, multi-compartment freezer; the television is, it goes without saying, always switched off at the mains, which means it does take rather a long time for the Sky listings to come up whenever you turn it on; and Ella persuaded me not to upgrade Phoebe and Kate's mobile phones on account of the mountains of perfectly functional but just-out-of-date handsets lying, unused, around people's homes. Phoebe has really struggled with that one, and is allegedly saving up the necessary funds herself, such is the intolerable shame of being seen to own an eighteen-month-old model.

The thing I'm personally struggling with is the tumble-dryer. No more warm fluffy towels straight from the dryer, just sheets of sandpaper with which to scrape yourself on emerging from the shower. And instead of T-shirts and jeans that can be easily smoothed and folded while still warm from the dryer, you get crumpled, stiffened articles that require ten minutes under a firm iron before they're wearable. Does the energy saved by line-drying make up for the extra energy consumed by the iron, not to mention the person standing there ironing? I'm not at all sure.

And compact fluorescent light bulbs! I don't doubt that they produce the same amount of light as a normal bulb for a quarter of the energy and last eight times longer, but the light they emit is hideous! Glaring, lacking in subtlety, undimmable. There has to be a compromise option.

Rob is still looking at me, and now shakes his head and sighs. A whisper of a smile creeps on to his lips. 'Come here,' he instructs, dropping his newspaper to the floor in a heap.

I move over to the sofa where he's sitting and he pulls me on to his lap.

'What am I going to do with you? When is this nonsense going to stop? I want my wife back.'

'I'm right here,' I say, kissing him. His lips taste of toast and marmite.

'You are, but you're not,' he says. 'You've turned into this crazed thing. A crazed green thing.'

'Is that so bad?'

I squirm as he squeezes my waist.

'Rob, is that so bad?' I persist.

'No, I suppose not,' he says, unconvincingly. His eyes scan my face, looking for clues. To what, I'm not sure.

'Good. Then I'll carry on,' I say brusquely, giving him another kiss and springing off his lap. 'In fact

I have to carry on today. There's a group of us meeting at two to get a few things done. Kate's at the stables – I'll pick her up when I've finished. Maybe you can fetch Ella at around three? She's at Charlotte's.'

'And Phoebe?'

'I'm not sure what she's up to today. Revising, hopefully. They've piled on the work for the Easter break and I hope she's not going to leave it all until the eleventh hour. She's in the shower right now,' I say. 'Hopefully a very short one,' I add, smiling.

I head towards the sitting-room door with the intention of swooping up some laundry from the utility room on my way upstairs.

'So who exactly are you meeting then?' Rob calls out to me.

I spin round to look at him, astonished. All these weeks I've been going to meetings and talking on the phone to Eloise or Daniel or Phyllis and he's not once expressed interest in knowing anything about them. Actually, none of my family has been very curious. Perhaps they've assumed, or hoped, it would be a passing fancy, something too short-lived to warrant any curiosity.

'I'm not sure who'll turn up today,' I say evasively. In actual fact, I know it will be just me and Daniel for the first hour or so. Phyllis cried off yesterday due to a surprise visit from her grandchildren, and Eloise can't come until later when her daughter takes over at the boutique. The younger ones might

189

come along at some point. There's always a core of people who drive these sorts of efforts forward, and I seem to have ended up as one of the handful of the Green Link group who are it.

'What are they like, though. Most of them?' He's obviously not going to let this one go. Oddly enough, having been irked by his disinterest for weeks, I'm now strangely uncomfortable with his probing.

'Oh, all sorts, really. A huge mix. There's that woman who works at the library, and another who owns a clothes shop. Then there's the local head-mistress and a couple of her students. And Barry from the Doll's House. You know that shop that sells miniature Victorian houses?'

'Ahh. And are they good sorts? Nice people?'

'Yes. They are. I mean, I hardly know them, really. But we work well together.' The memory of my lunch with Daniel makes me gulp noisily as the words escape my mouth.

'So what are you going to be doing today? Exactly?' he asks, focusing his gaze on me. He leans forward on the sofa, his elbows resting on his knees, as if in wait for something momentous to be revealed.

'Well, we have this plan. It includes stuff like the toxic product disposal drive, and the auto-pollution reduction scheme. And we're thinking of staging a sort of rally in the park on Hill Street – you know, a sort of mega-environmental day when we instigate all of this stuff. Some of us are a bit torn – there might be advantages to drip-feeding it into the community. Spreading it out a bit.'

'And you really think people are going to buy into this stuff?' There's no edge to his voice, and I don't think he means to be offensive. It's a bit like the lace underwear thing. He just can't see the attraction.

'Well, we can but try,' I say with forced chirpiness.

'Well, good luck. Just don't be too disappointed if your efforts don't come to much. People can be pretty cynical.'

'People, or you?' I say, with more animosity than I've intended.

'Hey, don't shoot the messenger!' he says, leaning forward to pick up the unruly sheets of newspaper lying around his feet. A crease forms on his brow as he concentrates fiercely on folding and straightening and stacking.

I stand at the door for a second or two, watching him. The newspapers invoke a picture of him, of us, from long ago. We were in our first house, lying on the floor in front of the fire reading the Sunday papers. There were sections of newspaper scattered everywhere, around and underneath us, under the chipped plates strewn with toast crumbs and marmalade rind. Kate, who was maybe a year old, was asleep beside us in her baby bouncer, and Phoebe must have been napping upstairs. We looked at each other, cheeks flushed by the heat of the fire, and decided to seize the moment, right there, on top of the *Sunday Times* Review section and less than five feet away from our sleeping baby. It was all very fast, but quite glorious. I remember how we laughed that night at the discovery of the black ink all over Rob's lower back – an instant tattoo; a reminder of a moment of abandonment stolen from the clutches of our lives as the exhausted parents of toddlers with a mortgage far beyond our means.

Now I think, When, exactly, did he become a person who feels compelled to reassemble a dishevelled newspaper with such care? Where is the optimistic, enthusiastic, passionate person who wanted to tend to the eyes of the world's poor, who would ravage his wife in the middle of the afternoon with just a few sheets of newspaper for padding, and how is it I didn't notice him slipping away? Has he really gone, or is he just hiding, like me?

I turn and walk out of the room in a conscious effort to escape the air in it, which has suddenly become heavy and claustrophobic. If I didn't know better, I'd swear the walls were moving in on one another, squeezing all the free space from the room.

PHOEBE

I'd never realised that you can look up 'Abortion' in the *Yellow Pages*. When you do, you are referred to the pages on Clinics or Pregnancy, and you have three whole pages of telephone numbers to choose from. I choose one at random. Teencare Abortion and Advice. I carry the number around with me for a week.

I decided that using the Internet was too risky. Mum signed up for a parental control service a couple of years ago, and I know she gets notified of every website we visit. I only discovered that when she freaked out about Kate having been on a site called Horsey Girls. Kate thought she'd discovered a new source of discounted jodhpurs. How was she to know she's be accosted with images of naked women doing bizarre things on (and with) horses?

Today's an ideal day to make the call. Dad's collecting Ella, and Mum's at some meeting, as usual. I sit on their bed with the phone in one hand and the little pink Post-it note inscribed with the telephone number in the other for at least ten minutes, trying to summon up the courage to call. My fingers tremble as I press the buttons on the phone, and even the deep breaths I take don't seem to fill my lungs.

The phone rings three times before a friendly female voice answers.

'Hello, you've reached Teencare Advisory. We're here to help you. If you would like to speak to an advisor, please call our freephone number, 0800 900 900. Otherwise please choose from one of the following options.'

I hang up quickly, and prepare to dial the freephone number but realise I've already forgotten it. 'Arseholes' I mutter as I stomp to my room in search of a pen. The only one I can find leaks bright turquoise ink. I dial the original number and scribble down the freephone number the friendly voice fires at me. 0800 900 900.

Another friendly voice answers. 'Hello, this is Becky Fisher speaking, executive assistant to the Chief Executive of Teencare Advisory'. Then a pause, during which I open my mouth to speak before realising that I've reached another answerphone message. 'I'm away from my desk at the moment, but please leave a name and number and I'll call you as soon as I can.'

Clearly, this is going to be just as difficult as I imagined, I think. How can I possibly leave a name and number? Who would ever do such a thing? Even my mobile would be a risk. The way I see it I have two options. I can wait a while and call this Becky person back, or I can look up another number and try them. I sit staring at the pink Post-it note with the two telephone numbers on it, one of them with little rivulets of turquoise ink bleeding from its digits. Then I pick up the phone again.

This time I get Becky in the flesh. I wait a second before speaking, just to make sure. 'Hello?' she says again, in a kind but insistent voice.

'Hello. I wonder if you can help me,' I say. My voice sounds weak and unsure, even to me. I can't think how it sounds filtered through several thousand metres of telephone wire and the inevitable cacophony of an office environment.

'Of course I can. That's what I'm here for.' How many times a day does she say these words? I wonder. 'Tell me how I can help.'

'Well, I'm not calling for me. I'm calling for my friend.' I bet she's heard *that* a thousand times before as well. I also bet that half the time it's complete crap.

If she does think it's crap, she doesn't let on. 'OK. And what kind of help does your friend need?'

'What do you mean?'

'I mean, is she looking for contraception advice, or is she pregnant?'

'She's pregnant. I think. She thinks.'

'And how old is she?'

'Fifteen.'

'Do you know how far along she is?'

Stupidly, I don't. 'No, I'm afraid I don't. I was just making this first call for her. She's kind of scared so I said I'd help her.'

'Well, that's very kind. But we really need to know what her situation is. I think it would be best if she

195

came in to see us for an initial consultation. Can you get her to do that? Maybe you can come with her.'

Omigod. I don't want to go with her.

'All right. When would that be?'

'Let me see . . .' I can hear her breathing heavily into the phone. 'Sorry, this new computerised diary system is taking me a while to get used to. I wish we still had the paper thing! There we are. Looks as though we have an opening next week, on Tuesday at four-thirty. Can you make that?'

'Sure, I think so. I'll check with my friend. Do we need to do anything before that?' I'm not sure what I'm thinking of, exactly. It just doesn't seem right that you can turn up for something as huge as an abortion consultation without any preparation at all.

'No, just bring yourselves. You are very kind to come with her. She will need your support. You must be a very good friend.'

But I'm not, I want to shout. I don't know how I got myself involved in this. Is it too late to uninvolve myself? Would it be too awful to hand Rebecca the pink Post-it note and tell her to get on with it?

'Yes, I guess so,' I say. 'We'll be there next Tuesday.'

Arseholes, I think, after hanging up. Next Tuesday I was supposed to be going with Mrs Thomason to watch Josh play, then we were going to have supper at their house. For a second I'm tempted to ring back the clinic and ask to rearrange the appointment, but then I think, What kind of person places a higher priority on a boyfriend's rugby game than on supporting someone through something as horrendous as this?

My deliberations are cut short by the slam of the front door and a cheery 'Hello' signalling Dad and Ella's return. I put the phone back in its cradle and scarper back to my room, shutting the door quietly behind me. I sit at my desk and arrange open books around me as if I've been deep in revision all along. When Dad pops his head around my door to say hello, I try to look worn-out and hard-done-by.

'Poor you,' he says. 'Have you got much more to do?'

'Loads,' I say, sighing. 'I'll be here all afternoon.'

He smiles sympathetically and ducks back out, shutting the door behind him.

I know that if he and Mum knew what I was doing they'd hit the roof. But I can't tell them or before you'd know it, Julia would know and then Andrew and then Rebecca would be done for. And anyway, what should I be guilty about, exactly? I'm not the one who's got herself pregnant. I'm not the one who's decided to have an abortion. It's nothing to do with me. I'm just helping someone, and where's the sin in that?

I lean back in my chair and glance at the Orlando Bloom calendar pinned to the bulletin board above my desk. The shot for April isn't up to much. The black T-shirt and jeans he's wearing make him look kind of sinister, and he's standing in a really awkward pose. In about a week I can flip over to the May picture, which is much better. It's a close-up in black and white, and the way he's leaning into the camera you could convince yourself that he's about to kiss you. I'm looking forward to having that one up for a month.

LIBBY

aniel and I are having a disagreement. Our first. It has to do with the question of whether we should hold a rally day to introduce the community to our proposed set of programmes, or just start initiating the programmes one by one in the hopes that they won't be overwhelmed by it all. It's all very mild, as disagreements go, but it's caught me off-guard.

'I really think we'd be better off waiting,' Daniel says as he stirs milk into my coffee. 'Do things close together so that people see it all as a coherent campaign.'

'You don't think people will be put off by the idea of a big campaign? Whereas if we sort of sneak in the initiatives one at a time they'll just get used to the idea.' I notice that he has a cut on the thumb of the hand holding the coffee cup, and find myself trying to picture how he got it. The thought of him preparing a meal makes me swoon a little, which in turn makes me feel incredibly juvenile.

'Well, that's true in theory. But it tends not to work like that. People need to see the big picture – it's too easy for them to rubbish the issues individually.' He allows a smile to creep on to his face, an antidote to his adamance.

I realise that the thing that has caught me off-guard is not the actual disagreement, but my unease at the thought of disagreeing with him about anything at all. I sigh. It all seems to be getting slightly complicated.

'Hey, who abducted Mrs Blue Sky?'

I look down at my feet, then peer shyly up at him through the strands of hair that have fallen loose from my clip.

'OK,' I say. 'I'll bow to your greater experience. We'll delay the toxic drop-off until we've sent out the flyers and announced it all at the awareness day. If we do it mid-July, that'd be perfect – warm enough, schools won't have broken up yet, so people will still be in organising mode rather than holiday mode.'

'Hallelujah! She's back in blue-sky mode again,' he says, throwing his head back and his hands into the air. Then he stands in front of me, locking his deep brown eyes on to mine.

Eloise walks through the doors just in time. She's wearing one of the long, multi-tiered skirts I've seen hanging in her shop window, and a wonderful pair of pink suede boots. She must have them in every colour.

'Here you are, you two. A little sustenance for the weary.' She plonks her wicker basket on the table in front of us and whips off its green checked cover to reveal a basketful of muffins. They're nothing like the ordinary store-bought variety, being a sumptuous golden brown and studded with enormous chunks of plump, fresh fruit.

'God, Eloise, are you expecting an army this afternoon, or trying to make us fat,' I say, leaning down to sniff the muffins. They are still warm.

'Neither, my love. Just looking after you.' She looks at me, then Daniel, then back again at me. I detect the slight raising of her right eyebrow.

'So what have you been up to?' she says, resting her bottom on the edge of the table and taking a muffin out of the basket. 'Tell me what's been going on.'

'Have you not noticed? There's definitely something going on,' she whispers as we sit separating ten thousand leaflets into carriable stacks. Daniel needs to make a call to Green Link headquarters and has gone outside to try to get some fresh air and a better signal.

'What do you mean?' I say, avoiding her eyes.

'I mean, he has a thing for you. It's plain as day.'

'Eloise, that's ridiculous. I'm fifteen years older than him. At least. And I'm married.'

'And when did that ever stop anyone? I'm not accusing you of anything, hon. I'm just pointing out the obvious.' Then she jokes, 'I blame Demi and that Ashton fellow. It's been a whole new ball game ever since they got together.'

I stop, a clutch of leaflets in each hand. I stare across the table at nothing in particular before responding.

Then I turn to her. 'Eloise, how obvious is it?'

'To most people? Probably not at all. To me, very. I have a sense for these things. And I'm telling you. He's falling fast.'

I put my two piles back together, then separate them again, staring at my hands as if the task requires my complete concentration. Eloise isn't the only one to have noticed something. The other day while we were breathlessly trailing after Hank, Gilly said to me, 'There's something different about you, Libby. I can't put my finger on it, but it's definitely there. A sort of gleam in your eyes. Come on, what is it?' She seemed to buy my story of a rekindling of my interest in all the things I studied so long ago, but even as I was recounting it all to her I had a sense of my own duplicity. Maybe duplicity is too strong a word; it was at least partly true.

'And what about you, hon?'

I swing urgently around to face her. 'What do you mean, what about me? I'm married, Eloise.'

'She reaches out and touches my forearm gently. 'Hey, no one's saying you're doing anything wrong, hon. No one's accusing you of anything. But you're only human. It's got to feel good to be admired by a fella like him. He's lovely.'

I rise from the table abruptly and walk over to stand in front of the bulletin board that stretches along the whole of one side of the room. Dozens of multicoloured lions and tigers, the loving creations of the morning playgroup children, stare back at me.

'I'm frightened, Eloise. That's the truth of it. In

seventeen years I've not fancied anyone else. I've not even been aware of anyone else. There's just been my family, Rob, the girls, me at the centre of it. Since joining this group, since meeting him, I feel, I don't know, like I'm at the edge of it. Outside of it, even. This isn't supposed to happen to someone like me.'

I turn around to face her. She's sitting cross-legged on her chair, her skirt piled up between her legs. She gives me a kind, knowing smile.

'Don't worry about it, hon. You're a good person. A good mother. You're going to do the right thing. Just don't beat yourself up if you happen to enjoy the attention of a lovely bloke for a little while. Where's the harm in that?'

Daniel enters the room just then. I try to look natural, but am certain I fail. Eloise leans against the back of her chair and segues seamlessly into a relaxed conversation with him.

'Hey, hon. What did they have to say at Head Office?'

I listen to them talking about feedback from Derek and the Green Link national group, and a spectacularly successful campaign in Southampton, but the words have no traction in my brain. I'm beginning to feel warm and light-headed. I need to sit down.

'You OK, Libby?' says Daniel, suddenly leaning over me.

'I just felt dizzy for a second. Must be coming down with something.'

'You should go home. You've worked hard enough. Hasn't she, Eloise?'

'Yes. You're right. I should go home,' I say, reaching for my jacket, which has slipped off the back of the chair and is curled around its legs.

'Do you want me to take you?' he says, concerned.

'No, no,' I say hurriedly. 'I just need to go home.' I really need to go home.

PHOEBE

I call Rebecca's mobile while I'm out shopping with Alice, waiting until she disappears into the changing room with a pair of skinny grey jeans so I won't be overheard.

'I've made an appointment for next Tuesday at two-thirty. I hope you can make it,' I whisper. Alice emerges from her curtained cubby-hole and stands at the far end of the changing room examining herself in the full-length mirror. She does a little pirouette then stands facing me, her upturned hands and raised eyebrows demanding a response. I give her the thumbs up from where I'm standing at the opposite end of the room.

'Oh my God,' Rebecca says. I imagine her pale, freckled face, eyes wide with alarm.

'What? I thought you wanted me to help you?'

'I did. I do. But an appointment so soon? It sounds quite scary. What are they going to do?'

'Just talk to you. Then I'm not sure what happens. I guess they'll tell us.'

'Us? You're going with me?'

'Sure. If you want me too.'

'Phoebe, what you're doing . . . it's really nice. Really kind. I'm going to remember it, always.'

This kind of over-the-top praise is a bit embarrassing for me. People have called me pretty or fun before, but I'm not used to being called kind. Quite the opposite, in fact. At home I'm usually being accused of committing heinous crimes towards Kate or Ella.

'Yeah, well. Don't mention it. Anyway, you'll have to tell your mum you're going shopping or something. Don't tell her you're at my house because she might check. And anyway, she would think that was kind of weird. You know what I mean. If you were suddenly coming to my house.'

I don't say this to be bitchy, but it occurs to me that she might hear it that way. But the fact is she never does come to my house; I've never invited her, and probably never would have if this hadn't happened.

'Right. OK,' she says hesitatingly, as if she's also trying to decide how to take my comment.

'Anyway, I have to go now. I'll call you so we can meet up on Tuesday,' I say, hurriedly hanging up just as Alice reaches me, skinny jeans in hand. I'm thinking she's going to ask me who I've been talking to and my mind is whirring away in an effort to fabricate something plausible. Luckily, self-absorption wins out over curiosity and all she says is, 'Do they really look nice? Are you sure?'

'They look gorgeous, Alice,' I say, dragging her

over to the till. 'Now come on, I'm dying for something to eat.'

Last night I had a dream. I was in some strange house, in a bedroom. At first I thought it was Josh's bedroom, but then I realised it was brown and green, not blue and covered floor to ceiling in Martin Johnson posters. Then suddenly I was on a bed and there was a guy on top of me pulling at my clothes and I was calling out Josh's name, but when he lifted his face I could see it wasn't him. It was the face of a guy I'd never seen before. I tried to push him off me, shouting, 'I've made a mistake. I've made a mistake.' But I couldn't shift him. He was just so heavy. And suddenly I was naked underneath him. Just like that.

I woke up sweating. At first I wasn't sure where I was, but gradually I made out the ponderous contours of the chair in the corner of the room and felt the bit of torn embroidery along the top of my duvet cover and realised I was at home, in my own bed. I couldn't get the image of that guy's face out of my mind. I shut my eyes tight and tried to picture Josh's face, his lovely blue eyes, his strong cheekbones, the lock of dark blonde hair falling across his forehead. But no matter how hard I tried I couldn't do it. The stranger's face kept popping up. Eventually I sat up and switched the light on and read for a while, until I was confident the face would have faded.

That's definitely not how it's going to be. The

207

first time, with Josh, there mustn't be any clawing of clothes, or the feeling of a heavy body on top of me, making it difficult to breathe. What I want is that scene in *Cold Mountain*, where Jude Law comes back to Nicole Kidman after years of searching for her, and they make love for the first time in a log cabin, bathed in the golden, glowing light of a low fire. I've never seen such a beautiful scene, never felt so tearful witnessing two people together. Somehow it was gentle and urgent at the same time. That's what I want.

I know I won't get the firelight, though. That's probably asking a bit much.

LIBBY

'Christ, what's that smell?' exclaims Rob as he walks into the kitchen.

'Peelings. For the compost heap. I just left them in here a little too long, and they've started to smell. Sorry.'

I reach inside the cupboard and retrieve the peelings bin, reminding myself to take it to the compost heap before we're all gassed.

'So, composting? In a London garden barely big enough to contain the garden chairs? Lib, do you think maybe this is going too far? I'm sure we've more than done our bit for the planet.'

'Rob, if you only knew what had to be done you'd never say that. You'd be after me to fill the bloody garden with compost heaps.'

Instead of arguing with me he opens the fridge and peers inside it. 'We've run out of Evian,' he announces.

'We haven't run out. I just stopped buying it. Have some tap water.'

'Tap water!'

'Rob, it's actually better for you than bottled stuff. *And* it doesn't involve transporting heavy bottles from one end of the country to the other.'

He gives me a tired stare, then peers into the fridge again, emerging with a jug of milk.

'Is milk OK, or shall I have tap water with my cereal too, on the grounds that dairy cows farting methane into the atmosphere is a leading cause of climate change?'

I decline to answer. He pours milk on his cereal and takes it over to the table where he sits down and opens the paper decisively. There's a brief silence, not an entirely comfortable one, before he looks up and says, 'I met one of your Green Link people the other day.'

I'm standing over the sink, with my back to Rob, peeling carrots for the carrot and raisin salad I'm taking in for Michelle and Courtney. I look up at the window but continue peeling.

'Really, who was that?'

'Fellow called Daniel. Seems a nice chap.'

The peeler clatters into the sink, along with the carrot. I pick the carrot up and rinse it under the tap.

'Really. How did you meet him, then?'

'He came into the clinic. Said he thought he might need to change the prescription for his lenses. He was right.'

'So how did Green Link come up? I mean, how did you get on to that?'

'Oh, you know. The usual way. We were chatting. I asked him what he did. Then we put two and two together and he realised you were my

210

wife. He said you were a real asset to the group.'

I can feel Rob's eyes on my back, so I turn to face him with what I hope is an inscrutable expression on my face.

'Really? That's nice of him.'

'Yeah. He seemed like a nice bloke. Not at all the grungy sandal-wearing type I would have imagined.' He smiles at me and arches one eyebrow. 'Quite good-looking, actually. You never told me you were spending so much time with young, good-looking blokes.'

A forced laugh rises quickly to my throat. I'm not sure whether he's joking, or whether he really suspects there might be something going on.

'Rob, don't be ridiculous. I'm not working with lots of young blokes. There are twenty of us and most of us are over forty. The young people are mostly Phoebe's age. We're just a good team, that's all.'

'Hmn. So your friend said. That's good,' says Rob, nodding. He's still staring at me. What is he waiting for? I have to move, to find something to do before I say something stupid.

'Anyway, I have to get these outside,' I say, whisking the compost bin off the counter.

As I walk out of the back door my face feels hot against the damp morning air. I trudge to the corner of the garden, a strange jittery feeling in my stomach. It's not guilt. It can't be – I haven't done anything wrong. It's something else.

Standing over the compost heap, scraping the

last of the congealed peelings from the insides of the bin, I realise what it feels like. It's like that unsettled feeling you get when you have to make a decision and you're torn. Indecision. That's what it feels like.

'Phoebe, I need you to do me a favour, please.' I'm standing on the libary steps, the only place to get a decent signal. There's an uncommon rush of people coming into the libary, and at one point I'm almost sent tumbling by two young boys with enormous backpacks.

'What?' she says, affronted before she even knows what I'm going to ask her.

'Ella's here with me. She usually comes with me to these meetings but tonight she's looking really tired. I think she might be coming down with something. I need you to walk down and collect her just before supper, give her something to eat. Maybe get something for the others.'

'Why can't she stay there and just lie down or something?' Phoebe whines.

'Because she needs some peace and quiet and some rest and this is going to go on for ages. Can you come and get her, please?'

'Oh, alright,' she agrees huffily, huffy ranking a close second to cynical in the list of her specialities.

'Thank you. I'll see you about six then. We're in the first room on the left inside the libary doors.'

I walk back inside to see Ella sitting at a table

with Gabriel, Harry, Courtney and Michelle. They are organising the leaflets Eloise and I started stacking the other day, putting them into little canvas bags ready for distribution.

'Hi mum. Courtney said she needed help.'

'Judging by these mountains of leaflets, she does,' I say, smiling at Courtney.

I leave them and wander over to the opposite side of the room, where Barry, Marla and Lynette are huddled over a poster.

'What do you think? Good result? We're about to go out and decorate the town with a few hundred of these!' enthuses Barry.

'I think they're great.' I really do. Everything's come together, the artwork, the lettering, the message. It looks like a real poster for a real cause, not some amateurish effort by a bunch of inexperienced enthusiasts.

'Right, I'm going to call the council again. Get them to confirm one way or another that we can have the park July the tenth. The buggers are prevaricating now.' I look over at the single phone. Daniel hangs up immediately, almost as if he's anticipated my request.

'You want this, Libby?' he shouts.

'Please,' I say, moving towards his table.

'Be my guest,' he says with mock ostentation, standing up and ushering me towards his chair. He watches me pick up the phone, then winks at me when I start to speak. I wish he wouldn't do that, I think. It's so off-putting.

The hour between five and six passes quickly. Leaflet stacking is followed swiftly by poster distribution, and Ella helps Lynnette to pin up the first few in and around the library. When Phoebe arrives, Ella pulls a sad face and pleads with me to let her stay longer. Phoebe looks angry at the prospect of having wasted her time, and begins to argue with Ella. I turn away to speak to Gabriel, who has an urgent question about where we've been granted permission to stick posters, and by the time I turn back, Phoebe's irritation seems to have vanished.

'It's OK. She can stay for a little while longer. I'll wait for her.'

I'm frankly flabbergasted. It's so unlike Herself.

'Oh, well, OK. But that will mean you both sitting in on the meeting. Why don't you stay until the coffee break, then go home. It will still be light out.'

'Sure,' says Phoebe, smiling sweetly.

I look curiously at her. 'Could you just give Kate a ring and let her know you'll be a bit late? You'll have to go outside. There's no signal in here.'

'No problem,' she says, fishing her phone out of her bag. As she walks towards the double doors I notice that she gives her head a little toss and runs her hands through her hair.

We have a full house tonight. The prospect of a rally in the park just two months away seems to have concentrated people's minds. Phyllis and Nancy, who missed the meeting last week, immediately take

214

Phoebe and Ella under their wings. The girls end up being wedged between the two older women and subjected to their almost constant ministrations. At one point, Daniel is forced to chastise them for making too much noise.

As a mother, you don't get many opportunities to just observe your children. There are school plays and sports days of course, but they are different. Staged. Unnatural. Tonight, after I've given an update on the council's response, and listened to Lynnette and Barry reporting on poster distribution, I watch my girls, sitting attentively, absorbing this novel experience, totally unaware that I'm watching them. Phoebe laughs politely when Phyllis leans over and tells her something, and Ella smiles back when Nancy gives her a knowing look in response to one of Barry's jokes. I feel the warm surge of pride within my chest.

We break for coffee just after seven and Phyllis escorts both girls over to me as if they are precious property requiring hand delivery. Herself is having some difficulty quashing the instinct to roll her eyes, I can tell.

'Lovely girls, Libby. It's been such a pleasure to meet them,' she says, smiling fondly at Ella then Phoebe.

'Oh, they're all right, I suppose,' I say.

'I've been trying to persuade them both to help us out. We'll need more hands on deck from now on, especially on rally day and toxic drop-off week.'

'I'm already helping,' says Ella triumphantly.

'So you are, dear,' says Phyllis.

'I'd love to help out too,' announces Phoebe.

I greet the announcement with stunned, open-mouthed silence.

'What?' she adds hastily. 'Don't you want me to?'

'Of course I want you to. I think it would be great. I'm just surprised, that's all.'

'Another recruit, Libby?' asks Daniel, coming up behind Phyllis.

'It looks that way,' I say. 'Daniel, you know Ella, obviously. This is Phoebe, my eldest.'

'Good to meet you, Phoebe,' he says, thrusting his hand in her direction.

Phoebe inclines her head shyly, then places her small, delicate hand in his larger, browner one. 'Hello,' she says, almost inaudibly. But she does, I notice, manage to look him in the eye, which is something of an improvement on the norm. I remember when the girls were little Rob and I were forever reminding them to look at people when greeting them or answering a question, and when they each reached the age of about six we thought they'd cracked it. We never dreamed that you had to start the whole process again once they became teenagers and began to look up, down, away – basically anywhere but into a person's eyes.

'Right, short coffee break tonight, folks,' Daniel says, clapping his hands together. 'Got a lot to tie up.'

'Slave-driver,' I quip. 'OK, girls I'll see you later. Ella really needs to get home now.'

'Sure, OK,' says Phoebe. 'Come on, Ells.' She touches Ella lightly on the arm and nods towards the doors. She listens attentively to Ella as they walk. When she reaches the doors she does a sort of Princess Diana dip of the head and looks up through her eyelashes as if playing to the paparazzi.

'Lovely to meet you two,' shouts Nancy as the girls leave the room. Then she walks over to where Phyllis is already seated and squeezes her shoulder. Phyllis looks up at her and smiles, then places her own hand on Nancy's, leaving it there for a good long moment. The look they exchange says 'loved-up' as unequivocally as a Mills & Boon front cover.

Well, hasn't this day been full of surprises, I think. First Herself comes over all enthusiastic and cooperative. Then Phyllis and Nancy. How is it I've not noticed that before? I must have been blind, for their every move seems to communicate it now. I feel a smile in my mind. It's lovely to watch people so obviously in love.

PHOEBE

So *this* is what it feels like. Can you die of it, I wonder?

LIBBY

A couple of months ago I would have given anything to have Rob or the girls ask me what I was doing, and actually listen to my answer for more than a nanosecond. I would have enjoyed hearing them express some pride in my efforts. Now, I feel strangely uncomfortable with it. Hemmed in. Threatened.

First there was Rob getting cosy with Daniel under the eye chart. Now there's Herself to deal with as well. My beautiful, ornery teenaged daughter has reached into my world, shown signs of wanting to share something with me, and instead of feeling excited at the prospect, I'm viewing it with apprehension and resentment.

What am I afraid of, I wonder? That she will embarrass me in front of my friends and colleagues? That she will let me down? Or is it her watchful eyes that make me nervous?

The evening after the meeting she asks me about everyone, starting with Phyllis and Nancy, whom she'd clocked as lovers before I did. She fires questions at me in rapid succession. Is Barry really the geek he first appears? (No.) Is Eloise married?

219

(Divorced.) What are those two girls like, the ones I make the food for, the ones who speak so badly? (Lovely, once you get beneath their defences.) How old is Daniel? (Twenty-seven, twenty-eight, I think.)

Her inquisitiveness exhausts me. In the end, I'm grateful for the trill of the phone, and for Liz's voice on the other end. (And *that* is saying something.) She's been to see Dad for the first time in weeks, and wants to report every disturbing detail of her visit. She expects me to be shocked, I think, but I'm not. I see it every week. The mismatched socks. The three pairs of underwear, worn one on top of the other. The butter dish stashed under the sink with the Brillo pads and the bleach. His wallet laid on the top shelf of the fridge, amidst the decaying celery and half-empty tins of baked beans.

That any of this is a surprise to Liz peeves me. If she were offering a solution, now that would be helpful. A solution must be found. Things can't go on as they are. The slow decline seems to have become a perilously alacritous descent. A descent that no amount of visiting from me, Mrs Tupper and the nice lady who plays chess can halt.

'What are we going to do?' she asks, accusingly. Did you catch that? *We.*

'I'm not sure. I guess we'll have to get more serious about looking for a home. Or maybe he'll have to live with one of us.'

Her response is immediate and dismissive. 'That's impossible. He can't stay here. It would never work.' Then she goes on to explain all the reasons it would never work.

When Liz embarks on her brief tirade I hold the phone slightly away from my ear and direct my eyes skyward. There's no one to witness my petulance, because Phoebe has moved across to the other side of the kitchen, where she's bending over her school bag in an apparently desperate search for something. When she finds what she's looking for (her phone, evidently) she stands and raises her arms like a footballer who's scored the wining goal, revealing an expanse of silky-skinned, flat stomach to the world. Leaning against the counter I can feel my own, softer, rounder tummy pressing against it. I try to remember the last time mine was like hers. I can't.

'I wasn't suggesting that, exactly, Liz. I'm well aware of your lifestyle.'

'You're not working, Libby. It would make more sense for him to stay with you.'

That's our Liz. Direct. For the jugular.

'Look, I'm really busy right now, Liz. I've got a lot going on. I know we have to sort this out, and we will. I just need a bit of space right now, OK?'

My words are greeted by a silence so stony I can almost feel its cold weight. Goodbyes are exchanged, along with reluctant promises to talk, later, about a plan.

Clearly, I'm not living up to Liz's view of how this family works. It occurs to me that this must be a jolt after all these years, and I admit that I take some pleasure in this. The fact that Liz is perturbed, ruffled, put out. By me.

PHOEBE

It only took me a minute to notice him. I walked through those double doors, found Mum and Ella, then, seconds later, spotted him across the room. He was leaning against the wall with one hand in his jeans pocket, laughing with some young guy with glasses who I'm sure I recognise from somewhere. He threw his head back in this abandoned, joyful laugh and all his hair, that gorgeous, thick, long, brown hair, sort of swished against his shoulders in a haphazard kind of way. From that moment I was hooked.

When he took my hand I thought my knees might buckle. I've never seen anyone quite so bloody gorgeous. So soulful. So intelligent. Next to him Orlando Bloom would look like Mr Bean.

I watched the way he ran the meeting and I thought, *He is incredible*. He has this way of speaking that pulls you in. You can't resist listening to him, even if he's talking about something as mundane as the toxicity of a bottle of Windowlene. He oozes charm and sex appeal and total and utter gorgeousness. It starts with his eyes, brown and piercing and perfectly balanced between a set of sharp

222

cheekbones and the elegant, wave-like swoop of his dark brows. And it ends with his long, muscular body. I could tell about the muscles when he leaned forward and his shirtsleeve sort of strained across the bicep to reveal a beautiful curve. Nothing too dramatic. Not a weightlifter's bicep. The bicep of the casually good-looking.

I could have looked at him all night. I wanted to stay, but I knew Mum needed me to take Ella home and I couldn't afford to make things too obvious. I've tried to avoid making things at all obvious, in general. I quiz Mum about everyone there, when all I really want to know is stuff about him. How old is he? Where is he from? Does he have a girlfriend? How can you stand being in the same room as him and not touch him? There must be something about getting older that makes you immune to these things.

It's a terrible thing to say, but Josh suddenly seemed so small and insignificant, so young, when I saw him. We met at Starbucks after school and sat next to each other on one of the benches. He stroked my hand at one point, down below the table, where no one could see. And you know what? I felt nothing. Absolutely nothing. All I can think about is Daniel's hand holding mine for that brief moment in the library. I've thought of practically nothing else since. I even dreamt about him. It wasn't a proper dream, with a beginning, middle and end, or even any action at all really. It was more like a single scene captured by the pause button: just me lying with my head on his chest, his hand stroking my hair. Utter bliss.

If I'd known that kind of perfection existed, I'd have stood for days in a queue of thousands for a chance to be in the same room as him. I'd have been at that first Green Link meeting with Mum like a shot.

And now, of course, it all makes sense to me – why I've been putting off sleeping with Josh, feeling so unsure about it. He isn't The One after all.

LIBBY

We are walking, he and I. Through some woods, evidently. I spot a reedy pond in a clearing just ahead of us. It's a hot day and we're both sweating just a little. He stops, under a shade tree, and pulls gently at my arm. I stop and turn to face him, and he brushes the hair back from my forehead. Then he smiles, and leans down to kiss me, pressing me against the tree trunk. The sensation is, well, sensational.

Suddenly, inexplicably, the woods have vanished and we are lying in a bed. The bed is vast (if there's such a thing as a super-deluxe-king, then this is surely it) and its acres of perfect, white sheets are caught up between and around our intertwined limbs. He is kissing my neck, running his hands along my arm. The tingling on my arm is so acute it hurts. I feel I'm about to explode. I'm finding it hard to breathe. His hand moves towards my breast and I emit an intense, gutteral moan.

I open my eyes with a start to see blinking red lights. 1:54 – 1:54 – 1:54 – 1:55. a.m. Did I do that out loud? I roll over to see the curve of Rob's head and shoulders, the line of his arm flung back across the covers. He's snoring gently, almost imperceptibly.

Lying on my back I stare at the patterns of light created by the moonlight seeping in at strange angles through the gaps in the curtains. I become aware of a wetness between my legs, and my hands rise to my face instinctively, to hide my shame. I look again at Rob, half expecting him to be staring at me censoriously, but the muscles of his back are still moving rhythmically.

I pull back the covers and slip out of bed. In the bathroom, I use three tissues to wipe away the evidence. Then I stuff them into the depths of the bin, underneath an empty contact lens box discarded by Rob this morning, and a spent tube of Colgate with Advanced Whitening and Stain Prevention.

I decide that I can't go back to bed immediately in case Rob senses my tears. If I'm in here, and he wakes up, at least I can claim to be on the loo, or getting a glass of water. I sit on the edge of the bath, shivering, waiting for my tear ducts to dry up and the choking heat at my throat to subside. When I think it's safe, I stand up to go back to bed. I catch sight of myself in the bathroom mirror, my face made ghostlike by the silvery early morning light. I hardly recognise myself.

PHOEBE

A lunch has been sprung upon us. Not just any lunch. A great big deal family lunch with *three* families. We used to do this sort of thing all the time when we were little, but we haven't done the multi-family neighbourhood Sunday lunch thing for years. Not since Rebecca and Kate and I grew up and started doing our own things at the weekends.

This one's going to be difficult, owing to the fact that Rebecca and I have this secret we're trying to keep from everyone else. We have to be careful not to act weird in any way, to make sure we don't draw attention to ourselves. Somehow we have to behave as we've always done, like people who once knew each other quite well but have settled into a sort of polite but distant acquaintanceship. Like people who aren't about to go off to an abortion clinic together.

Mum thinks the most challenging thing about this lunch will be meeting Fran's new boyfriend Paul. Apparently Fran thinks it's time. Mum thinks it would have been better if she'd met him on her own, over coffee or something, rather than at a lunch for twelve people, but apparently Fran insisted.

227

She said Paul is used to children (being a teacher, I guess he would be), and will absolutely not be put off by the rough and tumble of family life.

I love Fran, so I'm really happy for her. But I bet it's really difficult for Freddie and Jake. Especially Freddie. It's not that easy to think of your mum with someone else, even if, like Fran, she's been separated from your father for years. I don't see much of Freddie, seeing as he's over a year younger than me and goes to an all boys school, but I can still picture him all those years ago just after his dad left. I'll never forget it. He was playing rugby, and for some reason we were all there watching him. Maybe it was a big game, and Fran had commandeered us all to make up for the fact that Freddie's dad wouldn't be there. Anyway, Freddie made a try, and we were all cheering madly, and he got up and smiled and held the ball over his head. Then his face lit up, as if he'd seen someone or something amazing. He started running towards us, then suddenly stopped dead in his tracks. He fell to his knees and started crying, right there in front of his team, his coach, and all of the other parents. He stayed there, sobbing, until Fran ran on and put her arms around him then ushered him off the pitch.

Fran said she knew immediately what the problem was. Freddie'd thought he'd spotted his dad in the crowd, standing next to his mum. In fact it was only some guy with his dog who'd happened to stop and watch for a bit. I have to admit he did look spookily like Freddie's dad though.

LIBBY

Fran is hosting lunch for twelve. There will be all of us, plus Julia and Andrew and Rebecca, then Fran and her two boys. Most significantly of all, there will be Paul, Fran's boyfriend of just over a month.

I tried to persuade Fran that it might be better to introduce Paul to us one at a time, or at least one family at a time, but she was absolutely adamant that this was the way she wanted us to meet him. 'He's from a big family. And he spends his life around kids,' she said. 'It would be strange for him *not* to be in a slightly chaotic environment.'

Paul might well be the type of person who revels in domestic chaos, but I suspect the real reason Fran wants to introduce him to us all at once, during a long, drawn-out Sunday lunch during which the atmosphere and conver-sation will surely be lubri-cated and enlivened by several bottles of red wine, is for the theatre of it. She's in love, and she wants to show off to the world. She needs a supporting cast and some background scenery to display her new relationship in its best light. I wonder if, subcon-sciously, she's aware that her romance will glow even more brightly when set against relationships that have endured more than a decade and the birth of several children? For six years, Fran has had to suffer the ignominy of having been party to the most disastrous relationship of any of us; you can't blame her if she wants to look like a romantic sensation for a change.

Phoebe is reluctant to go, and Kate isn't thrilled about the prospect. As the children have got older, it's become more difficult to drag them, en masse, to gatherings of our friends and their offspring. When they are three and four years old, even ten, like Ella, they fall in quite readily and seem to be able to find common ground. As they get older a sort of self-consciousness sets in, and they find it harder to mingle with the other children, or to endure the seemingly torturous questioning of their embarrassing parents' embarrassing friends.

We walk the five hundred yards up the street to Fran's house. Unbelievably, and on account of the light drizzle, Herself suggests that we take the car, but not a single one of the rest of us even acknowledges her suggestion. We are each laden down with something: I carry the bread and butter pudding while Rob lugs the wine; Ella lovingly cradles the flowers, and Kate struggles under the weight of a pile of books I'm taking to lend to Fran. Herself is the only one to travel un-encumbered, unless you count the fact that she is forced to hold up her skirt as we navigate the potholes and puddles.

Paul answers the door. I like him immediately. He is tallish, maybe five foot eleven, slim, in a black shirt and dark grey jeans. He smiles a broad, friendly smile, a real smile, one that makes his eyes crinkle up under his black-rimmed glasses. His hair is jet-black and quite wayward. He looks exactly like the English and drama teacher that he is.

'Hellooo,' he says, ushering us inside. 'You must be Libby and Rob. Fran's told me all about you.'

'We are indeed,' says Rob, offering his hand. 'And you must be Paul. Really good to meet you.'

'Hi, Paul,' I say, shaking his hand. 'These are Phoebe, Kate and Ella.'

'Good to meet you, girls. Come on in.'

Fran is in the kitchen spooning juices over the lamb. 'Hi!' she says exuberantly as we walk in. Her cheeks are flushed pink, which could be a result of standing over a hot oven but I suspect is due to a combination of red wine and excitement. I notice that Paul gives her waist a little squeeze as he passes by her on the way to the cupboard where the glasses are kept.

It's funny to watch him moving about her kitchen with such ease. I know her kitchen so well, I could direct him to anything he might need: glasses, plates, candles, the good linen and the everyday stuff. But he clearly doesn't need directing. How has he managed to look like he belongs in such a short time?

'The others should be here in a minute,' Fran

231

explains as she bends to put the lamb back in the oven. 'I had to get them to pick up some extra bouillon cubes on the way. Why is it you never have the ones you need? Naturally I've got dozens of the green and yellow ones, but could I find even one red one? Of course not.'

'White or red, Libby?' asks Paul.

'Oh, white to start with,' I say. 'Rob will probably have red.'

I look over at Rob, who has found a seat on one of the bar stools at the centre island and is giving the thumbs-up in response to Paul's questioning glance. Judging by the matey way he's smiling at Paul, he's already pegged him as a good bloke, decided that there's no need to be suspicious on Fran's behalf.

'Freddie and Jake are in the other room playing some awful spy game on the PlayStation,' Fran says to the girls. 'Would you like to join them? We've also got a mini-billiards table in there.'

'Or you can stay here and chat,' I add quickly, conscious that Herself in particular may not want to be trapped in a room full of younger children. Things may or may not get easier once Rebecca arrives; Rebecca and Phoebe have never been close. At gatherings like these, which happen less and less often these days, I'm conscious of a sort of awkwardness between them. Because Julia and I know each other well, and because they are the same age, they know they ought to be friends, but somehow they've never really clicked.

Ella and Kate disappear and Phoebe hovers in the kitchen, pretending to be entranced by Fran's cat, an ancient marmalade creature named Simone (after Simone de Beauvoir, one of Fran's heroines) that spends most of its life curled up in a basket in the corner of the kitchen. Rob and Paul quickly become engrossed in conversation about something; I can't quite hear what's being said but the amount of physical energy being expended tells me the conversation is possibly sporting related.

'How's Josh?' Fran shouts to Phoebe from her position at the centre island where she is painstakingly laying pieces of smoked salmon on to little triangles of brown bread.

I throw Fran a meaningful look, which she studiously ignores. 'Bugger this. Where's Gordon Ramsay when you need him?' she moans. 'These things always look like a dog's breakfast when I do them.'

Phoebe says, 'He's fine,' then resumes the careful stroking of Simone.

'Here, let me do that. You do something else,' I say, moving round to where Fran is standing and gently shoving her aside. I busy myself cutting the salmon into perfect triangles to match the bread, and I'm just thinking how nice it is to be engaged in this sort of gentle domestic task with Vivaldi and the jovial tinkle of pre-Sunday lunch chat in the background, when suddenly a sort of chaos engulfs us all. The doorbell rings and Paul goes to answer it, then Fran drops a pan of boiling water in the sink and it splashes up in a great wave and burns her arm; her scream makes me jump and the knife I'm using slices through the end of my finger. When Andrew, Julia and Rebecca enter the kitchen, Fran is busy applying Savlon to her wrist and I am standing with my finger under running water while Rob roots around in the cupboard beside the fridge in search of a plaster. It's all a bit *Casualty*, and none of us is in any position to rush forward and hug the new arrivals.

'Sorry about this, you three,' says Fran, rolling her eyes. 'The good news is at least the lamb's all right and there's plenty of wine.'

'Oh poor you. What happened?' gushes Julia, coming over to inspect us both while Andrew hangs back looking slightly awkward. I don't think his expression has anything to do with shock at having stumbled upon a minor injuries unit; he's always slightly uncomfortable when he first enters a room. He's a very buttoned-up person; the sort you have to really work on before you get anything out of him. Then what you do get tends to be delivered in the form of mini-lectures. He's so unlike Julia it's always been a mystery to me how they ever found each other.

Before long the emergency room atmosphere has transmuted to the warm, relaxed mood of the Sunday lunch. The scent of rosemary and garlic fills the air, and the gentle clattering of lids on pots of boiling vegetables creates a soothing backdrop to the conversation. The adults hover around the central island, some of us on stools, while Phoebe and Rebecca sit cross-legged on the floor, both of them now assiduously stroking Simone as if to assuage the awkwardness between them. There's a sudden explosion of noise when Freddie, Jake, Kate and Ella, who've evidently tired of the PlayStation, burst out of the family room, through the kitchen and out of the back doors into the garden, football in hand.

Julia and I exchange the odd look as we observe Fran and Paul together. It amazes me, as it probably does her, to see them so relaxed in each other's company. He is wonderfully attentive, but not in that vaguely nauseating way some men have. With him it's all about small gestures: a swift kiss on her forehead as he helps her to lift the roasting pan from the oven; a gentle hand on her lower back as he refills her wine glass. I'd lay money on the fact that neither Andrew nor Rob even notices half the things Paul does to convey his adoration of Fran. But Julia and I must have inbuilt antennae for that sort of thing.

It all seems to be going swimmingly well until Julia says, quite innocently I'm sure, 'What did you think of that ruling on Friday? The one about parents not having the right to know if their daughter is seeking advice about contraception, or even having an abortion, no matter how old she is? I was livid when I read that.'

Being both a lawyer and someone with very firm

views on parenting, Andrew is very clear about what he thinks. 'It's a bloody travesty,' he pronounces. 'It makes no sense to insist that parents be responsible when their children play truant, then tell them they're to have absolutely no say in whether or not their teenage daughter terminates a pregnancy. Either parents are responsible or they're not.'

'But don't you think it's different where sex is concerned?' says Fran, lowering her voice. But the girls' interest has already been piqued; they have both turned their heads to listen, and Simone has rolled on to her back with her paws in the air as if to register her discontent at being so hastily abandoned.

I try to work out Phoebe's expression. There will, of course, be disapproval at our even deigning to discuss such a topic in her presence, but I wonder what other uncomfortable mix of emotions she'll be harbouring. Fear that she will be found out? Worry that she might be doing the wrong thing? Panic at the mere thought of being faced with a decision about an abortion herself?

'How do you mean?' persists Andrew, oblivious to the underlying tension in the room.

'I mean,' whispers Fran, 'that sex is one thing that kids and their parents find very uncomfortable discussing. Kids don't want their parents to know about their sex lives, and they *certainly* don't want to know about their parents' sex lives. Believe me, I know.'

I look over at Paul before I can stop myself; he smiles shyly at me. Poor bloke, I think. He must feel like a special interest attraction at a theme park.

'But don't you think they should discuss it, uncomfortable or not?' asks Julia just as Andrew opens his mouth to pronounce again. 'I mean, I would certainly want my daughter to discuss it with me. I'd hate the thought of her going through something as life-changing as an abortion without my even knowing. What would that say about our relationship?'

Rob, Paul and I are all silent. I daren't express an opinion, knowing how uncomfortable the whole thing must be making Phoebe. I'm also, I realise, a little ashamed, knowing what I know. What does it say about Phoebe's and my relationship that she hasn't told me about the pills? Would she tell me if she needed an abortion, or would she hide behind the provisions for confidentiality that the courts have just upheld?

'What do you think, girls?' says Paul. He may be right; it's probably rude to discuss something like this in front of them without asking for their input. At the same time, he's got to know that they're unlikely to want to contribute.

Rebecca bites her lip, and Phoebe shrugs. They look at each other, then back at all of us. Simone drapes herself over Phoebe's lap in the hopes of reinstigating her massage.

'Or is the whole thing too hideous to discuss?' I ask.

'Sort of,' says Rebecca, offering a weak smile.

Then Andrew blunders in again, his voice booming. 'All I know is that if I ever found out a child of mine were having underage sex, let alone having an abortion, there would be serious hell to pay. I really think you have to take a firm line on these things. If we don't set the standards, who will?'

None of us knows who will, evidently, because we let his question hang there unanswered while we scrabble around for some essential pre-lunch chores with which to busy ourselves. I think we'd all like to pretend it will never happen to us. It crosses my mind that the thing that might have made Rebecca most uncomfortable is being referred to as a child of his as if she were some sort of hypothetical concept.

When we turn back to the girls, they've disappeared, and I can't decide if Simone looks indignant or forlorn.

Thankfully, nothing as controversial as recent rulings on abortion come up over lunch. It all quite jolly, and the closest we get to a heated tussle is when we debate the merits of *Celebrity Big Brother*. (Poor Andrew. He's the only one to deem it unwatchable, worthless rubbish. I watch Rebecca exchange a glance with Julia then slide down in her chair as he argues his case.) Just before pudding, and in response to a polite inquiry from Paul, Ella describes our Green Link group

238

and delivers one of her mini-lectures on the merits of showers over baths and the importance of buying local produce and being sparing with electric light.

'Andrew is forever on at me about switching off lights,' says Julia. 'But I think it's the bills rather than the environ-ment he's thinking about,' she adds cheekily. 'And he's very much a bath man. Can't stand showers, can you, darling?'

Her dark blonde hair, normally so neat in its streamlined bob, is a little tousled, and her cheeks are puce, owing to the fact that she's had quite a lot to drink. Even so, she has the appearance of being strapped in, bound up. I long for her to rip open her mint-green cardigan with its row of perfect pearl buttons and reveal even the slightest whiff of a collarbone. Or for her to slouch, abandoned, across the table. But Julia doesn't really do abandoned. Andrew won't allow it.

'Well, we're all sinners in our house, aren't we, Ella?' Rob quips. 'We do take showers, but very, very long ones, apparently. Tell you what, Ella. That will be my belated new year's resolution. No shower longer than, what, two minutes? What do you think?'

'Or you could just try not running the water while you brush your teeth, and not running the shower for several hours prior to getting into it,' I suggest, smiling very obviously so that no one will take this as a genuine attack. I'm not about to ruin Fran's lunch with a domestic.

'Do you honestly believe that sort of thing can make a difference?' asks Andrew, sitting back in his chair with puffed-out chest and dabbing the sides of his mouth with a napkin. It's only a question, but it's delivered in a voice that so reeks of derision that all response is momentarily stifled. Ella's face has taken on a slightly crumpled expression.

I don't want Fran's lunch to be ruined by a heated debate about environmental disaster any more than I want it tainted by a domestic, so I bite my lip. The only person I'd actually expect to take Andrew on about something like this is Fran herself. I certainly don't expect it from Rob.

'But what's the alternative, Andrew? Just this morning there was another headline: *THE WORLD HAS JUST TWENTY YEARS TO STOP CLIMATE DISASTER*. Can we honestly continue to sit and read these sorts of things and then cast the papers aside and carry on as per usual? Increasingly that seems like a form of near-psychopathic denial.'

'Well, for a start, you'd be a fool to believe what you read in the papers, ninety per cent of which is simply untrue. Second, if the research is true, the more sensible approach, it seems to me, is to invest in the technology that will enable us to counteract the effects of climate change. And thirdly . . .' (Andrew's arguments almost always have three parts), 'what the vast majority of people don't realise is that adopting the strategies being promulgated by these crazy Greenpeace types is a sure-fire route to economic disaster, which would have far more negative consequences than the odd flood.'

I watch Rob's face as he considers whether or not to take on Andrew. At any other lunch, we might be able to have a considered debate about this, one devoid of heat or venom. But Andrew has made that impossible by his very tone and posture, as he so often does. We really shouldn't attempt these sorts of gatherings with him any more. I'd far rather see Julia on her own.

'Believe what you will, Andrew,' Rob says after a pause, taking a hearty swig from his wine glass and leaning back in a way that signals his early retirement from the argument. He clearly doesn't want to ruin Fran's lunch either, but Fran's not the only person he's thinking about. 'Personally, I think we should be eternally grateful to people like Ella and Libby for trying to shake us out of our complacency, and do some small things that will make a difference. May I suggest a toast to our very own crazy Greenpeace types.'

'Hear hear. To our Crazy Greenpeace Types,' shouts Fran, and we all raise our glasses with a great flourish. Rob smiles at me from beneath his arm. I feel a sudden rush of warmth and gratitude and wish I were sitting next to him so that he could feel it too.

'What do you think?' whispers Fran, sidling up to me as I take the bread and butter pudding from the oven. 'Isn't he lovely?'

I turn to face her. 'Oh, Fran, he is absolutely

gorgeous. I'm so happy for you.'

Fran shrugs her shoulders and smiles widely. 'I keep having to pinch myself. I'd honestly given up on ever having a second chance. You know, I think it's even better than the first time. After everything I've been through I think I really know myself now, and I know Doug was completely wrong for me, completely wrong full stop.'

Looking at her I'm almost jealous. Hope and excitement are oozing from every pore. There is nothing in this world quite like those initial, all-absorbing feelings at the beginning of a love affair. I look at her lips and think, Lucky you. The deliciousness of all those first kisses.

'Anyway, how are you? How is all your Green Link stuff going? You seem to spend a lot of time there.'

'Really well. I was very uneasy about it at the beginning, as you know. It felt sort of flaky and impossibly challenging at the same time, do you know what I mean? And I loathe being tied to large groups. Running with Gilly and the others every other Friday is about my limit. But I've surprised myself. I'm loving it now, and I think it's fantastic for Ella.'

'Rob seems to feel a bit better about it now, don't you think?'

'Maybe. He probably still thinks it's a bit of a crackpot cause, but he wasn't about to let Andrew get away with rubbishing it. I think the real problem, in the beginning at least, was that he couldn't stand for me to be so involved in and distracted by something that excluded him. He's had my full attention for all these years after all; he's got into some very bad habits.'

I look through the doors into Fran's cramped dining room, and see Rob laughing uproariously. Then he leans forward and starts telling a story that seems to have everyone else's rapt attention. Julia giggles and covers her eyes in response to something he says, and Phoebe comes up behind him and smacks him playfully on the head. Then she stands with her hands resting on his shoulders, listening.

'Fran, what do you think it means if you dream about being with someone who isn't your husband? Do you think it's significant?'

'That depends. How often have you had the dream?'

'Once.'

'Oh, that's nothing. I wouldn't give it another thought. What I would worry about more is if you think about whoever it is during the daytime.'

In response to my silence she asks. '*Do* you think about him in the daytime?'

'Sometimes,' I say, staring at the pudding's golden crust.

'Who is it?'

'Someone from Green Link. A guy called Daniel. I think about him more than I should and it bothers me.'

'God, you know Rob mentioned him to me. Do you think he suspects something?'

'What? What did he say?' I ask, sounding more panicked than I'd like.

'Nothing much, just that he's met him at the clinic and how nice he seemed. But then he mentioned how nice-looking he was, which I thought was a little odd. It's not the sort of thing you usually hear Rob say. But he was joking, he didn't sound really upset or anything.'

'Well, there's nothing to be upset about,' I say, suddenly feeling that I ought to sound indignant. 'Nothing's happened. Like you said, it's not a big deal, right?'

Fran looks at me. 'Of course it's not. You've been married for almost two decades. It'd be a bloody miracle if your head had never been turned by anyone else in all that time. It doesn't mean you're not in love with Rob any more. It doesn't mean anything. Besides, it will probably pass. Give it another couple of months and you'll probably wonder what you ever saw in this Daniel person. Crushes vanish as quickly as they appear. The sort of thing you have with Rob doesn't.'

Suddenly Rob is there, standing behind Fran with a pile of dirty plates.

'What are you two gossiping about?' he says good-naturedly.

'Oh, this and that,' says Fran, eyes wide with alarm.

'Did you ask Fran about the Phoebe thing, Lib?'

'Yes. She wasn't much help. Said thank Christ it wasn't her problem, or words to that effect.'

'I don't believe that for a second,' says Rob,

putting an arm around Fran's shoulders and drawing her to his side. 'Not our Fran, dispenser of wisdom on everything from *Big Brother* to the correct interpretation of X-rays.'

'Here you go, Robbie, my boy, you take the pudding, we'll take the bowls,' says Fran, handing Rob a pair of oven gloves.

'My pleasure,' says Rob, scooping the pudding dish up from the counter and heading back to the dining room, shouting 'Pudding is served' in a way that almost lays claim to his having made it.

Fran hands me some bowls and leans in towards me.

'Don't think that I haven't looked at you with envy during these past six years, Libby,' she whispers. 'What I have now might seem awfully lovely to you, but I've paid a huge price to have it. Don't think for a second I wouldn't rather have had what you two have had.'

When I volunteer to wash some pots, Julia leaps up from the table and offers to dry for me. Before I've even located the scouring pad she says, in a hushed voice, 'Can I ask you something?'

My initial reaction is to suspect that she's overheard Fran and me talking about Daniel and my dream. I know that's practically impossible because she was in the dining room the whole time, but it doesn't stop me from gulping slightly when I say, 'Of course. Fire away.'

'I'm worried about Rebecca. The past few weeks,

maybe longer, she's sort of retreated into herself. I know she's a quiet girl, maybe not as confident as someone like Phoebe, but she's been withdrawn even for her. And she's not eating properly. When I ask her what's wrong, she say's it's nothing. If I ask twice, she shouts at me. You know how they are at this age. I just don't know what to do.'

'Do you want me to get Phoebe to talk to her?'

'That's exactly what I was going to suggest. Do you think she would? Of course Rebecca must never know I've asked you to do this.'

'Well, I'll certainly ask her to. I don't think they see each other all that often at school, but they seem to be getting on really well today.'

'That's what I thought. You know, I'm worried sick about her, really. And Andrew is absolutely hopeless when it comes to things like this. He just berates her. His latest theory is that she's got an eating disorder, so he keeps forcing her to eat things. It's awful to watch.'

What is really awful to watch, for me, is how much Julia has had to accommodate Andrew all these years. I think at times it must tear her apart. Left to her own inclin-ations she'd be a more communicative, open sort of parent, but she's somehow been brainwashed into taking a very traditional view of marriage and parenting, one in which open disagreements between husband and wife just don't feature.

I reach out with my soap-suddy hands and give her a hug. 'Don't worry, Jules. I'm sure it's just a phase. God knows we've been through enough of them with Phoebe. Everyone tells me you get them back when they turn sixteen, which isn't so far away, after all.'

I'm quite exhausted by the lunch. Red wine makes me tired anyway, but I think it's the unusually high quota of quietly shared secrets that has worn me out. I started out feeling like an extra on the set of *Casualty*, and end up feeling like a central character in *Emmerdale*. Underage sex. Suspected eating disorders. Middle-aged women with inappropriate dreams. Whatever happened to schools and house prices, I wonder?

PHOEBE

There are two Teencare Advisory Centres in London, neither one of them all that close to where we live. Rebecca and I end up taking the tube, then the bus, to get to somewhere near Stockwell. We have to walk through some pretty rough streets to get there, but the clinic itself looks quite nice. Modern, clean. Safe.

No one paid much attention this morning when I told them I was going shopping after school. Mum was busy reprimanding Dad for leaving the TV on stand-by the night before. She accused him of being wasteful and he said at least he wasn't obsessive. She asked him why he couldn't just support her in her efforts to drag our family into the twenty-first century, and he asked her since when did slogging his guts out five and half days a week at the clinic not count as supporting the family?, to which she said, 'Don't be obtuse, you know exactly what I mean,' at which point I had to intervene. I said, 'Come on, you two, do you think the rest of us want to listen to this?' and made a big show of going to switch the TV off at the mains myself.

As soon as we walk into the clinic a woman sitting at the front desk looks up and smiles. 'Hello, girls, how can I help?' she says in the same voice that Becky used. Calm, welcoming, like a warm blanket. Perhaps they are trained to speak like that.

There are two other people in the waiting room, young girls on their own. One is flicking through a magazine with her eyes aimed firmly down; the other is staring blankly ahead. I'm conscious of trying not to be overheard.

'This is my friend Rebecca,' I say as quietly as I can without actually whispering. 'She – we – have an appointment at 4.30.'

'Oh yes, here it is,' says the smiling woman whose name tag identifies her as Tara. 'Hello, Rebecca.'

Rebecca is standing beside me but looking around nonchalantly, almost as if she's not with me. She doesn't seem to hear Tara. I look at her, annoyed. 'Rebecca!'

'Oh, what?' she says, startled.

Tara smiles, clearly unfazed by Rebecca's distractedness. It's probably normal under these circumstances.

'Just take a seat over there, girls. Someone will be with you shortly,' she says, gesturing towards the bank of seats against the far wall.

We choose chairs at the far end of the room, away from the two other girls. One looks up at us very briefly as we sit down, I notice, then resumes her protective, downward-facing posture. The still quiet is all-engulfing, despite the occasional beep of the telephone and the sound of Tara's cheerful voice.

Suddenly, there's the whoosh of a door opening at the far end of the room and a woman in white shirt and black trousers is marching briskly towards us. She kneels down in front of us and smiles, resting her clipboard on her knees.

'Hello, girls. I'm Caroline. I'm one of the counsellors here. I'm going to take you back and explain about how things work here, what we can offer you. OK?'

Rebecca and I both nod wordlessly. I don't much like the feeling I'm getting, the feeling of being part of this, tarred with the same brush as Rebecca. Even though there's no actual suggestion of tainting. The way we're being treated, it's as if we're here to peruse wallpaper samples, not talk about termination procedures.

We follow Caroline through the whooshing door and along a corridor towards a small room containing three armchairs. A consultation room, evidently. There's no examination table shrouded in crisp, white paper, no set of frightening stainless-steel implements.

'Now, we're here to talk about you, Rebecca, is that right?' asks Caroline. I've not been imagining it, then. She was keeping her mind open to the possibility that I might actually be the one in trouble, that this whole thing was some sort of double-bluff designed to protect my fragile dignity.

I rush to clarify. 'Yes, it's Rebecca.'

'OK then, Rebecca. I'd like to start by telling you about the kinds of services we offer here, and how we can help. Then I'd like to ask you a few questions. OK?'

Rebecca nods, her eyes transfixed on Caroline's face. Caroline's steady gaze looks like a lifeline, even to me.

Caroline spends a few minutes explaining how Teencare operates. I try to concentrate hard on what she's telling us, in case Rebecca is too nervous to take it in properly. I learn that there are ten loosely connected clinics across the country, all funded by charitable donation and therefore totally free to the client. You can meet with a nurse, a counsellor, a doctor, or all three if necessary. Counselling can be about anything related to sexual health – contraception, sexually transmitted disease, pregnancy – or indeed anything else you are having difficulty with, such as relationships. I briefly consider seeking her opinion on the advisability of relationships between irresistible twenty-seven-year-old activists and almost-sixteen-year-old girls, but think better of it.

Caroline pauses part way through her monologue. 'What is it you want to see us about, Rebecca? Which one of the things I mentioned?'

Rebecca turns to me. I incline my head towards Caroline encouragingly. 'Its . . . I think I'm pregnant.'

'You think? What makes you think so?'

'I've missed two periods in a row. That's never

251

happened to me before. And I've been feeling kind of sick, since last week.'

Caroline greets this information with complete equanimity. 'OK then. What we'll do first is a pregnancy test. We can do that today, if you like. If the test is positive, we would offer you counselling, so you can decide what you want to do. If you decide you want a termination, we would give you a referral to an NHS hospital that can carry out the procedure. Normally, you would expect to wait three to four weeks for that. Is that clear?'

'I don't want to keep it. I already know that. I can't.' Rebecca's voice is high-pitched, strangled by panic.

'That may be true. And no one is going to persuade you to have the baby if you don't want to. But we feel it's best for you to discuss the matter fully with a counsellor, to make sure you are completely happy with your decision.'

'Do you have to tell my parents?' This is the crucial question, of course, one I would have asked right at the beginning.

'Well, if you were over sixteen we wouldn't have to. As you are fifteen, it will be up to the doctor's discretion.'

'What does that mean?' shouts Rebecca, sitting forward in her chair. 'You can't tell my parents. They absolutely can't know.'

Caroline reaches across to Rebecca and places a hand on her knee. 'Relax, Rebecca. If it really will cause you difficulties to have your parents know, the doctor will take that into account. Let's take first things first, shall we? How about we do the pregnancy test?'

Rebecca nods and slumps back into her chair. Her eyes well up with tears, her face is pale almost to the point of translucency. Suddenly she lifts her hand to cover her mouth, and I'm sure she's going to cry out. But she doesn't. She vomits instead. Into her hand, so that sticky, lumpy rivulets drip through the gaps between her fingers and on to her lap.

Caroline is up like a shot, grabbing kitchen roll from a cupboard in the corner of the room. She rips off several sheets and places them on Rebecca's lap, then opens her hands and begins wiping the mess from her palms. Her expression never changes. She doesn't even wrinkle up her nose at the smell.

'There you go,' she says, when Rebecca is more or less cleaned up. 'You'll need to wash those trousers when you get home, but otherwise you'll be fine. We'll take care of you. That's what we're here for.'

It's wonderful, this place. Maybe a little too wonderful. If you're not careful, you might convince yourself that what you're about to do isn't significant and life-altering, or even a stupid mistake worth regretting.

Rebecca's test is positive. Her appointment with the counsellor is in a week's time, and keeping it will require the pretence of another lengthy shopping trip. On the train home she hardly says a word. Me, I'm on the lookout for tears, nervous breakdown, vomit. I know that, in the absence of the saintly Caroline, I'll be the one expected to clean it up, whatever it is. On balance, and stench notwithstanding, I think I'd rather deal with vomit.

When the silence becomes too oppressive, I try to think of something to say to fill it.

'I think Josh and I might break up,' I announce. This might even make her feel better, knowing that someone else is going through some sort of heartache, to know that she's not the only one not living in a perfect world.

She seems quite shocked by the revelation. 'Why?'

'Well, you can't say anything. I'm trusting you with this. Promise?'

She nods firmly. Given her current circumstances, I'm as sure as I've ever been that she won't betray me.

'I've met someone else. Someone I'm totally in love with. He's absolutely perfect. I wish you could see him.'

'Who? Is it someone at Kings?'

'No, nothing like that. Someone totally extraordinary. Like no one you'll have ever met,' I say, leaning in to whisper, '*Much* older.'

Rebecca emits a little gasp, followed by a weak smile. 'That's great, Phoebe. You're so lucky.' Then she sinks back into the worn, faux velvet seat and her silence.

It seems to me that what I've told her hasn't made her feel better after all.

LIBBY

ate looks Phoebe up and down, taking in her long flowing skirt and boots, the emroidered boho blouse, the waist-length necklace.

'Where are you going? It's a school night,' she asks.

'I'm going with Mum. To the meeting,' Herself announces.

'You are?' I say, standing up from where I've been wiping up a sticky patch on the floor. It's no wonder we have ants. We'll have mice next. Declining standards of household care and regularly overflowing under-sink compost bins can't be the best recipe for vermin control.

'Mum! We agreed this last week. I said I wanted to help, and you said fine,' she says indignantly, one hand on an outthrust hip, head tilted to one side so that her glorious hair cascades all the way down one arm.

'Oh, well, OK. I know you said you wanted to help, but I didn't realise you wanted to come to all the meetings. I thought maybe you'd help us on one of the rally days, or with leaflet distribution.'

'Well, I'll do that too. But I really feel I need to go to a few meetings so I understand what the whole thing's about. You know?'

'Sure, sounds sensible. I guess with this being your first week back at school you won't have too much homework?' I say.

'Exactly,' she replies, then floats off into the hall and towards the downstairs loo. This new-found fervour confounds me. It's what I've wanted, looked for, waited for. Now that I've got it, I don't trust it.

In a flash it comes to me. Phoebe has had a life-changing experience, something that has changed her view of the world. It's official. She's slept with Josh. Like it or not, it's happened, and I'll have to accept it. Could it be that it's actually been good for her? That we've seen the last of Herself? Perhaps there's something *really* special between her and Josh and they are doing the right thing.

'Mum? Did you hear me?' Kate is tugging at my arm.

'What?'

She sighs. 'I said I need a new tennis racket for school. Mrs Walker say's mine's too small. Can we go tomorrow after school and get one?

'OK, darling,' I say.

'What's with everybody? People sure are acting weird,' she says, shaking her head as she leaves the kitchen.

After she's gone, I realise I'm committed to

working with Michelle and Courtney tomorrow, and that I'd rather she used Phoebe's old racket in any case. But I'm not in the mood for a scene right now, so I let it slide.

Sitting in the meeting, amidst the Green Link crowd, I can't take my eyes off her. Suddenly she looks even younger to me, even more innocent. But of course she's not any more. I count the weeks until her sixteenth birthday in my head, rationalising with myself that once it arrives it really will be none of my business, out of my hands. That's what they say, isn't it? Our family doctor, the lovely Doctor Sarah, warned me that sixteen is the cut-off point for obligatory parental involvement in decisions about contraception, abortion, anything sex-related. Twenty-one weeks. That's all that stands between me and absolution.

Courtney, Michelle and I are about to start our tour of the neighbourhood. We have three heaving sacks of leaflets to deliver through residential letterboxes. We huddle together near the bus stop outside the library, allocating responsibility for streets.

Phoebe and Ella were initially earmarked to help us, but have somehow ended up with Gabriel, Harry and Daniel covering the streets on the west side of the park. I don't mind. They'll have more fun with Harry and Gabriel anyway. Phoebe finally realised where she'd seen Harry before. It was on a programme about the youngsters who'd spent their half-term break clearing up a forest. At the time, I recall Phoebe branding them 'pathetic'. She might still think that, for all I know, but she doesn't let on. She was all ears when Harry was explaining the different initiatives his school had put in place.

We agree to do the first two streets together, so I can keep an eye on the girls and we can all get the hang of the patter. Most of the time, we don't expect to be asked to deliver the patter, but we need to be prepared, just in case. If someone opens the door and actually takes a leaflet from our hot little hands, we don't want to miss an opportunity for a face-to-face sales pitch.

We've been through about a hundred houses when I spot one with a familiar car parked outside it. I'd know the car anywhere, because it's spotless. More spotless than any car in London deserves to be. It must be Claire Thomason's Mercedes. But this isn't her house.

The mystery is solved for me as I bend down to stuff the flyer through the shiny chrome letterbox. I hear the clink of the flap on the other side, followed by the swoosh of paper sliding across tile and the genteel tones of Claire Thomason's voice.

'Thank you so much, Anne. That was lovely,' she is saying as she opens the front door. 'Oh my goodness! What have we here?'

'Sorry to startle you,' I say quickly, anxious not to be taken for an itinerant, or someone from 3-mobile offering vastly reduced line-rental rates in addition to cheaper gas/electricity/water bills.

'I didn't expect to find you here. Anne, this is Libby. Her daughter goes out with Joshua.' Anne gives me a measured smile. 'And what's this?' she asks, brandishing the flyer.

'It's a ten-point action plan we're suggesting to all local households to help improve the environment in our area. Simple stuff, really easy to implement, but could make a huge difference. Just how much difference is explained on the back. There's also an invitation to join us at an awareness day on July the tenth in the park on Hill Road. We'd be so grateful if you came and supported the neighbourhood effort.'

The patter exhausts me. I think I've delivered it at top speed out of fear of losing their attention. In truth, I never really had it. The expressions on Claire's and Anne's faces inform me that they are very unlikely indeed to turn up on July the tenth, or indeed even to read the back of the flyer. They are also, I realise, not the types to get involved in anything as unseemly as door-to-door flyer delivery. Tables for twelve at £2,000 a pop is more their style.

When Claire does respond, her question has nothing to do with anything I've said.

'And who are these two young ladies?' she asks, gesturing towards Michelle and Courtney, who have somehow ended up behind me, cowering. They're not stupid. They recognise antipathy when they see it.

'These are Michelle and Courtney, students at Carlisle Lodge. They're part of the Green Link team organising all this.'

Claire looks the girls studiously up and down, her gaze dawdling on Courtney's tight, slicked-back ponytail. When the girls open their moths to say hello, I swear she almost shivers.

'Well, I'm sure it's a very good cause, aren't you, Anne?' she says condescendingly. 'Toodloo, everyone. Must run,' she says, sweeping past us.

'Thank you for this,' says Anne, waving the flyer and closing the door in our faces.

The girls and I stand there for a second and watch Claire get into her car and pull away.

'Poor Phoebe,' says Michelle cheekily, checking out my expression for signs of disapproval. I don't show any.

Courtney adds, 'Phoebe? What about poor Joshua?'

The girls link their arms thorough mine and we march out of the driveway and on up the hill.

The next evening I get a call from Mrs Walker. It's highly unusual to be called by a teacher, so I'm surprised. As soon as she mentions the word tennis I'm not.

'Yes, I know. I'm so sorry. We meant to get it yesterday, but I got tied up with something,' I explain.

'The thing is, Mrs Blake, I've been asking Kate to get a new racket since weeks ago, well before the Easter break. Has she not told you?'

'Er, no. Well, perhaps. I'm not sure. I might have forgotten,' I say, sounding like Herself caught red-handed at something. 'I've been very busy lately,' I add by way of acceptable adult excuse.

'I'm sure you have, Mrs Blake,' she replies, but her tone says, *Likely story*.

'Anyway, I'll make sure she has one by next week,' I offer. 'I'm terribly sorry.'

I am sorry. Not so much about the racket, but about the fact that I've so obviously not been paying attention to Kate. Has she really asked me about this several times? Have I forgotten, or failed to hear in the first place?

I open the little notebook I've taken to carrying around with me. I never used to need one; seemed to be able to keep on top of things without writing everything down. Clearly that's no longer the case. I write Friday in large capital letters at the top of the next clean page, and the words *Tennis Racket!!!* underneath it. Then I growl 'Get a grip, Libby, get a grip' to myself, much in the manner of a football coach to a team on a losing streak.

PHOEBE

This Saturday is May the sixth, once known as The Day I Plan to Have Sex with Josh, or possibly, and more momentously, The Day I Will Become a Woman, but henceforth to be remembered as The Day Josh Was Very, Very Disappointed.

Josh has been texting me all week, trying to arrange for us to do something at the weekend. He's pretty diligent, Josh, quite good at staying in touch, but five messages a day is excessive, even for him. Things haven't really looked very hopeful for him all week. Seems everyone in my family is going to be at home all weekend, commitment-less. And Josh's parents, who were planning to go out on Saturday night, are now prevaricating because Mr Thomason's disc problem has flared up again. Josh's desperation radiates from the letters on my screen. 'Don't worry. Not a problem,' I text back, which probably makes him feel worse.

I haven't quite worked out how to break it to him. I've never broken up with anyone before. With Ben Halliday things just sort of tailed off. The phone calls and texts just petered out to the point where it was obvious, and, with the help of a few whispered messages from mutual friends, everyone somehow got the message. I still see him sometimes, and it's like nothing ever happened. Like we never spent all those hours kissing until our lips were bruised.

I like Josh a whole lot more than I ever liked Ben, so this is going to be really hard. My initial plan was just to tell him I wasn't ready to Do It after all and just sort of let the rest of our relationship amble along. Then I decided nothing short of a clean break would do. Now that I've met Daniel, he's all I think about. I'm permanently agitated and unable to concentrate. When I hear the beep of a text arriving, my heart leaps and I imagine, just for second, that it's a message from Daniel. Of course it never is.

Mr Thomason's disc makes a partial recovery and the Thomasons are able to go out after all. It's a black-tie do at Grosvenor House, apparently. Carriages at *midnight*, Josh tells me gleefully.

Before I leave for his house, I have about an hour-long conversation with Rebecca, who's more distraught about next week's appointment than she was about going to the clinic the first time. I think the trouble is that now there's no doubt, whereas before she was probably holding on to the tiniest sliver of hope that she'd got the dates wrong or just not noticed her period, or that her queasiness was somehow down to a persistent tummy bug. Now she has the official word of an official person: she is definitely pregnant.

If only she'd thought about things a little more in advance. Hell, I'm kitted out with a double dose of contraception, and I'm not even sleeping with anyone.

Mum offers to give me a lift to Josh's house. I had actually planned to walk over, to give myself time to get my thoughts together, but she really seems to want to drive me, so I let her. As soon as we're strapped in it's clear she wanted to get me alone so she could initiate one of those carefully planned but seemingly spontaneous conversations while driving.

'Was that Rebecca you were talking to before?' she asks, staring straight ahead, hands gripping the wheel.

'Yes,' I say, with false nonchalance. I stare out of my window, pretending to be transfixed by the sight of an old couple trying to coax a tired old spaniel along for its evening walk. The man is frowning, tugging aggressively on the lead; his wife slaps him lightly on the arm, shuffles over to the dog and scoops her up in her arms.

'How is she?'

'What do you mean, how is she?'

'I mean, is she all right? In general? You seem to be speaking to her a bit more lately, which is lovely, and I just wondered if you'd noticed anything?'

'Mum, what are you talking about? What would I notice?'

'Oh God, I'm no good at this,' she says exasperatedly, turning to look at me. We have stopped, momentarily, to allow a silver Volvo to maneouvre its way into a narrow drive. 'Look, Phoebe, Julia is worried about Rebecca. Apparently she's much quieter than usual, and she's not eating much, and Julia is concerned that there's something seriously amiss. She wanted me to ask you to talk to her.'

When she says this I feel the lead weight of an enormous responsibility pressing down on me. I could so easily shift it by sharing what I know with Mum. But it's impossible to conceive of my telling her and her not feeling she has to tell Julia. Hell, even I feel something of an obligation to tell Julia. But I mustn't. Rebecca is adamant; if I had a father like Andrew I might feel the same.

'Well, I talk to her all the time,' I say, making a genuine effort to sound consoling as opposed to defensive. 'She has some issues, but nothing she can't deal with. She's not anorexic or anything, if that's what Julia is thinking.'

'So you don't think there's anything really serious? Nothing I should tell Julia about?'

I pause for what feels like for ever before responding. 'No. There's nothing.'

This is the worst lie I've ever had to tell. Worse, even, than hiding the pills and pretending I wasn't planning on sleeping with Josh. But it feels like a necessary lie, an unavoidable one. Telling it makes me feel instantly more remote from her; at the same time it seems to bridge the gap between us, because suddenly one thing, at least, is very clear to me: if I were in real trouble like Rebecca, Mum would be the first person I would tell.

As I ring the doorbell I peer in through one of the stained-glass windows at the side of the door. There's a warm, orange glow coming from inside. Then a shadow passes in front of the window, and Josh opens the door.

Behind him, the hallway is bathed in candle-light. There are candles on the table by the stairs, and on the stairs as well. There's another one in the little alcove where Mrs Thomason usually keeps a large urn. (I wonder what he's done with it.) Josh smiles shyly at me and takes my hand to pull me into the house. It occurs to me that I should have done this on the phone after all. At least a week ago.

'Do you like it?' he asks me.

'It's lovely,' I say, nodding gormlessly. My feet are rooted to the marble hall tiles.

'There are more in there,' he says, pointing to the sitting room. 'And upstairs,' he says with a naughty smile.

That, it seems, is the extent of his seduction plan, because he stands looking at me awkwardly for what seems like an age, then says 'What would you like to do first?'

'Shall we get something to eat?' I say, moving towards the kitchen, which as far as I can see is the only part of the house not twinkling with the light of a thousand burning candles.

'Oh, sure,' he says, a little put out. 'How about a drink of something? My mum left us some Cokes and stuff. And I know there's some beer too.'

'I'll just have Coke,' I say. I've no intention of getting legless and doing something I'll regret.

Josh sticks his head inside the fridge and roots around for two Cokes. He plonks both of them on the counter, then opens a drawer and searches noisily for an opener.

'Aha!' he announces. 'Here it is.

He pours a Coke into a glass and hands it to me. 'You look really lovely,' he says.

That's it. I can't stand this any more. It's breaking my heart already and I've only been here five minutes.

'Josh, I can't do this,' I blurt out before I've even taken a sip of my Coke.

'Oh, do you want some ice?' he says, reaching for my glass.

'No, I mean our plan. I can't do it tonight.'

He puts his Coke down on the counter and takes a step back. 'But we've planned it. It's the right time. What's wrong?' he asks, his voice small and unsure.

'I just can't. It doesn't feel right,' I say. Then comes the killer blow. I shut my eyes to deliver it. 'I've kind of met someone else. I don't think we can see each other any more.' I look down at my feet, then squeeze my eyes shut again. 'I'm really, really sorry.'

'Fuck,' is all he says before walking into the sitting

room and sitting down on the edge of one of the big stuffed sofas with his head in his hands. I notice that the candles in here are all a deep red, to match the walls, and that there's a fire burning.

I follow him over to the sofa and kneel on the floor in front of him. There's a band pulling tight across my chest, and I feel a hot, burning liquid rising in my throat. I put my hand on his knee. He stares at it.

'Josh, I'm really sorry. I like you so much. I was going to do this. But now I just can't. Please understand. We can . . .'

'Oh, don't say it, Phoebe!' he shouts, brushing my hand from his knee aggressively. 'Don't tell me we can be friends. I don't want to be fucking friends.'

I start to cry, and when I look up I see that he's crying too. For a moment I think that maybe I've made a terrible mistake. I want to take back what I've said. But any words I might use to do so bunch up in my throat. I am mute.

I'm about to stand up and go. He wipes one hand across his eyes and grabs mine with the other and says, in a soft voice. 'Sorry. It's just hard. Can't we talk about it?'

I look at him for a very long moment. During the long moment I work at picturing Daniel in my mind, as a sort of test. I wait for the rush of feeling that usually accompanies a mental image of Daniel, and when it comes, I shake my head resolvedly. 'I'm sorry,' I say again, wondering if there is a limit to how many times you can say the word without the other person hating you for it.

I stand up then and look down on his head, which is buried in his hands. I bend down and kiss the top of it. Even as I'm doing it I realise it's a bit patronising, like a gesture you'd bestow on a dog or a small child.

Then I turn and walk through the ruby glow of the sitting room into the ochre glow of the hallway and out through the front door. I make it to the end of his road, then collapse on the bench next to the postbox. I'm trying to dial Laura's number, but my vision is blurred by the water brimming from my eyes, and my fingers are shaking so much that I dial an eight instead of a seven and end up getting a restaurant. The woman at Chez Phillipe says 'May I help you' twice, but obviously she can't so I hang up without speaking.

Arseholes. I knew Josh would be hurt and disappointed, but I hadn't planned on feeling quite this crap myself.

LIBBY

Daisy takes a tumble just outside the library, going up the steps rather than down them as you would expect. Michelle and Courtney are the first of our lot to come upon her, when there is already a small crowd gathered and the ambulance has been called. Michelle goes with her to the hospital. She insists upon it, apparently, despite Daisy's protestations.

Daisy has been turning up religiously every week. She's such a reassuring presence, in her pretty flowered dresses and her perfectly polished leather court shoes; a reminder of the days before people had to worry about things like the carcinogens generated by a toaster, or the UK fridge mountain. And she almost always has something useful to add to the discussion. Barry is particularly fond of her. He's so gutted by the news that she's fallen and damaged her hip that he turns instantly ashen.

'My goodness, that's terrible. Where has she been taken?' he exclaims.

'The Royal,' I say. 'Michelle's with her. Don't worry.'

'Never mind. I'll go along anyway. They might need another adult to sort out the forms and things.

Can't expect poor Michelle to handle all that. Can you spare me here?' he asks.

'I think so,' I say, smiling only to myself. 'You go ahead.'

The numbers are down tonight, for all kinds of reasons. There's Daisy, Barry and Michelle at the hospital, obviously. Eloise is babysitting for her daughter Kelly (something to do with an urgent meeting between Kelly and her 'good-for-nothing prick of an ex-husband' Kevin). Phyllis is under the weather, according to Nancy. And Shelly, Marcie and Carole are sporadic attendees at the best of times. In the end, there are just eight of us, seated in a small circle, recounting our experiences of leaflet distribution.

'What was the reception like, do you think?' asks Daniel. 'Did you get the chance to talk to many people?'

'A few,' I reply. 'Most people were open-minded, pleased to listen. Whether they'll show up or not is another question. Tell you what, why don't we do a kind of reminder beforehand. On bikes or something. We have at least half a dozen bikes between us. We could use megaphones – strap them to our chests somehow. '

People like the bike and megaphone idea. Once we've agreed on the details, there's not a lot else to discuss. Most of the activity in the run-up to the rally has to be carried out in small groups during the day, so the meeting ends pretty quickly.

Herself is almost completely silent through it all.

She's been strangely down and irritable since Saturday. My gentle probing has been to no avail. I daren't enter into an intensive interrogation for fear of retaliation.

When we've finished stacking the chairs, Phoebe pops to the loo. Daniel walks towards me, his arm outstretched. He holds something out towards me. It looks like a newsletter.

'What's this?' I ask.

'It's a three-day conference in Brighton. I thought you might be interested.' He stands opposite me, waiting for me to skim the first page.

'It's a marine ecology conference,' I say, stating the obvious.

'Yeah. Green Link takes places every year. I thought maybe you'd enjoy it.' He sounds nervous, suddenly like a small boy.

I stare at the newsletter, not really taking it in. During this brief reprieve, he seems to recover some of his easy manner. 'I thought it would be good for you to get back to your roots.'

When I look up from the newsletter he adds, with a cheeky smile, 'You can't hide in suburban London for ever, you know.'

I long to reach out and touch him, any part of him, just to give some substance to the currents that are hovering between us. Instead I busy my hands with folding the newsletter and stuffing it into my bag. 'I'll think about it,' I say. 'It was nice of you to think of me.'

'Pleasure,' he says. Then he adds, with a

nonchalance as thin as rice paper, 'I was planning on going this year. We could go together.'

We stand there, absorbing the full impact of these words. Then a swishing noise, the noise of a door being opened, punctuates the silence and startles us both. He turns around.

'Hey, Phoebe,' he says with exaggerated exuberance. 'Thanks for coming tonight. Are you planning on being one of our bike-riding megaphonists?'

'If you want me to,' she says obligingly. I think back to this morning, when I asked her to take out the compost, and wonder at the difference in her response.

'Definitely,' he says. 'Most definitely. Come on, girls, how about I treat you to a latte and a brownie before we go home?'

I can't think of anything worse than sitting in a coffee shop with Phoebe and Daniel. But Phoebe's already nodding her head, and before I know it, it's a done deal.

Daniel is something of a chameleon, I discover. One minute he's issuing invitations for weekends in Brighton and throwing me meaningful looks, the next he's playing the good team leader laughing and joking with a pair of colleagues. There's hardly any sign of the first Daniel in the coffee shop. There's no knocking of knees as we struggle to fit round the small table, or brushing of fingertips as we reach for the sugar. The only glimpse I get of the other Daniel is when I go up to the glass-fronted counter to fetch a spoon and catch him looking at me as I walk back to the table. He averts his gaze deliberately, quickly.

Herself listens in a way she seldom listens to anyone over the age of twenty. When Daniel chastises her for wanting to discard her perfectly functional mobile in favour of an updated model, she laps up his arguments as if it's the first time she's ever heard them, and readily agrees to keep her old phone.

She doesn't register the look of disbelief I give her. All irony is lost on her.

PHOEBE

I'm glad I've got Rebecca's problem to take my mind off my own. I don't want to think about Josh – the candles and the tears and the sunken feeling that stayed with me afterwards.

I sent him a text the following day. 'Hope you're OK,' it said.

'Fucking fantastic,' he texted back.

'I still care about you,' I wrote, thinking it was a nice thing to say.

'???!!!,' he replied.

I decided maybe it was easier not to try to be nice.

Getting away to the clinic was trickier this week, engin-eered only with the aid of a hastily constructed lie about having to go to the British Museum to do some research.

'How are you feeling?' I say to Rebecca as we sit waiting for our consultation. Rebecca's asked to meet with a doctor and a counsellor at the same time, to speed things up.

'OK, I guess,' she replies, smiling weakly. She digs into her bag for a digestive biscuit, the only thing she's found to counteract the nausea. She's nibbling on her second biscuit when we are summoned.

We're taken to a different room than last time. Bigger, with more chairs, but otherwise almost identical. Still no surgical implements, which is something of a relief. I think the mere sight of them might be enough to persuade Rebecca to refuse termination just so she could postpone the pain by eight months or so.

The counsellor, who's named Judith, is young, with dark curly hair and a wide, open face. Dr Helen Peterson is short and sturdy-looking, with grey hair swept back into a clip. She looks horribly stern at first, but once we've sat down and she starts to speak, that impression is quickly dispersed.

The first thing they want to talk about is Rebecca's relationship with the father. I guess most girls who come in are in a long-term relationship, because that's what they assume at first. Rebecca seems to freeze up when they ask, then she says, 'I'm not with the father. I mean, we're not seeing each other. Any more.' This elicits expressions of concern and sympathy from Judith and Dr Peterson, but their questions (*How does she feel about that?*; *Is there a chance of a reconciliation?*; *Should the father be told?*) extract only monosyllabic responses from Rebecca. Finally she says, 'Please can we not talk about this any more.'

Dr Peterson and Judith take their cue, and we move on to talk about Rebecca's options. It takes about fifteen minutes to go through the pros and cons of each option, that's all. I watch Rebecca's face as she's told about the two termination options, medical and surgical. If it were me, I'd opt for the medical procedure involving taking a pill and waiting to spontaneously abort, but Rebecca winces when this is described to her. 'I want to be sedated. I don't want to feel it happening,' she says sheepishly, as if she's failed a test of some sort. Doctor Peterson tells her not to worry and scribbles something down on her clipboard. Perhaps a tick in the box marked 'Surgical Procedure'.

It seems to me to take longer to go through the 'Having the Baby' alternative. I always knew having a baby would be an involving, messy business. God knows it's been drummed into us enough at school. But somehow, hearing about it all here, when there is a real decision to be made, the monumental, life-changing aspect of it all seems to loom out of all proportion.

'You don't have to decide right now, Rebecca,' says Judith kindly. 'You can take a few days if you like.'

'No,' says Rebecca firmly. 'I can't. Can't have the baby, I mean. I just can't cope with all that on my own, and I know my parents would disown me. So there's no choice really.'

Dr Peterson and Judith exchange a glance, the meaning of which is decipherable only by them. These people are very good, so impeccably neutral.

Then Judith says, 'OK, Rebecca. We'll book you in for a termination at the hospital nearest your home. It will take about three weeks, most likely, so you'll have time to think about your decision. If, at any point, you want to reconsider, or just go over things again, you can call me. At any time.'

'Can't we get an appointment sooner?' pleads Rebecca. 'I really don't want to think about this any more. And I feel so ill.'

'The only way to speed things up is to go private. We can book you in at the Marler Clinic, but it will cost you almost £500. Do you have £500?' asks Judith.

Rebecca thinks hard for a second. 'I have around £200 saved up. That's all.'

'Well, I'm afraid that's not quite enough, dear,' says Dr Peterson, grimacing. 'The NHS option is the only one for you. Let's hope we can get you in before the three weeks is up.'

I'm not sure what makes me speak up then. Maybe something about Rebecca's joyless, desolate expression. Maybe the image that flashes briefly through my mind of me in her situation, and the feeling of wretchedness that washes over me when it does.

'I have £300 in my savings account,' I announce to all three of them. 'She can have that.' Then I turn to Rebecca. 'Please. Have that.'

Rebecca almost flinches in surprise. Judith and Dr Peterson smile warmly at me then look over at Rebecca, waiting for her response.

'Oh,' is all she says.

'That's a very kind offer,' says Judith to help her

along. 'Do you want to take it?'

'Yes. Please. Thank you.' Rebecca says, biting her lip and looking more worried than relieved.

'Good,' says Judith. 'That's good.'

Then Dr Peterson announces that Rebecca has the right to a short period of private consultation with her and asks me to leave the room and wait for her in the reception area. I'm certain Rebecca is going to reject this idea outright, given the extent to which she's relied on me the past couple of weeks, but surprisingly, she lets me go.

Even though she's asked me to leave I feel bad leaving her there. She looks so vulnerable, like she could break.

We are studying Keats. When Keats spotted his lady at Vauxhall he became tangled in her beauty's web and was unable to look upon a rose's dye without his soul taking flight. Sweet memories of the lady eclipsed every other delight. It occurs to me that Daniel has had a similar effect on me. Nothing has looked or felt the same since I first set eyes on him. I get a soaring feeling when I even think about him, and if that's not a soul taking flight I don't know what is.

He is, without question, the most wonderful person I've ever met. So principled, but not in that creepy evangelical way some people have. So full of knowledge, about everything it seems to me, but then so funny and light. One minute he's talking about the G8 summit and the Kyoto treaty, the next he's doing an imitation of those guys on *Little Britain* or tapping out a U2 song with the sugar spoons.

It never occurred to me that a person like him existed. All these years I've been staring at posters of Orlando Bloom and Heath Leger, and going out with boys like Ben and Josh, and I thought that was it. That the dazed, moony feeling I got from them was the extent of it. Now I know different. Now I know what it feels like to admire every fibre of a person's being, to want them to touch you so badly that the ache takes root in your body. As Tom once said to Jerry about a very attractive lady cat he'd fallen for, he sets my soul on fire.

Part of me wants to tell the whole world how I feel, but I'm guarding my secret closely, certain that Mum would not approve.

LIBBY

'**I** was thinking of going to Brighton for a conference in a couple of weeks' time,' I say quietly to the mirror, practising.

I'm standing in front of the mirror in the bedroom, red-faced and sweaty from my run. Rob is in the bathroom, shaving. I've decided this is a good time to bring up the conference. If I wait until the evening, the announcement will be laden with too much import. If I call him at work it will be even worse. A casual, throwaway remark in the midst of our hurried morning routine seems best.

'Rob, I was thinking of going to a conference in Brighton in a couple of weeks. What do you think?' I say, occupying myself with opening the laundry basket in the bathroom and stuffing my running clothes inside.

'What kind of conference?' he asks, stretching out his neck to give the razor a clean line.

'A Marine Ecology conference. A few of us from Green Link were thinking of going.' I swallow hard.

'What will you do there?' he asks, swishing his blade through the greyish soapy water in the sink.

'What do you mean? It's a conference.'

He turns to look at me. 'I mean, are you just going as an observer, or are you guys doing something there. Presenting something?' His tone is impatient.

'Oh. I see what you mean. Well, mostly observing really. But the thing is, it's an area I'll be at least vaguely familiar with. So there's a chance I could get involved in a few more national Green Link efforts on the marine side if I meet the right people, get back in the swing of things.'

'Is that what you want?'

'I don't know. But it would be nice to have the opportunity.'

'Yeah. I guess so,' he says, patting his face with a towel. I notice that the towel is filthy and grab it from him, stuffing it into the basket. There's so much in the basket that I can't press the lid down. How can that be? I'm sure I did some laundry a couple of days ago. The laundry basket is the antithesis of the fridge: no matter how often you empty it always seems to be full.

'So, would you mind if I went?'

He turns to look at me then. Eyeball to eyeball.

'Who's going?' he asks.

'A few of us,' I lie. 'Eloise, Daniel. Some people from the national movement.'

'Right.' He says. Just like that. 'Right.' Then he keeps staring at me, waiting for something.

'Anyway, if you really don't want me to go, I won't. But I would like to. It would be really interesting, and I would sort of like to kick-start some sort of career for myself.'

'Whatever you want,' he says, turning back to the mirror. He opens the cabinet and takes out a deodorant stick, which he rubs on his underarms.

'OK. I'll go then. I'll make sure everyone is catered for here. Don't worry.'

'Oh, I'm not worried about that,' he says, as I disappear back to the bedroom.

That night, when we are lying in bed, he turns to me and says, 'Lib, you do know that if you get involved with Green Link on a national level you'll be expected to travel all over the country. The demands on your time will increase. How's that going to work?'

I lay my book across my chest. 'I have no idea. But surely we can cross that bridge when we get to it. The important thing is that I really want to do this.' Then, when he doesn't give me the look of affirmation I want, I add, 'Isn't it?'

'I don't know. I suppose so. Yes.' He's more subdued than irritated. Resigned.

I pick up my book and resume reading. He does the same. We lie like this for about ten minutes. Then he drops his book and leans up on one elbow.

'Lib, tell me something. Does anything feel different to you? Do things feel different?'

I laugh nervously. 'What do you mean?'

'I mean us. You and me. Do you think we're different?'

'Since when?'

'Since, I don't know. Since a few months ago.

283

Since before you started this Green Link business.'

Why do people insist on calling it this Green Link business? Like it's some sort of child's play they're waiting for me to outgrow.

'Well, maybe. I'm busier, so we don't have as much time to talk. And I'm happy, and happy to be busy, but surely that's a good thing.'

'No, it's not just that,' he says. 'I don't know what it is. It's something else. You don't feel it?'

'No,' I lie. ' You're being silly.' Then I pull his face down towards me and kiss him.

'I love you,' I make myself say. I do love him. I've always loved him, even when we've been in the midst of a huge row, or when he's been distracted and inattentive. Even since his inattention became a pattern, just the way our marriage has become. But I still have to make myself say it now. I wonder if it comes out as awkwardly as it feels to me saying it.

Maybe it does, because instead of saying 'I love you too,' he says, 'I hope so.' Then he turns away from me and plumps up his pillows in readiness for sleep. Normally I wouldn't let him get away with this, the abrupt and single-handed termination of a conversation without resolution. But tonight I do.

Fran tells me she thinks there's something funny going on as well.

'Tell me I'm being paranoid if you like,' she says, laughing nervously, 'but it feels like you're holding something back from me. Is there something you want to say to me but you're afraid to? Do you think

284

I'm doing the wrong thing getting involved so quickly with Paul? Because if you do, I'll listen to you. I'm not saying I'll do everything you say, but I'll listen.'

I try to reassure her, tell her I think Paul is wonderful and the best thing that could have happened to her. Suitably reassured, she tries another angle. That's the thing about Fran: she doesn't give up easily.

'So it's not Paul. What is it then? Is all this stuff about saving the planet getting you down? Because maybe you're taking it a bit too seriously, Libby. You can do a lot of good without going quite as far as you're going, don't you think? It's not worth getting down over.'

'Of course it's worth getting down over!' I exclaim. My voice is light, but I mean it, nonetheless. I give her a short lecture on overflowing land-fills and CO_2 emissions much the same as the one Ella treated me to earlier in the week.

Throughout our conversation I'm conscious of trying not to mention Daniel. I certainly don't mention the invitation to Brighton. She doesn't mention Daniel either. She might not be one to give up easily, but she does have blind spots. She's never asked me again about the dream or my confessed obsession with him; she's probably not given it another thought since I first mentioned it. It's almost as though she didn't take it seriously, as though she refused to entertain the possibility of a real indiscretion on my part, or of any genuine rift in Rob's and my relationship. In her eyes we are perfect, and things like that just don't happen to us.

PHOEBE

I have almost four hundred pounds in my savings account. Grandpa has been putting in £10 a month for as long as I can remember, and I get the odd cheque for my birthday or Christmas. And I hardly ever take money out of it. The one big thing I did buy was my iPod, but that was ages ago, and the balance seems to have recovered since.

The girl behind the glass screen looks shocked when I tell her I want to withdraw three hundred pounds all at once. The old woman ahead of me only asked for twenty, and the man ahead of her deposited a cheque without withdrawing anything at all. I guess it's unusual to ask for so much cash.

'Three hundred, yeah?' she says, looking at me through the fringe that's draped across her forehead and over one eye. Her nails are long and pale pink with that tell-tale square-ended thickness at the tips. Acrylic.

'Hmn.' I nod.

'You going out shopping then?' she asks with a conspira-tional smile.

'Sort of,' I reply. I try to think of what I will tell her I'm shopping for if she asks me. I make a snap

286

decision to say I've planned an excursion to Top Shop and Urban Outfitters on Oxford Street, but in the end she doesn't ask.

'I bet you look gorgeous in everything you try on,' she says.

I smile.

She counts out the money in front of me, her thick nails clicking on the counter. 'There you go,' she says, pushing the notes through the gap under the glass partition. 'Have a nice time.'

She winks at me. I smile at her again and take the money. For about three seconds I think about what it would be like to spend £300 in one go at Top Shop and Urban Outfitters.

I give the money to Rebecca in the loos just before we catch the bus home. It feels a little like what I imagine a drug deal to be like. She's embarrassed by the envelope's thickness, I can tell. And having it in her hands seems to bring home the reality of what she's about to do, because she starts crying. It's not the same kind of crying as I've seen her doing before. The first time, in here, she was literally sobbing her guts out, as if her world had fallen apart. It's not like that now. These are quiet tears, making their way down her cheeks in a sort of slow, steady march.

'It will be OK,' I say, squeezing the top of her arm.

She looks at me, a single drop dangling from the end of her nose. Then she flings herself at my body and squeezes me, both arms around my waist, her head buried just beneath my shoulders. I stand there for a second or two, my arms dangling uselessly by my side. Then I hug her back.

That evening I'm almost certain that Dad suspects something because when we're in the kitchen he offers me a Coke and asks me if I'd like to sit and chat for a while. Most days, 'a chat' is code for 'a telling-off'.

But it seems he really does want a chat after all. When he's poured a Coke for me and a beer for himself, he says, 'So, listen. How's this Green Link business going? Are you enjoying going to these meetings with Mum?'

For a nanosecond I think he might have read my mind, that he knows about Daniel. Then I realise that would be impossible.

'Great,' I say. 'Really interesting.'

'And how's Mum? When she's there, I mean? What's she like?'

'What do you mean?' I say, puzzled.

He laughs then. 'I was just wondering what she's like when she's in committee mode. You know, debating, organising things. We don't get to see her like that very often.'

'Oh, I guess you're right,' I say. Now that I think about it, she is a bit different when she's there. Everyone loves her, for a start. People are always asking her opinion on things, and when she gives it, they act like she's dropping gold nuggets from her mouth. She seems to be in charge, somehow, and I once heard Daniel refer to her as his trusty deputy. When I tell Dad this he smiles, and then gets this sort of faraway look on his face.

'She was a bit like that when I first met her,' he says. Then he leans forward in his chair and takes a swig from his beer glass. 'She was pretty feisty back then. And so serious about her marine science. I remember when I first spotted her in the café where she used to work. She used to be a terrible waitress, because her mind was usually on something else. She didn't want to be there at all. She wanted to be on some beach somewhere, or in a lab, peering into glass jars full of seaweed.'

I listen to him tell me how they met and how they couldn't stand to be apart when she was working in Southampton, and how she gave up a whole lot of opportunities to move to London and be with him. I realise not only that it's the first time I've heard the story, but that it's the first time it's occurred to me that they *have* a story. A large part of me wants to say, Come off it, you're making this up.

When he's finished telling me about When They Were Young, the conversation meanders about, without a discernible direction, until suddenly, out of the blue, he mentions Daniel. This makes me sit up a bit straighter, I can tell you.

'So what do you make of this Daniel fellow?' he asks.

'Daniel?' I say casually, like Green Link meetings are full of fit blokes whose names I have trouble keeping straight.

'Yeah. You know, the one who's leading the whole thing? Is he any good?'

'Well, yes, I guess he is. He's very clever. Knows everything there is to know about this stuff. And people like him. They really want to do things for him. I guess you'd say he's kind of inspiring.'

'Really?' he says, nodding his head, like he's mulling something over. 'Mum and he get along?'

'Yeah, I guess so. Why?' I ask, thinking this is a very strange line of questioning.

'Well, I know they're all planning on going to this marine conference in Brighton, that's all. Eloise, Daniel, someone from the national group. I just thought, that's an awfully long time to spend with people if you don't really get on well with them.'

My mind takes leave of the room then. I can hear him talking, but the words just float around outside my head and drift off without registering. All I can think about is how insanely jealous I am that these people are going to be spending days on end with Daniel while I'm stuck here, in this house. I have to find a way of getting myself invited to that conference, whatever it is. I have to go instead of one of them, in Eloise's place maybe, or Mum's. It's just too perfect an opportunity to be missed.

After a minute or two he probably senses that I've lost interest because he says, 'Well, enough of that. I guess you'd better get moving on your homework,' and gets up from his chair, leaving his almost empty beer glass looking kind of forlorn on the counter.

LIBBY

Eloise and I arrive at the hospital for morning visiting time, our arms laden with marshmallow-pink peonies and cloud-white hollyhocks. We've brought along a couple of vases and a pair of scissors, which takes the sting out of the initially scathing looks we are thrown by the nurses on the duty desk.

When we pop our heads around the door, Daisy is sitting propped up in bed, looking pristine enough to be taking tea at the Ritz. Her hair's been back-combed, and she's wearing a pretty pink and white flowery smock nightie instead of the regulation washed-out grey hospital gown. Her face brightens when we enter the room.

'Oh, hello, girls. How lovely to see you,' she says in her sing-song voice. 'Oh my goodness! What lovely flowers.'

'To match your nightie, hon,' says Eloise, giving Daisy's hand a squeeze then holding the peonies out for Daisy to smell. Daisy inhales and then closes her eyes and lets her head fall back on the pillow. 'Heaven,' she pronounces. 'Absolute heaven.'

Eloise and I start filling the vases with water and

snipping off the ends of the flower stems. Daisy sits with her head resting back on the pillows, a peaceful smile on her face.

'So, Daisy, tell us how you are?' I say. 'Are you still in a lot of pain, or is it bearable?'

'Oh, it comes and goes, you know. It really depends where I am in the drugs cycle. But overall I can't complain. It's a lot better than it was a week ago.'

'I'll bet it was bloody awful a week ago!' exclaims Eloise.

'Yes, you're right, dear. Absolutely bloody awful,' Daisy says. Her refined, melodic voice gives the profanity an almost sacred quality.

'So what's the prognosis?' I ask, placing a vase full of pink and white blooms on the grubby window sill and standing back to admire my hand-iwork.

'Well, broken hips don't mend so quickly when you're my age, you know, so it will be a long while before I'm back to normal. But they say I'll be able to leave here next week. Provided I have the right set-up at home.'

'And do you? Who will look after you? How will you get up all those stairs?'

'Well, my guardian angel has sorted all that out for me. He's called Barry,' she says, a shy smile creeping across her face. 'He's a marvel, that man.'

'Apparently so,' says Eloise. 'So how's it going to work?'

'I'm moving in with him for a little while. He's

got a spare room on the ground floor of his house, and he's already moved a bed into it. He's got it all worked out. So kind, don't you think?'

Barry's a dark horse. I'd figured him for a nice man, a harmless man, an enthusiast, if one with a tendency towards too much chatter. I hadn't realised his heart was actually carved out of gold.

'It is kind. But you know, I bet he'll enjoy the company too, you know. Don't kid yourself this is all for your sake!' I joke.

'You think so, dear?' she says, a look of genuine bafflement on her face. Then she smooths out the sheet below her hands and says, 'So tell me, girls. What have I been missing? How's it all going?'

'Just terrific,' says Eloise in her hearty, generous way. 'We are making so much progress on this rally that's planned for the tenth. It's all coming together nicely. We've even had a few more people volunteer to help us run the thing. That flyer we did has made an impression, I think.'

'That's good to know,' Daisy says quietly. 'I do so wish I could be helping you.'

'Oh, don't you worry about that. We'll have you there in a wheelchair overseeing one of the stands on the tenth. You're not getting off that lightly!' I say.

Then Eloise announces, 'Libby here's turning all serious on us as well. She's planning on going to a marine ecology conference in Brighton, with all the Green Link bigwigs. Pretty soon she won't want anything to do with the rest of us amateurs.'

'So what's this conference, Libby? Tell me all about it,' says Daisy, pushing herself up a little higher on the pillows. Her bright blue eyes are gleaming, but her skin is pale and looks as though it might tear if you rubbed it too hard.

'Oh, it's something Daniel told me about. He'll be going, as well as all sorts of people from Green Link around the country. He thought I'd enjoy it because of my background, you know. Also, he seems to think I might be of some use to the national organisation if I get involved.'

'How exciting,' says Daisy, opening her eyes wide and hunching up her shoulders in a girlish display of delight.

'Very, very exciting,' echoes Eloise, giving me a knowing look.

'Anyway, I'm not a hundred per cent sure I'm going yet. It's a lot to organise, being away for three days. I'm not sure Rob and the girls will cope without me,' I say.

'Oh, they'll cope, hon. The question is, will you?' says Eloise. The look she shoots me is like a mirror-image of my own feelings about the weekend: neither condemning nor collusive but something in-between.

'Oh, Libby it will be fine,' pipes up Daisy, oblivious to Eloise's meaningful stares. 'Three days away from the cooking and the washing-up. It'll do you the world of good.'

Daniel was the one who told Eloise about the

conference. He dropped it into a conversation with her and Julia Harding and Michelle in the most throwaway, casual manner you can imagine. The way he said it, it was as if there really were nothing more to it than a couple of colleagues going away to indulge in a little marine ecology. The way he said it, it made perfect sense.

Half the time I can convince myself that it does make sense. Half the time, I'm not really sure there is anything more to it. Sometimes it feels as though we really are two people with an evolving friendship based on a shared interest and a shared sense of humour. Then suddenly there's a rush of something between us. Something invisible, I'm sure, to the outside world. But something real. Like an electric current transmitted without the aid of wires or magnetic fields. A current with enough inbuilt strength to leap across pure, empty space, unfacilitated.

Will I go to Brighton in two weeks' time? I still don't know. I've allowed him to register my name, pay my registration fee, but I've not booked a room. And I haven't told Fran. I didn't even tell Fran when she called to announce, in the giddy tone of an eighteen-year-old with a serious crush, that she and Paul were going away to Paris for the weekend. I particularly didn't tell her then.

I wish, in a way, I hadn't told Fran anything at all. She's always adored Rob, been fiercely loyal to him. I'm not sure I'd bear up under her scrutiny.

★   ★   ★

I've always thought that people who see connections between simultaneous but seemingly unrelated events are slightly deluded. I'm a big believer in coincidence. But my dream about Adam Cook – the ex-cabinet minister who left his wife of thirty years and set up shop with his (very) much younger secretary – really gets me thinking. He's not someone I'd normally even think about, much less dream about. And he hasn't been in the news for almost a year. But I have a full length, multicolour dream about him. He is descending a hillside as I am trekking up it. We exchange cordial hellos and resume our separate hikes.

The next morning I wake to the news that Adam Cook has died of a heart attack while on a hillside walk with his wife. *How weird is that?* I think. How could I have possibly known about his hiking in the hills ahead of time? Even *I* have to think there's something in the connection between my dream and the circumstances of his death – that he was somehow trying to send me a message, to warn me about something.

But what message, what warning? That's the difficult part. Avoid hiking holidays if you are over fifty-five and have a weak heart? Only go hiking with paramedic support in tow? Stick to politics?

Or is it: *Be wary of messing with someone half your age. They will only drag you up hillsides too steep for you to climb.*

PHOEBE

I've never been into Eloise's shop before. Her stuff is too expensive for me, and too old. Pretty, but meant for someone forty or fifty years old, not fifteen.

When I step inside the shop today there's no one there. But at the tinkling of the bell Eloise appears from behind a curtain, pen and paper in hand.

'Hello, hon. What brings you here?' she says warmly. I think, She is so what I'd love to be when I'm older.

'Oh, I thought I'd have a look around. I don't have much homework to do today.' I lie.

'Well, make yourself at home. I was just fixing myself a cup of tea to make this stock check a little more palatable. You fancy some?'

'No thanks,' I say, then,'Well, OK. Maybe I will.' Tea will draw out the visit, make it easier for me to say what I've planned.

Eloise disappears behind the curtain again and I browse through the racks of blouses, skirts, scarves. My fingers linger on the draped silks of the skirts, the soft knits of the little tops. I find something I absolutely love, might even consider wearing if I could afford it. It's a stunning long, strappy summer dress in some sort of multicoloured silky fabric. The hemline is choppy and uneven, and the overall impression is exotic. I hold it up against my body and admire myself in the mirror.

I think that maybe I was wrong and maybe this shop isn't so frumpy after all.

'Aha. I could have predicted you'd like that one,' Eloise says, holding out a cup of tea to me. 'It would look stunning on you. Or rather, you would look stunning in it. Then again, you could probably put on a sack and look stunning. Trouble is, I bet you don't have the £300 you'd need to buy it.'

I have a picture of myself handing over the white envelope to Rebecca.

She moves over towards a lime-green corduroy sofa that sits in front of the three small changing cubicles lining one wall. 'Come, come. Let's sit over here for a while. Business is pretty slow today.'

I follow her over to the sofa and sink down into its deep, squashy cushions. God knows how anyone ever gets out of this when it comes time to leave, I think. Maybe that's the idea. Maybe men get stuck here, so their wives just keep trying things on until they've exhausted all the stock.

'So, what's up? Shall we talk Green Link, or other stuff?' she asks, smiling at me. Her glasses, which are rimmed in a silvery purple metal, have slipped down on to the end of her nose and she is peering at me over the top of them. For a second it looks as if she might be going to interrogate me.

'Well, now that you mention it,' I say, 'there was something I was wondering about.'

'Fire away, hon,' she says, taking a sip from her tea. A small drop spills out over the edge of her mug and on to her skirt. 'Oh, bollocks,' she says quietly, rubbing at the spot.

'You know this marine conference my mum's going to? The one you're going to as well.'

'Er, yeah. I do,' she says. This time she gulps too much of her tea and almost chokes on it. 'Go on.'

'Well, I would be really fascinated to go. It's just the kind of thing I'd be interested in. Do you think I could go along?'

'Oh, hon. I'm not sure there'd be the space,' she says, just like I was afraid she would.

'Oh, that's too bad. Do you think maybe one of the others would want to give up their ticket? You know, maybe they're only going out of obligation or something.'

'Well, the thing is, hon, I think that the people who are going really want to go, you know?'

'Oh. So you really want to go, do you?'

'Sure do, hon. Can't wait.'

'And what about my mum? Do you think she's got her heart set on going?'

'Not only do I think she has her heart set on it, but I think it would be a crime to keep her away. Your mum has a whole wellful of knowledge and understanding in that area, and her passion for it has been sparked all over again. Would you honestly want to see her give that up?'

'No, I guess not,' I say, peering into my tea. My mum as a person with a whole wellful of knowledge and a huge passion for something. It's a concept I'm having some trouble absorbing.

'In any case,' says Eloise, leaning towards me and putting her hand on my knee, 'I'm pretty sure there's an age limit at this thing. I think you'll have to wait until you're eighteen.'

I can feel my opportunity slipping away. The opportun-ity to be in his company for three whole days. By the time we'd finished, I just know something would have happened. There'd be all those walks along the beach, all those slide shows in the dark where we'd be able to sit holding hands without anyone noticing. But instead of me enjoying all that, there will be my mother and her friends spending all that time with him.

Arseholes, I think. What a waste.

I must look more disappointed than I've meant to, because Eloise lifts up my chin with her index finger and says, with soft eyes, 'Come on, now. There's got to be more exciting things for a girl like you to do anyway? Tell me about this boyfriend of yours? Your mum says he's lovely.'

That's when I tell her all the things I haven't even told Mum yet. About Josh wanting to sleep with me, and me having thought I really wanted to, that I really might love him, then finding out that I didn't. I tell her about falling for someone else, and realising Josh wasn't for me, and about the way he looked when I broke up with him. I'm not sure why I tell her all this, except that she has this way of pulling you in. She's the sort of person you want to tell things to.

'But you absolutely can't tell my mother,' I say when I've finished, suddenly fearful that my indiscretion will lead to everything spiralling out of control. 'None of it. Especially the part about the new person.'

Eloise looks a little surprised, like she doesn't understand why I would tell her and not my mum. I don't fully understand it either.

'Please, Eloise. You have to promise.'

'Okay, hon. You have my word.' She rests her hand on top of mine. 'This guy has got to be pretty special to have turned your whole world upside down like this.'

'Oh, he is. He's so special sometimes I can't believe it when I look at him. He's not like anyone I've ever met.' Then I look down and feel my face redden at what I'm about to say. But I still say it, because somehow, saying it makes me feel just a little bit closer to having it. 'My heart feels full up when I'm around him. Like it could explode,' I say.

When I hear myself say these words, which immediately sound melodramatic and full of sentimentality to me, I'm half expecting her to laugh. But instead she just fans her face with her hand and says, 'My. That sure does sound like something special. Maybe you're right to keep that to yourself. The minute you tell anyone, sounds like they're all going to want a piece of him.'

LIBBY

The postman has to ring the doorbell as there's an oversized envelope in his stash. He greets me in the usual way ('All right, love?'), hands me the post, and marches off down the path. I stand watching him for a second. Actually, I'm not really watching him, I'm staring at the Morrisson's house across the street. It's rubbish collection day and there's a mountain of bulging black bin liners at the end of their path, not a single orange bag amongst them. I shake my head. The *Sunday Times* magazine's just informed us that we are all doomed, and the Morrissons don't even recycle!

Trying to contain my irritation, I head straight to the kitchen clutching my pile of envelopes. I've never been able to resist opening post the minute it arrives, with the eager anticipation of a child awaiting a birthday cheque. Most of the time it's a disappointment. Bills, circulars, bank statements, the odd catalogue. Today's post is more enticing than usual, with lots of different-sized envelopes. Tucked in the middle of the stack, in a slim white envelope, is the hotel confirmation. I recognise it immediately, before

I've even opened it, because of the pink Brighton Sands seal on the back – one of those that you can make at home with a kit. I run my finger along the seal, half expecting it to smear, and stand holding the envelope in my hands for a few minutes before I open it. I could chuck it, unopened, into the recycling bin, here and now. Instead, I open the envelope, retrieve the confirmation slip, and tuck it into my wallet behind the yellow Sparks Dry-Cleaning ticket, which reminds me to collect Rob's shirts.

Then I remember that I am supposed to be washing and ironing his shirts instead, because 'dry-cleaning means washing clothes in chemical solvents that are dangerous to workers in the dry-cleaning industry and harmful to the environment', and I suddenly feel quite tired.

Here's the question I've asked myself a thousand times: what am I going for? When my blood boils as I read an article about the destruction of marine species in the paper, I'm sure the reason has to do with marine ecology. As I sit in the study sifting through old research papers I've resurrected, papers I can hardly believe I had a hand in writing, I'm convinced it's professional pride making me go.

The reason I can't allow myself is Daniel. I cannot be going to Brighton for Daniel. When the fact of him confronts me, I shut it out with the force of a door being slammed shut. Sometimes I have to literally close my eyes, squeeze them together hard, to prevent my brain from being assaulted by his image.

PHOEBE

The day Rebecca goes into the clinic is the day of my French oral. I'm sure it's being conscious of being on time to meet her that makes me go blank when I reach the part where I have to describe my favourite film (It's *Cold Mountain* at the moment, for obvious reasons, but reasons that are obviously not going to be revealed during my French oral) and why it had an impact on me. Mme Lorizeau stares at me with hard eyes, not moving a muscle, and I can feel the words drifting further and further out of my reach. She must sense my panic, because her expression softens and she starts to prompt me with questions. Something clicks into place and I manage to stumble my way through to the end, though I forget to make the comparison with the book, which annoys me as it was the bit I'd worked hardest on.

The Marler Clinic is nice, a lot like the first clinic we went to, only much larger. It's so bright and upbeat you could almost convince yourself you're going in to have a pedicure instead of an abortion. Rebecca is already in a private room when I arrive. She's sitting up in a white gown on one of those metal beds with wheels, which will presumably be wheeled straight into the operating room. She's staring ahead with a kind of blank expression, like a barricade.

I stand by the side of the bed pulling the sheets straight. 'How are you feeling?' I ask, not knowing what else to say.

'All right, I guess,' she says, suddenly not looking all right at all. The blank expression has transformed into something altogether more wobbly.

'You don't have to go through with this if you don't want to. You can change your mind, you know,' I say. I'm not entirely sure this is true but it seems to me that she needs to feel she still has options. With something as momentous as this you just wouldn't want to feel trapped.

'No, I want to go through with it. I have to. I just want to get it over with so I can stop thinking about it. I just want to have it be over so I can go back to a normal life. Do you know what I mean?'

I smile and touch her gently on the arm. I can only imagine what she means, never having had to do anything this huge myself. Never having been in such an enormous mess that I was desperate to escape.

We are interrupted by two nurses. One of them tells me they're taking Rebecca to the operating room and asks me to wait for her down the hall. They quickly surround her, flicking levers and pushing buttons and arranging covers in preparation for wheeling the bed away, so it's difficult for me to get close to her to give her a hug. The best I can do is wave at her from the door before I disappear down the hall to the waiting room.

There are two other people in there. A woman about Mum's age, who's presumably waiting for her daughter. And a young bloke, no more than seventeen or eighteen. Maybe he's waiting for his girlfriend. What a thing to have to do. To wait while your girlfriend aborts the baby you've conceived together. I shudder at the thought of it, which seems somehow worse than the procedure itself. I can't imagine how a relationship would recover from it.

The woman is calmly flicking through magazines, just looking up every now and again when she hears someone pass by in the hall. The boy is agitated, his left leg jiggling up and down irritatingly. A couple of times he gets up and goes over to the water cooler and fills a plastic cup with water. He fills it right to the top and drinks it in one gulp, like he hasn't had a drink in days.

Looking at the woman makes me wonder how Mum would be in this situation. I close my eyes and try to imagine it, but I can't get a picture of it. I realise that I can't really get a picture of her at all at the moment. If someone asked me to describe her I'd be stuck, which is ridiculous because I've known her all my life, obviously. I used to think I had her figured out, and would be able to predict what she'd say or do in any given situation. Lately it seems she's become something amorphous that I just don't get.

None of us has to wait very long. It seems it doesn't take more than a few minutes to suck a foetus out of a womb. Within fifteen minutes both the woman and the boy have been summoned to the bedsides of their loved ones, and before long a nurse beckons to me from the door too.

The whole thing is quite surreal. One minute there's the possibility of a baby; fifteen minutes later, it's as if the whole thing never happened. Except that it's not. I can see that from Rebecca's face. There's outward relief in the set of her shoulders, the way she relaxes into the pillows rather than fighting against them, the way her hands are just lying in her lap rather than being wrung together. But there's something else alongside the relief. A kind of emptiness in her eyes.

I had wondered what I would be required to do, but it doesn't take me long to work it out. The doctor warned us that different girls react in different ways, some being immediately overcome with a kind of joyous relief, others feeling numbed by shock. It's clear that Rebecca's one of the latter, and that she'll not be capable of thinking for herself for the rest of the day. She sips the tea given to her by the nurses, puts on the clothes I lay out on the bed, and signs a bunch of forms that are placed in front of her as we leave. But she's not really all there. She leaves her copies of the forms on the counter and the nurse runs after us with them. She takes one look at Rebecca and hands them to me for safe-keeping.

We sit in silence for the whole of the train journey home. When we reach our stop, I have to prod Rebecca to get up. She'd probably be at bloody Stansted by now if I'd not been with her.

If anyone ever tries to tell you that abortion is no big deal, don't believe them. Take it from me: it's a big deal. I always knew that, in a way, from interviews I'd read, but now I really *know* it to be true. You only have to look into Rebecca's eyes to know.

The phone is ringing when I walk in the door, but by the time I reach it, the answering machine has clicked in and I can hear Auntie Liz's voice shouting. It sounds serious, so I pick up the receiver and cut into the message, even though the very last thing I feel like doing is speaking to someone, particularly when the someone is Auntie Liz.

'Hi, Liz? It's Phoebe? Liz, hello, it's me.'

There's a moment's confusion while Liz takes in the fact that she's now speaking to a person rather than a machine. Then she resumes her shouting where she'd left off.

'Phoebe, where's you mother? I need to speak to her.'

'I have no idea. I just got home,' I say, holding the receiver away from my ear and scowling at it. 'Can I give her a message?'

'Yes, you can. The sooner the better. Tell her

that her eighty-year-old father, who depends on her to visit every week, has been found wandering alone in the back streets of Winchester. Tell her the poor man was looking for her, because she was supposed to be there yesterday but she neglected to turn up. He was worried, so he went out looking for her, and nearly got himself run over in the process. Tell her I asked her what the bloody hell was she thinking!'

'Oh my God. Is Grandpa all right?'

'Just about, thank God. But he had a close call. More importantly, he's worried sick about Libby. Nothing anyone says to him can calm him down. He's convinced she's dead or in hospital some-where. Where the hell is she?'

'I don't know,' I say lamely, looking around for a note or any other sort of evidence as to Mum's whereabouts. My mind isn't working at top speed today, so I'm struggling to think what day it is, where she usually is. Then it occurs to me that I have no idea where she usually is anyway. She could be traipsing around handing out leaflets, or at the library, or in Brighton for all I know.

'Phoebe, this is important. She needs to call Dad. To see him, if she can. Can you find her?'

'I'll try,' I say, looking at my watch. It's five o'clock. Surely she'll be home soon. 'Maybe she's collecting Ella or Kate from somewhere. I'll try her mobile.'

'Don't bother. It's switched off, or she's just not responding. When she comes home, just tell her what's happened and get her to call me.' As an afterthought she adds, 'Please.'

This must be what it feels like to be on the opposite side to Auntie Liz in court. Bullied. Ready to do almost anything to get back on her good side. I'll bet even her clients are frightened of her. She doesn't even bother to say goodbye.

Mum finally gets home at nine o'clock, when everyone else has been back for hours. Kate gets dropped off from hockey, and Dad collects Ella from Lilly's then sets about making supper. He's getting quite good at it now, though it would be stretching the point to say he enjoys it.

When Mum walks in, all I have to say is, 'Liz called. She's very upset,' and she stops dead in her tracks, her hand flying to her open mouth to stifle a gasp. She knows what's happened before I tell her.

'Oh my God. I forgot all about Dad. Didn't I? Jesus, what's happened?'

So I tell her everything Auntie Liz told me. I'd expected to get some satisfaction from this, but when I see the colour drain from her face and her eyes crinkle up with worry and realise how sickened she is, I almost feel sorry for her. When she says, 'How could I have done that? How could I forget?' I'm tempted to tell her not to worry about it, that she's got a lot on her plate and forgetting is only human and Grandpa will be all right.

What comes out sounds more like Auntie Liz

310

than I intend. Even Dad sounds like Auntie Liz. Only Ella comes forward to take mum's side. She walks over to where mum's standing and leans against her, silently slipping her arm through mum's, as if to tell her it's a mistake anyone could make. The rest of us just stand there. It's like we're doing one big collective *I told you so.*

LIBBY

As if to emphasise my disgrace, the sun is glaring down from an unforgiving, cloud-free sky, conspiring with the malfunctioning air conditioning to turn the car into a mobile oven. It's only eleven in the morning but my chest is already sticky and glistening with sweat. Early June can be like that. Then the summer holidays come along and you get nothing but grey skies and drizzle.

It took me some time to amass the courage to call Liz last night. Hearing Phoebe describe how angry she'd been took me back to being eleven or twelve, listening to her berate me about something stupid I'd said, something ridiculous I was wearing. She's always had the ability to make me feel small and inadequate. The years have dampened the effects of her scorn, but not eradicated them.

I looked for some sign in the others' eyes, some signal that what I'd done was understandable if not completely forgivable. But none of them threw me the lifeline I wanted. None of them gave me any sympathy. Thinking about it now, I was naïve even to look for it. No one forgives a mother when she messes up, least of all her own children.

Almost as soon as I pull into the drive, Mrs Tupper is standing at the door. It was she who found Dad yesterday, wandering around the back-streets of Winchester looking for the daughter he was sure had been kidnapped or murdered. Apparently he went into M&S and asked for me; he'd remembered my stint there as a student twenty-six years before and was convinced he might still find me in Ladies' Underwear.

Mrs Tupper's disapproval of my modern-day green nonsense is nothing to the condemnation she's about to dish out, that much is clear. Instead of greeting me with her brusque but friendly hello, she stands leaning on the door frame with her substantial arms folded indignantly across her ample bosom like a couple of meaty chicken legs on a mound of mashed potato. There's not even the faintest trace of a smile on her lips.

'Hello, Mrs Tupper. I'm so sorry you've had to deal with all this,' I say as I climb out of the car. Surely if I apologise at the outset she'll be unable to maintain such a high level of animosity.

Not so, evidently. Her arms remain folded, her expression stern.

'Well, at least you're here now. At least he'll be able to rest some.'

I offer a feeble smile as I squeeze past her into the house. 'Dad?' I shout. 'I'm here.'

When I walk into the kitchen and see him sitting in his chair, that's when it hits me what I've put him through. He seems shrunken. His eyes are rimmed with red, his cheeks hollow. When I kneel down in front of him, he leans his forehead on mine and begins to shudder, tears streaming down his cheeks.

'Thank God you're here. I thought . . .'

'I know, Dad. I know. But I'm fine. Nothing has happened to me. I just . . .'

I just what? Forgot to come? Forgot about him? Temporarily lost my mind? Got so wrapped up in my own life that I didn't give him a second thought for an entire week?

'I had so much going on that I forgot what day it was,' I venture inadequately. 'How silly is that? Even Ella remembers what day it is!'

I squeeze his hands between mine, then reach up and wipe the tears from his face. 'I'm so sorry, Dad. I'm so sorry for the worry I've caused you. I love you so much.'

He smiles at these words. A generous smile that crinkles up the skin around his eyes into soft folds. All the others might hate me, I think, but he's going to forgive me instantly.

'I'm just glad you're safe, love,' he says, squeezing my hand this time.

His instant forgiveness has a strange, emboldening effect on me. Instead of feeling guilty but relieved, as you might expect, I experience a momentary flash of self-righteousness. I am the good girl, the one who never caused him and Mum any trouble, the kind one, the one who stayed home to help while the other two were out God knows where with Christ knows who. I'm the one who's turned up here every week without fail, while Jaime has had her hands deep in clay and Liz has hers chock-full of court summons. If he can see that so readily, why is it no one else can?

I straighten up from my kneeling position. 'Right. I'm going to go out to the car and get the things I brought,' I announce. 'I brought some lovely french bread and pâté and the sweetest cherry tomatoes you'll ever taste for lunch today. Would you like that?'

I feel steadily better as the day progresses. We eat a nice cheering lunch, at which even Mrs Tupper begrudgingly acknowledges the deliciousness of the tomatoes. Dad and I spend some time turning and compressing the compost heap in the garden and cutting up an old sheet into tiny squares for Mrs Tupper to use as dusters. Then we sit for a long while under the apple tree, sipping lemonade. By the end of the day he's fully recovered, as far as I can tell. By the end of the day, I've almost completely forgotten my misdemeanour.

Almost, but not quite. There's an aspect of the crime that lingers behind to haunt me. It's not that I forgot him, or that my forgetfulness caused him such distress. Anyone can be forgiven for being so busy and distracted that they occasionally lose the plot. What I can't forgive myself for is the thing that's distracted me.

Because although it's true that the preparations for the rally, the canvassing, the organising, the

endless phone calls to City Hall, even my nervousness at the prospect of attending a professional conference for the first time in almost
twenty years have made me remote and preoc-
cupied, that's not the whole truth. It's not even
half of it.

PHOEBE

The funniest thing has happened. I'd never have predicted it, not in a million years. Rebecca and Gabriel. In the space of a week they've become an item.

Gabriel's been growing on me. At first, when I realised he'd been one of those people I'd seen on that TV documentary, I figured we'd have nothing in common. He's quite shy and a bit awkward, which makes him difficult to talk to. But once he's been around you for a while he loosens up and you discover that he's actually really funny. A couple of weeks ago we had such a laugh, him, Harry, Courtney and me. Courtney was making fun of Harry's accent, then she started in on me. So Gabriel did an imitation of her that had us all rolling on the floor. The nice thing was, no one seemed to get offended. Courtney even did an impression of herself. They're a good bunch of people really. Not at all what you expect when you first meet them. I've even got used to Courtney's hair, though I would never wear it like that myself. And I swear her skin's been better since she's been eating the meals Mum brings her.

All of us were supposed to do some canvassing in the village. Daniel asked us to, and no one refuses Daniel, least of all me. At school that day Rebecca had seemed really down and she'd asked if she could come over, so I told her she could go along with the rest of us.

I could tell Gabriel fancied her from the minute we walked up to the rest of them. I think he could tell she wasn't feeling so hot, though of course he wouldn't have had a clue as to why. He invited her to go stand with him on the corner of Elm and Connor. When we all met up again an hour later it was as though they'd known each other for ever. He spoke to her really gently, like he knew that's what she needed.

I read somewhere that people always choose mates that look like them. Personally, I think people grow to look like each other. Like Brad Pitt and Jennifer Aniston. Suddenly, you noticed they had the same-shaped faces, the same pointy chins and hamster cheeks. And Sean Connery's wife seems to grow more like him every year – tanned and fierce-looking, only with hair.

Gabriel and Rebecca have both got this slightly wan, freckly, blonde look going on. And there's something a bit fragile about them both, but when they stand next to one another they look somehow stronger, like a whole. I'm happy for her. I know it's only been a week, and it could all go wrong, but it's just what she needs to take her mind off things and get her back on track.

My own mind (when it hasn't been dreaming up romantic scenarios involving me and Daniel) has been focused on the accumulation of knowledge. Not just any knowledge, but knowledge that will get me somewhere. I found two books by Mum's bed: *The Reluctant Environmentalist* and *Save the Planet*, of which I've committed large chunks to memory.

The information has already come in handy. The other day, when some of us were making fact sheets for the rally, we were having a conversation about what environmental facts and figures we ought to be putting on them. I suddenly remembered that the air indoors is ten times as polluted as the air outdoors, and that the average home contains thirty-five hazardous chemicals. When I said this out loud, Daniel stopped what he was doing at the table next to us and said, 'Well, look who's a fountain of knowledge now! What else have you got up your sleeve?'

So I kept going. All this stuff poured out of me, as though a tap had been turned on. Stuff about sustainable energy sources and water purification and GM foods. In the end we were all messing about, competing with each other to see who could come up with the best statistic. The entire time I was conscious of Daniel's body beside me. I could almost feel the heat from his legs, which were about a foot away from mine. Amidst the craziness of the competing voices, it was his I was always conscious of: strong, sensual, full of depth.

I love the way he laughs, throwing his head back like he really means it.

When I'm feeling wildly optimistic I tell myself something has *got* to happen between us. I've never once set my sights on someone and not had them fall for me. Not once. I only had to look at Josh and he was mine. Came over from where he was standing and talked to me like I was the only person in the room, for the whole evening. It was the same with Ben, who dropped Sally Prince the day after he heard I had a thing for him.

But I'm not always wildly optimistic. Quite often I'm depressed and discouraged. I'm not used to feeling so unsure, but then, the stakes have never been so high.

LIBBY

There's a box on my pillow. It's a tiny blue box adorned with a small white card tucked beneath a silver ribbon. There is obviously something small and expensive inside it.

I sit down heavily on the bed and try to recall all the times Rob has presented me with unexpected gifts during our marriage. When we were first together he would sometimes come home with odd little things – a beaded necklace from Camden market, or a gilded shell from an out-of-the-way gift shop he'd stumbled upon. After Phoebe was born and I was beside myself with exhaustion and the flat was littered with the little babygrows and cardigans people had given her, I remember he came home with a beautiful cashmere scarf for me. It was duck-egg-blue, and the softest, most luxurious thing I'd ever owned. He wrapped it around my neck and kissed the tip of my nose and said, 'Because I love you.' I remember it so clearly, almost as if it were yesterday.

But birthdays, anniversaries, Mother's Days – these have been hit-or-miss occasions. Sometimes he remembers and gives me something carefully chosen and lovely, other years it's a hurriedly chosen card and a pot plant. Once, just once, he came home with some plastic-looking pink mums wrapped in cellophane from the garage. I swear he looked shame-faced as he was presenting them to me, before I'd even begun to convey my own disapprobation. Nothing quite that awful has ever been proffered again, but I have had to learn to live with the ups and downs of gifts.

But gifts out of nowhere, for no apparent reason? These are rare indeed, and have been for at least ten years. Maybe more. The little blue box on my pillow is so surprising it's very nearly frightening.

I pick up the box and hold it in the palm of my hand. I pull at one end of the ribbon, but stop myself before the bow unravels completely and place the box on the bed. I can't open it just yet.

The rest of the bed is littered with T-shirts, jeans, a couple of skirts, a few pairs of knickers and a bra. On the floor lies the striped, multicoloured zip-up bag I plan to stuff it all into. That was a gift from Rob, for some occasion or other that I can't now recall.

The trip to Brighton is tomorrow, and before I spotted the little blue box I was quite happily packing for it. But now I'm paralysed, and suddenly the task of placing all these clothes into that bag seems inordinately challenging. I'm just not sure I can do it.

When I do finally open the box, I find a wide, angular, silver ring with a single topaz embedded in it. The stone is very nearly the same colour as the cashmere scarf, which I still have, though I hardly wear it any more.

The card says 'Because I love you' and I really wonder what to make of it.

PHOEBE

It's weird watching Mum heaving her bag into the taxi, turning to wave goodbye. I don't think it's a sight I've ever seen before. She's ever been away anywhere on her own without at least one of us in tow.

The good thing about the past few months is that her going isn't quite such a shock to the system as it would have been. She's been a little bit gone for a while now. Dad's quite adept at meal preparation, if you're willing to count eggs in all their variations as actual meals outside of breakfast time. Kate just gets on with things, and by some miracle, Ella seems able to find her own ballet shoes and gym kit when she needs them. *And* I've worked out how to use the washing machine. I got tired of finding the top I needed still squashed at the bottom of my laundry basket. Also, it has to be said that on one or two occasions, something that's gone into the wash has failed to come out of it. All things considered, looking after my own laundry has looked like the least painful option.

It's not really the physical stuff that's going to be difficult with her gone for three days. It's more that there's a kind of strange silence in the house when she's not in it. Don't get me wrong. There's plenty of actual noise, but it's like the soft hum that's normally at the centre of it disappears.

The worst thing was watching Dad say goodbye to her. She gave him a kiss and held up the chain around her neck to show him, the one where she's put the ring he just gave her. I don't know why she doesn't just wear it on her finger. He didn't seem to know what to do then. He stood there like some gauche teenage boy, smiling in a way that looked to me like a cross between worry and puzzlement. His mouth did a good impression of a smile but his eyes were squinty and narrow, the way they get when he's trying to work something out.

Me? All I can really think about is how Daniel is going to be a hundred miles away for three days. There's a lot going on. Laura's having some people over tomorrow night, and there's a big rowing regatta during the day. I'm going to check in on Rebecca at some point as well. So I'll be busy, but that's not really the point.

LIBBY

I've been so caught up in my story about going to Brighton with a crowd that I'm startled when I see him standing there alone on the platform at Victoria Station. It occurs to me that the story was for my benefit all along.

He's squinting up at the departures board like about a hundred other people, his rucksack lying on the ground at his feet. I come up beside him and give his waist a playful squeeze.

'Oh, hi,' he says, breaking into a grin. 'You shouldn't do that to people. You could give them a heart attack.'

'*Last call for the London to Brighton at sixteen thirty-five, departing from platform nine,*' says an invisible man over the loudspeaker, his instructions rendered almost inaudible by the crackling and whining of the microphone.

'Come on, we'd better hurry,' Daniel says, picking up his rucksack and grabbing me by the arm.

We tear along the concourse towards platform nine, only tearing is difficult for me because I've overpacked the striped zip-up bag. I had a last-minute panic attack about being the only one in a skirt when everyone else was in old T-shirts and jeans, or having only jeans to wear in the evening while everyone else struck just the right note of casual elegance in dresses and skirts, so I packed everything, or pretty damn near it. Round about platform six Daniel becomes aware of my difficulties and grabs the bag from me, which makes tearing immeasurably easier.

In fact the man with the loudspeaker was exaggerating, because we reach the train with plenty of time to spare. We actually sit there for at least five minutes before the clunking and grinding of the wheels signals our depart-ure.

The carriage is full, which is to be expected given the forecast of perfect weather. Who wouldn't want to be by the sea on a sunny weekend in June if they had the chance? Certainly, the family across the aisle from us are anticipating uninterrupted sunshine and blue skies. All six of them are wearing shorts and sun hats, and the group is kitted out with buckets, spades and fishing-net paraphernalia in every conceivable colour. I wonder how that's done, I think. Whenever we make an excursion to the sea, we can't seem to lay our hands on any of the buckets and spades we've purchased over the years, so we end up replacing the lot.

Daniel and I exchange a surreptitious smile about the bucket and spade brigade, then he fishes a bottle of water out of his knapsack. He takes a swig before offering it to me.

'Thanks, I'm parched,' I say, taking a sip. While

I'm drinking I experience a momentary flutter somewhere between my chest and stomach at the thought that my lips are going where his have just been. This is ridiculous, I think to myself. I can't keep this up for three whole days.

'It's going to be really great, this weekend,' he says. 'Do you want to see the programme? And the advance reading notes?'

'Oh, sure,' I say, taking the stack of papers he hands to me. 'How did you get hold of these?'

'Friends in high places,' he says, grinning. 'Most people will get them when they register tonight, but I asked a friend on the organising committee to send me a couple of sets in advance. I kind of like to know what I'm getting into.'

Yes. So do I, mate. So do I, I think, staring down at the papers on my lap. I don't know what unnerves me more at this moment: the prospect of having to take in all this information and make coherent conversation about it after all these years, or the sight of his hand resting on the leg of his jeans, just inches away from mine.

We sit reading for most of the journey, like an old married couple. Occasionally he offers me the water bottle, and twice I offer him a piece of Wrigley's spearmint gum, but we're otherwise pretty focused on our reading material.

At least that's the outward impression I'm giving. My insides are actually sloshing around like the poor fish in one of those plastic bags you win at fairgrounds. Only, unlike the fish, who can expect to be rescued from the child's hands and placed to rest on a firm surface before long, there will be no respite for me. I suspect I'll be struggling with insides that refuse to stay still for most of the weekend.

The conference is at the Brighton Centre, next door to an enormous, nondescript hotel – big, white, with hundreds of identical windows, half of which overlook the car park or the busy main road. It may be nondescript, but it's expensive, so we're not staying there. Brighton Sands is a small eight-room hotel run by a Mrs Bartholomew, about a mile to the west of the town centre near Hove.

Mrs Bartholomew is a sight to behold, not at all the broad-breasted homey woman with soft white curls and flowery apron that I expect her to be. She comes to reception in a strappy orange sundress that doesn't even pretend to cover the top of her black lace bra. Her hair is shoulder-length and bright, blinding blonde, and her tan looks as though it's been worked on in a booth. She smiles at us through shiny lips the colour of strawberry *Hubba Bubba*.

'Hello!' she says flamboyantly as she squeezes past us to stand behind the worn pine table that serves as a front desk. 'Welcome.'

'Hi,' we say, quietly and in unison. Then Daniel bends down to retrieve the letter confirming the booking from his rucksack, and Mrs Bartholomew takes the opportunity to stare at his bottom before smoothing her hair and patting her bosom in funny fluttery movements.

Daniel and I stand in the hall with our bags at our feet, not sure where to go next. She smiles at us both. 'I've reserved two lovely rooms for you. Mrs Blake, you are in the room just at the top of the stairs. Mr Carr, you are up another floor, first door on the right.'

I hate it when people call me Mrs. It makes me feel old.

'Will you both be wanting newspapers in the morning?' she asks, handing us each our keys. She's looking at us inquisitively, not because she's beside herself with curiosity about whether or not we will want papers, I'm sure, but because she can't figure out what we are to one another. Aunt and nephew? Friends? Mother and son? Surely not.

'That would be great,' I say, and Daniel nods. 'We'll head up and get ready now. We're going over to the marine conference at the Brighton Centre.'

'Oh!' she exclaims, obviously relieved to have us all worked out. 'You both work for one of those green organisations, do you?'

'Something like that,' says Daniel, who's already halfway up the stairs and seems in a hurry to escape Mrs Bartholomew's grasp.

Daniel drops my bag outside my door and continues along the hall towards the next set of stairs. 'There's registration over at the Centre this evening, and we can have a look around, get the lie of the land. We'll head over in about half an hour, yeah?' he says. He's turned to look at me and is walking backwards, straight into an artificial fern. 'Oops,' he says, smiling and patting the leaves as if to placate them. 'Better watch out for the foliage.'

'That's not all you'd better watch out for,' I say, stifling a smirk. 'I'd keep my door double-locked if I were you.'

'Too right,' he says.

At five to seven there's a knock on my bedroom door. I do a quick spin on the spot, checking to make sure I've left nothing intimate on display. Lucky I've thought to do so, because there's a pair of knickers on full view in the middle of the carpet. I reach down and stuff them in a drawer, then tuck my new ring on a chain inside my shirt before opening the door.

Daniel's leaning on the railings opposite my room, arms folded. He breaks into a broad grin when he sees me. 'All set?' he asks.

'Oh, sure. Just let me grab my bag,' I say, ducking back into my room. 'Do you think I need a sweater?' I shout from inside.

'I would. Can get pretty breezy by the water in the evening.' His voice is louder, closer than I expect. I turn to see him standing just inside the door. Actually in my bedroom. Where I'm going to sleep later. The implied intimacy makes me blush.

I grab the first sweater I find from the pink chair

in the corner of the room and hurry towards the door. As I shut it and turn the key in the lock he asks, 'Shall we take the bus or are you up for a walk?'

'How far is it, do you think?'

'About a mile. Give or take.'

'I can do that,' I say, flourishing my flat, comfortable loafers as evidence.

'Good. Let's go for it.'

Mrs Bartholomew is nowhere in sight, thank God, so our exit from the hotel is speedy and unwitnessed. I have no desire to be watched by Mrs Bartholomew, to have her ruminating over what I'm up to when I'm not even sure what I'm up to myself.

Our walk takes us along the quiet lane where the hotel is situated, along a slightly bigger lane and then on to a much busier main road. Daniel is convinced this will lead us directly to the waterfront, and he's right. As we near the end of the road, a bright blue vista opens up. The sea is twinkling with a thousand diamonds in the early evening sun. Tiny orange and yellow triangles are dotted about in the near distance, the sails of small boats heading back towards the shore.

We walk at a brisk pace along the waterfront, a shoulder-width apart, his hands in his jeans pockets, mine swinging by my side.

'You sail?' he asks after a few minutes of silence.

'A little. I used to. Not much opportunity now. How about you?'

'Same. I did it a lot as a kid, and I spent six months working as an instructor at a kid's camp in Canada when I was nineteen. That was a great summer.'

'You really love Canada, don't you?'

'Yeah. One day I might end up living there. Shame about the winter, though. Cold enough to freeze your balls off,' he says, dead pan.

I laugh. Then we are silent again.

'What will we do for dinner?' I say, stepping aside to avoid being ploughed down by a roller blading maniac coming up on my inside.

'There's a meet-and-greet dinner, buffet style, which we might want to go to.' He looks at me questioningly. 'Then again, maybe not?'

'Maybe not,' I say, laughing again.

We walk for around twenty minutes before spotting the massive grey stone building that is the Brighton Centre. Seeing it, I suddenly feel queasy with nerves. Probably like the girls all felt on their first day of school. Like I haven't felt in a very long time.

The lobby of the centre is busy but not overwhelmingly crowded, humming but not oppressively noisy. This calms me a little. We spot the registration desk, at which there is a small group of people milling around, and make our way towards it. Seemingly without thinking, Daniel takes my hand to lead me towards it. Without thinking, I let him. Then, obviously thinking very quickly, he drops my hand, and I see the reason why.

'Daniel, my son! How the hell are you?' exclaims Derek, giving Daniel a bear hug.

'Good, great. How are you?'

'Never better.' Then he turns to me. 'We've met before, haven't we?'

'Yes,' I reply, feeling a peculiar combination of pleasure and discomfort. On the one hand, I'm pleased to be someone worth remembering; on the other, I'm rather desperate for some anonymity this weekend. Just until I find my feet. (Also, it has to be said, because information has a way of leaking out into the atmosphere, making its mysterious way to remote places. Places like Richmond, for example.)

'Libby is a key member of the Green Link local action group in Richmond. Remember that meeting?' says Daniel eagerly. 'She's doing a fabulous job masterminding an environmental rally in a local park. And she's no slouch on the marine science front either.'

Masterminding? Me? I think.

'Pleased to meet you again, Libby. Listen, if all this really appeals, you should think about getting involved with our marine activity at a national level. We could use a spot of expertise,' he says generously, and apparently oblivious to my embarrassment in the wake of Daniel's gushing introduction. He suspects nothing beyond the obvious, obviously. Why would he?

'Anyway, I've a quick meeting to get to before supper. We'll catch up over the weekend,' says Barry, slapping Daniel on the shoulder. 'Really great to see you, my man.' Then he backs up and disappears through a group of new delegates crouching under the weight of their enormously intimidating backpacks. The sort of backpacks you carry when you've spurned the creature comforts the rest of us take for granted to spend your entire life on the road doing meaningful work for no material reward whatsoever.

I turn back towards the registration desk so as to avoid having to converse with the fiercely committed ones. Daniel must sense my discomfort, because he smiles and nods his head in their direction, rolling his eyes good-naturedly. I know for a fact that he'd be perfectly at home talking to any of them, just as he's perfectly comfortable working alongside the likes of Ron and Barry and Julia Harding. The eye-rolling is for my benefit, and mine alone.

After registration (which takes an age as they can't seem to find my name at first) we spend a few minutes gaping at the giant information board at the opposite side of the lobby, trying to decipher the itinerary for the next two days. There are lectures with titles like 'Successful Sustainability Programmes' and 'The Politics and Economics of Marine Ecology'. Daniel points out a couple of must-attend lectures and discussion groups – 'He's fantastic, that guy. Really knows his stuff' – and scribbles a few things down in his notebook. I'm so overwhelmed by the list of topics and session leaders that it's all I can do to continue gawking up at it. There are more M.Sc.s in Marine Botany and Ph.D.s in Aquatic Culture on that board than you can shake a test tube at. Did I really used to aspire to be one of them, and to understand this kind of stuff? And love it?

Itinerary absorbed, we head up the broad staircase towards the large room where the buffet supper is being served. We poke our noses into a room in which the chairs around the large round tables are gradually filling up with delegates bearing plates of cold meats and salads. Most people are talking quietly and reservedly, getting to know one another, but I notice one table near the buffet that is in positively raucous form, and it's only eight-thirty. We stand on the threshold of this horrifying sight for a few seconds, then Daniel leans down and whispers in my ear.

'Let's blow this pop stand. Find something smaller.'

Without even waiting for my answer, he places his hand on my lower back and gently pushes me away from the doors and in the direction of the staircase. Relief takes hold, and I sprint with him down the stairs, across the vast lobby and out of the building. We stand on its front steps for a few minutes, gazing out into the darkening night sky. To our left, twinkling like a jewelled palace, is the aptly named Palace Pier.

'Perfect,' he says. 'Let's head over there.'

Cosy in the sweaters we've thought to bring, we sit side by side at a café on the pier devouring fish and chips. My preschool nerves and fear of earnest backpackers are washed clear away by the bottles of Stella, the stars, and the tinkling of the merry-go-round nearby. Our conversation is easy and relaxed again, and I begin to feel like the woman I was yesterday.

This is absolutely perfect, I think. Then my heart does a little leap when he leans in towards me and I'm sure he's going to touch my cheek, perhaps even kiss me. Instead, he picks up the chip I've dropped in my lap and puts it in his mouth with a playful smile, and my heart does a big leap this time. At the mere idea of a shared chip. You have to wonder what would have happened if he'd fed the chip to me instead.

And it's then that it really hits me. What I've done. What I'm doing. What I'm planning to do. But I don't think I'm being too melodramatic when I say that I feel powerless to stop this train.

My pulse is racing. My heart is leaping about inside my chest, and my breathing is, I realise, quite shallow. My synapses are firing off wildly, making all sorts of random connections.

And this isn't because Daniel's thigh is gently pressing against mine, though that is admittedly very nice. Or because I can feel the rhythm of his breathing as he sits beside me, eyes fixed on the speaker at the front of the room. Rather, it seems to be a response to a lecture on a pollution control programme in the Baltic Sea.

My body is ecstatic at the opportunities now being presented to my brain. My brain itself, while perilously close to overload, is joining in the celebrations. Neither can quite believe their luck.

I can't remember the last time my brain was stretched, teased and played with this way. The last time I actually had to work at understanding something. The last time I felt that peculiar satisfaction of understanding dawning. I remember being pretty chuffed with myself when I finally mastered the art of sticky-back plastic-ing, getting my time down to one and a half minutes per book and without any swearing, but that was nothing compared with the feeling I have today.

It's the third session of the morning. The first was a presentation about a programme to rejuvenate some Canadian sponge gardens (uninspiringly titled 'British Columbian Sponge Gardens: Adverse Human Impacts and Human Interventions'), and the second was a session on the reintroduction of locally extinct life forms to some wet grasslands in Olendorf, Germany. The preservation and reintroduction of species was what I'd focused on at university, to the extent that you can focus on anything at B.A. level. So it isn't long into the session before I'm getting all hot and bothered by the sight of fire-bellied toads and warty newts cavorting in grassy wetlands from which they've been extinct for a decade.

We'd been a little late for the first session, having dawdled a trifle too long over our breakfast of coffee, toast and an egg boiled to perfection, under the watchful eye of Mrs Bartholomew ('Please,

338

call me Linda'). Linda served our breakfast wearing another cleavage-revealing sundress, this one in bright pink. When she bent over to place Daniel's egg in front of him, she hovered there for a moment straightening his napkin, her breasts heaving next to his ear. I think she is very, very disappointed not to have made any headway with Daniel despite her quite heroic efforts.

So absorbed have I been by the morning sessions that lunchtime takes me by surprise. We decide that lunch will be a sandwich each and a shared tub of strawberries, taken on the lush green grass of the Old Stein, a park with a beautiful view of the Royal Pavilion, with its stunning white domes and minarets. We find a spot under a chestnut tree which must be forty feet tall, and dive immediately into the plastic bags containing the sandwiches, both of us ravenous.

'So what did you make of that fellow, Doctor Verboost?' Daniel asks, wiping a spot of mayo from the side of his mouth. 'A bit hard to follow, wasn't he?'

'A bit, I suppose. Typical scientist. But I thought his project was amazing. I mean, the persistence of that team has to be applauded, if nothing else. All those frogs they lost, and all those people telling them it would never work, and they just ploughed on. Then their funds dried up but they somehow managed to magic up some money from somewhere else. Amazing.'

'Yeah, you're right. And when you think about

it, there must be thousands of teams like his, each working feverishly and against huge amounts of opposition and scepticism and just sheer indifference to preserve one small aspect of marine life. You'd think that with all that dedicated effort and brainpower we could bring about more change on a larger scale. You know, to stop fucking up the poor bastard fish and frogs in the first place.'

'Well, you're just like them,' I say.

'How do you mean?' he asks, raising his eyebrows.

'Dedicated. Ploughing on against all the odds and opposition. It's just that you do it on land.'

'Yeah, I guess. But I haven't been doing it very long. Six years is nothing. These guys have been at it for decades.'

'What did you do before. Before the six years? You've never told me.'

'I did a short stint at Procter and Gamble after university, if you can believe it. Lasted about eight months before cracking up.' He shakes his head and laughs. 'I mean, fuck me. Have you ever met anyone less likely to fit in at Procter and Gamble?'

'No, I don't think I have,' I say, laughing too. I try to picture him wearing a corporate haircut and a fine wool suit. I can't.

Daniel lies back and stretches out, his head resting on his folded arms. I lie on my side, propped up on my elbow. Above us, the sunlight filters through the clusters of pale green leaves hanging from drooping branches. Occasionally a gust parts the branches and the sun bursts through, splashing white and gold puddles on to the grass between us. We stay like this for a few minutes talking about the morning, some of the people we've talked to, the sessions we'll attend tomorrow. Then, out of the blue, he says, 'God, you're great, Libby. Really great.'

'Thank you,' I say. 'So are you.'

He looks away for a few seconds, apparently deep in thought. Then he leans up on his elbow and looks at me, hard, and I think that maybe he's going to say something profound and challenging about the ecosystem, but instead he says, 'Libby, is it just me, or is there something big going on here?'

I pause before replying, looking down. I could so easily deflect him, give us both a way out of this impossible situation.

'No, it's not just you,' I say. I know that these five tiny words have removed all doubt, and with it all hope of an easy, uncomplicated ending. But, like I said before, this train's going full throttle and I can't locate the emergency handle anywhere.

'I think I might go crazy if I don't kiss you soon,' he says next.

I smile at him, drawing out the moment. It's such a delicious thing to have someone say to you; I want to savour it. I repeat it in my head, twice. Finally I say, 'We can't have that. There's the lecture on Ethics in Science and Environmental Politics to get through yet. You'll need all of your faculties for that one.'

He laughs, then does the thing we've probably both been waiting for him to do for weeks. His lips hover close to mine for a minute, and I smell the strawberries on his breath, then he kisses me. A sweet, undemanding kiss, but enough of a kiss to make me think, Thank Christ we're in a crowded public park in broad daylight or we'd be in all kinds of trouble.

Which is what he says, collapsing back on to the grass.

PHOEBE

alf the free world will be at the regatta. I'm
sincerely hoping that Josh will be in the
other half. I don't want a scene. As insurance against a scene I plan to surround myself. I'm
going with Alice and Laura and Chloe. I've also
invited Rebecca, much to Alice's chagrin. Alice really
has a thing against Rebecca, but I've told her she
needs to get over it. Rebecca's nice, I've decided;
not nearly as bad as the impression she gives.

We need to take a bus to get to the best spot
on the river, where there are drinks stands and
loads of people. The girls come to my house first
to get ready, then we all head out together. It's
scorching hot. I make Rebecca wear sunscreen.
With her skin she'd be a beetroot in about five
seconds.

Kate asks if she can come, but I'm very firm.
She gets way more upset than she normally would,
maybe because Mum's away and she's got nothing
very much organised for the weekend. But it's still
a no. I can't be worried about watching out for
my little sister for the whole afternoon.

I sit next to Rebecca, and Laura and Alice sit

squashed into a seat on the opposite side of the aisle. We're lucky to get seats at all, because the bus is packed out with people, each of them lugging about five bags of shopping. There's a wailing baby in front of us. He's a really sweet little black child with big round eyes and fat cheeks. But he's very loud, so his allure wears off after a bit. I'm just thinking how I wish his mother would get off at the next stop when I look up and into a familiar face standing in the aisle.

'Hello, Phoebe! Fancy seeing you 'ere' says Michelle. 'Hey Courtney, look.'

'Hiya,' says Courtney. 'Where're you off to then?' She's wearing an insipid yellow tank top that's a bit too tight for her slightly plump body and doesn't look quite right with the pink velour tracky bottoms.

Talking on trains and buses is always tricky. The minute you speak it seems the whole place falls silent and ears are tuned for superior audio reception. Even the blessed baby stops crying, and his mother, the nerve of her, turns around and gives us a censorious look.

'We're going to a regatta,' I say. In the excruciating noiselessness of the bus, the words suddenly sound foreign, even to me.

'A wot?' says Michelle, laughing. 'What's a flamin' brigatta when it's at home?'

I can't see Alice and Chloe's faces, but Laura is peering through the triangle created by Courtney's hand-on-hip pose looking mildly horrified.

'Oh, it's a sort of boat race. Only they set up

stands where you can buy drinks and stuff. It's fun. You should come.'

Laura looks really horrified then. Like she might kill me. I'm not sure why I invited Michelle and Courtney to the regatta, except that it somehow felt churlish not to. But there's no way they'll come.

'Sounds great,' says Michelle unconvincingly, 'but we've gotta be somewhere else. My brother's having a barbecue later on. We're going to Asda to pick up some food for him.'

'Oh,' I say. Then I notice Alice leaning forward to get a look at Courtney and Michelle, and watch as an unkind smile creeps on to her lips. She turns to Laura and mouths something I make out as 'pikey'.

'Oh, Alice, Laura, Chloe and Rebecca, I should introduce you to Courtney and Michelle. They're friends of mine from Green Link.'

There's no handshaking, or even any actual exchange of hellos (except from Rebecca), just a lot of quiet nodding. The stern, disapproving look has gone from Laura's face though. They all look rather stunned.

'Anyway, we're off 'ere,' says Michelle, nudging Courtney towards the exit doors. 'Bye.'

'Bye,' I say, adding, 'See you next week,' and a wave for emphasis.

I'm expecting Alice to lean forward and say, 'Phoebe, *who* were *they*?' but she doesn't. No one says anything for a minute or two, until Rebecca announces, 'Gabriel says they're really good value, those two.'

345

Then she leans across me and whispers to the others, 'Gabriel is this guy I've been seeing. Did Phoebe tell you about him?'

The other three lean forward to listen to Rebecca, who is giddily eager to spill the beans. Only after the first sentence I can't really hear what she's saying on account of the burning sensation in my cheeks and the tightening of my throat. I grab on to the metal bar in front of my seat, just to feel something solid.

Then I look again, just to make sure. There, just opposite the place where the number 93 has stalled in traffic, arranging a pink and turquoise sundress on a mannequin in the window of her shop, is Eloise. She's not in Brighton after all.

Rebecca notices immediately that something is wrong, but I tell her it's nothing, that I must have eaten some squiffy prawns. Then, when we arrive, Laura says to me, 'Are you OK? You seem really quiet?' 'I'm fine,' I respond. 'Just really tired.'

It's a relief when we are swallowed up by the hoards of people milling about on the river banks and I can escape their scrutiny. We have to fight for a small patch of grass where we can lay out our pathetic picnic of store-bought sandwiches and crisps (other people have arrived equipped with elaborately constructed picnic tables and chairs and great hampers filled with smoked salmon and champagne). We've hardly been seated five seconds when we spot Charlie and his crowd standing by the river just ahead of us. Alice calls out to them and they beckon for us to join them.

All I really want to do is run home and bury my head in my pillow, but I manage some inane chat and completely pointless flirting over the course of the next half-hour or so. Then, just as I'm congratulating myself at being able to hold it all together, I'm knocked sideways by the sight of a lovely-looking blonde boy standing with his arm draped over the shoulders of a pretty blonde girl by the Pimms stand. She is tiny, a near-perfect fit for the space under his shoulder. Laura notices him too.

'That's the new girl, the one from Texas who joined just before Easter,' she whispers. 'I heard Josh had started seeing her, but I didn't want to tell you.'

The Texan girl throws her head back and laughs, then smacks Josh playfully on his bottom. Her own bottom is peach-like in dark blue low-rise jeans. My stomach lurches.

'Phoebe, are you OK?'

'We broke up less than a month ago and he's already with someone else,' I say quietly and without emotion, mainly, I guess, because I'm not entirely sure what emotion I'm feeling.

'Yeah, but you broke up with him, right? You didn't want to be with him any more?' Laura looks at me penetratingly, as if she's trying to work me out. The others are oblivious to us, having been distracted by a minor spectacle involving Charlie, Sam and a water bottle.

'Phoebe?' Laura says insistently. 'That's right, isn't it?'

I force myself to tear my gaze away from Josh and his new girlfriend as they head towards the river with clasped hands, and stare speechlessly at Laura for a few moments.

'Yeah, that's right. But we went together for almost a year. I just didn't expect to be forgotten quite so quickly, that's all.'

'Oh, Phoebe,' she says, putting her arm around my shoulder. 'He won't have forgotten you. It's probably all for show anyway. To make you jealous.'

I don't think so. He hasn't even seen me, couldn't possibly be doing anything for my benefit. He looks completely taken with her. I may as well not exist.

'I have to go,' I announce, turning on my heels without waiting to witness the confused expressions on Alice and Rebecca's faces. Laura can explain to them, tell them whatever she likes. All I know is that I have to get out of here. I'd anticipated the possibility of a scene, but this wasn't the scene I'd imagined.

I take the bus home, tell Dad I'm not feeling well and go straight to my room. When I am finally safely behind my bedroom door it's like someone taking a wrecking ball to a dam. I cry and cry and cry some more. Every time I think I'm finished, that I've wrung myself dry, it starts again. My nose gets so red and sore the Kleenex feels like sandpaper. My eyes become ugly and swollen, and my face is transformed into a mass of tiny red splotches. I don't look even a bit like a young Michelle Pfeiffer now. I don't think I've ever cried this much. Not when I broke up with Josh. Not even when Grandma died.

There's such a profusion of feelings whirring around inside me that I can't untangle them. Images flash in front of my eyes in quick succession, each one eliciting a confused jumble of intense responses: a white hot anger, a stabbing sense of betrayal, an unutterable sadness, all mixed up together. Mum and Daniel together. Josh draping himself over that awful, awful girl with her tiny waist and her exquisite bottom. Me breaking up with Josh, foolishly thinking he was really hurt, would actually miss me. Me sitting next to Daniel, breathing in the scents of his coconut shampoo and his old leather jacket, stupidly believing I might one day be with him.

The realisation that I'm not going to be with him comes over me in waves all evening, knocking me sideways again and again. My anger at Mum is pretty much a constant. *How could she?* I keep asking myself, sometimes out loud. *What the hell does she think she's doing?* Not only is it cruel and immoral, but it's gross. A woman of forty-one with three practically grown-up children fucking around with someone barely out of his mid-twenties. It's disgusting.

And that is what they're doing. Fucking around. Probably fucking right now, in some sordid little hotel room with a lumpy bed and crappy net curtains.

I wake up at one o'clock in the morning, lying fully clothed on top of my duvet. I glance at the sandwich that's been placed on my bedside table, its ham filling now hardened and yellowing at the edges, the bread dry. The sinking feeling inside tells me that the past twelve hours haven't been a dream. The white hot anger is gone, leaving just the stomach-churning sadness behind.

Now I *know* I really do love him. If I didn't, where would all this grief be coming from? He's all I've thought about for weeks and weeks, ever since I first met him, but now when I think about him all I can see is them together.

I don't know how I'm going to get up in the morning, I think, burying my face in my pillow. How can I possibly face the day? How can I possibly face Dad? He doesn't know, surely. He can't, or he'd never have let her go.

Part of me wants to tell him, to land her in it so that when she comes home she has to face the music. She'd not be able to defend herself. They'd have a row. He'd probably leave her.

Although the prospect of all that looks like sweet justice, it also scares me. I don't want to be the one responsible for hurting Dad, and I don't want our family to be like Gemma Hill's. Gemma and her sister Lottie have spent every Boxing Day for the past four years on the train between London and Norwich, and the last time I saw Gemma she was completely freaked out because her dad had just announced that he was having a baby with his new thirty-one-year-old wife.

I don't want to be like Gemma Hill. But I do want my mother to suffer. I lie for a while thinking of all the ways I could make her suffer and get an odd sort of satisfaction from this. I could let her know that I know, then threaten to reveal the truth to Dad any time she upsets me or tries to prevent me from doing something; I could leave sly little notes in places where she will gradually discover them, innocent enough things that, when finally pieced together, would finally reveal the full extent of my knowledge; or I could simply embarrass her – sit Daniel down and tell him stories of her worst transgressions, descriptions of her most unappealing habits. She doesn't paint her toenails or keep up her bikini-waxing in the winter, I'd say; and when she falls asleep on the sofa her mouth sometimes gapes open, making her look about a hundred and three. He couldn't possibly fancy her after that.

But the satisfaction I derive from these scenarios is short-lived, and what I end up thinking is this: what the hell use is it having hair like spun gold and a face like Michelle Pfeiffer's if the boyfriend you've been with for an entire year forgets you in five minutes, and the person you wish was your boyfriend is having sex with your own mother?

Or, to put it another way: what's the point, exactly, of me?

LIBBY

The day is almost over. Daniel and I have snuck back to the hotel under the guise of changing for dinner. The sexual tension between us on the walk home was unbearable, and by the time we reached the hotel we couldn't bear it. We walked up the stairs and stood outside my door, feverish with anticipation as I struggled with the key. There was no question he was coming in. It hadn't been discussed, but we both knew.

Once inside the room, the intensity of our desire overwhelmed us. Daniel shut the door with one hand and pushed me up against the wall with the other. Then he began kissing me, devouring me, his hands moving up from my waist and under my shirt. Expertly, his fingers found the hooks on my bra and it snapped open. He cupped my breast and my knees almost collapsed.

I pulled his hips towards me and he grabbed my legs. Wrapping them around his hips he carried me over to the bed. We fell down on to it, then he was tugging furiously at my jeans. He eased them down and I felt him hard, urgent, against me. He kissed me, a passionate, searching kiss, then looked deep into my eyes. My entire body shuddered, from the sheer, overwhelming joy of it.

No, not really. But it was a spectacularly steamy fantasy to have on a walk home through streets lined with statu-esque regency town houses, with cyclists and roller-bladers whipping past me by the dozen. It certainly made the journey pass quickly; I seemed to arrive at the hotel within minutes of leaving the conference centre. When I walked through the front door and chirruped an ostensibly innocent hello to Linda, I felt myself reddening, half convinced she could tell what I'd been thinking.

It's true, the day is almost over. Well, the serious part of it is, anyway. The last lecture finished at six and it's time for dinner. The possibility of joining the throng at the buffet table has not even been discussed. We are heading to Momma Cherri's Soul Food Shack, made famous by its proprietor's appearance on Gordon Ramsay's *Kitchen Nightmares*. It was Derek's idea. He's booked a table for seven, so I fully expect to have to hold my own in conversation with Derek, Daniel and four strangers, some of whom are bound to be of the worthy, backpacking variety. But I feel up to it now, less inconsequential. Besides, I'm famished and dying to tuck into some sticky ribs, black-eyed peas and sugared baked sweet potato.

Daniel stayed at the conference centre to meet with a couple of guys from the national movement. They collared him outside one of the lecture rooms at about four o clock, all a-twitter about something and desperate for him to give them some advice. He agreed, reluctantly I think, to meet them at six in some bar in the Lanes. He didn't have a lot of choice, really. What was he to say? Sorry, I'd planned to pop back to my hotel room for a spot of illicit intimacy with Libby? I don't think so.

But if he hadn't gone for the drink, it might have happened that way, mightn't it? We'd have come back to the hotel together, snuck past Linda, gone through the charade of some small talk outside my room, then made some excuse to go into it, together. And then what? I shudder with pleasure and shame in equal measure.

As it happens, I'm in my room on my own, getting dressed for dinner, which is at eight. I'll have to make my way there alone, but, being the type of woman who's masterminding an environmental rally in the park, that shouldn't be a problem. I'll get Linda to call me a taxi, though, as I don't fancy walking there alone in the dark. She'll be wild with curiosity, I'm sure. Probably hoping I'm going out on my own and that Daniel will return here, alone, at some point this evening. For all I know, she's sorting out her décolletage in readiness for a possible encounter at this very moment.

Speaking of décolletage, I'm in something of a quandary about my own, such as it is. You see,

I've been wearing a plain white bra and knickers all day, but I know that, sitting in the top drawer of the dresser, is a matching number in black and pink lace. One of the sets at which Rob sneered when I bought it a few years ago. I felt guilty packing them, but I did it anyway, telling myself I'd be wearing them, not for anyone else's benefit (in the spirit of a *Cosmo* girl) but for *me* (in the spirit, apparently, of your average French woman).

But packing them and wearing them are different matters entirely. Wearing them with intent is even worse. I sit naked on the bed for at least ten minutes trying to decide what to do, and in the end I opt for the plain white bra and knickers combo. Maybe I see the choice as some sort of insurance policy. Knowing I'm wearing such a patently unsexy, everywoman brand of underwear might be just what I need to help me keep control of the situation. On the flipside, if I fail to keep control of the situation, I'll have all that much less to be ashamed of.

I can't remember ever having been in the grip of such a dilemma, and it's not the underwear dilemma I'm talking about now. I want something to happen, but at the same time I very much don't. The thought of Daniel's hands on my body fills me with both pleasure and panic. I've never been so devoid of my rational powers, which is ironic given that I felt them to be so heightened in the lectures this morning.

In an attempt to persuade myself one way or

another, I've been actively trying to think about Rob, and to listen to the feelings that are awakened by my thoughts. But it's not working very well. For some reason, he's a bit of a blur to me at the moment. Coming here seems to have temporarily wiped out seventeen years of love, lust and shared experience. Not wiped it out, exactly. Just muffled it with a layer of cotton wool so it doesn't speak quite so loudly to me.

I hate walking into places alone. The more crowded and brimming with jollity they are, the worse I feel. I'm always afraid, for a brief second and in defiance of all logic, that whoever I'm supposed to be meeting won't be there (because they've had to work late/found something better to do/had a minor car accident) and I'll be left looking around, like a lemon, before eventually skulking, humiliated, back out into the night.

I feel this familiar fear when I walk into Momma Cherri's, but luckily I'm rescued by the sight of Daniel springing up from his seat and beckoning to me. So instead of walking through the restaurant sheepishly, anticipating humiliation, I actually walk through it with something like pride, secure in the knowledge that more than a few diners will have spotted the glorious good looks and charm of the fellow who's obviously so keen for me to join him.

There are only six of us after all, a person named Henry having had to rush back to London following a call from his wife about a minor domestic crisis. At the round table, Derek is seated between a fellow called Ed and a rather scary-looking woman called Angel. Daniel is next to Angel, and he's left a space for me between him and someone who is introduced at Terry. Based on first impressions, they all seem nice enough, except perhaps for Angel, who's fierce expression, short-cropped hair and sturdy build are a little intimidating. Not exactly a worthy backpacking type, but not that far off it, either.

After a few minutes' conversation, it's clear that Angel is, well, an angel, and that Terry is the one I need to be wary of. He's not overtly nasty, but there's a very subtle arrogance about him, and a few times I catch him regarding me with something that looks a little like condescension. He's probably wondering how someone like me, someone with hardly any credentials and only a few months' experience working with Green Link, has conned herself a place at a cosy dinner for a select few of the obviously dedicated. People like that are so weird, I think as I observe him. They spin a good yarn about wanting to spread the message and create a movement 'for the people', but when it comes right down to it, they don't actually want to be with any of 'the people', much less admit them to the inner sanctuary.

For the first half of the meal I don't say much. A couple of times Daniel turns and looks at me encouragingly, or sympathetically, or maybe a mixture of both, and I try to work up the courage to do more than dip my toe into the conversation. But as the wine intake increases and people start thumping the table for emphasis, I begin to think that it might be safe to speak, as anything stupid I say stands a good chance of slipping by unnoticed. So when Derek and Terry start debating about whether the green movement has become too remote and inaccessible to people, I hazard a few opinions.

Things seem to go well until Derek says, 'The key is, how do you make the *facts* more accessible to people? The research?', and Terry says, 'Well, people have to work at understanding. You can't always play to the lowest common denominator,' and then I say, 'Well, you can meet people halfway. For instance, that session today. What was it called? "Recolonisation of soft-sediment ice scours on an exposed Arctic coast?" I mean you can't get much more bloody remote than that!', and the table falls silent and Terry looks at me with ice picks in his eyes.

Daniel rushes to my defence. 'No offence, Terry, but she's right. We could learn a few things from the communications experts.' Then he turns to me and explains, 'That project was one of Terry's babies.'

I want to crawl under the table. Instead I excuse myself and head towards the ladies'. Angel excuses herself too and follows me, though she doesn't look like a woman who would normally go to the ladies' in a pack to stand giggling in front of the mirrors reapplying.

'So, how long have you and Daniel known each other?' she asks as we stand side by side in front of the sinks.

'About five months, I guess. Ever since the Green Link thing started up in our neighbourhood.'

'He's great, isn't he?' she says, and I wonder if the question is loaded. I nod and smile.

'The thing I love about him is that he's so dedicated, but so unpretentious with it. Not up his own arse, like Terry.' She laughs and smiles at me.

'Oh, Terry's all right,' I say. 'He's just a bit earnest, and a bit angry. Maybe that's what happens to you when you spend your whole life doing research that so many people refuse to pay attention to.'

'You're too nice, Libby,' Angel whispers, linking arms with me as we emerge from the loos. 'Are you always this nice?'

I laugh, which is good because it gives me the air of someone confident and carefree and not at all perturbed by the disapproval of the eminent scientist and activist at our table.

We say our goodnights at about eleven. I breathe a sigh of relief as we head towards our hotel and away from the others, who are still standing chatting under Momma Cherri's bright porch lanterns. The exhalation must be louder and give away more than I've intended because Daniel leans close to me as we walk and says, 'Don't worry about that thing back there. Terry can be a real arse sometimes.'

The rest of the way home, I'm acutely aware of the tension between us, which seems to be building with every footstep. But it seems to me it's not just sexual tension. Make no mistake, there's plenty of that, but it's intermingled with fear, on my part at least. And indecision. The whole thing is not yet inevitable.

About halfway home he takes my hand, and I look up at him and smile. A weak smile rather than an un-reservedly happy and abandoned one, but a smile none- theless. When we open the door to the hotel, the sounds of merriment issuing from the bar cause me to stop abruptly and hold my breath; the prospect of being dragged into the bar by Linda to make polite conversation with the other hotel guests is distinctly unappealing. We hurry quietly up the stairs before we are spotted. I fumble around searching for my key, find it, and unlock the door. But instead of just following me in automatically, like he did earlier in my head, he stands there while I enter the room and switch on the small bedside lamp, so I'm forced to say something.

'Do you want to come in for a moment? Have a drink?' I ask, indicating the mini-bar.

'If you're sure,' he says from his position leaning against the banisters, hands in pockets.

If I'm sure? Is it possible to be sure? Is he?

I nod, evidently unable to speak.

He closes the door behind him and goes over to the chair at the side of the chest of drawers. He removes my sweater from where I'd left it on the cushion, drapes it over the arm, then sits down, leaning forward with his elbows on his knees and his hands clasped in front of him.

'What would you like to drink?' I say with as much lightness as I can manage. 'Looks like Linda's stocked this thing with everything – gin, whisky, beer. Name your poison.'

'A whisky, please. Just a small one.'

I stand with my back to him, pouring a whisky for him. I hesitate, trying to decide whether I'd be better off sober or just a little bit more drunk for all of this, then pour myself a whisky too.

'Here you go,' I say, stretching out my arm. He takes the glass and smiles. The smile is so lovely that I retreat back to the bed for safety. I sit on the edge of it swirling the whisky around in my glass.

'How are you?' he says after a bit.

I look up, startled. It's a funny question, though in a way exactly the right one.

'Loving being here with you. Nervous. Worried. All of those things,' I say.

'We don't have to do this, you know,' he says.

'I know.'

Then we say nothing for a bit. The silence between us is thick with anticipation. So thick I'm afraid it might suffocate me, so I get up from the bed and move over to the window.

I can hear voices outside in the garden. Linda's guests must have retired to the patio. There's a loud guffaw, followed by the tinkling of female laughter. Then the low chatter continues as before. The sound of them there, just below the window, is vaguely surreal. It's hard to believe that they are all carrying on as if everything were normal, as if there were not something of enormous consequence about to happen in this room.

Then Daniel is behind me, pressing his lips into my hair. I lean back into his body, just to know what it feels like. He takes this as permission to lift my hair and kiss the back of my neck, the dip of my shoulder.

'I shouldn't be doing this,' I say breathlessly. Unconvincingly.

He says nothing.

For more than seventeen years no one but Rob has kissed my neck. Even Rob rarely does it now. He used to come up behind me and caress the small of my back as well. Sometimes we would stand there for minutes at a time, me stirring a sauce or sautéing something in a pan, him stroking my skin under my shirt. I can't remember when we last did that.

Daniel's lips are butterfly-like on my neck, but I can feel his hardness against my lower back. His left arm encircles me and begins caressing my collarbone. Then it slides down inside my shirt and strokes the goosebumps on the swell of flesh above my bra. (My plain white bra. Bloody useless insurance policy, in retrospect.) It takes all my will not to turn around, not to do all the things I have not done with another man for more than seventeen years.

But it turns out my will isn't the thing in control of this situation. Daniel pulls me around to face him, and now I can feel him hard against my stomach. I'm in real trouble here, I think, even as I welcome his tongue inside my mouth like a greedy child with a sugary lollipop.

But it's not until I open my eyes to see his own, intense with something more than just desire, that I know just how much trouble I'm in. That both of us are in. Does he know it too, at that moment? I think he must, because instead of kissing me again he presses his forehead against mine and closes his eyes.

'I can't do this, Daniel.'

'I know,' he says.

'I'm so afraid.'

'I know.'

'Do you?'

'Yes.'

'It would be a terrible thing to discover that we loved each other. Wouldn't it?'

He swallows hard and closes his eyes. 'Yes. It would.'

I push away from his chest at almost the same moment he pulls back. He turns away from me and walks towards the door. When he gets there he tips his head back and runs his hands through his hair. They grip his head like a vice.

Then he opens the door, walks out, and pulls the door shut behind him in one swift, decisive movement, leaving me to absorb all the shock and sadness that has filled the air in my small, dimly lit room.

It isn't at all how I'd imagined it earlier.

I ache for him all night. It's torture listening to the gay voices below my window, carrying on until the wee hours of the morning, while I lie in bed with nothing but a throbbing sadness for company. I'm tempted, a couple of times, to go upstairs and tell him I've made a mistake. But I never make it any further than the door. And I never open it.

The thing that holds me here is fear. Fear has proven a real match for lust, maybe even love. How about that? I'm afraid of so many things. That if I gave in I'd discover that I really did love him in a way that was impossible to relinquish. That whatever we did, there would be pain, all around, for everyone. That in an instant I could destroy everything about Rob's and my life. Everything about Rob.

It turns out that the cotton wool that was stifling the sound of my life wasn't all that dense after all. The sounds of Rob and our life together was pounding in my ears with the force of a thunderous ocean all the while Daniel was kissing me.

Eventually I fall asleep, though it can't be until very early in the morning because I wake up feeling shocking. Not hungover from all the beer and wine and whisky (which I never finished in any case); just grey and listless. My limbs are lead-like, and

I have to sit on the edge of the bed for a minute to muster up the strength to get up. I remember this feeling so well. After Mum died, a bleakness stayed with me for weeks. Every morning meant a repeat of the realisation that I had not dreamt her death, she was gone. Every morning I would drag myself out of bed and try to shake off the greyness and don something resembling a stoic demeanour.

Yes, I know what grief feels like, and this is something like it. And it intensifies when I see the note lying on the carpet just in front of the door. I know exactly what it is, and it isn't an express check-out slip from Linda.

Of course he had to go. How could we have chatted light-heartedly through breakfast then walked together to the conference centre and sat through 'Advanced Levels of Pollution Analysis in the Marine Environment' or 'The Future of Aquatic Cultures' as if nothing had happened? Impossible. His note is laced through with the same grief I'm feeling, and I can't blame him for slipping away to wallow in it.

I skip breakfast, being unable to face Linda's inquiries about Daniel's hasty departure, and I'm grateful beyond belief for the presence of some anonymous young girl, who evidently doubles as the chambermaid, at the reception desk when I check out. She orders me a taxi, into which I collapse and travel, zombie-like, to the convention centre. When I get there I realise that I've not actively decided to stay in Brighton for the day's sessions. I've just been operating on autopilot, taking one step at a time, and this is where I've ended up. Now that I'm here, I decide that I may as well attend the morning sessions. They might lift me out of myself for a bit, take my mind off the memory of Daniel's body against mine, and the mental image of his back, departing.

Sadly, pollution clean-up programmes off the coast of Newfoundland, no matter how dramatic their results, are no match for my dispiritedness. I hope no one's watching me, because they'll take me for a brainless idiot, or someone high on something, so absent is my expression.

At noon, I give up the pretence, collect my bags from left luggage and order a taxi to the train station. I'll have to dream up some plausible excuse for my earlier-than-planned arrival home, but I've an hour's train journey and a half-hour on the tube in which to do so.

The train carriage is empty, save for a young hippy couple a few seats ahead of me and a silver haired senior citizen opposite. He sits down there after I've already taken my seat, ignoring the two dozen empty seats beyond it. *Damn it*, I think, turning my face towards the window. *Now I can't even cry in private.*

But I don't cry, in any case. I think my misery has numbed my tear ducts as well as every other part of me. I sit, staring out of the window, trying to rationalise my feelings, to give them some sort of shape I can understand. After an hour spent interrogating myself, it occurs to me that I'm mourning not just everything that will never be with Daniel, but everything I've betrayed and called into question by wanting him.

Even though nothing really happened, everything's changed. I've always been buoyed up by the unquestioned belief that Rob and I were an indestructible combination. Now I realise we've been operating under false pretences all along: nothing's ever come along to test us. Then, the minute I stumble across someone I could love, a test, I very nearly fail it. What does that say about me? What does that say about the seventeen years I've spent with my soul mate, the love of my life, the father of my children?

It feels like a door has been flung wide open.

PHOEBE

I'm not at all prepared for Mum coming home early. All my upset and fury needs to be organised for maximum impact. As it is, I'm still in a bit of a state.

'Hello? Anyone home?' she shouts. I hear her walking from room to room.

'Up here,' I shout back eventually. No doubt she expects me to go downstairs and see her, but I sit it out. Five minutes later, she knocks on my door and comes in.

'Where is everyone?'

'Out.'

'Out where?'

'Tennis. Riding. Lilly's.'

'You didn't want to do anything?'

'No.'

Now I'm supposed to say something like 'How was your weekend?' or 'We missed you', but I keep my mouth shut and my eyes focused firmly on the book I'm pretending to read. Without even looking at her I can tell she's incredulous, wondering how even I could be this rude.

'Hellooo! I'm back,' she says sarcastically.

I look up. The first thing I think is that she doesn't really look like someone who's been away for a dirty weekend with someone who's not her husband. She looks worn-out, hollow. It occurs to me that maybe worn-out and hollow is what guilt looks like.

'I can see that. Welcome back,' I say in the most unwelcoming of tones.

She's obviously not up to dealing with this affront because she just sighs and walks out of the room. She goes into her own and shuts the door. Then the phone rings and I hear her talking, to Fran I think. At the sound of her laughter I'm filled with resentment. *How dare she?* I think. *How dare she laugh in the midst of destroying all of our lives?*

I manage a whole week of this stony silence. At one point she asks me whether there is anything wrong at school or with Josh, and I give her a glare of such significance that she actually flinches.

In the meantime, she and Dad resume a sort of eerie normality. It looks forced to me. One time I walk in on them in the kitchen, and she's got her arms around his waist and her head pressed against his chest. Normally I'd say something like 'Ah, bless' or 'Get a room'. Instead I just think *two-faced liar*.

LIBBY

'Why did you come home early?' Rob asked when we'd finished dinner and the girls had disappeared to watch TV.

'The last few sessions didn't look that interesting. And I was tired.'

'Did the others come back with you?'

'No.'

'Was it good? Did you enjoy it?'

'Yes. It was really fascinating. I met a lot of really nice people, learned a lot. All in all it was definitely worth going.'

'And do you think it will lead to anything?'

'I don't know. I'm not sure.'

Then an awkward pause.

'It's really good to have you home.'

'It's good to be back.'

He doesn't know about Daniel and the weekend, but he knows something. And it's the same thing I know. While he wasn't looking, a fault-line formed in our relationship. Now he's casting about trying to figure out what caused it and how to fix it.

'Hey,' he says, the first time I see him.

370

'Hey to you,' I say.

'You found your way back all right?'

'Yeah. I'm a big girl.' I smile to reassure him that I'm not angry.

' Sorry about leaving like that. It felt like the only thing I could do.'

'I understand.'

'I didn't sleep at all.'

'Neither did I.'

Then Barry and Phyllis walk in jabbering excitedly about something they've seen on the Discovery channel (I pick up the words 'climate' and 'disaster' so I know it wasn't something cheering like a documentary on the mating habits of big cats). They pause briefly when they see us, then carry on talking as if they've not noticed anything.

We don't have sex until four days after I come home. And then it's at my instigation. I need to know.

My assertiveness surprises him. It takes him a few minutes to catch up with me. But he does, and we slip into our familiar rhythm, only it doesn't feel so familiar. He feels foreign to me, and a little uncertain. It's nothing like those first times, but there's something of the first-time desperation about it.

I'm so mightily relieved that I almost shout out loud.

PHOEBE

I watch her all week. I make myself go to the Green Link meeting on Wednesday so I can observe her in context. I want to see what he looks like, too. Whether he's changed.

Neither of them gives anything away. They don't look like they're in the first throes of love, or as if they're sharing a smutty secret. In fact, they hardly speak to each other at the meeting. Daniel hardly speaks at all, to anyone, except to usher the meeting along. It's like he's lost some of his shine.

Then an idea occurs to me, a fantastically wonderful idea that lasts about three seconds. Maybe it didn't work out. Maybe they had a fight. Maybe there's hope for me after all.

When the three seconds are up I realise how impossible that is, and sink back into my gloom. Even if it didn't work out with them, I could never . . . Not after she'd had him. That would be just too sick for words. Almost as bad as that ancient politician who had sex with a mother and daughter *at the same time* and then recounted the whole sick tale in his best-selling diaries.

Feeling brazen I walk right up to Eloise and ask her why she didn't go to Brighton after all. Without missing a beat she says, 'Oh, things were pretty hairy at the shop so I decided I'd better not. It's our busy season, summer coming up.'

God, they're good, these people. Maybe that's what adulthood is: an honours degree in advanced lying.

I'm called upon to do a spot of lying myself. Mum's trying to finalise the list of responsibilities for the environ-mental rally in the park. Having had to endure the torture of being in the same room as Daniel for one hour knowing what I know, it's clear to me that I won't be capable of helping with the rally any more. I've certainly no intention of showing up on the day. So when Mum asks me whether I'd rather be stationed at the composting stall or the swap shop I say, bold as brass, 'The thing is, it turns out I've got a field outing that day, so I won't be able to help after all.'

'Why didn't you say something before?' asks Mum, her eyebrows crinkling in bewilderment.

'I didn't realise. Got the dates mixed up. Sorry,' I say, my tone unapologetic.

'That's too bad,' says Daniel.

'Yeah. What a bummer,' says Gabriel. 'After all the work you've put in.'

I shrug my shoulders as if in mature resignation at the inevitable.

On the way home Mum says, 'Phoebe, are you

sure about the date of that field day? Or is it that you've lost interest?'

'Of course I'm sure,' I shout with very convincing indignance. 'God, thanks for the vote of confidence, Mum. What do you think I am?'

She backs off immediately, completely unaware of the fact that she's sniffed out something close to the truth.

'Sorry, you're right. That wasn't fair. It's just that you've seemed kind of distant this week. Is everything OK?' she says, and I wonder why she has to be so reasonable.

'Mum, just leave it, OK?' I snap, pushing ahead of her to get through the front door.

Sometimes when I'm behaving insufferably I'm aware of it all along and I regret it within seconds. But on this occasion it's something to be revelled in.

LIBBY

A confrontation with Herself brews all week. I don't know when it will happen, or over precisely what, but I'm certain that, before too long, she and I will be locking horns over something.

It becomes apparent what the something will be on the Saturday morning after I return from Brighton, after I've endured six days of being alternatively ignored or treated like a lower form of life.

We are alone in the house. Rob's at the clinic, Kate's riding, and Ella's still at a sleepover. Phoebe rises at eleven, comes downstairs dressed and apparently ready to go out and finds me smothering a leg of lamb with garlic and rosemary ready for tonight's supper, in an unusually organised domestic moment for which I've already congratulated myself.

'God, it stinks in here,' she says, ever the charmer.

'It's just the garlic, Phoebe. You won't be complaining when you're eating it tonight.'

'I won't be eating it tonight.'

'Oh. I thought you were staying in.'

'I was, but I changed my mind. I'm going to a club in Twickenham.'

'A club? Not a proper club, surely?'

'What other kind of club would I be going to?'

'Phoebe, you're fifteen. You should be going to a club for fifteen-year-olds, one that doesn't sell alcohol.'

'Well, everyone's going. And so am I.'

'Is Josh going?' I ask, though it wouldn't make any difference. I'm still not happy about her going anywhere there might be alcohol and ecstacy in abundant supply.

She rolls her eyes impatiently as if I've just committed a sin of the most monumental proportions.

'Josh and I are history, in case you hadn't noticed.'

I hadn't, I'm ashamed to say. The news astonishes me, and I clasp a garlicky hand to my mouth, nearly asphyxiating myself.

'Phoebe! What happened?'

'We broke up. It's no big deal. Anyway, I'm going to the club with Alice and everyone.'

'Phoebe, I just don't think it's appropriate.'

She regards me with such a hateful expression I feel as though I've been stabbed.

'Oh puhleeeze. Do you really think you should be lecturing me about what's appropriate and what's not?'

'What is that supposed to mean?' I say. Before the words are out of my mouth I know exactly what she means, and I know this is going to get very, very ugly.

'What do you *think* I mean, *Mother*!' she screams

before turning on her heels and making for the front door.

'Phoebe!' I rub my olive-oily hands on my jeans and run after her, reaching her just as she's opening the front door. I reach out and push it shut. There's the sound of the door slamming shut, followed swiftly by the sound of a Christmas cracker being pulled. It's a second or two before I register that it isn't a cracker at all but my cheek being slapped. I touch my stinging cheek, checking it for blood. Then I experience one of those moments of great clarity. I know exactly what I have to do, and I know that if I don't do it, I will lose her.

I reach out and slap her, leaving a bright red hand-mark and a sprig of rosemary on her cheek.

The only other time I smacked Phoebe was when she was about four. She'd thrown a wobbly in a toy shop and refused to leave until I bought her the skydiving Barbie she'd set her sights on. I threatened her with a smack on the leg if she didn't stop, then had to follow through when her rage intensified and she threw herself on to the ground and held her breath.

I smacked Kate once too. I was trying the 'Time Out' method, which only works if the child in question will actually cooperate. If they refuse to sit on the damn step, there's not a thing you can do about it, short of binding and gagging them and tying them to the banisters. Or smacking them. Which I did.

On both occasions, smacking made me feel physically sick. (And that was before the government started debating the merits of throwing recalcitrant parents into prison.) I swore never to do it again, and I never did. Ella's never once felt the palm of my hand on her leg or bottom.

But this had to be done. It may even have to be done again, because Phoebe is coming at me now, arms flailing, eyes brimming with tears of rage. As I walk backwards she's pursuing me, punching my arms and screaming, 'I hate you. I hate you.'

It's reprehensible to engage in a physical fight with anyone, let alone your own daughter. All I can say, in my defence, is that it feels like the only sane response to the years spent silently absorbing the body-blows of her derision and the few seconds withstanding the force of her mad, waving arms. All this time she's been pushing me, trying to find out where my limits lie. Well, now she's going to find out, I think.

I grab her by the shoulders and steer her towards the sitting room, where I push her backwards on to the sofa. I'm about to say something rational like 'Can we please calm down and discuss this' when she leaps up and comes at me again. Suddenly we are both on the floor, rolling around with bodies entwined like a pair of mud-wrestlers on Sky Sports. At one point she gets the better of me and ends up sitting astride my stomach, wearing an expression that can only be described as venomous. I wouldn't put it past her to thump me in the nose, and I'm not going to lie around and let that happen, so I lift my hips and pull her arm and in one swift movement she's on the floor and I'm sitting on top of her. I pin her arms back over her head and she thrashes about, knashing her teeth like a trapped wolf. We stay like this for a few moments, and I make the mistake of thinking, This is over. I lighten my grip a fraction, and before I know what's happened I hear a thump and feel a sharp pain in the back of my head, and I realise I've been thrown backwards against the coffee table. I watch her disappear like a crazed thing up the stairs. When she reaches the top she shouts, 'I hate you, you filthy whore.'

If you think you can't imagine anything worse than being branded a filthy whore by your daughter you'd probably be right. I feel sickened, but also unrestrainedly enraged. Steaming. Foaming-at-the-mouth livid.

I chase her up the stairs and reach her room before she manages to lock the door.

'Don't you ever speak to me like that, Phoebe!' I scream, pushing open the door. She's pressing against it with her full bodyweight and for a second I think it's going to slam in my face, but somehow I find the strength, and, giving it an almighty shove, manage to push it open and send her tumbling backwards on to her carpet. This time the thump is the sound of her head banging against the edge of her desk. I hold my breath, waiting to see if she is badly hurt. She doesn't seem to be, but she is slightly stunned, so I take the opportunity to gain the upper hand. I rush over and fling my body on top of hers, pinning her hands back above her head again.

This time she doesn't flail around with bared teeth like a rabid animal. She closes her eyes and begins to emit small whimpering noises, like a puppy left alone at night for the first time, as tears slide down her cheeks. The sight of her collapsing like that sets me off as well, and soon we are both sobbing. I roll off her body and lie on the floor beside her. It's not easy to cry lying flat on your back, so before long I'm nearly choking on my tears. At more or less at the same moment, we roll towards one another and wrap our arms around one another. We stay like this, holding each other and crying for what must be ten minutes.

When I feel able, I say, 'Phoebe, I don't understand.'

She pushes my body away and looks at me through watery eyes.

'I love him, and you slept with him. Didn't you?'

And do you know something? The impact of these words is greater than the initial slap to my face, all the blows to my arm, and the bash to my head combined.

'Phoebe, I had no idea. I never knew.'

'But you did, didn't you? You slept with him. You're still sleeping with him. He doesn't want me. He wants you. And you already have someone.'

'Phoebe, I didn't. We didn't. Where did you get that idea?' Neither of us needs to ask who *he* is.

'You went away with him, to Brighton. I know you went alone, so don't try to deny it,' she hisses.

I lie back and cover my face with my hands. How do I begin to explain this? There is no way to explain this.

'I knew it,' she says triumphantly. But her triumph is quickly overshadowed by a resurgence of sobbing.

I remain lying on my back, staring at the ceiling, afraid of looking at her.

'Phoebe, I did go away with Daniel. But it isn't like you think. It's complicated.'

'Yeah, really complicated. Cry me a river.'

'You're right. I feel something for Daniel. I'm not going to deny that. We have this sort of connection. If things were different, maybe something would have happened between us. But things aren't different. I love Dad, and all of you. I wouldn't jeopardise that.'

'Really? Well maybe it's too late for that.'

I gulp, fear tightening my throat. If she's said something to Rob we're all done for.

'Phoebe. Nothing happened. You have to believe me. And if I'd known how you felt about him I'd never have considered going at all.'

She's staring at the ceiling now too, still and blank-eyed. We lie like this for a few minutes, then she drops a small bombshell into the silence.

'I broke up with Josh because I was sure Daniel and I would be together. Obviously, that was a mistake. Only he's already seeing someone else. A really pretty American girl who just moved here.'

'Oh, Pheobe.'

'All the time he was pretending I was special and begging me to sleep with him he didn't really care that much at all. It took him about two minutes to find someone else.'

She turns to face me.

'When I met Daniel I just knew he was the one. How wrong I was, huh? Why would he want me? Turns out nobody wants me.'

Then the tears start streaming again and she rolls over on to her side and into a tightly curled ball, facing away from me. Her sobs have an unreal, muffled sound beneath her hair.

I lie behind her, spooning her body, pressing my mouth into her hair, inhaling her pain. I deserve it, after all. If I could suck it all out of her and into me I would do it. What kind of mother doesn't notice her daughter falling in love? Or doesn't realise that she has split from the boyfriend she's been with for almost a year? What kind of mother misses all these signals?

Not one who's been paying close attention to her To-Do list, that's for sure.

PHOEBE

We lie there for ages, then Dad's cheery 'Hellooo' stirs us to life and Mum uncurls herself from behind me and gets up. If she feels anything like I feel, I think, she's going to have a hell of a time trying to small-talk her way through the rest of today.

Before she leaves my room we exchange a look. Longer than a glance but more fleeting than a stare. I take it as a pact. She won't humiliate me by saying anything about me and Daniel and the whole Josh thing, and I won't ruin all our lives by telling Dad about Daniel and the weekend. I'm not sure I believe her and I've certainly not forgiven her, but I'll let it go. For now.

I have to get out of here. So I wash my face, apply about ten tons of make-up, and prepare to go out to where I was going two hours ago. They'll probably all have left the coffee shop by now, gone off in search of something else to do. I don't care. Sitting alone over a vanilla latte and feeling the full weight of my misery has a certain appeal. Anything has to be better than sitting here playing happy families.

I shout goodbye and walk out without even speaking to Dad. I can just hear him. 'What's up with her?' 'Just leave her,' Mum will say. 'She's in a mood.'

And what a mood it is. You'd have thought thumping the living daylights out of Mum and being thumped in return might have beaten some of it out of my system. But it's not gone. It's just changed shape. Or rather, it's lost its shape and become something formless, boundary-less – at the core of it the knife wound of Josh's betrayal (because, oddly enough, that's what it feels like to me) and the impossibility of Daniel, and surrounding it, a kind of generalised hopelessness.

LIBBY

The weekend seems to drag on interminably. I'm desperate for the chance to lick my wounds in private and figure things out, but I don't get the chance until they've all left the house on Monday morning. Only once they've all gone I find I'm not comfortable sitting alone with my thoughts, which are in too much disarray to be good company. I pick up the phone to call Fran, then hang up again halfway through dialling. I'm not sure I can take Fran's support and understanding right now. She knows too much of Rob, and loves him too much. She also loves me too much; I'm not sure she deserves to be confronted with this nefarious side of me. I realise that what I need is Eloise.

The shop doesn't open until ten, but I can see her pottering about in the back. I knock on the door. She peeps through the curtains, a frown at the ready, then brightens when she sees that it's me.

'Hello, hon. What brings you here?' she says warmly as she opens the door and waves me inside. 'Can I sell you an outrageously expensive but absolutely to-die-for frock?'

'No, it's not a frock I need,' I say, heading over to the green sofa by the changing rooms.

'Oh dear. Sounds serious. Sit yourself down and I'll make us some coffee.'

I sit down and flip absent-mindedly through a copy of *Elle* I find lying on the sofa. The first article I turn to (about this season's must-have – a pair of skinny jeans that bunch up around your ankles) does nothing to improve my mood. Even Kate Moss looks terrible in skinny jeans.

Eloise returns with two steaming mugs of coffee just as a customer knocks on the door. She throws them a polite but firm smile and points at her watch. The customer looks puzzled, then notices the sign on the door and stomps off in the direction of the dry-cleaners.

'Now, tell me what's up. To be honest, I was expecting you to come all last week.'

'Why was that?'

'Aw, come on Libby. You can't expect to go away for a weekend in the company of someone like Daniel and not come back with something to talk about.'

'God, if you only knew.'

'I want to know. Tell me.'

So I do. I tell her about the whole weekend, including the bits about getting all excited about rescued toads and newts and my faux pas with Terry. I tell her about every moment spent with Daniel, and how I felt and how it ended.

'And you know, even though I didn't go through

with it I still feel like a terrible person.'

'For God's sake why?'

'Because I came *that* close, that's why. And because a large part of me still wants to.'

'The way I look at it, Libby, all that proves is that you are not a terrible person. In fact you may go down as the best person I know. You came *that* close, but you didn't. That makes you superhero material as far as I'm concerned.'

'Yes, but what does it say about me, about my marriage?'

'I'll tell you what it says. It says that you love your husband. It says you value your life with him too much to chuck it away. It also says that you are human. I mean, Christ almighty, you'd have to be a robot never to meet another person you were attracted to, never to want anyone else. There's no crime in wanting, Libby. The crime's in the having. And you know, sometimes that's not even a crime.'

'Yes, but there's more. Are you ready for this?'

'Go on. Shock me.'

'Phoebe knows. And she's in love with Daniel, or thinks she is, anyway, which, when you're fifteen, is the same thing.'

'Oh my God,' she exclaims, clapping her hand to her mouth. 'I should have seen that coming. She told me about it. It's just that I didn't realise it was him she was talking about.'

'Well it was,' I say. I'm not all that surprised at Phoebe having shared something with Eloise that she couldn't share with me, but it still smarts.

'And before you go getting all upset because she told me, that's perfectly normal. Young girls like that always need someone outside their family to share their darkest secrets with. It'd be totally unnatural for her to want to share them with you.'

'That's not how it is in the movies,' I quip.

'Yeah, well the movies ain't got nothin' on real life. Think about it. She's a beautiful girl, struggling to figure out who she is, who she wants to be, what people think of her. She doesn't really want *you* to have anything to do with who *she* is. And she certainly doesn't want you to be the first to know when she's met *the one*.'

Eloise sits back and sips her coffee, apparently exhausted by the delivery of this insight. Then she has another thought. 'And why would she tell you? You'd have only told her he was too old anyway. Admit it.'

'Well, he *is* too old for her. And I know what you're going to say: he's too *young* for me.'

'I would never say such a thing,' she says, a twinkle in her eye. 'You know me better than that.'

'Anyway, you haven't heard all of it yet. Not only does she see me as the thing that came between her and Daniel, but she's just discovered that her ex-boyfriend Josh has moved on to someone else within about a few weeks of their breaking up. Now she's thinking that maybe he never cared that much about her anyway – that he was just trying to get her to sleep with him - and that she was somehow deluded for a whole year of her life.'

'Lord, this is sounding more and more like *Neighbours* all the time.'

'I can only imagine the turmoil my poor girl is in. I mean, to learn these kinds of lessons at the tender age of fifteen? It's so cruel. It's so *adult*. Whatever happened to high-school proms where the kids danced at arm's length, and innocent dates at the drive-in?'

'They happened in America, that's what. And only in the movies. And you can be damn sure the guy had his hand up his best girl's blouse one night and was bonking another one in the back seat of his daddy's Cadillac the next.'

'Well it never happened to me like that.'

'I'll bet it did, honey. Think about it. I'll bet you had your heart broken somewhere along the way, or discovered you'd been betrayed by some guy. Maybe not at fifteen, but at seventeen, or eighteen. It's inevitable. And in a way, it's necessary. How do you recognise the prince if you've never had any frogs to compare him with?'

I remember Craig, who made me feel like a non-person. Maybe the joy of meeting Rob, who made me feel like a whole person, was that much greater after Craig. Maybe I'd never have recognised the treasure that Rob was if I hadn't suffered at the hands of a boy who had disdain woven into his DNA.

'You know what?' I hear her saying, pulling me back to the present, 'it might not seem like it right now, but Phoebe will be all right. She might even be better off. A very pretty girl who's never had her heart broken is a danger, to herself and everyone else. Just think about that the next time you're tempted to beat yourself with the bad mother's handbook.'

Fortified by my hour with Eloise I head over to the library, hoping to find Daniel there. Part of me thinks this could be a very bad move. But I tell myself I'm going for closure, that's all.

But closure is never easy. You usually have to work for it. He's not there, so I have to call him.

'Libby!' he says, unable to mask his delight.

'Hey,' I say. When did I start being a person that said 'Hey'? What's wrong with 'Hello', or 'Hi'?

'Daniel, I think we need to talk. We've a lot of work to do together, and I'd hate the thing that happened to get in the way. And I don't want to . . .' An involuntary sob prevents me from finishing. It takes me totally by surprise, as it does him.

'Libby?'

'Sorry. I don't want to lose you totally. That's what I meant to say. I want us to be able to be proper friends.'

'Yeah, OK,' he says quietly.

'So, can I see you?'

'Sure. We could go for a walk in Richmond Park.' Then, as if he's read my mind, 'On second thoughts, why don't we meet at Amandine for coffee in half an hour. We'll be safe there.'

It's true, you can't really get into any trouble over coffee. You have to keep yourself all zipped up for the sake of the other cappuccino drinkers. There can be no shaking or sobbing, no last-minute changes of heart leading you to leap over the table and into the lap of the person opposite you.

But inside, you can be breaking apart. And when you touch his hand across the table, just the once, you can still feel the pain shooting up your arm and into your chest like a lightning bolt. And you can still cry discreet tears all the way home so that by the time you arrive there you feel so emptied out that you head straight up to bed, letting the phone ring and ring.

I was wrong. There is, after all, something worse than being called a filthy whore by your own daughter. It's the call from your daughter telling you that her sister has been knocked down by a car and is lying in a hospital bed with concussion, a broken leg and several broken ribs.

The accident happens at 8.45 but Phoebe doesn't reach me until noon. My mobile was turned off for most of the morning, and when I returned home I went upstairs and decided to ignore the house phone. I do that when I'm in the middle of something or I can't face talking to people, but I usually manage to check for messages before too much time has passed. Today I didn't do that. I was so wrapped up in my own stupid misery that it slipped my mind.

When I do pick up and hear Phoebe's voice, the tightening in my chest is immediate, instinctive.

'Mum,' she says urgently. 'You have to come quickly. There's been an accident, and I can't get hold of Dad, either.'

'What? What is it, Phoebe? Who is it?'

'It's Kate. She's been hit by a car. She's at the Royal Free in Richmond.'

'Jesus. I'll be right there,' I say, slamming the phone down.

'Oh God, Oh God, please make her be all right. I'll do anything for her to be all right,' I mutter to myself as I fumble around trying to find my bag, some shoes, the car keys.

It's a miracle I make it to the hospital in one piece. It's not that I drive particularly fast, but that my concentration is shot to pieces, and I very nearly run over a mother with a child in one hand and a pushchair in the other at a zebra crossing. Christ, that's probably just how it happened, I think.

All the way there, pictures of me and Kate jostle for space in my mind. Me sitting gossiping in Eloise's shop while Kate is being rushed to the hospital in an ambulance; me sitting opposite Daniel, with my phone turned off, while they are wheeling the stretcher into emergency. I think I will never be able to forgive myself. Then I remember that I hung up on Phoebe without even asking her how she was coping, and I think I probably shouldn't forgive myself for that, either.

PHOEBE

Mrs Harlow came to find me in the common room. She rushed up to me in a frenzy. 'Phoebe, you need to come with me. There's been an accident.' She caught hold of my arm and started tugging me towards the doors. 'Don't panic, dear. Stay calm,' she'd said, in such an obvious state of agitation that I began to panic instantly.

'Who is it?' I said, feeling lost without this critical piece of information. I wasn't sure just how upset I should be getting.

'It's Kate, dear. She's been hit.'

Jesus, the woman was useless as a transmitter of vital details. Hit by what? A sixth former? A runaway lunch trolley? An eighteen-wheel lorry?

'What do you mean hit?' I said impatiently, by this time running behind her.

'A car, dear. Kate's been hit by a car and we need you to go with her in the ambulance.'

The rest is a blur. I remember seeing her on the stretcher, pale and still like she was already dead. Someone, and I'm pretty sure it wasn't Mrs Harlow, gave me an explanation of what had happened. I tried to listen but could only take in small, unconnected bits of it. Kate goes to cross when the green man is flashing, the car tries to stop but owing to a puncture suddenly skids and catches her halfway across the crossing. 'Why the hell was she at the crossing in the first place?' I asked the policewoman. She didn't know. Then I saw the wrapper of a packet of Cherry Twizzlers protruding from Kate's school bag and surmised that she must have gone shopping for tuck after getting off the school bus.

Then I was bundled into the ambulance to sit beside her, and I sat holding her small, limp hand while two paramedics fed about a million tubes into her and checked her pulse. I've no idea how long we were in the ambulance, or whether they had to use the sirens. I felt so numbed by seeing Kate in that state that it was like the rest was happening to someone else. At one point I realised that the paramedic was shaking me, trying to say something. I wondered how long I'd been ignoring her.

'Listen, sweetheart, listen to me. Can you contact your parents?'

'I don't know where they are.'

'Can you try? Do they have mobile phones?'

'Yes.'

'Please, can you call them. One of them.'

At first my fingers wouldn't even move. I just stared at the phone in my palm like it was an object that had been hurled at me from outer space. Then I looked at Kate's pale face and the will to be useful to her seemed to come to life in me. I remember thinking that I was all she had right then.

First I called Mum, who wasn't picking up. I didn't leave a message because I thought that could be dangerous. You read about people getting messages like that and then driving off bridges because of the shock. I tried Dad, but then I remembered that he was in Birmingham at a laser eye-surgery conference. The receptionist at the clinic told me she'd try to reach him for me. This time I threw caution to the wind and told her to tell him the reason. He'd travelled by train so he wouldn't be driving a car anywhere near a bridge.

Then I tried Mum again. And again and again. On her mobile and the home phone. *Arseholes,* I thought. *Why the hell aren't you picking up?* I even tried her at the library, where Phyllis answered the phone and informed me that she had popped in earlier, but only briefly. I was so angry at her for not being available. I was also scared that I'd end up being the only person around when Kate woke up and the doctors had to tell us the news, so I called Alice's mum and asked if she and Alice could come down. But when I finally did get hold of Mum all the anger I'd wanted to hurl at her seemed to disintegrate, and I just wanted her to come, quickly.

Now Kate is in surgery and I'm sitting here alone in the waiting room. Another waiting room. This time is infinitely worse than the time at the clinic.

They're patching Kate up, that's what they said. Attending to the broken bones, wrapping her in stuff. I know that the bones aren't the really big deal, though. It's the concussion and the insides that really matter, and no one is saying anything about those.

At one-thirty Dad rings me on my mobile. All the signs tell me I'm not supposed to have my mobile on in here, but that seems like a stupid rule to me so I've kept it on silent. If you don't need your mobile when you're in a hospital waiting room on your own and your sister's being attended to by an army of medical people and you can't find your parents, when, exactly, would you need it?

'Phoebe. It's Dad. I just got your message. How's Kate?'

'I don't know. They've not come out yet. But they did tell me not to worry. Do they always say that?'

'No, I'm sure they wouldn't say it if it wasn't true. Hang in there, sweetheart, I'm on my way. There's a train in thirty minutes so I should be there in about three hours. Is Mum with you?'

'No. But she's coming. Her mobile battery was dead but I got her at home.' I surprise myself by not wanting him to think badly of her.

'Right. Call me if there's any news. I love you, sweetheart.'

Just as I hang up I see Mum hurtling through the double doors and down the hall towards me.

Her hair has that dragged-through-a-hedge-backwards look, like she hasn't brushed it for three days. Her face is pale and blotchy at the same time, as if she's been crying for the same three days that she hasn't been brushing her hair. And her trainers, which she must have grabbed in a hurry, don't match. One of them, I see as she gets closer, is mine. The sight of her brings on a peculiar sort of tenderness.

'Phoebe,' she says when she reaches me. We stand there awkwardly for a few moments, as if we've just been introduced and don't know whether it's an air kiss or a handshake that's called for. Then she stretches out her arms and I fall into them, pressing my face against her shoulder. I have to lean down to do this as she's a bit shorter than me.

'Where is Kate? How is she?'

'She's in surgery. They're fixing her bones up, whatever that means. They said not to worry, and Dad said they wouldn't say that if it weren't true.'

She doesn't look convinced. She's probably thinking about *Casualty*, when they always tell people not to worry about their loved one just before they come out and tell them their loved one has unexpectedly died.

'So we just have to wait?'

'That's what they said.'

'Oh boy,' she says, collapsing into a chair while still holding on to my hand so that I'm forced to collapse into the chair next to her. She stares at the clock on the wall in front of us for a minute, then she turns to me and says, 'Phoebe, thank God you were there. You were there, weren't you? With Kate?'

'Well, I wasn't there when the accident happened, but I was at school. They came and got me and I came in the ambulance with her. But she didn't even know I was there because she never woke up.' At this I begin blubbering loudly. The other two people in the waiting room, an elderly man and a middle aged woman who's probably his daughter, look towards us and assume sympathetic expressions before taking hold of each other's hands and resuming their straight ahead posture. I noticed before that the man is wearing a thick tweed jacket, despite the June warmth, and that the woman's hair is squashed dark and flat against the back of her head, as if she's just slept on it. It seems Mum's not the only one whose sartorial standards flew out the window on the way to the emergency room.

Mum puts her arm around my shoulders and gently pulls my head down to lean on her shoulder. She begins stroking my hair and the side of my face.

'I bet she did know you were there. She was probably partly conscious, you know. And having you there would have given her strength.'

Then the doors burst open and Alice's face appears. When she sees me she turns and says 'In here', then pushes the doors wide open. Her mum follows her into the room and makes her way over to us.

Even though I don't really need them to be here now, it's nice that they are. Their presence is reassuring, I suppose in the same way that having lots of people around at a wake makes you feel better. It doesn't exactly eradicate your worry or your grief, but it sort of dilutes it with everyday things like cups of tea and sausages on sticks. Mum doesn't look anywhere near as pleased to see them as I am, which I attribute to the shock of everything She's actually a bit rude to Christine, not at all grateful. It's not until Christine actually sits down beside her and takes her hands in her own that Mum warms up.

LIBBY

It's the Adam Cook thing again, I think when I see Christine walk into the waiting room. I wasn't sure what he'd been trying to tell me, but *this* message is coming through loud and clear.

Phoebe tells me she called Christine when she couldn't reach me. It was a perfectly reasonable thing to do. And it was perfectly reasonable, and kind, for her to come. But her presence here is like a bellowing condemnation of me. *Look who had to come because you weren't paying attention*, the moraliser in the sky who choreographs the sending of these sorts of cosmic communications is saying.

Christine wears me down. She's a nice person after all, so she doesn't take my initial coldness for resentment at her for almost being the mother I almost wasn't today. She takes it as a sign of shock, out of which she gently lulls me with compassionate words and sympathetic looks. She fetches coffee which goes cold, and sandwiches that we don't eat, and stops a nurse to ask her for news when I don't have the strength to do it.

After about an hour I say to her, 'I should have been there when Phoebe rang. I should have been here with her.' And she says, 'Libby, you can't be everywhere. It's physically impossible. Unless you're going to be the sort of person who just sits at home waiting for bad news calls, these things are going to happen, and it's not your fault.'

I knew she would say that, but it's nice to hear it anyway. It doesn't make me feel all that much better inside, but it's comforting to believe that the impression of me that other people carry around will not necessarily be one of carelessness and indifference.

After what seems like days, a Dr Phillips comes in. He tells us in an infuriatingly calm voice that they have managed to stabilise Kate and treat her broken bones and do tests on all her other vital organs. She is not awake, but they hope she'll come round, and we can see her. (Doctors are supposed to talk in terms of percentages and chances and predictions, not use words like hope, so I'm not overly reassured by these words.) Probably best to go in a couple at a time he says, glancing at Christine and Alice.

'Don't worry. We'll wait here,' Christine says without hesitation.

I turn away from her to follow Dr Phillips and suddenly remember something. 'Oh my God, Ella.'

'Where is she?' asks Christine, springing up from her chair.

'She'll be home from school soon. On the bus.'

''I'll go for her. She can stay with us,' says Christine, bending to pick up her bag. 'Don't worry, Libby. I'll look after everything. You just concentrate on what you have to do.'

And with that, the mother of all angels and her daughter disappear, swooping up half-empty plastic cups and sandwich wrappers as they go.

Phoebe and I sit on opposite sides of Kate's bed, each of us holding one of her hands. I watch her eyeballs fluttering under her lids and take that as a good sign. I don't know if people destined to remain in seven-year-long comas have eyeballs that move, but I'm hoping not.

Phoebe is staring at Kate in a fiercely determined way, as if she's single-handedly willing her to wake up. As if she fears that the moment she looks away Kate might just quietly slip away from us. I know how she feels. I look at Kate, so pale and fragile you'd never believe that a few days ago she was coaxing a reluctant fifteen-hand gelding over a three-foot jump. I look at Phoebe, who, oddly enough, has never looked so beautiful.

When I was about thirteen I got hit in the eye with a football. It was a freak accident: I was watching the game, not playing it. The impact of the ball didn't just result in a bump, but sliced the entire corner of my eye. And the boy who kicked the ball was the very same one who'd dumped me painfully and publicly at a party the previous month. At the time, I saw it as a message to him, something to make him feel really, really guilty.

Sitting in emergency with a bloodied, makeshift patch on my eye, waiting to be seen by a doctor, I'd leaned on my father's shoulder and unselfconsciously revealed the deepest secrets of my recent life. There was something about the atmosphere in that room, where time seemed suspended, and the drama of my brush with death, or at any rate, my brush with partial blindness, that induced me to tell him things I'd gone to enormous lengths to conceal from him before.

I told him about being mad about Teddy (the errant footballer), then humiliated and heartbroken when he no longer wanted me; I told him about getting over Teddy when I came to suspect that he was shallow and selfish and sometimes even smelt bad, and about having spotted someone much nicer called Evan, for whom I had high hopes; I confessed to being worried that Felicity Hampton wasn't destined to be my best friend for much longer because she'd recently shown herself to be mean-spirited and vindictive; I even told him about finally getting my period (and bearing in mind that he was very firmly of the belief that periods were women's matters, along with female body parts and training bras, this will have been excruciating for him) and not understanding why Felicity's mother kept calling it the curse when it felt more to me like the coveted key to membership of an exotic club. To his credit, he didn't flinch once, not even at the mention of the word menstruation.

Something a little like this begins to happen to

Phoebe and me while we sit waiting for Kate to wake up and Rob to arrive. The shock and the waiting and the immediate sound of Kate's breathing, fused with the distant sounds of nurses scurrying along the starkly lit hospital corridors shouting instructions, conspire to create a sort of vacuum in which it is safe to say things that would otherwise be startling in their intimacy.

I say, 'Phoebe, I'm sorry I've been so distracted these past months. It wasn't my intention.'

She says, 'It's OK,' without taking her eyes off Kate's face. Then she adds, 'You weren't that bad,' offering me a small, conciliatory smile before resuming her vigil.

Then, in a kind of re-enactment of my emergency room confessional twenty-eight years before, I say, 'I never slept with Daniel, Phoebe. I discovered that I'm not cut out for infidelity. You have to believe me.'

'I do,' she says.

'The thing is, he's the first person that's really noticed who I am in years and it was intoxicating. Then I became even more of the person he saw, and I remembered what it felt like to be her. Does that make sense?'

She nods, biting her lip.

'I've made a big mistake by allowing myself to become so diluted. It all happened so gradually that I didn't even really realise it was happening. And it doesn't help anyone. Not me, or Dad, or you. I won't do that again.'

Phoebe turns her gaze towards me and nods again. Her expression – eyes in a half-squint, mouth pulled slightly to one side – says that she's trying to understand me. I appreciate the effort, because I'm not sure I completely understand myself. And I might be rambling. I plough on regardless.

'I think that all I really want is to have something for myself, and something of myself, as well as being what I am to all of you. Being with him, and getting involved in Green Link, felt like a way for that to happen.'

Then it suddenly feels urgent that I make this about her as well as me. 'Don't ever think it has to be a choice, Phoebe. You *or* the rest of life. You *or* your family. Promise me that.'

'I won't.'

Then, as if party to a completely parallel conversation rather than the one we've been having, she says, 'The thing that's really hard is that he didn't really notice me at all. Not really.'

I think, If this were a film or a play the audience would be bemused by the apparent disconnection between the mother talking about holding on to herself and the daughter's lament about unreciprocated affections. But to Phoebe and me, the points of intersection are perfectly clear.

'That's not true.'

'It is. It's OK, Mum,' she says looking at me sympathetically, as though the bad news is hers to give me. Then we sit in silence for a few moments, watching Kate's eyelids flicker.

'You know what's weird? It just never occurred to me that this could happen *to someone like me.* It was the one thing that I thought would never happen.'

I look at her, wondering if I'm expected to respond. Then she says, 'People are always telling me how lucky I am. They think I have it so easy. But they've no idea. But looking like this, it's not anywhere near enough. Is it?'

'No, it's not. But that's all right, because you are so much more than that,' I say.

PHOEBE

Dad walks into the room at about six. When he does, both Mum and I react as though he's woken us from a deep sleep. His voice, while not all that loud, is a startling contrast to the pattern we've established. Intense but quiet conversation interspersed with long periods of silence.

He comes up behind Mum first, putting his hands on her shoulders. She leans her head back, with her eyes closed, and he leans over her and kisses her forehead. They stay like that for half a minute, maybe longer. I think it's the most intimate gesture I've witnessed between them in years. Maybe ever.

After a short while he comes around to the other side of the bed. I stand up and he folds me deep inside his arms. 'How are you holding up?' he asks.

'All right,' I say looking over at Mum. 'Aren't we?'

She raises her eyebrows, then sighs and nods.

Then there are a few moments of talk about what the doctors have said and what we've noticed while sitting here watching Kate. He says, 'You both look knackered. You want something to eat?'

407

We shake our heads vigorously and with an uncanny synchronicity that makes Dad laugh, and makes me think, Hey, we are actually experiencing something as one. How about that?

We establish a new pattern. One that includes Dad. At some point during the evening, he persuades Mum to sit in the red fake leather chair in the corner and try to get some rest. He sits down in her chair to watch Kate. I stay exactly where I've been the whole time. None of us speaks much. Every now and then Dad says, 'Her eyes are moving,' like we did when we first noticed it, and I say, 'Good.'

After a while I hear Mum's gentle snoring from behind me. Dad and I exchange a look. I'm not sure what his look means, but mine is saying I'm grateful for the reassuring normality of Mum's snoring. At this moment it has something of the sublime about it.

When Mum wakes up from her power-nap, she and Dad decide to go out into the corridor and seek out the opinion of someone who knows something. They also need to call Christine to let her know what's going on, and ask if she can have Ella for the night. They're gone for quite a while, so I guess that they must also be talking to Ella. I experi-ence a pang of wanting to talk to Ella myself, and I debate with myself whether it's safe to leave the bedside unattended for a minute and go out to find Mum and Dad. I decide that it might be, and am just about to go when I notice Kate's eyes doing something more than flickering. They are struggling to open. I blink, and she does too, and then she is awake.

I smile at her and whisper, 'Hi.'

I can see that she's struggling to smile herself and not quite managing it. I say, 'You're going to be fine,' quickly, to fill the gap where her smile should be, and also to make sure she has something positive to take with her if she slips back under again. I'm dying to run out and fetch Mum and Dad, but I'm terrified that if I leave her she'll go again so I stay and hope they'll reappear by themselves. Not knowing what to do, I opt to keep up a running commentary, thinking that this will help to prod all those brain cells back to life. I tell her how long we've been here and what she's been doing and how the doctors say she'll be fine, and where Ella is and how many sandwiches we left uneaten earlier. I tell her about Dad's laser eye-surgery conference and how he'd rushed away from it to be with her. The one thing I don't say is how she ended up here in the first place, because I'm afraid the memory of that might catapult her back into a comatose state, or be the cause of some sort of panic attack.

The whole time she just lies there with her eyes open, stretching her mouth into an attempted smile. Eventually, she manages to stretch it out quite wide, so that it actually does resemble a smile, and this is what Mum and Dad see when they push open the door and come back into the room. Mum says, 'Oh Kate, darling,' and Dad says, 'Hey, Kate,' and in those few seconds the room is transformed from one in which time has been standing still into one in which life is, obviously, going to go on. It's such a lovely feeling that I have to hug everyone, including the nurse who comes in to change the water jug but spills it all because she's so excited by the sight of Kate's fully stretched-out smile.

LIBBY

In the two weeks following the accident, Kate endures untold pain and indignity with the same quiet forbearance she displays towards everything. For the first few days she is forced to wear a soft cast, a sort of cotton-wool creation. Then they have to stand her up to fit her into a rigid plaster-of-Paris number that stops her ribs and back from moving even a millimetre. Apart from the standing up, which is sheer agony for her, she is more comfortable in the rigid cast. But the cast makes it impossible for her bed to be inclined even an inch, so she has to lie flat on her back almost all of the time. After a few days she requests a book to read, but discovers that holding it above her fully reclined body makes her arms ache, so Rob constructs a makeshift book support from some washing-line wire and clothes pegs. At first we take turns unclipping and turning the pages for her, but after the first week she gets the hang of doing this for herself.

One morning I'm making my way to the water fountain to refill Kate's jug when I notice a frail, white-haired old man hovering nervously by the nurse's station. I don't know why or how, but I sense immediately that he is Charles Bailey, the man who lost control of his car and hit Kate. He checks the top button of his tweed jacket and straightens up as I approach him. His eyes are sad, his expression unsure.

'Mr Bailey?' I say, trying to sound convivial. I want him to know that we don't blame him. We've never blamed him. In the beginning we were too caught up in Kate's welfare to worry about how the accident had happened and who might have been at fault. By the time we got around to questioning these things the police had provided a detailed account of the event that fully exonerated the driver of the car, a seventy-one-year-old man. They told us that he'd been extremely shaken by the event, and would probably not be in any state to contact us directly for the timebeing.

'Yes. Mrs Blake, I assume,' he says. 'I've come to see your daughter. And you, of course. I hope you don't mind. I wasn't at all sure I would manage it.'

'Of course I don't mind. I'm pleased. It's very good of you to come.' Then I take his hands in mine. 'We know exactly how it happened. We understand.'

He starts to shudder then, and tears slide down his cheeks. I think of Dad, overcome with relief when he realised I was safe. Suddenly, holding Charles Bailey's hands seems a wholly inadequate gesture, so I wrap my arms around him and hold tight until I think he's calm enough to go into Kate's room.

Masterminding takes a bit of a back seat to all of this, obviously. During the two weeks Kate is in hospital, I barely show my face at the library. Daniel organises for the others to divvy up my job list, which they all do with amazingly good grace. The younger ones are magnificent. They come in every day after school and stay late getting everything organised, somehow fitting their homework into the gaps. Michelle says not to worry about the tuna salads any more; she knows how to make them herself. Gabriel says just shout and he'll look after Ella, an offer I take him up on at least three times in the two weeks.

Despite working the awkward early evening shift at the hospital and having to comfort Paul through his own father's sudden illness, Fran organises a rota for cooking meals and looking after the girls when Rob's not around. Fran, Julia, Christine – they all take turns. Most days, the angels Gabriel and Christine have Ella covered: if Gabriel isn't in charge, Christine collects Ella from the bus stop, feeds her and supervises her homework, then delivers her safely to our doorstep. On the weekends Lilly's mum swoops Ella up and takes her on outings to the cinema or the pool and back to her house to stay with Lilly.

Daniel calls me every few days to update me. The first time his name pops up in the window I

413

hear myself gasp and I have to gather myself together before I answer. After that it gets easier. He is warm, calm, reassuring, undemanding. If my heart and head weren't so full right now I'd find it harder to accept his friendly reasonableness, but as it is I can.

Eloise devotes her energy to me rather than to Green Link. When she's not at the shop. she's traipsing down to the hospital to replenish the basket of muffins and restock the vases with tulips or primroses. 'Go and get some fresh air,' she always says when she arrives. 'I want to find out what sort of disaster is going to befall Harry today.' She and Kate are steadily making their way through *Harry Potter and the Prisoner of Azkaban*, Kate for the second time, Eloise for the first.

Phoebe herself is a revelation. We take shifts at the hospital, and when she's not there she steps up her effort at Green Link. There are a million annoying little things to do to ensure that the rally runs smoothly, and she goes through the lot with a doggedness and good humour I haven't often seen before. Eloise tells me she how she stays on the phone for close to two hours one day trying to get confirmation of police support at the park perimeter. Apparently she is given other numbers three times and placed on hold at least five, but she emerges smiling and triumphant.

The other revelation is Liz. Obviously I can't make the usual weekly trek to Dad's, so she goes. I don't ask her how she's going to free herself up from the relentless demands of her clients because

I don't want to know. I just want her to go, and she does, if with something less than good grace. After the first visit she rings me to tell me what a saint I've been to go down on my own all this time. The next time she calls and says, 'I know you don't have time to talk about this right now, but I think we need to do something about Dad.'

'I know we do, Liz. I've been saying that for months.'

'I know you have, only now we really have to do something. Before he sets himself on fire or something.'

There's a pause, and I don't jump in to fill it.

'I was thinking,' she says, 'that we could take turns. Sort of like joint custody.' She laughs nervously. 'A month with me, then a month with you. If he'll have it, that is. It won't be easy to shift him from the cottage.'

'So long as we bring his beloved bin he should be all right,' I joke.

'And I could get the kids to start putting the milk in the cupboard under the sink just to make him feel at home,' she says.

We agree that it's a good idea in principle, and that we'll talk about it next week when things have settled down with Kate. I feel strangely elated when I hang up, like a person with influence and authority, and I realise it must be because she finally thinks I have some.

And Rob? Rob is working short days at the clinic so that he can spend time at the hospital and get

415

home in time to cook us all something in the evening. It's a pretty limited menu: scrambled eggs on toast, baked potatoes with tuna, scrambled eggs with sausage, but that doesn't stop me from wanting to kiss him every time he places a plate in front of me. I usually resist, knowing how Phoebe hates parental displays of affection, but one time I risk it. I grab his hand and pull him towards me and plant a huge display of affection right on his lips.

We are all, I think, afloat on relief. We cannot believe the good fortune involved in Kate having been delivered back to us, broken in parts but still essentially in one piece, and, most importantly, wide awake. After she woke up, Dr Phillips confessed that he'd had to entertain the possibility that her concussion would lead to a coma of indefinite duration, but that he'd not wanted to worry us by telling us that at such an early stage. 'She's had a very lucky escape indeed,' he said. *Jesus, haven't we all?* I think.

PHOEBE

In those few hours when it looked as if Kate might not wake up, I made a few deals with God. As a rule, I don't really speak to God except in an off-hand kind of way. *Oh God, I've got my period. God help us all if Mrs Devlin gets Deputy Head.* That sort of thing. So I imagine God will have been pretty surprised by my effort to engage him in conversation. The deals I've made probably knocked him right off his cloud.

Deal number one: If Kate wakes up before tomorrow I promise I'll be the best sister anyone could ever have. This will include tolerance for intensely irritating behaviour and a moratorium on snide comments as well as unlimited access to my closet.

Deal number two: If Kate wakes up before tomorrow *and* is perfectly all right (ie. she's not gone crazy or lost her entire memory), I promise to be the best daughter I can be as well. That means limited eye-rolling, being here as much as I can to support Mum and Dad, and helping Mum out with Green Link even if it means I have to face Daniel again. (I couldn't decide whether it would also mean forgiving her for going away with Daniel.)

Of course, Kate woke up within a few hours and didn't seem to have lost her marbles, which effectively meant that both deals came into play. With the blink of her eye, the bar on my life was suddenly raised. Perfect sister, good daughter. Forgiver of all sins. Stoic hard-worker of immense maturity even in presence of unrequited love of life.

It's a tall order, but one I feel I've lived up to pretty well so far. In two weeks I've managed to clear most of Mum's To-do list for the rally, admittedly with the help of the others, to visit Kate every day, and to restrain myself from saying things just to annoy people. I've been extra nice to Dad, assisting him with scrambled egg prepar-ation on more than one occasion and even washing up the pan.

When the going gets tough I think about the deals I made and repeat them in my head. I've never made promises before, not that I can remember, anyway, and there's something quite sobering about these ones. Let's face it, the guy knows when you're faking it.

Every now and again I catch sight of the bruise on my upper arm, and that's pretty sobering too. I realise that Mum must have a matching bruise somewhere, maybe even a full set. She bruises incredibly easily. Whenever I notice mine I hold on to it, like a reminder.

LIBBY

It transpires that the hospital is the easy bit. Bringing Kate home and making her comfortable, starting to manage our life on my own when the deluge of help dwindles, inevitably and properly, to a steady trickle, this is the hard part.

Washing Kate's hair for the first time is a family event. She can't sit, stand or make it up the stairs, so we have to do it with her lying down on the bed we've installed in the sitting room for the duration of her incapacitation. We shuffle her backwards so that her head can hang over the back edge, supported by Phoebe. Then we place a bucket under her head; I shampoo then Rob rinses using water scooped from the bucket. Ella stands at the ready with a towel, dabbing stray soap suds and water from Kate's face. At one point the phone rings and there's not one of us free to answer it. Rob says, 'How many Blakes does it take to wash one person's hair?' and I say, 'More than the number of elephants it takes to change a light bulb,' and even Phoebe laughs.

'What am I going to do for the next two months while I'm in this cast?' Kate says. She may well ask. There'll be no riding or hockey or going on the bus to school, that's for sure. I arrange daily tutoring from a nice chap called Phillip, a bean-pole of a fellow with Harry Potter glasses, a beak-like nose and a reputation as a whiz with the year eight curriculum. Kate is suspicious and a little resentful of him at first, but can't sustain it. It's just not within her nature to be difficult. She only has to endure it for a few weeks in any case, as school breaks up on the eighteenth of July.

With Kate immobilised, I don't have much time to myself during the day, so trips to the library are out of the question. But the rally is less than a week away, and I feel the need to be part of it again.

When I mention this to Phoebe the first Tuesday after Kate comes home, her response is immediate. 'Why don't you go down there? You can go every evening this week if you like. I'll make sure I'm home.'

'Are you sure?'

'Sure I'm sure. Dad will be home anyway. Between us we'll manage.'

'You know, she won't be able to move around for at least another two weeks. You have to do everything for her.'

'Mum, I'm not blind, you know,' she says playfully.

'Sorry. I know you're not.'

So on Wednesday I make the familiar journey up Church Road towards the magnificent spire and beyond it to the library. When I reach the steps I suddenly feel queasy and weak-kneed, knowing that Daniel will be inside. The past two weeks I've been operating in some sort of unreal territory. The life I had before the two weeks seems as if it belongs to someone else.

When I poke my head through the doors I see them all, deep in conversation or deep in thought, or, in Barry's case, up to his knees in cardboard boxes. He's the first to spot me, and shouts out from his cardboard sea. 'Well hello, stranger!'

On hearing Barry's greeting everyone else looks up from what they are doing and turns towards the doors. The sight of fifteen pairs of eyes aimed at me makes me burst out laughing. From their startled expressions, you'd swear a three-headed alien had just walked through the doors.

Within seconds, Eloise rushes up to me. 'Libby, it's great to have you back, hon. We've missed you.'

She ushers me over to the table where she's working with Gabriel on the final layout of the stalls. A hand-drawn map of the park is laid out on the table, and Gabriel is experimenting with different configurations by arranging and rear-ranging small rectangles of yellow paper.

'How's Kate?' he says, frowning.

'She'll be fine,' I say. 'She's going to have a very uncomfortable few months until the body and leg cast come off, but they think she'll recover.'

'Must have been a huge shock,' he says, unable to erase the frown from his brow.

'You could say that. But honestly, we're all coping just fine with it now,' I say. But his frown tells me he doesn't yet believe me, so I stretch out my arms in a triumphant gesture of resilience and say, 'I mean, look, I'm here, aren't I?'

Finally he cracks. A smile of relief. 'Yeah. That's great.'

'Listen,' I say to Eloise. 'Do you think you could update me so I'm in the picture? Would you mind?'

'Not at all, hon. Let's go over and grab a coffee and I'll talk you through where we're at. Gab, honey, are you OK with this for a while?'

'Sure. I'll call you if I get stuck,' he says, flashing another smile at me.

We walk to the other side of the room passing a couple of other tables on the way. Courtney says 'All right, Libby?' and Barry pats me on the shoulder as he rushes by in search of something. Phyllis and Nancy look up from their crouched positions over a banner from which they appear to be removing a stain, and say, 'Good to have you back, Libby,' in unison. All the while I'm acutely aware of the voice I can't hear, the face I can't see.

Eloise thrusts a cup of lukewarm coffee into my hands. 'Sorry, hon, looks like we've got the dregs,' she apologises. 'Now, where's that list.' She rifles through some papers scattered across the desk, finally landing on the one she wants. 'Here we go.'

We sit down in front of the desk and she studies the paper in front of her. I look around the room.

He's definitely not here. Without lifting her eyes from the paper on her lap, she says, 'He's not here, hon.'

I close my eyes and exhale loudly, then open them again and smile at her. 'OK. You caught me.'

'He had to be with his Oxford group today. He'll be here tomorrow.' She squeezes my hand. 'How *are* you?'

'I'm not sure,' I say. And I'm not. For the past two weeks I've put everything on hold, and now I have to deal with it.

'You'll figure it out,' she says confidently. 'I have faith.'

Now I remember that I have figured it out, and that figuring it out isn't the difficult bit. The difficult bit is living with it.

'I know,' I say. 'The thing is, it would be nice if I could fast-forward everything, you know? I want to get to that place where I can look back unemotionally on everything he taught me, about the world, about myself, and think fondly about how he made me appreciate my life and delivered me safely back to my husband. How long before I reach that place, do you think?'

'Hon, that place is probably miles away right now. Maybe you should take some baby steps. At the beginning, maybe pat yourself on the back every time you stand next to him for more than five minutes without wanting to jump him.'

We break into a conspirational giggle that turns out to be more conspicuous than conspirational because it attracts everyone's attention. They smile indulgently at us, probably relieved to see me apparently so lighthearted.

I finally see Daniel two evenings later. 'Hey,' he says shyly as he comes up behind me on the library steps.

'Hey yourself,' I say.

'Really great to have you back on board. You sure you're up to it?'

'Of course. It's a good distraction. And Kate's going to be fine.'

We stand facing one another in front of the doors for a second or two. He looks deep into my eyes as if he's searching for something. The answer to a question, maybe? Have you changed your mind? Or maybe, Who are we to each other now? Then he smiles unconvincingly and pushes open the door and we both walk through it.

PHOEBE

Of course Mum knows that the story about the field day was total crap, just an excuse to prevent me from having to turn up to the rally. But no one else does, so I am forced to invent another tale about how the teacher who was supposed to lead the field day has come down with acute appendicitis and her deputy's disappeared on stress-related sick leave, just so I can be around on the tenth of July after all.

They don't really need me, despite all their talk about more hands on deck and the more the merrier. The time they really needed me was when Mum was spending all her time at the hospital and I had to fill in for her. I guess I just got used to being involved, and now it would feel like an anticlimax to drop back again.

I thought I would have a really hard time dealing with the Daniel thing. The first time I saw him after the fight with Mum and Kate's accident I was afraid I'd give myself away. But it's amazing what you can do when you set your mind to it. When I feel myself weakening I try to focus on the things about him that aren't perfect. I think his hair's getting a little long, for instance, and beginning to drag down his face. If you wanted to be really picky you'd say he was a little too tall and thin, in a sort of rangy, Daniel Day-Lewis kind of a way. I never understood the fuss about Daniel Day-Lewis.

The first time I saw him he came straight over to me and pulled up a chair and I thought I might just fall off my own. He said, 'How are you?' and I said, 'Fine, considering,' and then he said, 'How's your mum?' and there was something about the way he said it that made me think, This is not just your average inquiry after someone's well-being. We talked for a while, about the accident and how Kate was getting on, and somehow he always seemed to work the conversation round so he could use Mum's name. I can't think why I never noticed it before.

It's not his fault, and I guess it's not hers either. It just is.

When I look at Dad my heart breaks just a little, and it makes it easier for me to play down the breakage of my own. He's got no idea, or maybe he has some idea but not a firm enough one to be useful, or dangerous. I'm amazed at how competent he's become at all the things he used to be useless at, and I tell him. I say, 'Those are great eggs, Dad,' or 'Mum must be really pleased about the way you're looking after her compost,' and he gives me a sort of lopsided smile of thanks and puffs out his chest.

The other day Phyllis was telling a story about her brother and how he's such a slob his wife now refuses to share a bedroom with him any more, and she said, 'I'm always telling her, Helen, you can't teach an old dog new tricks.' I said, 'Oh yes you can.' She had no idea what I was talking about and I didn't explain.

LIBBY

The day of the rally starts out grey and watery and stays that way until about nine o'clock. I have two cups of tea and will it to change. At ten past nine the sun breaks through and the clouds dissolve and it begins to feel like the day they promised on the ten o'clock news the night before.

I make toast but can't eat it. Rob says, 'That's just nerves,' just in case I hadn't figured that out for myself. Then he comes up behind me and wraps me in his arms and whispers into my hair, 'It's all going to go great. You'll see.'

The only person who's not going is Kate. The logistics involved were just too huge to contemplate. I asked Jaime if she could come up for the day and stay with her, but she's manically preparing for an exhibit and is twelve pieces short, so apparently the logistics of that were too huge to contemplate as well. Christine must have heard about my quandary through Phoebe. She rang and said she'd be happy to look after Kate. She said it would give her a chance to escape the chaos in her own house and it would feel like a day's holiday and no way was I going to deprive her of that.

I set out at nine-thirty to help with set-up. We managed to do quite a bit yesterday, so it's only the last-minute stuff that's left. The nervous fluttering in my stomach is overtaken by a rush of adrenalin when I get within two hundred yards of the park gates and I start to see the signs directing people to the rally, then spot the enormous green-and-white-striped banner strung across the top of the gates. WORKING FOR A GREENER RICHMOND. This is, after all, what we've spent the past five months working towards. All the door-to-door canvassing and harassing strangers on street corners and the posters will come to nothing if we can't raise awareness and enthusiasm here today. We won't stand a chance of implementing the schemes we've got planned for the next year.

The place is a beehive of activity even now. There must be fifty people milling around in various parts of the park, setting up signs, hanging banners from the edges of tables, shifting boxes from one place to another. I can't yet see any of our own core crew, except for Peter Ekenberry, who appears to be assisting the chaps running the composting demonstration stand. I shout out to him and he looks up and makes a visor with his hand. When he makes out my face he waves his arms wildly like an overenthusiastic child.

I find some of our gang in the marquee near the entrance that we're treating as a sort of head-quarters. Lynnette, David Peabody, Barry, Daisy, Nancy, Phyllis and Daniel are sitting on flimsy-looking blue plastic chairs sipping coffee out of recyclable paper cups. That's not strictly true. Barry and Daisy are sipping from fine bone china cups from the National Trust because Barry thinks it's important to maintain some standards in life.

'Hey,' says Daniel brightly when he sees me.

'Hey everyone,' I say back. 'How are things?'

'So far so good. The guys with the composting stand are setting up now, with Peter's help. The Jolly Green Gardener wanted more space at the last minute, which we managed to find by shuffling a couple of the organic veg stands around. Let's see, what else?' Daniel says, looking at the others for input.

'The woman from Natural Beauty called me last night to say she thought she might be late. Something about the lorry carrying her stuff being involved in an accident. But she just rang to say she's on her way after all,' says Lynnette.

'AA Skip Hire came up with two extra skips for the toxic product dump, at no extra charge. Eight-litre ones too,' announces Barry proudly, as if his formidable persuasive powers are responsible for AA Skips' sudden attack of largesse.

'And the weather's fantastic, which is a real bonus,' says a voice from behind me. I turn around to see Derek, who puts his arm around my shoulders as if he's known me for decades. 'Did you organise that?'

'Sure. I take my masterminding very seriously,' I say. 'It's very good of you to be here to support us.'

'I wouldn't miss it,' he says, then leans in towards

me and says quietly, 'Truth be known, I wanted to have a word with you later as well.'

'Oh,' I say, unable to conceal my surprise. I automatically look at Daniel for an explanation, but he gets up from his chair and heads towards the coffee urn without even looking at me. A moment later he comes back with a coffee in one hand and a list, *the* list, in the other. He offers me both. His face is impassive.

'You're just in time for the briefing. Why don't you lead us through it. Remind us all where we're supposed to be and what we're supposed to do.'

'OK,' I say. 'Only, with my not having been around so much for the past little while, maybe someone else should do it.'

'Don't be ridiculous, Libby,' says Phyllis. 'You'd be able to recite this stuff in your sleep.'

'You do it, Libby,' says Daniel. His voice is quiet but insistent.

'OK then,' I say, trying to hold the list with some natural authority. I notice that he has dark circles under his eyes, which I've never seen before. I also notice that a mile-wide chasm has opened up between us, though we're standing less than twelve inches apart. A second later when I see Eloise, Rob, Phoebe and Ella walking into the marquee, bright-eyed and eager for direction, I feel the chasm get even wider.

'Hello, you lot. You're just in time. Pour yourself a cup of lukewarm coffee and pull up a crappy plastic chair and we'll get started.'

At one point during the afternoon I find myself standing next to the transport stand sipping Pimms with Rob. He's taking a break from his tour of the park with the sign-up sheet for the Richmond Car Challenge. Having persuaded a hundred and fifty families to pledge to reduce their weekly car journeys by twenty per cent, he figures he's earned it.

'This must be surpassing all your expectations, isn't it, Lib?' he says, surveying the crowds. He tugs my sleeve and nods in the direction of a couple dragging two trolleys towards the Toxic Dump stall, one containing a toddler with bright red curly hair, the other stocked full of plastic bottles.

I'm a little giddy. With relief and pride and Pimms. 'Yeah, it's amazing what you can do with a bunch of cynics,' I say. 'Even the Morrissons have come.' He smiles and kisses me on the nose.

'I'm so proud of you, you have no idea,' he says next, then re-embarks on his rounds, clipboard in one hand, a Pimms in the other, before I have time to fully absorb how this makes me feel.

The high-point of the day is the rousing speech delivered by Jemima Scott, the Richmond-based actress renowned for her Green bent. The crowd, gently sozzled and with spirits high on sunshine and good intentions, join her in reciting a poem she's written for the occasion. Then she introduces her friend Sam, as in Sam Wilkes of the teen band *Handful of Dust*, and the under fifteens go wild. Sam only spent the first few years of his young life in Richmond, but that's good enough for the locals, who claim him as their own.

The low-point of the day is when Derek pulls me aside and tells me that he wants me to take over the leadership of the Green Link efforts in Richmond, and possibly become more involved at a national level.

'Why me? I ask innocently. 'What will Daniel do?'

'Oh, didn't he tell you? He's leaving.'

Just at that moment, Rob and Phoebe stroll past arm in arm about fifty yards ahead of me. I look at them, then at Derek, who is staring at me, waiting for my reaction to his proposal.

'I'm flattered, thank you. Can I think about it for a bit?' I say.

'Absolutely. Why don't we catch up later, chat about the details,' he says, patting me on the shoulder before heading back towards the marquee. He's only gone a few steps when I shout out, 'Where's he going? Daniel, I mean?'

'Canada,' Derek shouts back.

Of course he is, I think.

Later, when we find ourselves alone in the marquee, I ask Daniel why he didn't tell me first.

He says, 'Because I was afraid I might change my mind.'

'But I'd never have tried to change your mind. Not if it's what you want.'

'It wasn't you changing my mind I was afraid of,' he says.

'Oh.'

Then we are silent, busying ourselves with the collection of the cardboard cups that litter the tables and the bits of paper strewn on the floor.

'It's a good thing, Libby,' he says then. 'I could never have gone back to the way it was, and there is no other way.'

I want so much to walk over and wrap my arms around his waist and bury my face in his chest. Instead of doing it, I tell him it's what I want to do.

He laughs sadly and puts up his hands as if to defend himself. 'Don't,' he says. 'Just wish me luck.'

'Good luck,' I say.

'To you too,' he says.

PHOEBE

The summer is a good time to get over things. You don't have to face the people you don't want to, or even face anyone if you don't want to. People go away, sometimes for the whole seven-week break. The days stop being so full and passing in a rush and you find yourself trying to work out if it's Monday or Wednesday then realising it doesn't matter anyway.

The Green Link people are taking a break over the summer, so I don't even see much of them. Just Gabriel and Harry a few times; Eloise when I pass her shop. The really weird thing is, I miss those people almost more than anyone.

The only family in the whole of Richmond who don't seem to have gone away yet are the Thomasons. I've seen Josh twice. The first time he and his dad were in Amandine buying croissants. His Dad said, 'Hello, Phoebe,' in a not overly friendly way. Josh looked down at his feet; he might have said 'Hi' but if he did I didn't hear him.

The second time I saw him he was with that girl. I saw them walking along in Richmond Park one Sunday when I was riding my bike. He pretended not to see me, but he gave her a kiss on the cheek at the precise moment I sped by them so I think he did.

The other family who haven't gone away, of course, is ours. With Kate's leg still in a cast and her back and ribs still being in such poor shape, Mum and Dad decided a vacation would be too much of a trauma. So we're going to wait, maybe go to Cornwall just before school starts again in September.

When Daniel's postcard arrived, the picture of the North Vancouver lake on the front made me wish, momentarily, for a lakeside holiday like the one we took in Tuscany last summer. The postcard was addressed to all of us, so I didn't feel like I was snooping reading it. It didn't say any of the usual stuff about having a good time and wishing we were there, which is, I guess, because he's not actually on holiday. Instead, it said

Dear Blakes,
Settling in well.
Some great work going on out here – enough to keep me busy for years.
Libby, you'd love it.
Hope you're having a good time being in charge.
XOX Daniel

Other people wouldn't think anything of it, but to me it said a lot. I watched Mum reading it, and

I know that it said a lot to her as well. He may as well have said 'Dear Libby, I miss you.'

When she'd finished reading it she put it on the kitchen table and pretended to smile. I surprised myself by walking over and giving her a hug, and we stayed like that for a long while.

LIBBY

The postcard says nothing much but speaks volumes. *Don't worry about me. Don't worry that I might be coming home either, because I plan to stay here a long time, until we're out of the danger zone. You'd love the work. You'd love being here with me? I'd love you to be here with me?*

I look at it every day for a week, then I tear it up. There's no return address anyway.

Since we aren't taking a family holiday until later in the year, I've been able to make a couple of trips up north to meet with Derek and a few of his colleagues. We're still talking about my involvement, and I'm still interested. I've a feeling that the Richmond branch may be all I can handle for now, but we'll see. I'm not closing any doors.

Eloise keeps telling me, All things pass. I tell her, Could they hurry up, please. She says, Patience is a virtue. I say, Bugger patience, I'd prefer peace of mind. She says, You mastermind rallies involving thousands of people and receive invitations to mix with important folks who make important things happen, why do you want peace of mind? Peace of mind is overrated. In a way she's right. I realise

438

I used to have something like peace of mind and it had begun to feel a little like a living death.

I'm assuming some sort of peace of mind will appear, eventually. I'm assuming that with every day that passes, the memory of him will become more faint and ill-defined until it's hardly a real memory at all. Or maybe what happens is that the memory remains but just loses its sting.

While I'm waiting for the fading process to set in and the stinging to stop, I try to think cup-half-full thoughts, like how *even* the Morrissons are recycling now; how well Kate is recovering and how fantastically lucky we are that she's still here; how I can't remember the last time Rob or I referred to Phoebe as Herself, or the last time Ella needed me to sit on her bed and banish night fears; and how Rob's been kissing my neck every so often ever since I reminded him he never did it any more.

It's not a fabulous summer, but we do get the odd day with a bright blue sky. When we do, I try to really appreciate it. I hold my face up to it and try to imagine that some of it is rubbing off on me, and that helps too.